SLAUGHTERHOUSE
HIGH

SLAUGHTERHOUSE
HIGH

A TALE OF LOVE AND SACRIFICE

ROBERT DEVEREAUX

DEADITE PRESS
Portland, OR

DEADITE PRESS
an imprint of Eraserhead Press

ERASERHEAD PRESS
205 NE BRYANT
PORTLAND, OR 97211

WWW.ERASERHEADPRESS.COM

ISBN: 1-936383-10-1

Printed in the USA.

For Those Saints Among Us
Who Labor Tirelessly and Selflessly
Over the De-Dementification
Of This Seriously Demented World

PART ONE
Designated Slasher

1
Special Delivery

Sheriff Dewey Blackburn had a soft spot in his heart for the week leading up to prom night.

He never told anyone, though.

Wouldn't have been professional.

As Blackburn cruised the streets of Corundum, Kansas, scanning parks and sidewalks for ne'er-do-wells, he felt mighty glad that his hand gripped the tiller of the law, keeping the more deranged impulses of the citizenry in check. Corundum was a thriving town, not so small as to bore one to tears, yet not so large as to lose its charm.

In the back seat, his charges shifted.

The woman released a low moan. The prom gown into which she had been tucked—a waste of fabric, to Blackburn's way of thinking—whispered and crinkled like Christmas wrapping paper. She had been a real scrapper in the holding tank, resisting the needle with every ounce of strength.

Not so her male counterpart, some aimless drifter who stank of sewage until Blackburn's junior deputies washed, coiffed, cologned, and tuxedo'd him. Obligingly had he hazed toward his fate, a sheen of resignation smoothed over his eyes. The blunt, ragged remnants of his earlobes betrayed the shame of his past: ducking out on his prom ("promjumping," kids called it these days), being arrested and ostracized, having his lobes crudely docked before being thrust out to fend on his own.

Along the trim-lawned street, gawkers gawked from picture windows. Blackburn idled by, casual fingers guiding the steering

11

wheel, an elbow bent at his rolled-down window, siren quiet. But folks knew he would be out and about. This neighborhood burst at the seams with teachers, and a squad car with a drugged-out, dressed-up couple in the back and a plastic trough cinched to its top meant only one thing on prom night.

The sheriff hung a right.

A left.

Down the way, a porchlight blazed. The house's big black digits matched the address on his clipboard. Blackburn angled into the driveway and killed the cruiser.

Art teacher's residence.

Plenty of strange rumors circulated about Zane Fronemeyer and his wives. The man coaxed perverse paintings out of his students at Corundum High. Scuttlebutt had it he had entered the teaching profession for the sole purpose of being chosen. It had taken years, but the sick bastard's wish had finally come true.

Blackburn got out.

The doped-up couple had at least an hour of grog on the meter, but they'd be checking out long before *that* timer popped.

The sheriff strode up the walkway, highly tuned to the neighborhood geeks and gawkers.

He raised a warning finger to the threesome on the lawn across the street. They ducked back into their house, two scrawny joes and a fat she-bitch, all three buck-nekkid except for their lobebags. Them and their fellow rubberneckers would keep their traps shut. They always did, on account of the heap of penitentiary time they'd face if word leaked early which teacher had been chosen.

One ring. Two heartbeats. The door swung back.

"Zane Fronemeyer?"

"You're looking at him." Fucker smiled in oil. Behind him, like a matched pair of aproned bowling pins, huddled his wives, their left lobes decently bagged, their right ones chewed up more than most folks would consider proper. "You brought me a couple o' good ones, I hope."

Christ, what a creep, thought Blackburn. "Here's the paperwork," he said. "Help me with the trough."

Fronemeyer passed the bulging packet to his creamier-skinned spouse and followed Blackburn to the squad car. The sheriff reached up and slipped the knots. In the old days, the steel troughs had been gut busters. These new plastic jobbies with their squat fat legs were a hell of a lot easier on the back.

Hefting the front end, Fronemeyer led the way into his house. "Sheriff," he said, "this here's Camille. That's Hedda."

The sheriff nodded without registering which wife was which, so badly did he want this part of his prom night duties over.

In the front hall, the art teacher sported a matched set of stuffed parents, upon whom an inept fluxidermist hadn't bothered to make his sex-ready alterations at all subtle. What had been done to them was strictly against the law, but the statute was so honored in the breach that Blackburn would be laughed out of court if he tried to call these three on it.

Fronemeyer led the way to the basement steps. The air cooled as they descended.

Tweed Megrim, eighteen, naked, and brimming with anticipation straight down to her tippytoes, stepped through tickling bursts of bubbles into a steamy-hot bath.

With a wince she withdrew her big toe, then slipped it all the way in. The rest of her in an abundance of glory swiftly followed.

As the water rose to embrace her, visions of Dexter Poindexter danced in Tweed's head. At this very moment, just a few blocks away, Dex was stepping into his tub too.

No, wait.

Showers were Dex's preferred mode of bathing. He was standing beneath the punishing blast of a shower, yes that was it, his eyes shut, his mouth open against the downpour. She pictured Dex's sweet head angled right, his left earlobe buttoned cutely at the base of his ear, looking (this all in her imagination of course) like a fat blunt thumb bereft of nail and bone.

Tweed gasped.

Don't go there. In the bathroom, both her lobes were naked, as were his. On the right the friendship lobe, kissable, touchable, and viewable in public. And on the left? The secret, naughty lobe that her classmates cracked jokes about by their gym lockers.

Funny how it was okay for it to be unbagged when you were alone. And it was okay for little kids' lobes to be exposed until they grew breasts or their voices lowered.

But otherwise, only wedded twos or threes in the dim-lit privacy of their bedrooms were allowed to fondle that concealed length of flesh. Only there could it be pinched and licked and sucked so that their love partner gasped with surprise and delight, going all gooshy in the down-there place.

A devilish grin widened upon her face.

Everyone thought pretty little Tweed Megrim so innocent. Such a goody-goody.

They were right, of course. Plenty of girls at school, from all reports, were supremely slutty (Peach Popkin came to mind). And it was true that she, Tweed, had only *thought* exciting thoughts. Never had she dared act upon them.

Until tonight.

She had decided. To get Dex's motor running, she had even hinted.

If he futtered off a choice bit of flesh for her—a nose tip, a lobe, half a nipple, something like that—if he emerged from the frenzied crowd with his miniature cleaver dripping and a special prize clutched in his hand, why then, in the dark quiet of his parents' car, she would let him touch her lovelobe through her lobebag. Maybe she would even let him brush his nose against it.

Or rub his . . .

By God, she gasped, floating up through the bubbles and exposing the tips of her nipples.

. . . rub his bagged lovelobe against hers.

Tweed panted and laughed.

Enough of that. She felt light-headed. It wouldn't do to get herself all worked up so early in the evening.

She forced herself to concentrate on the pink-sequined dress that waited on a hanger in her bedroom. On the matching lobebag clipped to the hanger. And on her soft pastel pumps.

Her dad had spared no expense in decking her out.

Why should he? There was only one prom night in anyone's life. Well, okay, if you didn't count teachers, principals, janitors, school nurses, and such. *They* had one every year.

But they were grown-ups. Odd old folks whose generation didn't matter worth a hoot.

Nope. Tonight belonged to the kids.

She and Dex would survive. They hadn't been chosen to fall

beneath the slasher's knife. Some other couple had.

A full life lay ahead for Dex and her, and cruel fate would not step in to cut it short.

The day before, Dex bragged that he would punch the slasher's lights out, he would defend her, if by freakishly bad luck they had in fact been chosen. But Tweed put a finger to his lips and told him, "Hush up now, we won't be."

And she was right.

There was no question.

Tonight would be the most wondrous night of their lives. And many more nights of wonder lay before them.

Downstairs, her dad was singing.

"Take 'er easy," grumbled the sheriff, his shoulders stooped as he footed his cumbrous way down the stairs. The back end of the trough was wide and unwieldy.

Fronemeyer, struggling with the front end, nodded and slowed.

Doggy smell. A high soft whine like the plaintive *scree* of a clothesline pulley.

In the dim spill of light, the pup looked pitiful. Rib-winded, sick-eyed, underfed. It strained at its tether, eager for companionship.

But the sinkpipe held. Puppy claws scrabbled ineffectually on concrete. Light brown whips of turd swirled up from the floor by the dryer. A long-handled axe lay across the washing machine lid.

Blackburn's eyebrows rose. "You're practicing on a pooch?" he asked.

"There's no law against it." Defensive scum. "I used my own money. At the pound. They'd've snuffed him anyway. They'd've entered him in a dog-cracking contest, sure as we're standing here."

"Maybe so." The sheriff's tone betrayed him.

"I'm planning to work up. Most first-timers do, don't they?"

Blackburn's ears burned but he said nothing.

When they had set the trough near the drain in the floor, Fronemeyer arched his back and let out an exaggerated groan.

The sheriff glared at him and headed for the stairs. "Let's bring 'em in."

Upstairs, Fronemeyer's mates were draped in wifewear ten years out of date. Red-pink checks. Frilly aprons.

Blackburn nodded at them. He passed an end table that held the school's instruction packet, doing his best to ignore the fluxed elders in the vestibule.

It was a relief to hit the air outside. But the art teacher dogged his heels, putting in one small-talk goad after another.

When they reached the cruiser, Blackburn opened the back door. "I'll hand you the guy. "Walk him to the basement. Me and his date'll be right behind you."

The woman was propped against the man, both of them doped to the gills. It was a deal and a half to set her straight and wangle the man out, his ungainly shoes struggling for balance as the sheriff propped him up.

Fronemeyer, his eyes agleam in the moonlight, staggered beneath the passed burden. Shouldering one of the man's arms, he poured soused-relative, coaxy soothings into his ear and steered him toward the house.

The woman groaned. Blackburn shifted her out, her gown rustling like wads of packing. A prom pass was pinned to her dress. At her side hung a miniature cleaver and a small Futterware container, green-lidded.

Authenticity, they said.

As far as Blackburn was concerned, it was nothing but a waste of taxpayer money and a huge boondoggle to the Futter family empire.

The woman reeked of perfume. She had a nice shape to her, fleshed-out and curvy, twenty-five tops. Were it not for the freakish dye-job done on her exposed friendship lobe—pale green from some fringe group's absurd protest against the sexification of the lobes, as if God had intended anything *else*, for the love of Christ—the lawman would have thought her attractive.

"Where am I?" she ventured, slow-tossing her head, unable to open her eyes.

"Just a little further," he said, guiding her past Camille and Hedda. "There's a nice couch for you downstairs."

Yeah. Old. Dusty. Discolored foam poking out of threadbare fabric. But in her state, she wouldn't notice. And in nine-ten minutes tops, to judge from the art teacher's zeal, she'd be way past the point of noticing anything.

Again the dog.

Scree of a clothesline pulley.

Fronemeyer panted at the couch. Snailtracks of sweat eased down his cheeks. The seated man's head lolled back, his mouth agape as if preparing to break into snores.

Blackburn placed the woman beside her date. Whipping the receipt from his pants pocket, he pushed the axe aside and smoothed the paper on the washing machine lid. On it he scrawled the time of delivery and his signature.

"Sign here," he said, "and here."

"No problem," said Fronemeyer, taking up the pen. The ratswim of hair on the back of his hand Blackburn found repulsive.

When he was through, the sheriff tore off the pink copy, left it on the lid, and clipped the pen to his shirt pocket. The mutt's soft high whine had gouged a killer headache into his skull.

"It's done then?" asked Fronemeyer.

What was this citizen's problem?

Did he burgle beyond the Maximum Swag Rate? Did he run red lights? Clearly he felt guilty about *something*.

One could never tell about folks. What went on inside them was a mystery.

"A deputy'll be by in the morning to pick up the corpses. All three. Leave 'em here in the trough. We do autopsies, so nobody'd better try any shenanigans—"

"Oh, we'd never—"

"—not before, not after. No diddle, no fondle, no lobeplay. Am I clear?"

"We're not the sort to—"

"*Am I clear?*"

"Yes, sheriff." A nasty glare. "You are."

"I'm going to check these two out myself." He pointed a harsh finger at the teacher, feeling bombs land and detonate, bullseye, bullseye. "The dog's part of it too. I'll be scrutinizing Fido here *real close*, you hear what I'm saying?"

"Yes, sir." Deflation.

"I'll see myself out."

And that he did. Fronemeyer's wives, in the midst of a fondle on the upstairs couch, bade him good night. The blonde one mumbled it around a nipple.

Blackburn's squad car, even with a linger of the drugged

woman's perfume, hugged him like home. Firing it up, he headed for Corundum High and his duties there, the lockup, the speech.

If there was any justice in the world, he would never have to see Zane Fronemeyer or his wives again.

Shyler Bleak and his wife Bitsy sat on their bed, propped up against pillows. Their cardigans matched, their black patent leather loafers had been spit-polished to a bright sheen, and their fingers were lovingly entwined.

The TV on the dresser claimed pretty much the Bleaks' entire attention.

Ceremonies at the Shite House.

Down the hall there sounded a steady blast of shower water.

Gerber Waddell was Corundum High's feeb head janitor. Shyler and Bitsy Bleak housed, clothed, and fed him. Tonight, of course, he would be very much on duty.

The Bleaks got plenty of mileage out of the community for their sacrifices on Gerber's behalf. Store discounts, pleasant ego strokes, sympathetic words of encouragement and looks that said better-you-than-me.

But right now, on the heels of applause for the puppet president's introductory remarks about the nation's need for divine guidance, the Right Reverend Sparky Reezor bounded up to the podium and seized the lectern with his huge hands as if to rip it clean off its base.

"Mister President, distinguished guests, and all o' you sinners out there in this great nation of ours," intoned the burly churchman in his deep bass voice. "Got-*damm*it! Let us pray!"

He bowed his great white head. His eyelids clamped down tight, as if doing so tuned his mind to the eternal frequency.

Behind him, a TV camera caught Cholly Bork, crack puppetmaster and the brains—such as they were—behind the President. His masterful hands worked an elaborate airplane control. He mince-walked President Windfucker to a plush chair and angled his head as though he were listening in respect. Then that head bowed. The President's delicate oaken fingers steepled piously betwixt chest and belly.

"Dear God-in-heaven," thundered Sparky, "once again, as the year rolleth around like that vast immovable boulder (ha! but we know better, don't we, my friends?) that shut air and sunlight out of Thy Son's tomb, into our hearts and minds and pleasingly proud bosoms hast Thou rolled the marvel that is prom night.

"We in these Demented States of America are blessed to live in the greatest got-damned country on the greatest got-damned planet in this triple-got-damned wonder we fondly call the universe, my fellow citizens, ain't it a piece of work? And we have Thee, dear Lord, to thank for that.

"JEEsus—when He roamed the earth with those penetratin' eyes o' his—tugged with a harsh hand upon his friendship lobe and condemned us sinners, every one.

"JEEsus, the only man unfallen, swept His glarin' gaze, those condemnatory orbs whose sting we know so well, across the race of the fallen and He shouted, 'Let the little children suffer.'

"Got-dammit, let them suffer."

Shyler Bleak and his wife whispered the words along with Sparky Reezor.

"And JEEsus the Lion, He ramped back upon His great hind legs, His thighs tawny and muscular and slick with sweat. Across the tenuous fabric—that warp and woeful weft, my friends—of our smug complacency, JEEsus the Lion clawed bloody rents, roaring out: 'Cursed be the meek, for they shall eat camel dung.

"'Cursed be the poor, for money, the measure of all worth, proclaimeth their unworthiness.

"'Cursed be the peacemakers, for war alone has the power to set rods of steel in backbones that are otherwise fa-a-ar too bendable.

"'Cursed be the cowards and the whiners, for rage and fear alone nourish the human heart.

"Lord, I'm not gonna recite every one o' Your glorious be-RAY-titudes, much as I'd like to. No! For we are gathered here this evening to celebrate the annual sacrifice of our young.

"Here in Washington and aw-w-l up'n'down our eastern shore, from the great state o' Maine to that blinkered backwater we call Florida, senior proms are just itching to begin. Our brave boys and girls're champing at the bit like the prize studs and fillies we've raised them up to be. Their hooves are digging up divots from the dirt and flinging 'em skyward, as they wait for the starting gate to clang on back and for their death knell to sound.

"So I'll simply say THANK YOU, LORD, for the wisdom

of our forefathers. THANK YOU, LORD, for this marvelous rite of spring, established in antiquity upon our great got-damned land to honor the spirit of your Son. For His rage and hatred, we give abundant and abiding thanks. His ferocity we worship. We strive to emulate it. Every year on this aw-w-l important night, we seek to renew that living dogma, so as to kickstart our nation out of the dying days—out of the morally suspect doldrums—of winter and on into the rejuvenatory times of spring and summer.

"All of us, old, young, and in-between, bow our heads. Some small number of those heads shall roll, never again to rise upon the youthful necks that bear them.

"Their bodies shall, by their sorrowin' school chums, be futtered, so that reminders, dried and preserved, disseminate across the land and on into the future of this great and pow'ful nation. Mementos of prom night. Mementos too of those brave young souls, unaware—until the abrupt unlooked-for fall of that short sharp shock o' death—that they have been so chosen, that they have been so honored.

"Honored may they be.

"Honored, their parents.

"And may vast new hordes of talented seniors be unleashed upon this land, upon an economy in dire need of their skills, upon this close-knit community of sinners known as the Demented States of America.

"Got-damn, got-damn, in all manner of ways I say, got-damn!

"In JEEsus' name. Amen."

2
Slasher Slashed

Bastard sheriff. Damned gun-totin' goof had tried to throw a kink into this special night.

Couldn't. Not the essence of it anyway.

Zane ribbed the squealing mutt with a swift kick to stop its noise, but that only cranked up the volume.

Zane knelt before the couple, his knees cracking in protest. Through layers of fabric, he squeezed the woman's breasts, the man's organ.

The bag that clung stubbornly to the base of the man's left ear convinced you there might be something beneath. But his lack of a *right* earlobe—the sole blat in an otherwise persuasive visual symphony—told the real story.

Promjumper.

Even so, his exposed lobe-stump was quite the turn-on. Ditto the woman's undocked friendship lobe, whose faux-chartreuse dye-job reminded Zane of the crushed kernels of pistachios. And this doped-up duo was completely at his mercy.

The mutt's whimpers began again to grate on him. Zane checked his watch. Time to shake it.

He kissed the two of them on the lips, the man pretty much out, but the woman responding as in a dream, her pretty pink tonguetip starting to show.

They couldn't trace lipmarks.

Zane was sure of it.

Further play could wait until just before he axed them, once the

21

dog was dead.

After he'd had his practice? The young pair at the prom, whose names and place of death waited inside the packet upstairs.

Zane untied the leash from the sink trap.

Stupid mutt tried to lick his face, had to be batted away. He slack-jerked it into the light, then retied its leash to the trough leg closest to the drain.

That would minimize cleanup.

"Zane? You need anything?" Top of the cellar stairs.

Bitch wife wanted to watch. She had tried to coax him into taking her to the prom. Hedda would lick blood if he let her.

"For the zillionth time, I'm fine. Leave it alone, Hedda. You're staying home."

A hurt pause, then petulance: "Just trying to be helpful."

She shut the door.

The promise of the evening flared in Zane's body. Fired up by blood lust, he would come home from his killings at Corundum High and undo his worst mistake. Into the dustbin of memory would he drop-kick his sorry-ass wives. Then he and his lover would run off, assume new identities, and begin afresh.

When he let go of the leash, the dog's dumb exuberance yanked at the empty trough.

Damned thing needed ballast.

Zane's eyes lighted on the drugged couple. "What the heck."

The man alone might suffice.

They had shaved him at the jail. Homeless men typically had stubble or beards, but for prom practice they tended to clean up nicely.

Zane tugged at the man's right biceps.

"Come on, junior," he coaxed, shouldering the lulled deloused carton-dweller off the couch. The woman slid along the cushions, soft moans issuing from her lips. "You'll feel right at home in here."

It took several tries to get him into the trough. Zane knee'd one tuxedo'd leg over the rim, then the other, and lay the bastard down. He was heavy, more a matter of large than well-fed.

But this was the last time Zane would have to lift him.

More puppy tugs. More whimpers. More scrape and movement of the trough away from the drain.

Zane sighed.

The woman was in a bad way, her perm crushed against a couch arm as her fingers fretted at her brow. "Come on, honey. Your turn."

"Please, no." She was as listless as a sack of tapioca.

Zane drew her off the couch. A corsage of white carnations edged in blue tickled his nose. He snaked a hand beneath her gown, felt hot thigh, a bikini'd rump, hints of a slit.

Maneuvering her troughward, he wondered why no one this sexy had ever come on to him when he was her age.

He had her *now* though and, the law be damned, he would use her in some undetectable way, her and her companion both, before he was finished.

Zane positioned her atop her date, felled refugees from a wedding cake. The man's lobestub glistened like a dare. Zane pressed his lips to it.

The thrill of it blooded him below. Were time not pressing, he would have slipped off his lobebag and stroked himself to head-heaven.

The trough, which he pushed back into place by the drain, now had sufficient weight to anchor the dog's ardor. But the couple was showing signs of revival.

The medicine cabinet.

He raced for the steps. Hedda stood at the door, Camille topless beside her.

Zane glared at them. "Stay out of the basement," he warned, leaving the door ajar.

"Do you need anything?" Hedda asked.

"I'm fine."

Hallway. A snap of the light. Tired old sink. He clicked the mirror open and swung it aside. Medicines, sleeping pills, laxatives, a generous supply of Tuffskin-in-a-Tub.

Ah.

Chloroform.

Sampler drug-baskets had been the rage among realtors when he and the wives had traded up in houses two years before. Zane snatched the bottle up, shoved a few gauze pads into his back pocket, and returned to the basement.

The couple, still groggy, had begun to shift about in the trough, struggling for the energy to open their eyes. Zane knocked the man out first, then the woman, same pad on both. He had bought himself maybe ten minutes.

Keep focus on the mutt, keep his nerves calm, don't jinx his aim. Those were his goals.

Ready.

Ice Ghoul? *He'd* give them Ice Ghoul.

The axe seated itself in his hands, palm-wrap behind its blade. He walked about the drain until he faced the wag-tailed, droopy-tongued pup in the dim light, the gray trough stuffed with a heap of prom costumes.

Zane's practice chops in the woods outside of Corundum had been a cakewalk. Flinders flew. His arms sang to the rhythm of exertion, and the scent of tree sap swirled in his nostrils.

Here? Nothing but a chore.

Zane gritted his teeth, raised the sucker, and let fly. Missed the ribcage. Caught a paw instead. Blood bloomed where toes had been. The dog's whine rose to a freakish yelp.

Focus. Focus.

He inhaled on the upswing, then brought it down with a huff, slamming the dog back into the trough, gashing its belly. Out gushed a geyser of crimson, spilling across the concrete.

As the fur blackened around the blow, Zane lifted the axe once more, fine droplets in the air, that same stench that bullied its way down the school hallways when butchery class let out.

Again!

A hind leg, sliced, dangled awry. Those eyes, the panicked yelps; he should have chloroformed the damned *dog*.

Finish him, why don't you?

The next blow struck an artery. Blood fountained up and out, drenching Zane's pantleg. It splashed hot, then went cold and clingy. Such *life* there was in the mutt, struggling out of the carnage as if to undo it.

Zane caught its eyes, held them as he brought the blade straight down between them, burying it so that the skull collapsed and fell—a bleached steerhead in the desert—to the cement floor.

Zane's heart was pounding.

He laughed and cried with joy.

Through the cellar door, he heard a doorbell chime.

Let the bitches get it.

Despite an overpowering need to be chosen as the school's

designated slasher, Zane had always preferred violence at one remove.

The televised electrocutions on *Notorious* were just his speed. Indeed, he often used the show's soundtrack, its screams tracking the rise and fall of electricity through the victims, to draw the most amazing artwork from his students.

Now, he wasn't so sure.

This dog weren't no cord of wood. This had been life *itself*, and no more direct contact with life had Zane Fronemeyer had than in ending it.

First step, doggiedom.

Next, the homeless.

But could he endure their eyes? Damned straight he could!

Zane planted himself on the couch and sat forward, the axe angled like a leaf rake between his jittery knees.

Come on, come on, he thought, I didn't give you *that* much chloroform. Open your frigging eyes so I can finish you off and be on my way.

The cellar door unlatched.

Zane looked up in annoyance.

Dexter Poindexter averted his gaze from the mirror. He was a shy guy. Too shy for his own good, some people said.

That's what Mommy and Daddy told him, though Daddy Owen, the spouse they had divorced the year before, disagreed.

Dex fluffed the wide ends of his bone-white bowtie, nice smooth ripples. Its color and satin sheen matched his lobebag, a tight garter band right around the base of the ear and a generous splay below.

He sincerely hoped these things were dry-cleaned between rentals. It grossed Dex out to think of some other guy's lovelobe in this same bag. Maybe *many* guys, though styles changed often enough that it wasn't likely.

Dex shrugged into the coat, buttoned a button at his waist, and shot the sleeves.

His tux looked sharp.

Tweed would whistle at it. Her eyes would go wide. Of course, Dex would be busy admiring what a knockout *she* was in her gown, which she had described again and again these past few weeks in great detail.

It was fortunate they were in the dance band. Running through one chart after another would take their minds off the general terror.

As sophomores and juniors, he and Tweed had played senior proms, learning first hand what it was like to see the murdered couple carried into the gym, laid out beside the centerpiece, danced around, and at midnight torn apart.

That reminded him.

He went to the dresser and lifted the cleaver, its blade no longer than his index finger and not much wider. His church group—all church groups across the nation did this—had given him and Tweed practice. An expendable sheepdog. Dex had gotten a cross-section of tufted ear and only been nicked once.

Of course, tonight there would be more kids diving in to futter the couple. And their state of mind would be way more agitated.

That was for sure.

Dex's right leg twitched.

You had to be brave, cram in there, push and shove and lunge, praying that some doofus did not, by design or accident, clip your lobes, or slice off your fingers, or slash your face.

Dex raised his suitcoat's right flap.

These tuxes, the more expensive ones anyway, had a special pair of loops. On the right loop, he secured the handle of his cleaver. On the left, his Futterware container.

The cuffs caught his attention, as wide as high collars, and as flappy.

Cufflinks.

As stern as Dex's father was, he always had his son's welfare at heart. Dex removed the lid from the white box on his bureau. On top of a layer of cotton waited the gold-skull cufflinks his father had worn, and Dex's grampa before him.

Signs of love.

Mommy and Daddy had that ferocious look stitched to their faces. Harsh words spilled in profusion from their mouths. They were quick with the whip and Christlike in their savagery.

But they were proud of him, pleased in his choice of Tweed as a girlfriend, and bursting with joy that tonight was Dex's prom night.

He would brave the slasher, cut his way through the brambles, and emerge triumphant and ready to take his place as a useful citizen.

What more could he ask of life than that?

Dex poked a cufflink through a stiff ironed hole and snapped it into place.

The principal of Corundum High was taking his sweet time getting ready.

He wasn't showering.

He wasn't dressing.

Nor was he busy thinking mean thoughts about the little shits who would get their comeuppance tonight.

In point of fact, Peyton "Futzy" Buttweiler was on his hands and knees in the playroom, being whipped senseless by his lacklove wives.

"I'm sorry," sniveled Futzy.

Torment sneered. "Far as I'm concerned, you're not nearly sorry enough. He isn't, is he, Trusk? Lay into the fucker!"

And Trusk, the heftier wife, did as she was told.

Frayed and beaded whip-ends sizzled through the air and snapped away, interwoven with the high smack of Torment's bullwhip, crosswise upon naughty little Futzy Buttweiler's back.

Bloodspray spattered the walls, an abstract mural in progress.

Futzy's much deserved flaying fired up his brain. But his dead daughter's image burned as bright as ever.

"Harder," he pleaded. "Harder!"

"You miserable little shit-smoocher," said Torment. "Don't you *dare* order me and Trusk about. We're not a couple of high school tramps. You see all those blood flecks on the wall?" She bunched up twists of Futzy's sweat-slicked hair and yanked his head back. "Tomorrow, first thing, you're going to lick 'em all off, every damned one of them. No breakfast for old Futzy-Wutzy till he gets these walls spanking clean."

"His wounds are closing," observed Trusk.

"Well, fuck," said Torment, "we can't have that now, can we? Open 'em back up. Make new ones. Real fierce and frenzied, Trusk. Slice the scumwipe some indelible memories. Volley!"

With that, Trusk and Torment redoubled their effort. Grunting into their swings, they so minced the skin covering Futzy's shoulders and ribs, that wide expanses of bone peered through. Seas of red rushed in, to be parted by renewed whipsmacks.

"*Fuck* the little bastard!" shouted Torment. "*Fuck* his sorry ass!"

Futzy wept.

Kitty's young face shone bright and smiling. Her senior picture.

But around the edges of her smile peered an accusatory look, a look of shame and disgust at her father's inaction at her senior prom.

She was right to scorn him.

Do it, he thought to the two bitches he had taken in to punish him after Kitty's death.

A marital masochist, that's what he was.

Do it. Do it!

He dared not say it aloud, lest they withhold his punishment entirely.

"Now," said lean and mean Torment, the brains of the duo. "Give off. Man the machine."

Trusk's whip handle clattered to the floor.

Futzy braced himself for the pain.

Spang went the release mechanism and *hush-hush-hush* the grains of salt from the funnel above. They pinging and stippled against his skin, finding their way, much of them, into the V's of his wounds.

Salt knifed into him everywhere. Pain waved through his body like the unending misery twenty years before, the thoughts he could not shut off no matter how hard he tried.

Futzy passed out, the harsh words of his wives ringing in his ears, longing for death but knowing it would not yet be his.

The blue clunker pulled up to the curb and parked two blocks from Zane Fronemeyer's house.

A quiet walk past manicured lawns, no faces peering out. The doorbell chimed. Zane would be in the basement. But if not, if he was finished already, knifing three of them wouldn't pose too great a problem.

All planned, all smooth.

Familiar heads appeared at the decorative window in the door: Hedda and Camille, taste of sex on the lips, a threeway suckle on left lobes until they had gone giddily into simultaneous oral orgasm.

The deadbolt snapped and the door swung open.

Surprise lit their faces.

"Hello, you two." Casual. Not too loud.

"Zane's home," said Hedda. "Are you sure—"

"It's all right. If he comes upstairs, I'll offer an excuse. I have a few things I wanted to give you. Is it all right if I come in?"

Better be.

Discretion cautioned against the ruckus of forced entry.

Empty boxes in the clutched paper bag hid the shape of the knife.

Camille fretted. "Well I don't—"

"Sure," said Hedda.

Snap judgment.

That and her sex drive, a burning focus on whatever flesh happened to be at hand, were Hedda's most alluring traits.

The door settled snug in its frame as Hedda surged forward into a kiss.

Camille went nonlinear: "Hedda, what are you doing? Zane could pop up any minute!"

Hedda's hunger was palpable. "Take us away," she urged. "Tonight."

"Soon. I promise."

"Zane's a prize bore," said Hedda, her eyes hard and fiery. Amazing how such an attractive woman now held no interest at all, had become so guiltlessly killable.

"We don't like him," Camille offered.

"The three of us will be dynamite together. It'll happen soon, not much longer. But for now, I've got to go. I only wanted to drop these gifts off."

Beyond the art teacher's fluxed mother, the vestibule arched into the family room, where heavy curtains shut out the night.

As they approached the couch, they passed an end table that held a thick packet with Corundum High's clocktower logo in its upper left corner and "Z. Fronemeyer" scrawled across it in loopy ballpoint.

"What's the occasion?" asked Camille.

"Nothing special. I just wanted to express my love for you both. Hedda, sit here. Camille, beside her. That's it."

The bagtop uncrumpled. No footsteps clumped up the cellar stairs. A free shot at Fronemeyer's wives.

Inside the bag, the duct-taped boxes split on a hinge to yield the knife handle.

"Close your eyes and open your hands."

"Oh come on!" Blond-haired Hedda gave a practiced flick to her head that tossed just so her shoulder-length shag-cut. But she grinned.

"Humor me. Please."

They did.

The razored edge opened Hedda's throat to the bone, savage and deep, no need to grip a hank of hair. Just as well, since Camille's eyes sprang open at the sudden gesture. Her mouth sucked in air for a scream.

Clamp that mouth.

Press her back into the couch, off-balance.

Putty.

Once more the knife blade. Its swift passage reflected in Camille's eyes. She pitched right, dying, as the weapon was wiped clean on an end-cushion.

Doing Zane in was the goal, which wasn't yet a sure thing. No time to savor his wives' death throes. These two were mere pawns.

Kill Zane.

Then tackle the packet.

Game plans were always easier when you knew what your enemy had in mind. Besides, a map of the school's secret backways would be a welcomed refresher.

The kitchen flashed by in bright fluorescent light. Racing heartbeats erased all detail.

Stay calm. Set things right.

An image of the Lion of God slaughtering the moneychangers flared up. Some sanitized filmstrip from Bible school long ago.

Love owed, love denied.

These moved the world.

The knob felt cool. The flimsy cellar door, flung back, gave onto blue-painted steps.

Exasperation: "Hedda, for the last time—"

"It's me, Zane." Conceal the knife behind a pantleg. In the subdued light on the stairs, it would look perhaps like an injured arm.

Zane puzzled out his lover's name. His voice turned surprised and annoyed. Halfway down, Zane became visible, the washing machine behind him.

He rose from the couch, holding a bloody axe. The trough was dimly lit, but a bare lightbulb above the dryer caught glistens of gore threading into the drain. "But we were going to meet at *your* place after I . . . what kind of a . . . hey wait, what do you think you're—"

The axe looked tricky, a sharp thing that might fall in a scuffle. Go for the bold move, came the thought. A left-handed grip on the axe handle. Done!

Zane clenched tighter to counter.

The knife flew up and over. It caught on something hard in his chest, then slipped past to stab deep.

A Greek mask frowned upon his face: a bunched brow, anguished eyes, lips fizzling like a limp balloon, all of it in motion. Flares of life flashing by tried to stick and hold. But something vital had been skewered.

Zane collapsed, a house of cards falling inward. The axehead hung abruptly left, his fingers releasing their grip on the handle. The axe clattered to the floor. Then Zane, drifting downward, took to the tattered couch.

"Why—" he wheezed.

"Call it payback."

A glimpse aside into obscurity. The cellar smelled like meat and sewage. You would think the homeless would catch on. But they were as dumb as Thanksgiving turkeys.

Zane had just snuffed two more here.

Close to fifteen thousand nationwide bought the farm every year, if the networks told the truth.

Fifteen thousand more in prom couples.

A chill took hold, then burgeoning heat.

The blade angled from Zane's chest, the stir of a gelatinous stew. Its grim handle gristled in strained grip, curving and turning as the killer carved.

It wouldn't do to risk the possibility of revival. Zane would pay the price, as his spouses had done.

And the payments would continue, multiplying toward midnight, until healing took hold and love thrilled the heart once more.

Upstairs waited the packet. Keys, maps, agendas, the naming of the couple.

Not that this last was more than a curiosity.

One couple alone would not suffice.

Nothing near.

Still, they were names to bear in mind if ruin threatened and they fell to hand.

Fronemeyer's wristwatch, upside-down and spattered, read 6:20. Time to move on. The worn cushions soaked up his blood. But the stairs beckoned.

Music rose out of memory's ashes, slap'n'smack mixed with terrified slow-shuffling embraces on the dance floor.

Moving on, feeling high, sailing toward fated waters.

Tonight would be beautiful indeed.

PART TWO
Invitation to a Dance

"High school is closer to the core of the
American experience than anything else
I can think of."
   —Kurt Vonnegut, Jr.

"In skating over thin ice, our safety is in
our speed."
   —Ralph Waldo Emerson

3

A Delectible Frenzy

Whap-whap-whap, went the blades of the chopper, off-camera.

On a wall-sized screen at the far end of the Cabinet Room, toy houses on winding streets drifted past far below. Inset on the lower left, a woman with a mission waved to her husbands and drove off in a late-model car.

This year, a school in a suburb of Dallas had been chosen for the high mucky-mucks' delectation.

The designated slasher?

Karn Flentrop, a Home Ec teacher with killer gams, a clench-fisted upjut of breasts, taut and tantalizing lobes, and the perkiest bloodlust in her every glance.

For the camera's benefit, Ms. Flentrop's threesome had lingered over a love-hug in their living room.

Hunched, head turned, glued to the tube as he had been for hours sat Willy Wanker, the Secretary of Cultural Impoverishment.

Wanker seldom spoke in meetings, nor did anyone interact with him. His preferred mode of communication consisted of an unending stream of pontifications e-mailed out to all and sundry.

The Secretary of War, a chubby boozer named Barnaby Sloper, he of the bullet head and outsized belly, cracked a joke and wangled his bulk into a chair. Cabinet appointees on either side of him gave polite chuckles.

Then the door opened and a Shite House lackey with a red face and a rumpled suitcoat bellowed, "President Hargill Windfucker."

All rose to acknowledge their commander in chief. As Cholly

Bork tiptoed Windfucker through the door and across the carpet, the elected marionette's limbs lightly clacked like hanging beads parted by a sylph's hand. The Vice President and his entourage followed.

"Be seated, gentlemen. And lady," said the President in Bork's voice, his hands magnanimous, his back angled in a ceremonial bow.

They took seats.

A raised finger, a twist of the neck. "Brief us, Mr. Hix."

Chief of Staff Blathery Hix, a fat folder beneath one arm and a headset on his head, stood next to the President's chair. "Top right, Mister President, coming into view, is Choke Cherry High. Built in the forties. Nicely run down, not enough money, fuck the kids. They lobbied hard this year for the privilege of a presidential viewing, hoping for funding in return. I gave them our usual empty promises."

"Never commit when you can waffle, Hix."

"Yes, sir. Activate tunnel cameras." The helicopter view vanished. The screen jumped to a slow infrared glide through the secret backways of Choke Cherry High.

Delia Gaskin rinsed off the whipped suds she had worked up. Then she toweled dry and squeezed a dip of skin cream into her right hand. The cream went on smooth, circled along her cheekbones and sharped back and forth over her nose with one flexing palm.

Delia wore her thirty-eight years well. As one approached forty, one's face tended to take on spots and blemishes. Nothing near as unsightly as the blotch-bursts of sexagenarians like Futzy Buttweiler. But the vibrancy of youth inevitably faded. That hadn't yet happened to Delia, and for that she was grateful.

Skin care paid off.

Wigwag padded into the bathroom, gave a doleful double-*wumpf* in protest, and padded out, his message delivered.

The fur which rimmed the lop-ends of Wigwag's ears bore toothmarks. Delia reminded herself to brush them out before leaving for the prom. It wouldn't do to fuel, with the kindling of truth, student rumors of her peculiar ways.

In a distant room, a TV newscaster droned on unintelligibly.

Delia buried her face in a thick towel, not bothering to pull it off the rack. Before paper towels and blowers, restrooms had sported unending tugs of linen. The unrolling, eternally dreamy swatch of students passing through Corundum High reminded her of those endless linen strips. They passed along patterns of speech, class notes, cruelties, and rumors, one generation to the next.

Especially rumors.

But Delia wasn't simply a pet lover.

She had a much more interesting life than anyone might suspect. Brest Donner, the tenth grade biology teacher, had stolen a moment with her in the infirmary yesterday.

Brest was a sweet armful.

Her lips had sucked at Delia's friendship lobe, then brushed past her mouth to nuzzle and nip at the bagged left lobe, while Brest's own stylish lobebag swayed a tantalizing few inches away.

Brest's and Trilby's marriage to Bix Donner was crumbling, she had confided. She thought it conceivable that they might whisk Trilby's little girl away with them and go it alone.

If they were circumspect, a female threeway, despite its risk and illegality, might be in the offing.

Bix. Bothersome Bix. Two years before, he had hit on Delia at a faculty-staff retreat. Boorish lump. It never ceased to amaze one, the mates people chose.

The Donner family was slated to chaperone tonight. No doubt, beady-eyed Bix would laser-beam an unwanted glare of lust again and again across Delia's body. That would make things more difficult by half.

But if she cut the sucker down early, she could scoop out some breathing room. Enough, perhaps, that she might manage to set aside the trauma of her *own* prom, two decades past, and ease into the evening's festivities.

Delia dried her lobes vigorously, musing at how plain and unarousing lefties were when one was alone. Really, lefties weren't all that different from righties. Yet the world made such a big deal of covering them at puberty.

America did, anyway. Europe was, as usual, far more enlightened.

Bold upon the beaches.

Delia switched off the bathroom light and strode through her apartment. Her low-slung pup trotted after, a swinging hammock of dogflesh.

The TV voice grew louder: "Here on the eastern seaboard, it's ten to eight. High school doors are about to close. In the more westerly timezones, students and faculty prepare for the evening's events. DBC will provide comprehensive coverage throughout the night, as schools report in. Turnabouts, bizarre methods of slaughter, live updates from selected high schools—it's all here for you, all evening and on into the night, at News Central on DBC's Prom Night Special.

"Tuck Winter has news elsewhere. Tuck?"

Delia glanced at the set. Her body flexed as she walked, more buff than her school uniform led people to suspect.

Dewy-eyed Watt MacQuarrie, standing before a map of the nation, had just swiveled his head toward prankster Tuck Winter, a dumb weather jock whose smug mannerisms Delia hated.

Tuck Winter clearly had aspirations beyond weatherboy. Tonight, he wore a somber face. His left earlobe sported a staid lobebag, unlike the flamboyant ones fans of his weather report were forever sending in.

"Thanks, Watt," he began. "The RepellingCant primary took a nasty turn today, as Carty boosters released a videotape in which Bork Berenson kneels to—"

Delia tuned the sucker out. She left the bedroom door open, in case a sound-snippet lashed in to tantalize.

But as she shrugged into a dressy outfit, not her perennial school-nurse whites, she caught only snippets of the odd report. Plans for the next day's corporate picnics, where the deadwood would be picked off to make way for the previous night's grads. The uptick in stocks tied to mortuaries and crematoria. And some dull editorial on back-biting and finger-pointing among members of the Committee to Assassinate the President.

Commercial music blared.

Delia snugged a blue chiffon bag up about her left lobe. The bow that concealed its elastic tickled her lower helix.

She examined herself in the mirror above her dresser. Dark hair, short and styled. Skin pale and smooth.

A quick rummage through her gym bag. Yep, everything in its place.

The TV audio shifted into the languid unwinding of a saxophone melody.

Delia rushed out to watch.

Resentment toward the rules that dictated who could serve as a designated slasher routinely seethed in her head. Now, that resentment was augmented by the excitement these controversial new perfume ads produced in her.

The eye of the camera caressed the bare sleek cocoa back of a model. As her provocative voice pressed all sorts of sensual buttons, her delicate fingers toyed with a drawstring. The top of the model's lobebag loosened.

She coyly smiled.

Abruptly, the lobebag fell free, a daring stretch of skin coming into view. And as the uncovered tip threatened to hit the eye, the camera cut to a sea anemone provocatively waving its tentacles.

Killer.

Delia's mouth watered and her rage grew.

The fuckwits at the FCC had threatened to pull the plug on this daring ad campaign.

At Corundum High, an equally arbitrary and infuriating imposition of authority dictated that teachers alone—no staff, no principals, and never a school nurse—could off the prom couple.

As far as Delia was concerned, the airwaves belonged to everyone and should be entirely free. Lobesucking orgies on TV ought to be, if demand required, the order of the day.

And *all* adult employees of a high school ought to have an equal chance at being chosen.

Indeed, it was her opinion that passion and zeal should favor those who would put fire and fury into the kill. Delia had vast stores of rage in need of release, both from the student ridicule she had to endure each day and from the painful memories of a love dismembered.

Perhaps tonight would be different.

Things might work out for her.

Maybe Bix would bite it big-time. Brest and Trilby would love her. And she would see the nastiest students sprawled dead upon the Ice Ghoul's lap, ready for a well-deserved futtering at midnight.

Or perhaps the night held greater wonders than Delia dared imagine.

Somewhere in America's heartland, deep in an urban pustule, a cadre of anti-slasher terrorists, clad in black, slinked along back alleys to gather in the basement of an abandoned elementary school building.

Their leader, lit by moonlight streaming through a caked window, peeled off her ski mask and tucked it into her belt.

Emboldened, her co-conspirators unmasked too.

Eyes flashed from face to face. Great fear dwelt in them. Pride and excitement. The black-clad crew numbered seven, a spinoff from an above-ground anti-slasher organization the government begrudgingly tolerated.

"Let's review the plan," she said. "You and you will detain Sheriff Boltz once he has locked down the school. Gag him, secure his arms, hurry him into the passageways, sedate him, then give me the word."

"What if he puts up a fight?"

She paused, then steeled herself. "Years of talk have gone nowhere. They've shrugged off our protests and petitions." She laughed. "Listen to me. You guys have it memorized."

Eyes on fire, she addressed the questioner: "Use any means necessary. That's why I chose the two of you for this mission. Minimize his pain, but don't hesitate to inflict it. If you have to, waste him. We cannot afford to raise an alarm. The syringe will make him docile but its effects are not instantaneous."

She glanced up into the moonlight, her face tense. Had she heard something?

No.

"You three take the east wing of the school. By now, each of us has burned into our brains a map of the backways. Me and my hubbies will handle the west wing. With luck, we'll be there before the slasher and catch him coming off the elevator from the underground garage. They've secured the garage with a punch code, alarms after the third wrong sequence, so that's out. Other questions?"

She scanned them, her jet-black mop of hair clinging to her scalp.

"I'm proud of you all. Our kids are at stake, their lives yes but also their minds. They will *not* be inured to violence; we and folks like us will see to that. With luck and the grace of a reasonable God, we will end this horror in our generation. There I go again!"

"One last check of the walkie talkies."

They tugged them from their belts.

Dexter Poindexter's senses had never been more attuned to his surroundings.

The coupe's interior swirled with seeped-in aromas: cheeseburger wrappings, gym sweat, whiffs of adolescent horniness. Gleams of moonlight shot knife-sharp across the dashboard. The plastic steering wheel slid cool and stippled through his fingers.

A twelve-year stint of classes had come to an end, the last exam passed, the last cafeteria meal chowed down, the last homeroom roster called.

Tonight was the culmination of so many months of attending school that Dex's memory knew nothing else.

True, summer vacations had supplied breathers that, at their best, stretched to eternity—beaches and boat houses and waterskiing on upstate lakes.

But every September, new looseleaf notebooks were purchased, their pungent faux-leather smell beguiling the nose. Book covers were bought as well, Corundum High's colors, a fierce-eyed gray-and-green ram surrounded by ornate shields scrawled with latinate sayings.

Strange as it seemed, the terror Dex felt about school's not resuming in the fall seemed far more heart-stopping than tonight's slim chance at being hacked to death.

No matter whose life ended at the tip of the slasher's blade, he and Tweed would be touched by the killing. Worse if two of their best buds, or particularly bright-futured seniors, bought it.

But they had been steeled for that.

The victims' names, engraved in proud italic, would be added to the gold plaque in the display case at Corundum High's entranceway, their lives lauded in the newspaper and in local churches the morning after.

And life would go on.

Familiar streets peeled away, the same houses he passed whenever he drove to Tweed's place, rang her doorbell, and gave a "Hello, sir" to her dad, Mr. Megrim, Dex's eleventh-grade history teacher.

Tonight, house fronts glistened with street light. Clusters of people peered from windows or lingered on front porches, watching passing cars and wondering about who rode in them.

Moms and dads driving their kids to the prom? Spiffed-up promgoers possibly high on drugs? Or some over-curious night-cruisers?

Perhaps they relived their own memories of prom night, memories that fiercely glowed or gave off pale flares of longing for lost loved ones.

Dex released a sigh, not realizing how tight he had held his breath in. He checked his face in the rearview mirror, lobebag stylishly rakish, his skin zit-free from hairline to jaw.

He smoothed through a turn.

The headlights of an approaching car blinded him and passed by.

Dex checked his watch.

Time to spare.

In ten minutes, Tweed would float into his arms, her pink-sequined gown swaying as they went out the door and headed toward the prom and a new life together.

4

Relinquishment

Tweed Megrim twirled before the mirrored door of her rumble-back closet. A pink-sequined vision twirled there in reverse.

Such fluffery looked weird on her, yet she found it strangely beguiling.

She knew her boyfriend felt likewise about his tuxedo. She and Dex were Christmas baubles, gussied up for one another, for public display, and, God help them, for potential sacrifice. It gave Tweed a whole heap of scaring.

To be honest, it thrilled her too.

Dex. Dear Dex.

Elsewhere in the house, Daddy was singing as always a happy song. Visions of Dexter Poindexter swam dreamily before her. Awkward in lobeplay, a heartmelt whenever they engaged in secret bouts of flay'n'heal, Dex was the guy she wanted to cling to forever.

Soon he would arrive.

Tweed scrutinized her face and hair. Not a strand out of place, her complexion peach-perfect all over, her lips bowed and demure.

Condor Plasch, arm in arm with Blayne Coom, intruded on her thoughts. The pierced-in zippers along *their* lips made her shudder.

Pierced skin was one thing. But one's lips were permanent, neither growing nor healing with the removal of earring or barbell. Once disfigured, they remained so.

Worse rumors had spread about Altoona and Pimlico, a couple of female punks who had the hots for Condor and Blayne. What *they* had done to themselves . . .

Her father knocked.

The door opened a crack. "Hon?"

"It's okay," Tweed said. "Come in."

Daddy lumbered through the door like a burly brown bear. "Tweed, O Tweed, my daughter Tweed," he sang, "I saw your boyfriend's car pull up. And by the bye, you move the night to tears."

Daddy looked none the worse for his non-stop activity: dropping her kid sister off at school for parking duty (Jenna's prom was a year away, but a healthy streak of morbidity had drawn her to the periphery of this one), and spending an exhausting day at the mall with Tweed, having to put up with the consumerist orgasms of screaming mallgoers, not to mention the tiny squeakers Tweed had done her best to squelch.

She gave her dad a peck on the cheek. "I'll be down in a minute."

He trilled an okay and was gone.

For the umpteenth time, Tweed gave herself the once-over.

Downstairs, a doorbell chimed.

The lights in the mirror seemed suddenly to dim. A premonition passed through her.

Out of hundreds of couples—those that had naturally coalesced and the pairs decreed by the principal the week before—she and Dex had been chosen.

Tonight was their last night on earth. They would be murdered by some teacher, a colleague of her father's and maybe a favorite of hers, oh let it not be Claude Versailles.

Laid before the Ice Ghoul, they would bleed and release. Then, as midnight chimed, they would be hacked and futtered into a frenzy of pieces, their blood staining survivors' garments, their sundered flesh sun-dried and saved as mementos of escape.

Tweed flushed.

Light rushed back in around her.

It *couldn't* be them.

The odds favored their survival.

The same odds favored *everyone's* survival.

In a rare moment of mean spirit, she wished that Cobra and Peach, the couple least liked by anyone at school, had been chosen. Then she nixed the thought, touched a fingertip to her friendship lobe for luck, and swished out the bedroom door.

Dex was standing near the piano in his white tux, holding a corsage, looking spiffed up and out of place and beautiful. As her father beamed and hummed, she let her boyfriend's warm lips cup the tip of her right lobe, then did likewise to him, a chaste gesture of public affection.

Above her left breast, Dex pinned the pastel carnations.

"Perfect, perfect," sang her father.

He whipped out his camera, a mercifully brief moment, Dex's arm around her and a goofy grin on his face. Snap. Whirr. Her father's song turned grim, a rolling barcarole: "If they kill you, you know, I'll just *have* to *kill* them *back*!"

People found her father's habitual singing strange. His history students especially. But though he claimed he had spoken normally before he turned twenty, his singing was all Tweed had ever known.

It seemed perfectly . . . well . . . like *Dad* to her.

"Don't worry, sir," said Dex. "We're not the ones. We can't be. But if we are, we'll survive it. I've been working on my moves. Any teacher who touches Tweed is dead meat."

Dex exuded more confidence than Tweed thought justified, but she blushed with pride.

Dad sang about the TV show *Notorious*, how they saved the yummiest executions for prom night. Tonight's fry of a pair of mass murderers promised to be extra special, he told them.

Then Dex shook his hand, assured him he would have Tweed back by midnight, and they were out the front door.

"You okay?" he asked.

"Oh, sure." Tweed swept her prom dress clear of the passenger door slam.

When Dex slid behind the wheel, she felt impelled to elaborate. "To tell you the truth, I'm scared. Not about the prom so much as about losing you. But if I have to go through this, and jeez I guess I do, you're the one I want beside me more than anybody in the whole wide world."

Dex kissed her. "Me too." His left hand gave her lobebag a quick feel. Tweed gasped at her sudden arousal and turned away. "Not here," she said. "Not yet."

He mumbled an apology.

"No problem," she said.

After the ordeal—once they had used the tiny cleavers hanging at their waists, once the mass futtering had stained their clothing, their legs were danced to exhaustion, and they sat side by side parked on some bluff—only then would she sanction Dex's loving feints toward lobeplay. Perhaps she would initiate a few herself.

Dex fired up his coupe and grinned. "Your dad sure is hyped."

"He's nervous. He really hates prom night."

"Of course," Dex said. "There's you and your sister."

Tweed shook her head. "He's never liked it. We make it worse, of course, me being in jeopardy this year, Jenna next. But Dad contributes to the anti-slasher cause. Sometimes, he attends their meetings." She raised a finger to her lips. "Our secret."

"Sure thing." Dex signaled a turn.

"There's no telling with parents," he went on. My mom's really into dog-cracking. We went to a contest at the fairgrounds last week and she screamed her lungs out for this swung sheepdog. Poor thing didn't have a prayer against a Saint Bernard maneuvered by a Scotsman. At home, Jesus the Lion is forever on her lips. She likes to shout at sit-com characters to 'throw the other fist.' But get her off by herself, just you and her? She's as quiet and kind and considerate as anybody you could name."

"I like your mom," Tweed said.

Dex took his eyes off the road. "She likes you too."

"I'm glad." She snuggled closer. "Do you think Mr. Jones'll make us play a lot?"

"Nah," said Dex. "He's rehearsed our butts off, but I think he'll do like last year. Give us a solid hour of playing, bust our chops, then let the seniors go, and play the remaining sets with a smaller group, him on trumpet—"

Tweed groaned. "He's so awful!"

"Old blubber lips." Dex laughed. "Around ten, he'll throw in the towel and give the rest of the night over to slap'n'smack and dreamy ballads off the turntable."

Tweed caressed Dex's tuxedo'd arm. "I hope he plays *loads* of dreamy ballads."

Dex smiled. "It's going to be a special night, isn't it?"

"We get past the ordeal, you *bet* it will be." She put lots of promise in her look. Elation rose in her sweetheart's eyes.

They had their whole lives ahead of them. Once the fear lifted, the chosen couple had been slaughtered and futtered, and they knew what positions the killings at tomorrow's corporate picnics opened up, she and Dex could think about directions.

About the future.

About tripling up with someone known or not yet known, someone who would augment their twosome in a splendid new way.

"I love you, Dex," she said, and he shyly said, "Well shucks, me too, right back at ya."

Gerber Waddell loved taking showers. Hot water thundered down. Nobody swatted his hand away from his naked sexlobe. And he didn't have to hide his anger behind a benign smile.

Gerber tugged at his roused lefty like a bell-pull. In his mind's eye, the generous lips of Jonquil Brindisi, teacher of big sins, teased his sexlobe.

This phantom Jonquil rose from the billowing steam, slurping him in, disgorging him. Her eyes hungered for payback.

Like a panther she padded before him, one hand spanning to finger her nipples, the other down-and-in where she rocked.

But as she sucked his lobe, her skin veined, red and cracked, falling in chunks to the stippled floor. The scalding water needled her until she bled, pain everywhere upon that gorgeous body.

Still, she endured it, her lips fixed on his pleasure, though every suck trebled her agony and plashed the floor hot with crimson.

"Eat it, you snooty little bitch!" he muttered. How she deserved her pain, after years of an aloofness that screamed, I'm better than any lowlife janitor.

Then Gerber Waddell rose heavenward, careful to damp down his howls of joy. Beating streams of water sculpted perfect orgasm from the oval of his mouth.

Drifting down, Gerber stayed with his hatred. Tiles cooled along his spine as he bent at the waist, a jogger stitched for wind. His hair twisted in thunderous waterfalls.

Past torments paraded by.

The corporate heights from which he had once judged others.

The picnic murder of a woman he had loved, his own hand on the knife, and a lethal slash at the jealous bastard who had contrived for her to be chosen.

The petitions.

The forgiveness.

Sojourns in white rooms where they pried out chunks of his brain, taught him docility, thrust a mop and a bucket into his hands. And, after many years, tools.

Tools had their uses. Lately, Gerber had pondered them, how they might express impulses too long damped down and denied.

He slammed the faucet shut. Blasts of water shuddered to a halt.

Gerber rumbled the opaque door open and snagged a towel off the rack. Them green-coated scumsuckers had made a mistake. For all their hacking and hewing, they had missed a spot.

The urge.

Mild Gerber, feeble yes-man at Corundum High.

He'd teach *them*. He'd whip their fannies. Any more cheek and he would reach into his utility belt and tin-snip their lovelobes off.

Gerber stood before the steam-coated mirror, savagely brushing his teeth. His left hand sawed vigorous and wild across his jaw. The fingers of his right hand stilted against the counter, bamboo shoots white with tension.

When he emerged, the Bleaks were watching TV in their bedroom at the end of the hall. Missus Bleak chirped, "Water okay, Gerber?" and he said "Yes'm, it was," a hand concealing his left lobe, a towel tucked about his waist.

Gerber went into his room, where Mister and Missus Bleak's grown son had lived. Blue-black janitor duds lay like a dead flat man on the bed, undies and socks beside them. Off days, he wore Salvation Army crap, clothes that felt more like him than these did. Deceptive comfort for the normals. Put Gerber in somebody else's house, somebody else's uniform. Peg him. Make him safe for mobocracy.

But when he wore thrift store hand-me-downs, his thoughts came more easily. And when he wore nothing at all, they tumbled about in his head, wild, nasty, and free. Lull the bastards. Put him in safe togs, slip a denim lobebag over his lefty.

But a game had two players, he thought. One day, one *night*, he would break a few rules and loose the demon again.

Maybe tonight. Prom night. A night of beauty and savagery. It would be easy to throw a wrench or two into the cogs. All it would take was simply to give in. To act, once more, upon those suppressed urges.

Gerber pictured Missus Bleak coming through the door. Like a pork-bomb, she flew straight apart, warming the air with outflung spews of gore as her pudgy face exploded.

Somehow, it made this more like home.

More inviting.

Shiverful, spineful.

Mia Jenner gave her younger husband Bonn a look, then tossed barbs at Pelf, who sat cozy in his favorite armchair, pooled in lamplight.

"I can't believe you're doing that," she scolded. "Really, Pelf."

The older man peered over his glasses, one finger stuck in the library book. "Doing what?"

Exasperated eyes. "Reading."

"I read *every* night."

Bonn chimed in. "This is Fido's prom night. He'll be down soon in his tuxedo. Bowser will be showing up in *his* tuxedo. Look at you, sitting there in your robe and slippers."

"Like this was any old weekend," added Mia, snaking an arm around Bonn's waist.

"To hell with Bowser McPhee." Pelf's familiar grin slung above his jowls. "I *luxuriate* on Saturday nights: a soothing bath, a good book, a tumble in the hay and a perfect lobesuck with you two fine folks." He brushed aside the world. "People make too much of prom night. Let Fido and Bowser have fun, let blood be spilt, but for gosh sakes, let lovable old Pelf read his thriller."

Mia turned to Bonn. "He's begging for it."

"I think so too." Bonn eyed the instruments of pleasure on the coffee table.

"Isn't he begging for it?" asked Mia.

Bonn reached to retrieve.

A pair of stiff riding crops stuck out from between his fingers like black leather drumsticks. "Yes honeybunch, no question."

He handed Mia her weapon of choice.

"I'm *not* begging for it," Pelf insisted, grinning as he closed his book.

He probed deep into the cushion crack and coaxed out a hand-tooled, vegetable-tanned, sharkskin beauty, the riding crop his spouses had given him on his fiftieth birthday. Despite eleven years of wear, the thing had staying power and a humming *thwack* that sang of quality. It shone with crusted weltflow. Pelf gripped its handle and hunched forward.

Bonn said, "Let's get him," and charged in.

Mia followed, raising her lustiest yowl to the rafters. Her crop whistled down hard on Pelf's terryclothed buttocks as he rose to meet his attackers.

Back into the armchair they drove him, riding its floorward arc but not missing a battering beat as they tumbled across the carpet.

Mia lost herself in gaiety and torn clothing, ending up in her favorite position: cushioned by soft pillows, plugged below, her crop hand free to punish her lovers.

Bonn crouched to rouse her as his lickables bobbed hot against her lips.

Their laughter stopped when Fido yelled, not for the first time, "Dad, Mom, Dad. Bowser just drove up."

Mia, unBonning her mouth, angled toward her son. Spiffed and slicked to steal the heart of any youngster, Fido, class clown, stood there waiting for his special night to begin.

Door chimes rang out *bing-bong-bing-bong*, followed at once by Bowser McPhee's irritating shave-and-a-haircut rap.

The skin on Pelf's shoulder was red and raw. He slipped out of her, pulled about himself the tatters of his bathrobe, cinched it, and said he would get the door.

Mia righted the armchair and sat down.

She'd be *damned* if she would bother getting up to greet a belligerent little no-account like Bowser McPhee.

She touched the gaping flesh of one welt and made sizzling-lips sound and a face of pain. As the door opened, her fingers shot up to check her left lobe.

No problem, nothing showing, bag in place. But it never hurt to be sure.

Bowser McPhee was as fleshy and dark as ever. "Good evening, sir. Good evening, sir." He waved at Mia and she nodded. "Ma'am."

Fido came into the creepy kid's arms as they traded perfunctory right-lobe kisses.

Her husbands engaged in small talk, half-nods and smiles in her direction, until her son and his date were out the door. Mia crossed her legs. Her fingers fidgeted on the chair's arms.

Bonn misinterpreted. "Worried?"

"Nope," she said. "My son's from a charmed line. Fido will come home with a choice slice of flesh in his Futterware. But my God, he could do so much better than Bowser McPhee."

"Bowser *is* a bucket of slime, isn't he?" said Pelf. "But our boy is young. He's testing the waters. I don't believe the McPhee kid will be his final choice."

"We shouldn't have picked a dog's name," said Mia.

Bonn spoke up. "Something more normal may have helped."

Easy for Bonn to say, thought Mia, since he had had nothing to do with the decision.

"Dog names were all the rage back then," said Pelf in their defense. "Mia and I had no way of knowing. Besides, we've met plenty of Rexes and Spots, even another Fido our son's age, who have all been super kids. Nope, I don't think his name's the problem."

After a glum pause, Bonn offered, "At least he has a date. The school didn't have to pair him up."

"Small favors," Mia said. Her younger spouse was a handsome brute, juicy with passion, but his mind was as limp as week-old lettuce.

"Don't worry," said Pelf, massaging her shoulders. "He'll turn out fine."

"Once he dumps that walking embarrassment."

Pelf gave Mia's right cheek a resounding swat, raising a blush there. "For the love of Christ, sweetie, relax. Fido has more sense than people credit him with. Sure he's in tight with Bowser McPhee now. But it's more a buddy-buddy thing than love, from what I can see."

Mia took the hand that had struck her. "You think so?" She raised it to her mouth and bit deep into Pelf's thumb. Blood welled bitter upon her lips.

Pelf winced. "I'm betting that Fido goes into the prom with his eyes open and scavenging. Jesus, honey, that hurts."

Mia reseated her jaw and hit the nerves, again, again.

Bonn, having stripped off his lobebag, now fumbled at the

drawstrings of Mia's.

Pelf seethed upon a savage in-breath. He lifted his wife's hand toward his face so that her fingers claimed the dangle of his lobebag, a taut tug and rustle as it shimmied down and off.

For as long as their dalliance lasted, all thoughts of Mia's son, and what might happen to him at the prom and beyond, quite deserted her.

Peyton "Futzy" Buttweiler, for thirty years the principal of Corundum High, sat alone in his office.

The rolltop desk, his bookshelves, the stark paneling that covered the office walls, were all a dark delicious rosewood. This place was Futzy's arena of shame. So it had been for twenty years, since his daughter's prom.

That year, Kitty's final year of high school, Futzy had refused all knowledge of who the victims would be. The handful of teachers in the know had displayed nothing but impenetrable pokerfaces.

Futzy had had them dismissed or transferred, the image of Kitty, slain and futtered, burning into his brain.

Propped on his desk blotter, Kitty's senior picture was framed in fake-gold. The velvet fuzz at its back bore a shine from frequent handling.

Funny how, when her portrait lay facedown in his desk drawer, Futzy's office hummed with academic concerns. But as soon as he raised it into view, this place became a sanctuary of guilt, a quiet confessional, all of his administrative woes momentarily set aside.

It wasn't the dark dress, angled tastefully between shoulders and cleavage, that caught his attention. Neither was it her matching lobebag, the firmness of her young flesh, nor the sweet innocence of that hope-filled gaze into a future she would never live.

No, it was the knockout impact of the whole, the way it brought back a world of promise taken from him in one vicious night. Kitty had been its linchpin, her natural vibrancy infusing him and his wives, Freia and Keech, with what had seemed a deep and abiding commitment to their marriage.

When Kitty and her date were carried lifeless to the Ice Ghoul at the center of the gym, Futzy had borne for hours the sight of her slain body.

At midnight, the cleavers had come out.

Futzy Buttweiler sat among the chaperones a destroyed man, watching in disbelief the mayhem.

When he came home that night, it felt as if their house were kept together with spit and baling wire. Worse, his gradual drift away from Freia and Keech—long unsuspected beneath their shared happiness in Kitty—made itself plain.

Two weeks later, they left him.

His new wives Futzy had found lurking outside the bereavement clinic waiting to snag some guilt-eyed masochist. They had pounced, Futzy had let them pounce, and from that moment his house had become an abattoir of love.

Drive to school.

Bark admonitions and orders over the PA system.

Preside at assemblies where he would introduce a speaker and sit there despising the wretched rabble.

Cuff, swat, batter, and smack the foul little shits sent to his office for misbehavior.

The weary round had been enough to satisfy. That and a properly distant commiseration every year with the dead promgoers' parents, a perfunctory few phone calls between the slaughter and the futtering.

As he listened to their sobs, their quavering pride in son or daughter, he wondered if they felt one-tenth of the agony he, in renewal, felt every time he made such a call.

He would go home, post-prom, and let his wives rip into him, savage pain doled out, pain that often involved neither lobes nor gens.

But this year was different.

The Ice Ghoul had somehow fit perfectly into the underseas theme of Kitty's prom. For hours, the creature of tin foil, mesh, and papier-mache had towered over the slain couple. Icicles thrust into his little girl's eyes had capped the hidden mayhem of her death.

Year after year, in deference to Futzy's feelings, prom planners had shied away from the Ice Ghoul as a centerpiece, even as the tradition of using him to scare the vinegar out of incoming Corundum High kids caught hold.

But the world had darkened.

Devolving breeds of senior had turned more cruel.

Futzy peered into Kitty's eyes. Innocence. Kindness. Nothing like that existed any more at Corundum High.

This year, over Brest Donner's objections, the student committee had in defiance chosen the Ice Ghoul. They had even appropriated an area of the cool room, among ineptly butchered haunches of beef and pork, Lily Foddereau's senior projects, to store ice sculptures of the monster for a late-evening contest.

The little shits were not going to get away with this outrage. They would pay in spades for this nose-thumbing.

Futzy had shone no upset. He had remained a miracle of calm. At tonight's prom, he planned to continue in that vein, at least at first.

"Am I doing the right thing, sweetheart?" he asked his daughter's portrait. "Is Daddy on the right track?"

Typhoons of assent raged in his head, as they did whenever he posed the question. Over Kitty's permed helmet of auburn hair, from the strands of which peered a baby-soft right earlobe, a diffuse halo of light shone.

Yes, he would sour their evening.

Soon, though not soon enough, they would wish they had kept their Ice Ghoul as nothing more than a joke to frighten wide-eyed tenth graders with.

Futzy recalled Kitty's mothers, a rising duet of wincing squeals as he whipped them, the joyous anger that billowed inside him as he meted out their begged-for punishment. Hen scratchings. The *nertz* of a gnat at the ear. Nothing compared to the rage now astir in him, a rage he thought had dissipated in the years since Kitty's death, but which, it was now clear, had only lay dormant, waiting for its main chance.

He gripped the knot of his tie. Too loose. He tightened it.

This, thought Futzy, was going to be one humdinger of an evening.

Rhythming behind the wheel of her high-tuned piece of crap, Altoona tooled down the main drag of Corundum, Kansas.

The radio blasted slap'n'smack, tweedling her ears straight down to the lobes. Ballsy Pink Lady rockers scalloped out come-need there. Inside her leather pants, their voices tweedled her gens.

Zipper teeth, sewn along Altoona's labia at Easter and bunched up now like a slumped toddler's jacket, spit fire across her vulval gap.

She prided herself in being able to sing and sway and pummel the steering wheel with rhythmic slams of her right palm, even as she obeyed every damned traffic law on the books.

Sheriff Blackburn passed Altoona going the other way. In response to her cheery wave, he glared and made an abrupt turn-it-down gesture.

Huh. Blackburn.

He was cool though. It didn't tear her. For reasons beyond her ken, Blackburn had chosen to play a stern-daddy role. But inside, he was a good and fair humper of his mother.

Not like some of the geekoids she and Pimlico had had to teach how to behave.

Chub jokes and female-threesome innuendoes rolled off their backs. The Mathers twins, for instance. Less than head lice they'd been in their attempts to draw verbal razors across the girls' brains.

But as soon as she and Pim heard how Ig and Opie Mathers had bullied Nils Fancher, they invoked their November pact, secured the testimony of reliable witnesses, tracked the slugnuts down, told them what was about to happen and why, and flogged the living shit out of them to within a hair's breadth of what the law allowed.

Ig and Opie's flesh had sizzled beneath a white-hot brand, high flutes of pain issuing from split lips as U for Unkind seared deep into their foreheads.

It had been nothing like the violence normal people dole out to remind one another that life is cool, that they're alive, and that they have "a whipped kind of love to share," as the Pink Ladies so righteously belted out on the radio.

Altoona sang along.

Nearly too late, she spied the street sign. She turned wide on a *screeech*—what the hell, nothing coming her way.

Pimlico's house was five down on the right, where Stardust Place teed in. She roared into the driveway, jerked up hard on the brake, and killed the engine.

The sound of her black leather skirt shifting over the seat was covered by a vigorous shake of trees outside the car. That and the blare of a TV inside Pim's house turned the night as crisp and alive as cathedral air.

On the umpteenth ring, one of Pim's moms came to the door. It was the scraggly one, whose hair reminded Altoona of tossed straw.

"Oh yeah, right," she said, "come in."

She was thin and naked, fresh welts raised across her belly. Dark puffy bags slung beneath her eyes—not the morning hangover ones that fade with coffee, fresh air, and locomotion, but the sort that endure and define. A hastily pulled-up lobebag hid her lefty.

In the vestibule, the straw-haired mom angled her head back as if readying a sneeze. Her mouth widened. "*Pimmie! Your date's here!*" A wasted gaze at Altoona. "She'll be down."

"Thanks."

Pim's pop shouted from the TV room, "*Hey, Nola. Get your scrawny ass* in *here!*" Nola was already on the move. "I'm coming fast as I can, buttfuck," she mumbled, casting an all-men-are-scum look toward Altoona.

Pim yelled, "Be right down!"

"*Jesus, where the fuck you think* you're *going?*" Again the man's voice, apparently to Pim's other mom.

Altoona had never met her girlfriend's father. All she knew about him was that he cared not the whit of a shit about his daughters.

From the TV room, Pim's kid sisters made gross-out sounds. Altoona recognized the political spot. Oink-oinks blared from a hefty porker. Its throat caught on something. Then a blurt of spew hit an empty trough, replay, replay, replay. The camera jittered through a series of ugly jumpcuts as a stern DoleMoreCrap announcer intoned Fenny Boyle's sins.

And it was only primary season.

Things were certain to heat up, the vitriol

eating away at an already frayed political fabric, from now to November, Jesus God!

Onscreen, Fenny Boyle's digital clone, as convincing as technology could make him, knelt and (the kids fake-wretched again) bobbed, coming up with a dripping grin of brownish gunk and saying, "Mmmmm, tastes great!!!"

Passing it off as true wasn't as important as convincing voters it was a plausible scenario—*that* was what the game was about.

Pim's other mom burst into view, naked as well but with fewer welts. She pumped Altoona's hand, her lobes right out there in plain sight. "How ya doin'?"

As urbane as Altoona prided herself in being, she was always startled to see Britt Franken's left lobe exposed like that, wet with recent chewing.

But she liked Britt a lot.

There was plenty of heart behind her hard-edged exterior, and no room for bullshit.

Not waiting for Altoona's reply, Britt opened the hall closet, her reach stretching the blue-veined backs of her thighs and lifting her right foot off the carpet. When she turned, two items were squat-towered in her hands, a yearbook and a dated Futterware container, the orange-lidded kind that had been popular when Pim and Altoona were in grade school.

"*For shit's sake, Britt, you gotta see this!*" More a command than a suggestion.

"*In a minute*, you smelly heap of sewage," said Britt, her last phrase dropped way low and delivered with a grin in Altoona's direction.

Britt's hands worked at the lid.

"He loved me then. Kent Bodeen and Mimsie Chesk were chosen our year, pretty much nothing-people nobody in the class gave a damn about, so it worked out pretty well. The Frankenburger in there," Britt indicated the TV room, "kept looking over at them once they were draped out for all to see. He kept talking strategy, talking about the hunks of flesh he'd go after. His hands, when he wasn't fondling me, drifted to his cleaver. 'Just slice off something good,' I told him, 'something our kids can be proud of.' And when midnight struck, my fella dove straight in and got us some upper lip and the tip of, I'm not fooling now no not a bit, Mimsie's left earlobe."

Sure enough, as the lid drew back, a hefty lobe, shrunken in the process of being preserved and capped at the stump like a rabbit's foot, lay there in all its glory. It may or may not have been a lefty. But right or left, the *possibility* that he had slashed through to hack off a dead student's lobebag, claimed the coveted tip, and not kept it himself, spoke volumes about their puppy love.

"Wow!" said Altoona.

Britt nodded. "Don't it just beat all?"

Upstairs a door slammed.

"*Hey, little miss fat fuck, my lefty's throbbing and my whip hand's getting real itchy.*" Deadly warning.

"*All right, all right.* Gotta go. You two chickies have a swell time." She shrugged at the blood-smeared yearbook in her hands, resealed the Futterware, replaced both items in the closet, and buttocked off out of sight.

"Pretty sorry excuse, ain't she?"

Altoona turned to her descending date.

The pain having at last subsided in her crotch, Pim's sexy slink was back. She wore fishnet stockings, a tight black killer dress that ended a hand's breadth above her knees, and a face whose frail wounded wince burned deep in Altoona's heart.

"Your mom's not all that bad."

Scrunch about the eyes: "Give me a break." A cleaver dangled beside the Futterware on Pim's hip.

"Uh, sure, sweets," said Altoona.

"On second thought, give me a hug."

Leather brushed against leather as Pim cozied into her arms and angled up, engulfing in sweet lip-warmth Altoona's friendship lobe.

People said the lobes weren't connected. But she'd be damned if, every time her girlfriend's mouth closed on her right lobe, she didn't feel heat tingle in the left.

"You're walking just fine, hon."

Pim shrugged. "I took longer to heal than you, I guess. Last night helped."

Altoona remembered wet slides of niobium cathedraling at either side of her mouth as she softly dug for the love nub between. "Yum. You were okay a *week* ago, from what I could see."

"Yeah, possibly. But I didn't want to tear anything before Cabrille checked me out one last time."

Altoona laughed. "She was really coming on to us."

"Again!" Eyes wide for emphasis.

"Right."

"Cabrille's good. You can tell when she touches you, when she slips the needle in and explains how to clean the piercings and put on the Polysporin. But man, the way she looked at us that night . . . ."

"Yeah, it was pretty sick."

Altoona had held Pim, comforted her, wiping drops of sweat from her brow, and knowing as the woman proceeded upward—left right, left right, like a saleswoman threading bootlace—that she would be next.

Cabrille, thirty miles away in Topeka, showed, even that night, a glimmer of interest beyond professionalism. But years and a life

(Altoona suspected) too weird to contemplate had put the bag-breasted, crow-footed piercer beyond the reach of desire.

Besides, she *was* a woman, and a female threesome was illegal, not to mention yucky even to contemplate.

"She must've thought we were pervies."

"Yeah," Altoona said, "or potential ones."

"Some folks don't listen," said Pim, taking Altoona's hand and leading her out into the cool quiet night. "I told her about Condor and Blayne, how we thought their mouths were way cool when they showed up all swollen and pus-y from Christmas break."

"*They* sure took a razzing."

"Kids and teachers both." Pimlico opened the passenger door. "But folks changed their tune when everything healed up and Blayne started to work his zipper, slow and idle, right there in history class."

Altoona settled behind the wheel. "He kissed me, you know."

"The heck he did." Pim peered over to test her. "Oh bullshit! You're such a bullshitter!"

"He *did!*"

"Yeah, right." She slid closer. "Was it like this?" Pim's feisty bod overlaid hers, her fingers up under Altoona's lobes, her lips coming down to pillow against her mouth.

Pim broke the kiss, smiling, her right hand drifting down to grope Altoona's leather-mounded left breast.

"More metal in it," said Altoona. "More tentative, but real sexy. We were between classes."

"The *fuck* he kissed you. Did he really?"

"You'll see." She fired up the rattletrap, giving it extra pedal to make to vroom. "I wanted to surprise you. They're in a receptive mood. I got 'em horny for the big fourway."

"*Both* of 'em? Oh bullshit, bullshit, bullshit!" She hit the seat with the flat of her hand. "Come on Altoona, I don't like it when you tease."

"It's not a tease. We set it up. During the search for the dead couple, in the costume shop behind the stage. All you've gotta do is bring along your enthusiasm and your killer bod."

Pim countered with a renewed volley of bullshits, but it was clear she was starting to buy in. Altoona hoped Blayne had been able to persuade Condor, and that what both she and Pim longed for might begin tonight.

She flashed again upon their piercer, on Cabrille's calculated ramblings about the delights of female threesomes. No, they weren't pervies by *that* standard, but Altoona guessed more than a few prudish eyebrows would be raised—and the law brought thundering down—were word to leak that a foursome was in the offing amongst those who had bought big-time into the zipper craze.

Well fuck 'em, she thought, zooming backward into the street from the driveway. Love was love, whatever shape it took. Praise be to God for a world that could produce Pimlico, and praise abounding for the possibility of digging their talons into two super guys like Condor Plasch and Blayne Coom, brilliant, weird, dark, brooding sons of their mamas' most bizarre and urgent dreams.

"Hang on, hon," Altoona said. She pushed on into the promise of night, her brain radiant with possibility.

5
High School Secured

There was a split focus in the cabinet room: the video screen that covered an entire wall, and President Hargill Windfucker's asinine comments.

Although the Shite House video feed was and would remain private, famed sportscaster Blennuth Ponger had, this year, been shanghaied into the role of TV announcer. Ponger's laconic delivery betrayed his feeling that he was clearly out of his league.

"Here come the seniors."

Long silence.

"Our saucy little Home Ec teacher, behind the wheel of her killer car, is just a mile from Choke Cherry High."

Long silence.

"Right here, beneath this scrawled number, a big black fifty-seven, will the chosen couple meet their destined fate."

That sort of thing.

President Windfucker filled in Ponger's long stretches of silence with "Cute couple o' kids" or "That Home Ec gal's out for bear, isn't she?"

Whenever Cholly Bork voiced these inanities, angling the strings so that the presidential head shifted thoughtfully, the twelve cabinet officers turned from the screen and toward Gilly Windfucker to murmur and mutter "*Very* cute" or "She sure is, Mister President."

They sounded like churchgoers mumbling the phrases of a litany. They looked like spectators at a tennis match.

In her shiny red sports car, Karn Flentrop preened for the camera.

Her hair was perfectly coiffed, her nails long and pearl-sheened as the steering wheel rotated this way and that. She came to a stop, yanked up on the handbrake, and slid her sultry legs out of the car, taking the elevator to the backways as she patted her perm.

"Her moment of glory," mused Windfucker.

"Glory indeed, Mister President."

Camera switch. The young victim, a fresh-faced boy with much promise and no future, was helping his date out of the car, swish of a prom dress, her hand lifted like a swan's neck to his. The shot of them as they crossed the parking lot and entered the school wasn't the clearest, but it was critical not to arouse their suspicions.

Gilly Windfucker noted, "That gal would have made somebody a wonderful mom. Nice lobes on her, she's packing quite a pair."

"It's a crying shame, sir." "She's a gem." "Her young man could be in pictures." "They make us proud to be Americans."

As the doomed couple passed through locker-lined hallways to the gymnasium, Blennuth Ponger launched into the usual canned bios. In the upper right part of the screen, an inset series of stills and home videos tracked their childhoods, first steps, pony rides, birthday parties, theme park vacations.

"It kinda reddens the lobes, dunnit, watching them kids grow up, knowing what we're gonna see in a while, getting caught up in the anticipation?"

"It does, Mister President."

There was a hushed shuffle of chair legs upon the carpet as the twelve followed the President's lead and started to stroke their sexlobes through their lobebags.

They kept it up, turning their attention more intently toward the doomed pair and the tight fox who taught Home Ec. And thus did the presidential party slither down into the muck and goo of their private fantasies about this boy, this girl, and the buff teacher with murder in her eye and an itchy knife hand, compelling players in a national drama.

Weight against his left side.

That was the impression that first seeped in, that and the stench of death. The weight was warm and inert, in contrast to the cramped chill that wracked the rest of him.

The deadweight pressed down, then lifted free as cool air rushed in. His head was spinning. On every inhale, death smells rushed in to nauseate him and ride the next breath out.

He tested his eyelids. They cautioned open, lashes stuck, then free.

A vague notion of pipes swam high overhead. Crisscrosses of unpainted lumber. And blocking some harsh halo of light, the slumped form of a woman, dressed in finery, sitting on the side of whatever rough-edged coffin they had been jammed into.

"What . . . ," he tried, but only a modulated moan emerged.

The woman's head turned, partially uncovering a lightbulb. Its harshness delivered her profile, but with too sharp an edge to afford him a clear view of much beyond her dyed friendship lobe, some futile protest against the way things were.

He raised his fingers and wiped his eyes.

"You're awake."

His white stiff cuff came into view, as did the gold cross-gleam of cufflink backs and a coat arm's abrupt edge.

Accompanying the woman's words was a sudden certainty about where he was, memories of abduction and jail, a king's feast of food and a shower. Of submission to soap and scissors and being dressed.

And then the needle.

"But we're not—"

"Someone saved us," she said, standing up, one hand on the trough. "Saved us and did *him* in."

Working himself unsteadily to a sitting position, he followed the woman's gaze.

A bloated couch, stained crimson, cradled a dead man, the buffed hilt of a knife slanting up from his chest as if it had burst a huge balloon filled with raspberry jam.

The odor said otherwise, of course, mingled aromas of blurted heartpumps and the release of bladder and bowel.

"Poor boob ran into trouble," he said.

Rising, he spotted the dog.

"He deserved it," said the woman. "Christ, where's your head? He would've killed us. That axe lying on the floor was meant for us."

He nodded. "We got caught. Then *he* got caught."

63

"Damn deputy at the jailhouse nearly lost his nuts to my knee. If he hadn't had backup, I'd've gotten away."

"You from Topeka?" he asked.

"Kansas City. They surprised us at dawn."

"I thought I'd be safe behind the library. I wasn't. Do you think anyone's upstairs?"

"Doubtful," she said.

As the puffiness lifted from his head, he noticed her lobebag. His own state-provided bag knocked at the neck skin below his cropped lefty. He groped it, smooth cloth that no doubt matched his tux, and at the top, elastic and probably some kind of adhesive to clamp it lightly to the stub.

"Any idea how we lucked out?" he asked.

"My brain was real hazy, but I heard somebody say something, or *thought* I did. And I saw the killer's arm come up with a tightly gripped knife. A shirt of dark blue. Maybe denim."

Fear rushed through him. "You don't think he's upstairs?"

She laughed. "If he were, I'd shake his hand."

"He's probably a maniac. Maybe he's a black sheep wasting his entire family, and he's sitting upstairs right now at the kitchen table eating a sandwich." His voice fell to a whisper. "Maybe he's stopped chewing on account of now he can hear our voices and realizes we're not dead."

"You don't get it, do you? What we have here is one of the anti-slasher crowd who's decided to make a point: Kill the school's designated slasher. Crash the prom. Then, when no couple is slaughtered, reveal the deed and deal another blow to a savage system of sacrifice. What *we've* got to do is support him. We need to go to the prom, hang out through the time allotted for the killing and the search, and reveal ourselves once nobody's killed and our guy stands up and gives his speech."

She's joking, he thought.

Then it occurred to him that she was serious.

"Are you crazy?" he asked. "Even if you're right, *we'd* become martyrs along with the killer."

"I don't think so. We'd be national heroes. There might be a trial. But we'd be too hot to convict, and we're certainly not accomplices to his crime. Then there'd be speaking and signing tours—"

"Signing what?"

"Our book of course. I'm Winnie Hauser, by the way." A hand shot out. His rose and he let Winnie shake it. "The barbarity of prom night would be over and there'd've been created a link between housed and homeless that maybe just might get people's attention."

"You *are* crazy."

"There'd be food and warmth, showers and a fresh change of clothes every day dependably. The anti's would see to it. We would be their poster children. And when the power shifted, we'd be in an ideal spot to make sure things were done right."

He considered.

Then he shook his head, the dummy lobebag tapping stupidly at his neck. "I'll tell you what *I'm* going to do. I'm going to take this dead guy's cash, a closetful of clothes, and as much food as I can cram into his car, and head south, to Fort Lauderdale maybe. Give up your stupid dreams, that's my advice, before you get killed."

She tacked upon him. "If I'm wrong about our savior, they'll think *we* butchered Poor Mister Teacher and they'll come after us. They'll catch us. And the tortures they put us through will seem unending. Even after they've exposed and frayed our nerve ends to the edge of boredom, they'll hang onto us for the next prom night so they can slowly juice us on *Notorious*. And while . . . hey wait . . ."

Shit. She'd noticed.

"Come over here. Into the light."

He didn't move.

Winnie grabbed his arm. Yanking him toward the bulb, she turned his head and stared at his right ear.

He avoided her eyes, knowing what she saw.

Not the smooth stub of normal folks, but the imperfect tuck, like the knot atop an orange, of a dodger.

"You're a promjumper," she said. Contempt there. His silence confirmed it. "You grew up among them, attended their schools, enjoyed every advantage . . . and then you ran!"

"Spare me the litany," he said, pulling away. "I chickened out, okay? I paid and paid plenty."

Pursuit, capture, and two savage lobectomies raced through his memory.

Winnie approached him.

Softer: "What's your name?"

"Brayton. Kittridge."

"Well, Brayton Kittridge," her hands were warm on his neck, "this is your chance, don't you see, to make things right again. You come with me, confront the demons of the prom, and you can redeem the past. But if you shy away, I promise you, when they track us down and torture us and we find ourselves strapped in on *Notorious*, I'm gonna fix you with such a glare of hatred as we burn, that it'll put their physical torments to shame.

"And I can do it, too!"

Poor feisty woman. Winnie thought she could read him and fix him—fix ordinary folks too, no doubt—as easily as she might mend a broken toy.

But he had been there.

Unlike Winnie, who had been brought up among the proudly rejected and knew nothing of the ones who rejected her, he understood their vile little hearts, the beast she expected to confront and best in one night.

Without him, she would do something dangerous, maybe even try to attend the dance unchaperoned.

"I . . . I guess you're right," he said, noting the attractive combination of strength and naivete in Winnie's eyes. "We'll give it a try. Oh but what about these?" He fingered his right stub and her pale-green friendship lobe, liking the way hers felt.

"I'm betting there's a supply of Tuffskin somewhere in the house, give you some heft and cover my coloring," she said. "It's not ideal. But what with the subdued lighting at the dance, and given that we'll try to avoid others until the moment of revelation, it just might work. Come on, Brayton, let's look for it."

"Call me Bray," he said.

She huffed and grabbed his hand and yanked him stairward. He followed, admiring her thigh-swish and ankle-turn as they climbed the steps.

In the kitchen, the air cleared of death stench. But there were whiffs of gore that didn't vanish even when he closed the cellar door, and a quick search of the house brought them face to face with the teacher's wives.

"I think," said Bray, staring down at the fresh corpses, "we ought to consider revising our opinion of our savior."

"Poor things," said Winnie. "But sometimes pawns must be sacrificed for the greater good. He had to kill the teacher. Maybe these two put up a struggle."

"Does it *look* like they struggled? Phew, it's amazing how quickly dead folks start to stink. Besides which, why didn't he just truss them up? Why didn't he lock that guy down there in a closet or something, roped many times over as tight as a mummy so he had no way to escape?"

"Beats me." She picked up a packet from the end table. Its contents started to spill out the open end, but Winnie caught them in time. "Instructions for the designated slasher."

"I think the wacko family member theory is starting to make a lot of sense. Either it's totally coincidental our couch guy was murdered tonight, or his being chosen as slasher finally drove, I don't know, maybe his son over the edge."

Ignoring him, Winnie leafed through the documents.

"I bet the killer's hundreds of miles away by now."

Shuffle, shuffle, shuffle.

"He won't be anywhere near the prom."

Winnie glared at him. "Either way," she said, "no couple will be sacrificed tonight. So either we'll back what our savior has to say; or, if he doesn't show, we'll step forward to put our best spin on the student slaughter that wasn't."

End of discussion.

"While you've been standing there flapping your lips," she went on, "I discovered some things: The dead guy's name is Fronemeyer. An art teacher. Ah. Here's a map of the town. They've even circled the school for us, thoughtful of them. Corundum High."

No surprise. The deputies's shoulder patches had had "Corundum, Kansas" sewn into them.

"Here are the intended victims' names. Tweed Megrim and . . . Dexter Poindexter. Jeepers, what a name. And where they'll be sitting during the stalking phase. Now, while I find the Tuffskin, you use the phone book—there can't be too many Fronemeyers—and the map to figure out where we are in relation to the high school. Also, call the parents of these two kids and tell them their targeted darlings are safe."

That seemed pointless. "I don't think we—"

"Just do it," Winnie said. "The more committed anti-slasher folks we can count on coming out of this, the better. If I have to plant terror in the hearts of hundreds of complacent mommies and daddies, so be it."

She headed off.

It was a relief to regain the kitchen, away from the sight of neck slashes and the spills of blood that idled down the slain wives' bodies.

In a cabinet above the wall phone, Bray found the white pages. Thin. One Fronemeyer. Moonglow Street, so short its name ran its length, no more than four miles from school.

Finding the numbers for the Megrims and the Poindexters was just as easy. But mustering the will to dial them was another matter.

Winnie returned with a tub of Tuffskin in her hand, a prize from her rummage through bathroom cabinets. She carried as well a thick wad of bills and a set of keys on a chain, both of which she stuffed into Bray's pants pockets. "Well?"

Bray pointed to the map. "We're here. Over here's Corundum High. It's seven ten now. Apply the Tuffskin, let the stuff seal, hit the road at seven thirty, and we should be right on time."

"Did you call them?"

"Not exactly, I—"

"Wimp!" She grabbed the pad and punched in a number. Six rings. "That's right," muttered Winnie, "catch some fast food and go bowling while your son dies."

She hung up and punched in the other number, her index finger moving with strength and purpose. Ring one, ring two, ring three, followed by a click, and a singing voice, to which she began to say something, stopping when she realized it was a recording.

She drummed on the counter, then, "Yeah, hi, listen up. You don't know me, but your daughter Tweed and her date were chosen as tonight's prom victims. I have reason to believe they'll be spared. Trust me, this is not a hoax. You'll learn about it later this evening, but really now . . . don't you think you should have done more to stop this outrage before it went this far?"

Winnie hung up. "That oughta jolt someone's complacency."

"You were unnecessarily cruel."

"Tell it to the judge, Mister Promjumper." She pried the lid off the tub and dipped a hand into the soft goo. "Turn your head left." It burned going on, but Bray felt it harden and penetrate his skin as she kneaded and shaped it.

Thinned, Tuffskin concealed blemishes.

Applied more thickly, it gave heft to breast or cock.

A famous pianist had been said to extend his fingers this way, but anyone who understood music knew that had to be a wild lie.

"Now you do me," she said, "and by God you'd better get it right."

Her harshness had begun to amuse more than shame him, which was just as well. His hand held steady. He did his best to thin the Tuffskin and coat her lobe, concealing the pale green beneath flesh tones. Curiously, the more it reminded him of the lobes of girls he had lusted after when he was whole, the greater the urge grew to kiss it.

He planted a light one.

Winnie drew back. "What do you think you're doing?"

"Kissing my date's friendship lobe."

"Don't you friendship *me*!" she retorted. "Let's see what's to eat. Ten minutes tops."

Bray visited the john first.

When he returned, Winnie had a variety of meats and cheeses laid out on the table, along with three types of juice. He lifted a Jonathan from the fruit bowl, alternating bites of mozzarella and apple and feeling how weird it was to have a fake lobe moving to match his concealed stuffed lobebag on the left.

He'd give anything, he thought, to have it be real, to have this prom be his abandoned prom nine years before.

Between bites, he tried to filter his breath through his hand. The stench of death made eating an iffy proposition. Winnie, a thin shapely woman of fierce determination, chowed down oblivious of the smell. Her eyes darted between the wall clock and the sheaf of papers.

Bray grabbed another apple. One bite in, his date announced that it was garage time and headed back through the house. He tossed the apple in the trash.

Winnie's instincts were unerring. At the end of the hall was the door to the garage, a standard three-car structure with a couple of cars and some boxes stacked against a side wall.

"Which one is least likely to have belonged to Fronemeyer?" she asked. "We don't want to rouse suspicions in the parking lot."

"This one's got to be his." Bray pointed to a newer foreign jobbie whose license plate frame read PAINTERS DO IT WITH

ACRYLICRITY. A parking pass hung from its inside mirror.

"Good guess. We'll take the other." She started to open the passenger door. "What are you doing?"

"Holding the door for you." Winnie looked creamy and scrumptious.

"Get the heck over to the other side of the car. And get serious, will you? There are three dead people inside that house. And we're on a mission to turn things around in this cockeyed world."

"Okay, okay, I'll drive."

"That's right. You drive, I ride, I do the thinking, you follow orders. It's that simple."

Sliding in beside her, Brayton *nit-nit-nitted* the garage door open.

In this light, Winnie almost looked like Bonnie Dolan, the date he had disgraced through his cowardice. Maybe if he pretended as hard as he could, he might save himself and counterbalance the misery he had put the Dolans and his parents through so many years before.

He leaned toward her.

"Watch it!" she said.

"Fine." He smiled. "But before this evening's over, I bet you're going to want to kiss me."

"Bet away. Dream on. Hit the road."

Brayton did.

All three.

Their babysitter had finked out on them, so they had her daughter Pill to contend with.

Even so, Trilby Donner thought that having the three of them, her and her spouses Bix and Brest, chaperone the prom was a swell idea.

In public Brest displayed much love for Bix, even as she spoke privately to Trilby of dumping him in favor of an all-girl threesome with Delia Gaskin. But Trilby felt that if only they could do more together as a triple and as a family, if they made the effort to identify common threads in their lives and intertwine them to gain tensile strength, their marriage was still salvageable.

That's why she insisted so vehemently that they take Pill with them. It was, she felt a great idea, despite her embarrassment when

Bix passed a bribe to Elwood Dunsmore and the lynx-eyed student inside the door checking passes. Hush-hush, no need to let anyone know an eight-year-old was on the grounds, she would be mouse-quiet in the faculty lounge and out of sight as the slasher stalks.

Dunsmore, a coffee-skinned shop teacher with a bristle mustache and a bulbous friendship lobe, winked, okay'd his fingers, and folded the bills into his coat pocket. "That's called hush money," he told the junior, who nodded and said, "Yeah, we learned about that stuff in Mr. Versailles' class in the lesser vices."

Now Pill was being difficult.

"Why the long face, honey? I'll come in to check on you every half hour," Trilby assured.

The child kept her head bent, her pre-adolescent earlobes forlorn in their naked innocence. In three or four years, when puberty struck, her baby Pill would need to be fitted for a lobebag.

"You've got your books, Gigi the goat, and a nice plush chair. There's pear juice in the mini-fridge whenever you want it."

Whiny voice, yet thank God no tears: "But I want *you,* Mommy."

Brest and Bix stood by the door.

Trilby sensed them behind her, impatience and loverly interest intermingled. Later, in bed, she had no doubt they would use the delay caused by Pill's whining as an excuse to vent their pent-up affection toward her. And she would do her best to counter with her worn riding crop.

"You'll be a big girl, won't you?" she asked. "You'll take care of yourself?"

Pill nodded, hugging her stuffed goat.

"That's my girl. Now remember, if you hear footsteps, what do you do before the people come in?"

The corners of Pill's mouth flexed. "I miss Puff," she said. Puff was her kitty.

"What do you do?" repeated Trilby.

Pill looked glum. "Hide in the coat closet."

"That's right. In your little corner of pillows. Leave a tiny crack for air, and when you're sure they're gone, it's okay to come out again."

The faculty lounge was brightly lit and off-limits for the slaughter. Pill would, as Trilby had instructed her, keep her hands off the paper cutter and out of the supply drawer. Leaving her here would be perfectly safe.

"That's my girl," Bix offered.

Brest, beside him, said nothing.

Trilby kissed her index fingers and touched them to Pill's lobes. "Give your mommy a hug, honey."

Thick wool from Gigi the goat tickled Trilby's neck as her daughter's slip of a body moored against her and the butterfly mouth she so loved closed about the maternal tip of her friendship lobe.

Gerber Waddell arrived in his beat-up truck and his best coveralls.

As he crossed the parking lot and entered the school building, early promgoers gave him a wide berth. The teacher who sat at the front table, Mr. Dunsmore, and the short line of students being checked in ignored him.

Pond scum.

Oughta be snuffed, all of them.

Gerber went without ceremony to the supply closet near the band room. He used his ring of keys to let himself in.

It was close in here, the lone pull-bulb dim and dusty with age. Shelf upon shelf of tools and duct tape and extension cords in impossible orange tangles passed beneath his gaze.

Gerber paused.

Why am I here? he wondered. *There was a reason I came in here.*

Letting his fingers rise before him like so many pale stalagmites, he pointed them toward the school entrance and with great effort traced his steps until they were back where they had begun.

Oh yeah. Tin snips. An axe. An ice pick. A graduated, pan-piped pouch of screwdrivers.

He loaded his utility belt with these items, repeating their names over and over in a whisper until they dangled there.

Flag. Gotta do the flag.

Damned students didn't appreciate the work involved in the flag task. Mornings, they shot spitwads at him while the pulley at the top gave the odd groan and the parallel cords sang in high slaps against the flagpole and the heavy furls of the flag moved, jerk by jerk, into the sky like a huge slumbering dinosaur head roused from sleep.

Gotta take it down.

Night time comin' on.

Later, there would be blood to clean up, lots of blood.

And stray body parts from the futtering, flung into ill-lit corners of the gym.

But the night was still young, and plenty of mayhem simmered across the brainscape of Corundum High's head janitor.

Gerber Waddell locked the closet. He paused outside in the hall to remember again where he was headed.

Some gussied-up young snotwads swished by, wide-eyed and agiggle. They made a joke at his expense, but Gerber paid them no never-mind.

Flag. Fuckin' Ol' Glory. Fuckin' flag.

Yep.

Sheriff Blackburn watched the flag rise, giving it a smart salute as the head janitor watusi'd beside the white flagpole, the *ling ling ling* of the pulls slapping metal.

This night flag, designed by an artist of his grandparents' generation, had gradually replaced the day version, unofficially and then by an act of Congress. When it was first introduced, some had called it sacrilege. But most folks honored truth when they saw it: Fifty gloom-white skulls on a field of blue, bloody furrows alternating with flayed flesh, the skulls like Honest Abe looking drawn and haggard in his last photos, the flayings like sexual lashes gone mad, the whole a vivid rendering of the nation's dark side, the nation dubbed the Demented States of America scarcely twenty years before by an otherwise forgettable pop musician. The moniker had stuck, gone into common parlance, and was used more often than the original now—except by the President, though he too lapsed at times into the vernacular.

"Hi there," said Gerber Waddell, ducking and nodding at the sheriff from the flagpole.

Poor halfwit always said, Hi there.

Irritating.

"Looking good, Gerber."

The janitor mumbled his thanks, a catch in his throat as he figure-eighted the twin cord about its stay and yanked it tight. Benign feeb. Gone nutso years back at a corporate picnic the day after prom night. Killed one more than the law and custom allowed. But some judicious brain slicing had redeemed what could be redeemed, and Gerber Waddell, with the aid of his guardians the Bleaks, had become once more a productive member of society.

"Take care now, hear?"

"Thank you, Mister Sheriff." Gerber nodded politely, a grin on his face. Then he picked up the triangulated day flag, did a one-eighty, and headed for the school entrance.

Young couples were cascading now through the double doors, bottlenecked at the table Blackburn had just left. He had entrusted a padlock to the bristle-lipped shop teacher, Elwood Dunsmore—the final padlock that would be snapped on right at the stroke of eight, no more students allowed in after that, no more anybody. The only keys were in the packet he had left with Zane Fronemeyer and on the ring of metal hanging from the sheriff's belt.

A limousine drew up to disgorge another young couple, fear and anticipation on their faces.

Blackburn clucked and shook his head. Waste of money, as far as he was concerned. Most people made do with their own vehicles, parking in the lot on his left. But there were always some, too extravagant for their own damn good, who saw fit to hire fancy-dan automobiles, hoping to impress their dimbulb classmates with a display of gold-plated rungs up life's ladders.

Yeah, he remembered the kind from his own high school days. One of that crowd had reached his last red-gold rung a tad early, on prom night. The sheriff had a dried piece of pancreas at home to prove it.

Blackburn crossed the grass on his left and found the sidewalk. From his right fist swayed three padlocks.

Kids with flashlights, sketched shadows in the darkness, waved cars in off the street and left or right along a gauntlet of volunteers who handled the parking proper. Overhead, a pallid moon drifted in and out of pewter-gray clouds.

Passing the iron-barred windows of several classrooms, Blackburn rounded the corner of the building and headed for the gym's emergency exit door. When one lock's hasp slid snugly into place there, its firm snap sealed off the exit as a means of escape. There would be no promjumpers on *his* watch, at least not the kind that signed in and slipped out.

High exuberant shouts erupted in the parking lot at the sheriff's back. He thought of his son and two daughters, how in two short years Blitz, a sophomore, would drive or be driven into this very parking lot for *her* prom. Yesterday, a slight injury in gym class had brought Daddy to school, where he received assurances from Nurse Gaskin and a handshake from Principal Buttweiler. The whole encounter had given Blackburn a chill.

But they said it built character, this prom ordeal. And *he* had survived it, him and his wives.

"Hello, Sheriff!" Kids passed by, crossing the lot, a hint of challenge in their voices, but respect too.

He raised a hand to them. "Be careful now, you hear? Don't go catching any stray knives!"

"We won't!" But they well might. Only a few teachers, and the principal of course, knew which couple would die tonight.

Two padlocks remained.

Blackburn hummed as he rounded the building's next corner, low bristly shrubs keeping him clear of the wall. The back entrance was used only by driver ed kids and those who lived north of the school. It yielded to his efforts, a sturdy door now made impassable.

Nobody here. He started to feel creepy in spite of himself. *Whistle a happy tune.*

Right.

He resumed his walk around the building. On the east side was an emergency exit from the band room, hidden in moon shadows. The floods on this side hadn't been flicked on!

Damn that dimwit janitor.

Every year for the last three, the sheriff had chewed Gerber out about this, making up some crap about ordinances, safety regulations. But the truth was, Blackburn would somehow always manage to spook himself by the time he got around to the back of the school on prom night.

No houses. Just some weeds and a fence, a lazy stream bubbling along behind it.

Detaching the flashlight from his utility belt, Blackburn trained it on the door. The padlock fell from his hands and clattered on the concrete. Then it was up again, a cool inverted U of metal sliding against metal, a solid steel snap that sealed off the school's east exit.

Yes. How easy it was to feel satisfied by a simple sound.

Now to complete his journey around the school perimeter, get the hell out of here, and lambaste that dweeb janitor.

Someone touched him on the shoulder. The boy in him yelped. His skin bristled with fear as he whirled and went for his gun. Foolish gesture, on hold and relaxing even as he touched the gun butt.

Blackburn saw who it was. "Jesus Christ, don't you *ever* do that to me again!"

"Sorry, Sheriff."

"Creepy enough out here as it is." His hand returned to his side. "So, we meet again."

"Sheriff, I need your help." Oddly cool.

"You don't sound quite—"

His instincts flared. Then the dark arm rose, as though detached from its body's stasis, swiftly curving about and impossibly long.

A grimace betrayed the usually complacent face before him, exertion abruptly concentrated.

But before Blackburn could raise his hands to ward off whatever it was, the wind whipped up in the restless branches above him and an impossible weight snuffed all awareness swiftly out.

6
Limos, Volvos, and Jalopies

Dexter Poindexter's coupe eased through the night. Its headlights knifed through the darkness, which swept behind him and grew whole again.

Dex finally felt like a grown-up. A man in charge of his own decisions. Protective of his wife-to-be. On his way unshackled.

Starting in the fall of his junior year, there had been inklings, stirrings of adulthood: his voice growing deeper and more confident; the soft brillo'ing of his pubic hair; an obligatory stint as a zit farmer; the wary way adults had of staring at you, prunish joes and biddy-janes whose youth had long gone sour and who tottered, a whole heap of 'em, on the lip of the grave.

But tonight was different.

Tonight Dex sat behind the wheel of his car, Tweed by his side. Upon the tips of her earlobes and no doubt between her breasts, she had dabbed a scent that drove him wild.

Once they had enjoyed and survived the prom, wedded bliss would be theirs. A third would come along to complete them—male or female, it didn't much matter.

Then a couple of jobs to sustain them, and some kids underfoot in there somewhere.

But what if they had been chosen?

"It's a beautiful night," Tweed said.

"The best," he said.

What if the designated slasher were staring at their photos right now, laying plans to be right behind where they were seated, removing screws in advance so that he could pop out in an instant and draw his blade across Dex's throat? My God, he would die gasping for a breath that never came, even as he watched Tweed suffer the same fate. In the slasher's eyes would shine a bead of hatred, its gleam the last thing Dex saw as his vision faded.

Grown-ups hate kids, thought Dex. They envy us our youth. They love to snuff two of us every year. And I'll be just like them, now that I'm nearly a man.

But he quickly nixed that thought, letting righteous rage at the adult world again assert itself.

They would not touch his Tweedie-bird.

They would not harm a hair on her head.

Nor would they hurt Dex. He had been working on his reflexes, visualizing alone in his basement against the wall where Mom and Dad couldn't make fun of him. There, he pictured over and over the abrupt appearance of the slasher. Dex would push Tweed out of harm's way, then seize the knife arm of the emerging teacher, even if it proved to be gum-chewing Coach Frink of the gorilla arms and the dumb blunt brow and the beady eyes, even that musclebound dolt—and with his miniature cleaver sever the man's jugular.

In his imaginings, Dex effortlessly disarmed the bastard, saw him struggle in his death throes, threw an arm around Tweed, and said, "We got him, honey. He's dying and we're free."

Now, in the car, Tweed nestled closer and put a hand on his right arm. "I love you, Dex."

"I love you too."

And he did. He loved Tweed with his entire heart. "His spleen 'n' liver too," as the song had it. "We're going to have a *great* time tonight, you and me and all of us. This prom's gonna kick some serious butt."

"No question," she said, laying her head against his arm. "It's such a dreamy night."

His instincts were honed. No need to fret. Just live each harrowing moment for all it was worth. Screw up his nerves and be on high alert during the twenty minutes' ordeal, as the seniors hurried off to their designated spots, sat beneath big black numbers, and waited.

Afterward, the survivors would return elated and relieved to the gym, eaten up with curiosity. Which couple, they'd be wondering, would shortly be laid in the lap of the Ice Ghoul to be hacked and futtered at midnight?

It wouldn't be him and Tweed.

The odds *favored* them.

Then Dex's confidence hit the inevitable speed bump.

The odds favored *everyone*.

"I see it!" screamed Pim.

Altoona clucked. "'Course you see it, dummy. 'Swhere it's been for a billion years."

"Yeah, I know. But it's the *prom* and it's *night time* and you and me've got one more hurdle to go before we're *free*."

"So?" Altoona stopped behind some car whose left blinker was flashing. She checked her watch. Twenty minutes before the doors closed, and three blocks to the parking lot. "It ain't like it's an exam or nothin', Pim, so don't crap your knickers, okay? It's more like, in fact it's *precisely* like, two luckless fuckers are forced to cash in their chips and the rest of us are allowed to breathe again finally. Who's in that rustbucket ahead of us?"

Pim craned forward. "Oh jeez!"

"What?"

Pim giggled and clapped her black-mitted hands. "One's the loser babe from butchery who almost lost a thumb."

"Hairy-lobed Lulu?"

"Yeah. And look. Good old Futzy stuck her with that triple-bellied bozo with the corduroy pants who hangs over his lunch like pigs over a trough. The kid nobody in their right mind ever sits with." Pim glowered with ratlike malice. "I sincerely hope they're not the chosen ones, cuz no one I know would want to rush in and futter *them*. Too many goddamn cooties."

"Couple o' friggin' losers," said Altoona. "You wonder how they *live* with themselves. 'Course, if anybody had bullied either of these twits, we'd've held the bullies down and branded 'em. So go figure. Leave losers alone? Hey, we tolerate that. Cause 'em grief? We flog you to beat the band."

"Cuz we understand how it feels. The being mocked, I mean."

"Right."

Clouds scudded behind the school building as they approached the lot. Jacketed students directed with flashlights. Altoona saw Tweed Megrim's kid sister, Jenna, a peppery little junior, splitting cars off this way and that.

"Jesus fuck, it's the prom!" screamed Pim, jiggling fit to burst out of her dress.

What a love bunny, thought Altoona.

And what interesting times lay ahead later tonight, when they bared their nether parts for those yummy zippermouths, Condor and Blayne.

Altoona's lobes peppered and zinged like a string of pinched Christmas lights.

At the punchbowl, Jonquil Brindisi, teacher of the greater vices, ladled orange glop into the outheld cup of Claude Versailles, teacher of the lesser vices.

Jiminy Jones, ignored in a bow tie, roved on the risers, setting out thick binders of charts on the dance band's unsteady black stands. Poor sad Jiminy. Such a humorless stub of a fellow, short, bristle-browed, full of gray bland business grit in faculty meetings. His demeanor had surely had the effect of turning off potential mates, as now they turned off Jonquil.

Artificial fog drifted across the floor from that towering effrontery in the center of the gym, the Ice Ghoul.

"Thank you," said Claude. He took a sip of punch. "And yes, Jonquil, I concur. This year's crop of seniors showed execrable taste in choosing as the centerpiece of their prom the hoary old Ice Ghoul. He's not only a slap-in-the-face to a fine principal, our poor dear Futzy chum. But as much as, to the adolescents who while away a mere four years here the Ice Ghoul seems a source of endless merriment, to those of us logging our third decade and counting, he's dull, dull, dull."

Jonquil smiled. Wordy bugger, hair starting to thin. But Claude was tall, arguably handsome, all-in-all a not inconsiderably sexy man. "Maybe they took your lessons in Sloth to heart."

"Indeed," said Claude, licking orange foam from his upper lip. His suit was bright yellow with bold black stitching, his lobebag the same. "The Ice Ghoul *is* the easiest choice, isn't he, barring the inconsideration it shows for Futzy's feelings, which held back previous classes for twenty years but did not it seems hold back *this* class. A particularly vicious bunch this year, perhaps?"

"I try, Claude, I try."

Knock off a few years, ungray a few streaks at the temples, plunk him in a singles bar, and Jonquil would jump him in an instant. A pity she had stricken colleagues from her list of possible playmates. Pity too that the bar fodder, men and women both, came nowhere near Claude's quality and allure.

"In my lessons on Rage," she noted, "a full six *weeks* we dig and delve into that fine and unjustly maligned passion, I do my best to instill a love of the vicious."

"One would think it natural."

"One would think so."

Across the gym, Jonquil saw Adora Phipps nod her tight-bunned head and excuse herself from an early gaggle of seniors. She headed their way, young but dressed in a spiffed-up version of the granny clothes that marked her off as one of the oddest of the odd.

To Claude: "But men and women are vicious in so predictable and plastic a way, and they're no better as kids. In class, I work myself up—you know how I get—but they stare back, as dull as a crusted plate, these hormone-pumped wonders. Take *Notorious*, for example. Sure it's sexy to see someone fry on TV."

Miss Phipps nodded to them, listening as she poured herself some refreshment. A wormy seam, as she leaned, ran up the back of her stocking from fat-heeled black shoes. When she straightened, the seam was abruptly hidden, her long severe frock falling to cover it.

"Watching someone fry," continued Jonquil, "invariably gets me off."

"Me too," said Claude. He waved to Miss Phipps, who gave him a fuck-off nod and stared over her cup at Jonquil in mid-peroration.

"My point, though, is that *Notorious*, for all its supposed in-your-face violence, finks out when it comes to the stunning arousal of a fully-sensed kill. True, you get the look and feel of it. You get the sizzle and the screams. Their holographic expertise can't be faulted, and the porno flicks they superimpose over the frying flesh are chosen for optimal build and climax. But the *smell* they give us!" Cluck of the tongue, roll of the eyes.

"Surely you don't want the real thing?"

"Of *course* I do! You've been to enough of these proms, you and Adora both, to know that the aroma of burnt pork—or whatever the frig it is the networks use—is nowhere *near* the amazing smell of a corpse. For heaven's sake, if you're going to get people off, you really shouldn't cheat the most critical sense of all with cheap cosmetic substitutes. For all the distaste TV viewers claim, there's nothing like the aroma of victims, freshly butchered or fried, to bypass the veneer of civilization and go straight for the beast in the brain—nothing like it to snag one's lust and turn it positively ravenous."

Jiminy Jones bobbled a low sour blat out of his trumpet.

"I wonder," said Adora Phipps, taking another sip.

"Don't wonder," Jonquil said. "Believe it."

The lobebag Miss Phipps wore had that second-generation feel to it, as if it had been rummaged out of her grandmother's hope chest.

Her right lobe, thank goodness, was bare. A year ago, Jonquil and Ms. Foddereau had taken the English teacher aside, hoping to persuade her out of repression's past in *that* regard at least, and the resumption of school in September had seen Miss Phipps abandon the antiquated right bag that the rest of Demented States society had trashed so decisively in the mid-sixties.

Claude said in annoyance, "Where's Gerber Waddell when you need him?"

She followed his gaze to the wetness plashing down the papier-mache and chicken-wire face of the Ice Ghoul.

The creature half-knelt, half-crouched. It was daunting in its crudeness but so overdone as to be laughable: buttocks doughy and split apart, a thick spearhead erection beribboned and far too huge, bright red everywhere except where brush had missed newsprint.

Its musclebound arms lofted skyward—the knife, the torch, an obvious parody of the Statue of Liberty—and its massive head was bent to peer triumphantly at the dead couple soon to be laid before it.

Jonquil's gaze returned to the splash of drops, slow but predictable, that hit the concave crimp in its brow, sorrowed along its cheek, and dripped down the muscled chest before it passed out of view.

"Rained all night, didn't it?" she said.

"It woke me up," agreed Miss Phipps.

Jonquil took in the seething gush of dry-ice fog issuing from vents cut in the figure's broad pedestal.

"Yes it rained," said Claude. "But Futzy had the roof redone just last year. I told him—past experience ought to be trusted!—not to switch to Flashpoint & Sons based on bid alone. He ignored me. Now this."

"You think there's standing water up there? Perhaps a puddle?" Jonquil pictured a dark mirror of water rippled with night breezes, spread wide over ineptly tarred swatches of roof.

"More like a lagoon!" he answered. "As my favorite bumper sticker puts it, 'Life's a bitch, and then she whelps.' On this of all nights, the roof has chosen to fail. Water is trickling along crossbeams and onto the runways of the slasher's typically dry modes of access up there. Should he or she have an occasion to employ them tonight, he or she will be in for a case, at the very least, of wet knee. Early onset of gout, arthritis, or chilblains is not out of the question. Where the devil is our esteemed head janitor?"

Another of Claude's rhetorical questions.

Maybe he would go in search of the janitor. Or he might stoically wait for him to wander in. More likely, he would gnaw on this new peeve all evening, spinning elaborate rhetorical flourishes to feed his upset. None of it would diminish him in Jonquil's sight.

At the far door, a threesome strode in: Brest Donner, arm in arm with her man Bix, and Trilby, their third, bringing up the rear.

"Brest!" Jonquil called out, waving her toward the refreshment table when she got her attention.

Clusters of early seniors looked up too. But with the lights on full and the dance band only beginning to assemble, it felt not yet as though the prom had quite begun.

More kids, lights gone low and colorful, the front entrance padlocked shut, a cymbal whisk as the first notes of an old classic sounded: such signals would mark the real start of the evening, when these dressy stragglers on strews of sawdust would shift from out-of-place to right-at-home.

Brest tugged Bix along and Trilby followed after. Here, thought Jonquil, is a marriage in trouble.

Out of the madhouse at last and on the road, thought Condor Plasch. His buddy Blayne had one fucked-up family. "You have one fucked-up family, Blayne-O," he said.

83

"The shit they don't eat, they are." Stoic, dark, an anodyne for Condor's worldly woes, Blayne glanced out the passenger side and dug idly into a coat pocket.

"One last hurdle, we head west."

No comment from Blayne.

Condor wove from street to street out of the housing development. His tongue barbell knocked against the inside edge of his zipper mouth. He pictured lightning jags over wet enamel. "Yep, that's where we be headed. Put in our time tonight, pack up, ride way the fuck over to San Fran, where the funny papers are sayin' all good zipheads congregate." Blayne nodded but said nothing. "What's up, my good bud?"

Blayne stared over: "Me and Altoona did the lip thing today." He fetched out a kerchief, blue and white checked, rubberbanded at the middle and pulled into rabbit ears at the top.

"She just another sneerfuck privately pining to kiss metal?"

Blayne reared back. "Get real. This is Altoona you're talking about."

"So did she spill? Whether her and Pim did it, I mean."

"She *implied*." Blayne unbanded the kerchief. "Real strong."

"They've been walking funny since Easter."

Once, thought Condor, those two chicks had been a stone-cold drag. Couple o' wannabes.

Lately, they'd started getting interesting.

First, Pim had sidled up to him outside the cafeteria and brazenly requested their piercer's phone number. That had been followed by obsessive stares and all, capped by rumors of what she and Altoona had done over Easter.

"Not too raunchy in the visual way neither, them two," said Condor. "Cute lobes, big swellers beneath their sweaters, killer curves that narrow down into a tight clench below."

Blayne dropped a compliment: "They'd be hot and finger-rocking good in the sack."

"But wait up," said Condor. "We had to go through whole heaping gobs of pain when we had our *mouths* done. No *way* them girls'd let that shit be perpetrated on them you-know-where. I can still smell that cream-white oval pan with the red drool and spit, me goggle-eyed over it with my wuttering head on wobbly like I was fit to pass out. And I can feel the crimp of that skin-punch as my blood sprayed out over Cabrille's fist."

Condor signaled a turn.

"And those were my *lips*, Blayne-O, just my fucking *lips*! You think I'd let anyone do that to my gens?"

Blayne shrugged. "Believe what you want. I think they did it. Anyway, we get to find out tonight."

Yeah, right. "What's with the pills?"

"Some heady stuff," Blayne replied. "Brain revealers, Altoona calls 'em. While they were in Topeka, before they drove to Cabrille's parlor, they met this guy in a bar whose brother used the university labs in Lawrence to make it pure. No shit, no cut, no speed. Just a smooth high hit."

Condor's stomach flexed. "I dunno. Last time, my gut took a turn, loops of *no-no-no* and a quick uncatchable ralph or two, floors to mop in a dead-dog stupor the next morning, and pain, pain, pain. So I'm gonna beg off."

"That was Cobra's street-scam crap, cut six ways from Sunday with baby powder and strychnine, more'n likely. This stuff's the genuine article. Altoona says she and Pim took hits, got naked, it went on forever. She told me, get this, she told me her pussy tingled like a fizzing sizzling hot tub and that her sexlobe felt like it had swelled up and stretched out near three feet long and that soft wet hot invisible slave-tongues were lapping and sucking every goddamn cubic inch of it, hour after hour of yummy sexy shit, and I ain't lyin'."

"Altoona said *that*?"

"In so many words."

What the fuck.

He and Blayne had gotten into black candles a year before. They had written bleak poetry to the loneliness, sharing the verses before they engaged in yet one more bout of fruitless suck and flay.

They had stood by one another in Kansas City twice while a well-paid felony-risker had taken a tattoo needle to their underaged skin.

And they had gone together through the pain of zipper installation, a Christmas break Condor would never forget, the unending stairstep of hurt across his mouth and back again, the blood, the swelling, somehow managing to coax Blayne through the same.

The other kids' taunts thereafter were as nothing. They were as the *bip-bip-bip* of the zipper handle against his right chinflesh as he walked, a tickle soon become custom.

Now his buddy and lover (the one kid in the world who likewise had his ear attuned to the suck-tunnel of emptiness, who grokked that the probability of truly sharing anything with anyone anywhere *ever* was zip zero zilch) held forth a pill to pixie-dust the next several hours away.

Prom shit would unfold its truth, the lows lower, the highs higher.

And possibly in there, he and Blayne would get to gawk at two stripped chicks, blend flesh, Pim's unbagged sexlobe inside his mouth, her letting out little girlish gasps as his steel barbell brushed her forbidden lobe and his greedy fingers parted her zipper-teeth below and snugged their way into her moist hot clench.

"Well okay, give it here," he said. "Will we make it to the lot before buzz-time?"

"Five minutes after gulpdown, it kicks in."

"Works for me."

The pale yellow pill lay bitter on Condor's tongue. It took two hard swallows. Even then, the damned thing stuck in his throatpipe. But its bitter taste finally melted away, and Condor asked Blayne where they were supposed to do the girls.

"In the costume shop, during the search for the stiffs. She and Pim'll be pilling out too. Oughta be dropping it right about now."

Four minutes later, when Condor steered into the parking lot entrance, he felt a giggle bubble up out of his gut. "Oh jeez." It was a wavelet, yep, and he could see *huge* waves, shiny blue, way far out but edging closer.

"Yeah, I know," said Blayne. "But keep it tamped down till we get past Tweed's tight little kid sister and flash our passes at ol' Dunsmore. Once we're past the front table and into the gym, we can giggle as much as we freakin' feel like it, 'midst the dimness and death-terror and the whole dad-blamed fucked-up mess of a world."

"Blayne?" Condor said.

"Yeah?" The dark blue niobium in Blayne's puffy lips gleamed like a blueberry blintz.

"Tonight," he laughed, then bottled it up and jammed in a stopper. "I have a super-strong feeling that we're going to have the best goddamn time of our whole entire friggin' motherfuckin' lives!"

"Could be, buddy. Could be."

"Blayne?"

"Yeah?"

"I love you, Blayne."

The smile vanished. "Yeah. Love."

Blayne looked out the windshield. "Come on, my man, she's waving you on. Don't blow it."

Zane Fronemeyer'd been a warmup. Offing him and his wives had simply swept obtrusive clutter into the dustbin, which made for clearer lines of action ahead.

But they were peripheral victims.

Sheriff Blackburn, revived to offer up his voice for capture on tape, had given a foretaste of the main event. He, after all, had made the ultimate sacrifice in the school building, and roping him into place had led to a perfect and tasty omniscience.

But even Blackburn was mere prologue.

Now, to watch them arrive, to peer from the heart of concealment, an architectural honeycomb entwined above, beneath, around, and through the school proper—this sanctioned voyeurism drew *then* and *now* together.

It pointed the way toward healing.

How natural it was to identify with this building, a caretaker of the young and a presider over their slaughter. But tonight, this place of brick and mortar seethed with resentment at the pinch and crimp of the law.

One couple and no more?

Too strict.

Healing demanded free rein, and tonight that demand would be met.

Beyond a shelf of trophies, the seated shop teacher's hair shone. Opposite him, kids spiffed in tuxedo satins or fluffed in corsaged ball gowns flashed their pinned-on passes to the teacher and his junior helper and accepted the sealed envelope that bore their names.

At their waists dangled the mini-cleavers awarded them by Lily Foddereau upon successful completion of butchery class, these and the cloudy pastel-lidded Futterware containers.

But above the finery, between each dazzling lobebag and its companion earlobe on the right, their fresh-scrubbed faces wore the same devilish looks that mischievized the hallways, day in, day out. Mayhem directed outward, sex thoughts abuzz inside, as their jaws vacantly snapped gum.

Cobra passed by with Peach Popkin, owning her with a few fingers at the neck, his eyes dead with hatred.

Fido Jenner and Bowser McPhee hove next into view, Bowser's eager eyes glued to Peach's twitch of a rump.

Then the huge bulk of Kyla Gorg and Patrice Menuci, an item since eighth grade, blocked out the twosome waiting behind.

It didn't matter who they were, some of them victims, some victimizers. Every one of them had the play of holes on the brain. Mouth hole over lobe, pussy hole over prick, shove it in, yank it out.

Diversion from deadmarch.

Ah but tonight, how pleasing it would be to taste their fear, see it unclench, seize it right back up, and dole out death—enough to free their minds, those that survived, enough to salve the wounds that every prom night reopened, heal them at last, and find release.

When Kyla and Patrice were gone, a white limo drove away outside. Rocky Stark waved to it, and Sandy Gunderloy tugged at his sleeve. He turned, grinned at the shop teacher, and offered his hand.

Top jock.

Head cheerleader.

The momentary flash of a fuck. Imaginary. But every damned bitch-bastard in school flashed likewise whenever these two walked by.

Tonight's places of slaughter had been firmed up. But Jesus Fucking God it'd be such a pleasure to trash Rocky Stark and Sandy Gunderloy, even if meant veering off-plan in order to do it.

They were finalists for prom king and queen, as indeed were Brandy Crowe and Flann Beckwith. Most prom nights, that brought immunity. Broad, fearless grins.

Not tonight.

In a pig's eye were they safe tonight.

Time to move on. Doors would be locked soon. Lights would dim. Music would play.

The sort of music the little shits danced to.

The sort of music they faced.

Jenna Megrim waved another car left.

The breeze against Jenna's face was cool but not chilly. Armed with instructions and flashlights, she and the other volunteers had fanned out across the parking lot to direct arriving seniors.

Her father would be home, stepping out of the shower and preparing to sit before the tube.

Gravel scrunched at her back, a low motor, as some parent's car moved off down the blacktop, guided by the next flashlight-wielding junior. Moonlight caught its bumpersticker: "Have you kissed your child's friendship lobe today?"

Jenna had thought she might be bored. But simply knowing that the designated slasher was roaming the secret byways *right now* thrilled her.

The slasher *knew*!

It might be her Spanish teacher, Senora Westmore. Or Lily Foddereau. Or that handsome choir director with the killer eyes and the thick tanned lobes.

Whoever it was knew where the doomed couple would be sitting *and who they were*.

Even now, as she signaled them on, this pair of tuxedo'd boys blowing kisses at her might, in a little while, be lying, gutted open, at the base of the towering fiend she had helped construct.

Jenna knew she should feel frightened.

But she didn't.

Not even for Dex and her sister. They'd be safe. And her own prom night was an entire year away.

Besides, maybe she'd be a finalist for prom queen. Sure, she wasn't the best looking girl in the junior class. She wasn't claiming she was.

But Rocky Stark had flirted with her once, a smile and a smart slap across the face. As flirts go, it wasn't much. But it was enough of one that Sandy—who had let it be known that their twosome would be looking for male completion only—felt compelled to give Jenna a public dressing-down.

Even if a nomination wasn't in the cards, her birthdate would make her a tender on prom night. For three days on either side of one's birthdate each month (in Jenna's case, the twenty-third), any sort of physical harm was strictly forbidden.

Well, okay, except for *half* the high school seniors in that category on prom night. Grown-ups weren't *about* to give anybody a free ride from birth. Still, she had a fifty-fifty chance of being sent by lottery to the girl's gym, thereby escaping all possibility of slaughter.

If that were true, Pish Balthasar, the brainy beauty with the smoky eyes and a growing interest in her, would almost surely want to be her date.

Horn blips from the street.

Dexter drove, Tweed in mid-wave beside him.

Jenna's coat rustled as her arm shot up. She waved them on, blowing a kiss.

Dex stopped, roll down. "Don't let the Ice Ghoul get you!"

Roll up as Jenna's big sister said, "And have a good time at—" The window cut Tweed off, but Jenna saw her lips form *Pumper's house*.

"I will," she yelled, "and *you* keep away from the Ice Ghoul too!" Tweed looked grand in pink, and Dex would make a darling brother-in-law.

It wouldn't be long now.

Another quarter hour, and Mrs. Gosler or one of her husbands would drive Jenna and Pumper home for a sleepover. Jenna waved at Pumper across the lot, fingers captured by her flashlight beams, and Pumper waved back.

Later in Pumper's bedroom, they would listen, mock shock on their faces, to the Goslers watching the electrocution on *Notorious*. All the while, the two girls would keep the radio low, listening intently to the Midwest returns, heaving sighs of relief and bursting into giggles as Corundum High's victims were announced and it became clear that their older siblings had been spared.

Another car arced in.

An increase in frantic frowns meant the eight o'clock deadline must be drawing near.

Stay on the ball, Jenna told herself.

She had to concentrate, these last minutes, lest her fumbling lose someone their lobes.

Where before had been free highway, cars clogged in backup. Tough times ahead. Behind her, the ten minute bell sounded.

A wrench in her gut.

Get it on, she thought, relax the wrist, stay alert, give Tweed's classmates every fair chance.

Over driveway and blacktop, Jenna's fragile cone of light moved in deadly earnest.

Tweed walked arm in arm with Dex to the band room. In the empty hallways, her dress rustled an unbearable rustle.

Silent lockers serried by.

In her free hand she held the sealed envelope Wattle Murch's brother Daub had given Dex at the front table. It had grown sticky with palm-sweat.

The band room door wasn't locked.

They ventured in.

No one there.

A dim bulb on a lamp pole with a pullchain struggled to throw light over the wooden risers where the French horn section sat. Dark shadows choked the rest of the fan-shaped room, and Tweed had to trust to sense memory to know when to step up and when not.

"You see okay?" asked Dex. He had reached the cache of saxophones in back, set midway in the tall gray doors angled polygonally about the outer edge of the room.

He fumbled out his key.

"Yes, if I don't look at the lightbulb."

Tweed threaded through a tangled forest of stands, shoving the black nuisances aside. She touched the leather thong of her key, unpursed it, and felt for the right orientation.

The trombone closet unlocked.

Musty odor inside always, like the inside of a ventriloquist's dummy's mouth. There stood her trombone case.

Tweed hesitated, an irrational fear gripping her that someone was hiding a few feet inside the closet. She and Dex had once knocked on its back wall. Knowing that the slasher's secret byways wrapped around the band room, they had heard then the hollow reverb and wondered if this very panel had ever afforded him entry for the kill.

Eight years past, a couple had been butchered by Mr. Dunsmore right where the trombone players sat. Just yesterday, Tweed had emptied her spit valve upon a painted-over blood patch.

But fear was absurd.

It wasn't yet time for the kill, nor was it likely that she and Dex had been assigned to sit in the band room. Still, this *might* be the place again. Preparations may have been underway before they had interrupted them.

Something touched the back of her hand. A sound strained in her throat.

"Hey, it's okay, it's just me." Dex squeezed her hand.

"Don't scare me like that," she said.

"Sorry," he said. "Here." He lay down his alto sax case and snapped it open, *flan flan*, right-angling the lid. "I'll put the envelope in my case. Get your axe and let's go. Mr. Jones will start worrying about us."

Swooping her instrument out of the closet, Tweed walked cautiously with Dex to the band room door, breathing easier when it had swung-to behind them.

Rather than circle back past the front table to get to the gym, they continued counterclockwise along the first floor corridor.

On the left, science labs gloomed by, site of the hillside creep and the polar creep in geology, memorable goads-to-learning, and the place as well where chem, bio, and physics had been crammed into their skulls.

On the right, thick glass doors to the barn and the slaughterhouse areas made a valiant effort to hold in the stench. Not so long ago, that area of the school had terrified Tweed, despite the gradual progression from primary school petting zoo, to junior high's dissection of frogs and pig embryos, to high school's more demanding course of instruction in slaughter, rendering, meat-packing, tanning, butchery, and taxidermy. But now these skills were old hat. She felt as if part of her life was over. She would miss the down-to-earth Lily Foddereau, her loamy wisdom, her steady hand, her lethal axe-blade.

They turned left at the water fountain.

Far ahead, by the gym door nearest the front of the school, a clump of seniors congregated, the boys high-fiving and lobe-tugging as though they were wearing jeans and jerseys and topsiders, not tuxes and ruffed shirts.

No reason not to go in. They were waiting, it seemed, for the lights and the music to draw them out of the hallway.

That's us, she thought.

"My God, Tweed, look at it!" said Dex as they reached the entrance to the gym.

She paused beside him, her eyes at once drawn to the Ice Ghoul.

Even with the lights not yet low, he seemed suddenly larger and more menacing. Fog swirled about him from pedestal vents, a low white roll of guile and menace.

"Jenna told me over dinner that they'd filled in detail." The vast gymnasium seemed to swallow her voice.

"Yeah I know. You mentioned it," Dex said. "Some brushwielder, some real sicko, understands what high school is all about. That face really captures the feeling."

It made her shiver. She wondered, once they survived the stalking, whether it would seem less horrific. "Why's it . . . oh look, Dex, the roof must be leaking."

"Too bad," he said. "But when the lights change, it'll look like just another effect."

A voice called to them from the bandstand, off to the right. Festus Targer at his drumset softened a cymbal and twirled a brush at them. The bass drum thumped.

Farther along the same top riser, Butch and Zinc were de-belling low furious arpeggios from their down-directed trumpets. They were seniors, a couple in the throes of breaking up on account of being college-bound in different directions, Butch to the east coast, Zinc to the west.

Zinc had the blush-pink look of a tender, unflogged for days, and it was clear, had been clear since last week's lottery, that Butch felt guilty piggybacking his salvation on his lover's monthly reprieve from beatings and the luck of the draw. Some students resented those who escaped the slasher's knife that way, but Butch was much harsher on *himself* than were any of Tweed's friends.

Tweed took her seat on the middle riser. Dex sat below and to the left, next to Wyche Fowler, ego insufferable, but man could he blow Dex out of the water on the sax.

Tweed snapped open the case and threaded her horn together. Colored lights toggled at random. As she sprayed mist along the length of her cold-creamed slide, Tweed glanced up and saw, at the far end of the gym, Gerber Waddell by the light bank struggling to recall, with his genial feeble half-mind, the precise combination intended for this part of prom night.

"Where the fuck's Buttweiler?" Bongo asked in her right ear, an unruly low F struggling to speak at the end of his arm.

"Um." Tweed looked around. No sign of their principal. Not

93

at the punch bowl where the other chaperones clustered. Not at the longer stretch of table near the janitor, where the seniors would pig out and glug down.

A blue vision crossed the gym on a diagonal.

Nurse Gaskin.

She stopped on the sawdust to stare up at the Ice Ghoul bore continuing toward the other chaperones.

Tweed and Dex had a crush on Delia Gaskin. If only she weren't so old.

"I don't see him yet," said Tweed. "Maybe he's doing paperwork in his office."

"Yeah, or in the bafroom." Dimbulb Bongo. Still some years of growing to do, and he was nobody's genius.

"Tweed." Dex caught her eye, his neckband a shiny black against the white tux. He glanced at the nurse, then back at Tweed.

Tweed nodded, resigned.

The lights took on harsh red and green casts. At the far door, fluff and fine lines of clothing began to drift in.

Warming the mouthpiece with her hand, Tweed set it into the horn, tried for saliva she seemed not to have, bobbled a few notes, licked her lips and the rim of the mouthpiece cup, woodshedded the opening riff for "I'll Be Around," opened the spit valve, and shook out not a drop.

She was scared out of her wits. Half the band was a wreck pretending not to be. They would try to lose themselves in the charts, and maybe they would succeed.

But maybe they'd just have to wait for the prom kill to be over before they would find any kind of groove tonight.

Jiminy Jones glanced this way and that.

The lights at play in his thinning hair lent him weirdly shifting coronas. He held the light-tipped baton tight in one chubby hand.

A last look at the score, smiles darting into the band, a "Hi there Dex, easy on the triplets," his bowtie blue-sequined like his suitcoat edging, like his lobebag, his head raised to the air like a bull sensing slaughter as the eight o'clock bell sounded, the lights clicked precisely into place, and Jiminy Jones' baton came down upon the first terrified note of the evening.

7

Violence, Sweet Violence

Willy Wanker, President Gilly Windfucker's Secretary of Cultural Impoverishment, had slipped his lobebag off and was idly stroking his sexlobe as he watched the video feed.

In this, he was no different from any other cabinet member around the conference table. Even the President's lobebag lay limp on the polished tabletop, his slim wooden hand chop-cutting the air below his left ear in a semblance of stroking.

His manufacturers had made him a majestic sexlobe. Its bold presence suggested great power, though the general public would only be privy to its *implied* heft when bagged. They had even stained it with cedar blush, though they must have known—the protocol long established and drooled over in the media—that prom night was the only time it came into view and then only for members of the cabinet and their staff.

Up until tonight.

Wanker kept his counsel.

Close to the chest was his nature, a mode of being accepted by the others. But it also helped him keep confidential his role on the Committee to Assassinate the President, which issued periodic updates, under strictest wraps and with the utmost anonymity, to the press.

Secretary Wanker had served on that committee in many past administrations, but this one posed a special challenge.

Would clipping Gilly Windfucker's strings and snapping his limbs for kindling, duly videotaped for the national archives of course, do the trick? Or would they need to murder Cholly Bork as well? Kill the brains or simply the brainless twit of a figurehead?

In committee, Wanker had argued long and with great gusto that it was their patriotic duty to do them *both* in, indeed that *failing* to do so would surely throw the government into a Constitutional crisis from which it might never emerge unscathed. And his arguments, lo these many months, had eaten their way toward persuasion.

As to *when* the assassination would occur, Wanker had been convincing on that front as well. This very private moment in a president's tenure, the annual viewing of a hand-picked high-school slaughter, would at last be made public.

By god, thought Wanker with a wicked grin, I'll go down in history.

This, in part, fueled his lobestrokes, as the roomful of suited men, and one pants-suited woman, watched Karn Flentrop sharpen her blade in the machine shop and sashay through dusty backways that had hosted scores of slashers before her.

When the lobebags dropped to the table and the slow rip of opening zippers circled about the conference room, generous holes had irised open in the table directly above their laps.

Busy indeed were the hands of the nation's caretakers, left ones above the tabletop stroking their sexlobes, right ones below.

Even the President's left arm clacked against the edge of the table as though he were grasping something stiff below. But no gens did Gilly Windfucker sport.

Onscreen, a school bell sounded.

The cameras tracked, as best they could, the doomed couple's walk to the science classroom. That bold black number 57 again came into view.

They seated themselves beneath it.

The girl's date had been a quarter off-camera as he took his place. But she tugged him over by the padded shoulder of his suit, a loving gesture which he shook off, then accepted.

"I'm a little nervous," he said, by way of apology, and she said, "I know."

Just above their heads was a metal plate that seemed to be screwed into the wall and painted in place. But earlier footage had shown the viewers how it would abruptly open, footage replayed in slo-mo. A stunning stand-in enacted the role of the slasher, her arm coming in with a wavy-bladed dagger against the throats of a pair of doped-up vagrants.

"Those two young people," said Cholly Bork, "make my bosom swell with patriotic zeal." Gasps edged the presidential voice, though Bork's hands were engaged in manipulating Gilly Windfucker's limbs and mouth only.

"My bosom too, Mister President," intoned those in attendance.

Willy Wanker, as usual, said nothing. But his eyes were trained on the kids, his hands on his swollen tiller, and his mind on the crew of thugs that would, at his nod, burst through the cabinet room door.

Their final check of the walkie-talkies was nearly complete.

The woman who led them had gone down the line from one black-clad conspirator to the next. Each voice spoke clearly through the equipment she held to her ear.

No betraying squawks.

Top-of-the-line contraband.

"Hold on," she said, looking at the last man. "I'm getting sine wave distortion."

Then she realized the sound was outside, not in the equipment. Spotlights splashed the window thick with opacity. The drone of a helicopter whirlygigged down from above.

An electronic bullhorn snapped on: "WE'VE GOT YOU SURROUNDED."

Terror flooded her. Her eyes darted about the basement.

Who was looking away?

Who wasn't surprised?

But the light was too dim to make such a judgment, and most of her soldiers were already pulling on ski masks and drawing knives.

Then the door burst open and a choke of armed men in helmets and padded gear swarmed in, ganging up to drag down her people, tearing off ski masks, yanking heads back by hanks of hair, opening wide red grins in exposed necks.

Blood gushed onto concrete. Black fountains glistened in the silver night, turning the close air foul.

Then they attacked her, one young thug's boot slipping in blood but at once recovering. A young hotheaded soldier wrenched her down from where she stood. His foul-mouthed companion tore her lobebag off. Then three men rushed in to grab at her clothing, wrenching it apart like savages, her skin slick with sweat as the black fabric took on hole after hole and stretched into nothing.

"Teach the bitch a lesson," someone snarled, and that lesson, and many others, began to be most vigorously taught.

Butch rose for his solo in "Gettin' Off."

Back arched, trumpet lofted, a lick of hair swept across his brow, he made that horn wail, a weave of cool crisp notes bolting out like cliff beneath the frantic paws of a coyote.

Odd how his mind shuttled among chords while his fingers flurried out melodies above them. Yet somehow it always sounded new, some fresh-whelped beast that burst, sharp-clawed and yowling, out of the brass bell on rolling sweeps of passion.

The solo was flawless.

This was Butch's farewell gig, his last time through most of the charts, and he had no slasher worries to cramp his playing. Notes ripped aside like calendar days in a convict's cell.

But when he sat down and the saxes took the melody from him, the applause was tepid.

He knew why.

Zinc, Butch's date and fellow trumpeter, was a tender who had chosen a white ball on the stage in assembly a week before. They had gone steady for two years, but that didn't matter.

Zinc had lucked out.

Therefore, Butch had lucked out.

His classmates hadn't.

It was that simple. In their heads they knew he was cool. But their hearts screamed wimp, and he would carry to his grave the disgrace of having escaped the risk of slaughter.

Worse than that: Butch himself felt no less resentful toward the *others* whose dates were exempt tenders. Toward Ig and Stan and Lida Sue, even these, his friends.

They would be herded, the saved ones, into the girls' gym while their classmates faced real terror.

Somehow, Butch vowed, he would endure the summer months,

thinking only of Gryder College and his future there and beyond. There, before this night's shame caught up with him, he would stake out a brunt of friends, hoping they'd be steadfast under the communal pressure to shun him.

He pictured the trampoline in the girls' gym. When he had muttered something about trying it out tonight, the grown-ups standing nearby during the band's first break threw him looks of disapproval.

Fuck 'em, he thought. They had passed their test of courage centuries ago, the test he would be known forever to have weaseled out of.

Zinc leaned in to him at an eight-bar rest. "Super solo," he said. Butch nodded.

(*THREE-two-three-four*)

Monday, his lover would be fair game for flogging again and Butch planned a glorious one to celebrate their escape. When Zinc had been among the tenders lotteried free of danger a week ago in assembly (kids called them promstiffers), Zinc's mom and dad had embarrassed them both with a grand feast in thanksgiving. Grown-ups, face it, were gross and alien. They had no clue nor were they like to get one any time soon.

(*SEVEN-two-three-four*)

Tonight, Zinc displayed what had proven to be his and Butch's salvation: that thin-wristed, thin-lobed, smooth-skinned look of the unrecently flogged, which diminished him, which shrank him inward, making him look simultaneously hoary and tabula-rastic.

(*EIGHT-two-three*) *da-da-da DWEE!*

And Butch's bitchin' countermelody soared above the 'bones.

8
Unclosable Wounds

"They're *on* to us," muttered Bray.

Block by block on the drive from Fronemeyer's house, Bray's fear had grown. Now, as they stood at the refreshment table, it felt as if it surely must blare.

"Get a grip," Winnie replied.

Though the paper plate he held was sturdy, not the thin pitiful bendy kind that buckles or lulls under the least weight, his hand trembled. He transferred cheese cubes to the plate, orange and pale yellow ones with frilled toothpicks, then a fistful of wheat crackers.

Across the food, a senior girl with hard eyes and perky lobes stared at him, then shifted her glare onto the cheerleader bubblehead chatterbox with whom she had entered the gym.

"We're not *blending*," Bray agonized.

"Stick with the program."

Behind her smile, Winnie was miffed.

By the program, Bray knew she meant the plan she had laid out on the way over, the cover story the fuzzy-lipped teacher at the entrance table had swallowed without question.

Yes, Winnie had told Old Fuzzy Lip, they were correspondence students, had driven a fair stretch to celebrate their graduation from Corundum High. And yes, much obliged to accept one of a small stack of generic packets and wait out the stalking in the girls' gym with the tenders. He hadn't even checked their names, the pinned passes enough verification for him, and a frantic press of young people close behind.

But dumb luck could only hold for so long.

Winnie guided them away from the refreshments toward a darker patch of gym, not too close to the kids yet not so distant that they stuck out.

"This is right," she said, through a steam-heat shimmer of music. "I can feel it."

Sapphires, dark and gleaming, drifted across her face. It amazed him. Winnie was in her element here. She really believed they would pull it off, that tonight they would save the world.

"We're going to have our heads handed to us." He bit into sharp cheddar, wishing for apples to augment.

"You *are* a coward, aren't you?"

"Hey, never beaten, never flayed."

Between them and the Ice Ghoul, a few brave early couples danced, close and clingy. Many more were bleachered and bunched, plates and cups in hand, nibbling, sipping, and trading sick jokes.

A couple of chaperones circled the sculpted figure, a tall man and a shapely woman. Teachers, Bray guessed. Their shoes moved in and out of a rolling blanket of fog.

"The killer's nearby," said Winnie. "I can feel it."

"Our hero."

"He saved our lives."

"Three murders. So far. That's quite the humanitarian walking among us. I can't wait to shake his hand."

Tugging at his right lobe, the tall man nodded to the shapely woman without shifting his gaze from the rampant red Ice Ghoul. She broke off, her eyes suddenly on Bray and Winnie, and headed their way.

"I can see you're determined to be difficult, no matter how—"

"Save it," he broke in. "I believe we're about to have company." He made a point of not glancing at the approaching woman, hoping she'd veer off.

Winnie said, "I'll do the talking."

But the woman charged in. "Pardon my social ineptitude," she said, pumping Bray's hand. "Excuse my nosiness, but I can always spot grads-by-mail a mile away. You are . . . ?"

She stared right into him, a bold beautiful face with thick rich lips and lobes that sang.

"I, um, Brayton is the name," he said, out before he could warn himself to mumble something or to make up a name.

He was a goner, and Winnie would be dragged down too, just as, years before, Bonnie Dolan had fallen with him when they'd jumped the prom.

But the woman seized on his name, a snag in her head as she mulled.

"Brayton, Brayton," she said, an internal Rolodex flipping, then, "of course, Brayton Con-something, Connors, no Conyers! I had you last fall. Miss Brindisi? The Greater Vices, Pride, Anger, and Lust?"

"Of course," he said. "A wonderful class."

"And you must be our *other* student from Coffinville, Bray's co-worker, Raven Barnes." She shook Winnie's hand.

"That's right," said Winnie, matching the woman's brazen stance.

For one of society's outcasts, Bray thought, Winnie was admirably feisty.

"I'm pleased to welcome you both. I always find more in common with correspondents than with the youngsters."

"We have more focus," prompted Winnie. "We know what we want."

"Precisely." The woman's face lit up. "Say what you will about the merits of the annual prom kill, it does tend to distract the teenage mind from the task of learning. But get beyond that, venture out into the world for a spell, and well by golly, experience gives a correspondent a much clearer perspective on life—not to mention the legal exemption for returning students."

He chuckled. "No slasher."

"Not for you two."

"We'd submit to it if we had to," he assured.

Miss Brindisi moved in to confide, her right breast against Bray's sleeve: "It's for the young." Her smile overwhelmed. "They need it."

Bray nodded. "I understand."

"It's good for them. It toughens the fiber. And it's one hell of a tonic for us post-teens as well, to witness it."

"Yes." His lip corners felt as if they would crack. The woman's lobes looked delectable. "I'm sure it is."

"Well," she said, almost as if they'd shared a dance. "Brayton, Raven, I'll leave you to it. Stop by and say hello, after all the excitement dies down."

"We will," said Winnie.

"Several of your teachers are here tonight, and I know they'd love to meet you."

Bray waved. "We'll be around."

"Enjoy yourselves." She eased off. "And eat up!"

A whirl and she was away, heading back toward the tall man.

"Lion of God be praised," muttered Bray.

"Amen," said Winnie, turning her smile to him.

"Let's hope the *real* Bray and Raven aren't here."

"Are you kidding? Coffinville's at the southern end of the state. I've seen maybe four other older couples. A school this size probably has, oh, I'd guess thirty or forty grads-by-mail each year. They rarely show up on prom night."

"Only the vultures," he said. "The ghouls."

"Yeah, the ones I've seen seem pretty seedy. I say we avoid 'em. There's more virtue in the prom-jumping coward and his societally challenged date than in any hundred of those folks."

"We'll open their eyes," said Bray, scanning for them.

"Damned straight we will."

"Or die trying."

"Will you quit harping on death? Nobody's gonna die. Not tonight and maybe at no other prom ever again."

The layout of the gym was different than it had been at Bray's school. Bigger too. But the hard knot that was high school had tied itself tight in his stomach.

The feeling was the same.

Stifled growls of pent-up fury.

Naked fear.

"We'll see," he said and endured her seethed volley, comforted— even as she had her verbal way with him—at having Winnie by his side.

The fear was delicious.

Thick as oil paint gobbed on with a palette knife.

It rose out of the kids Jonquil passed on the dance floor. It fell in waves from the bleachers, rich and blunt and thrilling beside the music's brassy panic. Claude, captivated by the wicked red ogre towering at the center of the gym, had moved not at all.

"And the purveyor of lesser vices," she said, "having made the mistake of calling the Ice Ghoul dull, found that he could no longer tear his eyes away, forever ensnared in its charms."

Claude smiled at her. "Oh, hello. So who were they, the correspondents who have somehow managed not to look as unsavory as they've got, most certainly, to be?"

Jonquil touched his arm. "Our secret, okay? I don't have the slightest idea. The young man's name is Brayton, I'm fairly sure. The woman went along with my offer of Raven, so you can call her that if the need arises."

"Crashers," he said, bored. "Passes real?"

"Pretty convincing if not. Elwood would've caught an obvious fake at the door."

Claude gestured upward. "You know, in the right mood, and with a certain sinister fall of shadows across its body, this monstrous mound of kitsch has an undeniably creepy allure."

Moisture continued to drip down the sides of the Ice Ghoul's head.

"Does it stack up against the one in seventy-six?"

"This one easily outstrips the other," he said. "It's bigger. More height, more bulk, more menace. I get the uncanny feeling that it's aware of the outrage perpetrated against Futzy. Speaking of which, where is our illustrious leader hiding himself? Doesn't he realize we're all starting to extend the gossip about him?"

Mister Weight-of-the-World Principal.

Old Futzy would be in his element tonight, the focus of punishment, wallowing in misery. A fitting climax to weeks of increased student floggings, his admission of impotence after the prom committee announced the Ice Ghoul as its centerpiece at the dance.

"In his office is my guess. He'll slip in under low lights, keep himself apart from the kids, maybe even from us, until the ceremonies."

"A prom he'll never forget," said Claude.

"Yes. Expect new bylaws next year. No more Ice Ghoul at the prom as long as he's in charge."

Claude nodded. "The one in seventy-six was appalling, but only after Futzy's daughter and her date lay dead before it. The teacher who slashed them worked out a transfer. He'd really gone to town that night."

Jonquil thought back. "Let's see. I was all of fifteen then. My prom took place two years after that in seventy-eight." Someone, after the bodies had been retrieved, had arranged Quill and Dane arm-in-arm, their staved heads angled together, against the hard concavity of a black angel's sorrowing embrace. The deaths of her dearest friends had given Jonquil a backbone of steel.

"So are we going to blow the whistle on these two?"

"Let's not," she said.

"By which I take it, the left lobe of one or both of our crashers—the genitalia as well?—are at risk of being loved, for lack of a better word, by a certain sexy, horny instructress of my near acquaintance."

"Cruel, cutting, and unkind," she demurred, "and quite possibly true."

"I minored in the study of Jonquils."

"Who knows? The night's young. Survivors grow unusually festive at these things, and the spirit's infectious. Let me observe them, maybe have a little fun with them. We've seen really ugly souls buy prom passes from correspondents in the past. There's nothing new about that."

"It provides an additional pinch of terror."

"Which is all to the good," she said. "Let 'em hover at the periphery, add atmosphere, then throw 'em out after the futtering's done and the padlocks have come off. But what *is* new is this: These two don't strike me as your typical bogus grads-by-mail. There's something different about them."

"A new mix of body parts, Jonquil dear?"

"Never discount it, Claude. People don't couple enough in my opinion—which is the *right* opinion. They don't inflict enough violence. And when they do, there's no creativity, no spirit of inventiveness to it."

"My wives yammer on the same way, at least about indulging in the crude fluidities of sex," he said. "Your take on cruelty is, I hasten to admit, entirely your own—and a vast part of what draws me to you as a friend. That and your lobes of course."

"Kidder." She knuckled his shoulder, enough to make him wince. "But beyond that, they're out for something, and I can't tell what. They seem wholesome and apart, somehow. Here in body, yes, but headwise elsewhere. I'm determined to tease out their little secret before the night is over."

"May the Ice Ghoul watch over you," he said, patting the rough red rump of the beast.

"And you, Claude."

"More cheese!" he demanded, heading off into the music toward the chaperones' corner, swirling up wisps of dry-ice fog as he went, not bothering to see if she followed.

Futzy Buttweiler sat alone in his spacious office, an ache of loneliness echoing inside him with each muffled thump of the bass drum. Below him lay the gym and its vague layers of sculpted sound. As he stared through muted darkness, Futzy fingered the cache of confiscation strewn across his desk.

A bolas from one ferret-eyed defier whose spine had nearly cracked beneath the payback of its stones.

Cattle prods, thumbscrews, portable planers and sanders, the paraphernalia of torture lifted from the parental bedroom.

Pornocrap that would have raised Jonquil Brindisi's ire, so inept were its staged bloodlettings, so low and lackadaisical its standards for cruelty. These sorry tapes dulled a wondrous world of hurt into the turn of a fast buck.

Futzy had left the lights off.

Parallel slats of moonglow fell in cream slants across the carpet before his desk. Welts of moonlight that recalled to mind the flaying he had endured beneath his wives' fury, lacking only the wounds and the cutting words.

But inside his head, words came, redirected words as he redirected daily the abuse he got at home.

A victim there, a victimizer here.

They were all scum, thought Futzy. School culture artificially divided the student body into good kids and bad kids. A false divide. He saw that now.

It hadn't all been flogging and flaying, his exercise of discipline here.

Yet not one student, not one beneficiary of his many kindnesses, had objected to an affront so egregious and humiliating as the Ice Ghoul's return to Corundum High's senior prom.

Futzy forced himself to his feet.

His anger at them was greater than he had thought possible.

The walk to the barred window seemed beyond bearing, so wild and dense with passion the night made the air. Ordinarily, daylight contained his savagery in this office, giving it sanction and a blessing.

But tonight, lunacy edged everything.

Below, in the parking lot, vehicles gleamed.

This was his last chance at them.

He imagined the little shits revving up after midnight, backing out, tracing light-swept trails across blacktop, moving out into traffic, removing themselves and their pointless lives forever from his grasp.

Ah, but what if night went and morning came, and still the cars stayed?

What if something unspeakable swept through the school and fixed them there forever?

What if no key found its way to any padlock? And the air, this same air, grew still, stale, not moved by convection, by the bustle of bodies, by a riding crop descending, nor by the monotonously multiplied insuck and expulsion of air from young lungs?

Conceivable.

More than conceivable.

Matthew Megrim, Tweed's dad, found himself unsettled in the extreme tonight.

His bath seemed to last forever. Yet every check of the sweep-second-hand clock propped on the sink counter surprised him. Surely he had been idling here a good year, contemplating the polderesque rise and fall of his belly from the surrounding water.

Come-ons for *Notorious*, a week of teasers, had replayed in his mind. Endless views of the condemned duo mingled somehow with memories of his first wives, Cam and Arly, as they had been before they had drowned. Their fluxidermed corpses, the stuffed shells-of-themselves which duly graced his vestibule, came nowhere near those memories.

This parade of souls occasionally parted to allow him glimpses of his history class—folds of batter endlessly turned, the same damned desks, students seated according to chart, slated to pass through this year-end terror he so despised and tonight *feared* with a fear that had no limit.

Above all, his daughter Tweed recurred in his thoughts a thousand times. Again and again, her parting smile and "Good night" blessed his inner vision.

She would be killed. Jenna would comfort him in his grief. Then, next year, they would kill *her* and he'd go out of his mind.

Why hadn't he thrown himself wholeheartedly into the anti-slasher cause? He could have contributed more, done with less, "come out" as Krantor Berryman had done two years before, shared the spite and scorn with him, yes, but perhaps set more protests snowballing.

Too late now.

Too late for Tweed anyway.

He got out of the bathtub, vowing something decisive come Monday, some way to keep Jenna from having to run the gauntlet next year.

A milling hallway of seniors whipped up in his mind, dressed in tux and gown finery, massed in a forward hurtling plane. Ahead lay a brick wall, but only one of the bricks was real: one couple creamed, the rest bursting through illusions of brick, thinking afterward that maybe it hadn't been so bad, that it was something all kids ought to go through.

Jesus, his mind was snapping.

Matthew bent to peer into an unsteamed wedge of mirror. His calm eyes amazed him, not a hint of agitation.

He cupped his earlobes, then gripped them tight. Nothing sexual. Not yet. He remembered his childhood years, the comfort that surrounded and enclosed them. All of it a mad delusion that firm ground and not the thinnest of high wires lay between the wobbled balance-and-step of life, and certain death below.

He wrapped a towel around his waist and went out into the hallway. Entering his bedroom, he closed the door after him, feeling more cocoon-like that way. That was the way his parents had watched the show, and it was the way, shut off from their daughters, that Matthew and his wives had watched it.

Thank God for *Notorious*, he thought, realizing the addictive purpose it served even as he craved the hit.

Thank God there were folks rotten enough to fry in public each year, not just for the sexual thrill it provided—considerable, certainly—but also to divert the minds of anxious moms and dads across the nation.

Removing the towel, Matthew strapped on his Private Flogger, molded like a slug to his back, and turned it to Warmup. It sensed the contours of his muscles and their firmness, reminding him of heating pads applied to stiff necks as a boy.

Grabbing a Futterware container of coconut-oil on his nightstand, he made a nest out of his pillows and zapped on the TV.

National coverage of prom night. An East Coast map smattered with sporadic dots of early returns. At this point, the commentary consisted mainly of glib history and idle chatter.

Another station, a local Topeka business channel, scream-gabbled a pitch to survivors, showing a slashed red X simultaneously crossing out a cartoon picnicker and a box on an org-chart, urging its viewers to Call This Number Now!

Then Matthew found the channel he wanted.

Boggs Fleester, hair gray and combed back in perfect coif, sprang into his bedroom not two feet from the foot of the bed.

"Over my shoulder," he said in measured tones, "you can see the electric chair in which our two reprobates will fry."

Fleester wasn't really in the execution room. You could tell that. Soon, the distinguished newsman would fade. The electric chair and its surround would surge out of a flat background into vivid holographic prominence.

As Fleester's voice jauntily recounted the couples' rampage upon a Rhode Island school bus of elementary kids, Matthew glared feverishly at the clock. Come on, he thought. Stuck at twenty-five past eight. Get the damned show on the road.

Tweed, a vision in pink chiffon, beamed at the front door. "Good night."

She was dancing now, fearful at Corundum High, slow and close and clinging to Dex, or giving and getting blows in a frenzied bout of slap'n'smack prior to dispersal twenty minutes away, the slash achieved by nine.

She might, his pride and joy might . . . no, shut it out.

Fleester wrapped up and faded. The music took on intensity. The grim cell moved forward, the chair growing greater both wide and tall, like the Christmas tree in *The Nutcracker*.

Off to the left, an inset bubble hovered, inside it the executioner beside her dials and the two men chosen to pleasure her, naked except for the obligatory lobebags the FCC and common decency insisted upon.

Matthew sobbed.

A cell door opened on the right. In were marched the twosome, stripped, passive, doped up, and resigned.

Gritting his teeth, Matthew turned his Flogger to Low. The first lash fell with a pain that stung and diverted. He oiled his bare left lobe and his gens until the flesh flushed and stiffened. To the suggestiveness of the music he surrendered himself.

The aroma coming from the TV had a sufficient dankness about it to be convincing.

A sizzle of fire flared across Matthew's right shoulder, Cam's favorite place to flog him.

His darling wife Cam had birthed Tweed into the world, then Jenna, and loved them both dearly. Now she was gone, Arly with her, in that awful accident.

Soon *Tweed* would . . . no!

Matthew's hand fumbled as he notched it up, wincing at the increase in depth and frequency.

The couple were strapped in, the woman belted upside down, mouth to groin, groin to mouth. The executioner, her nipples hidden by two rotating male scalps, began to play with the dials.

They writhed as Matthew focused desperately on his own arousal. Uncensored black and white projections danced over their skin.

Funny, how the image of naked lovelobes posed no problem if they were grainy and contorted on curves of flesh. Yet the *couple's* lobes were crudely bagged. And the executioner's, bared now for action, had been expertly cubed out.

The condemned couple—scum bitch and bastard, by any measure—might in other circumstances have enjoyed the pain. But it was one thing to choose to have a lover inflict torment in measured doses within established limits. It was quite another to endure punishment, that would only worsen unto death, from that grim-faced invasive third called The State.

Matthew's arousal was progressing well. A lovely commonality of pull and tug, complementary and compelling, had arisen between his hands.

But the executioner's tinny voice, catching rhythm from another realm, threw a grit of grain into the turning cogs. Tweed at the door. "Good night." A vision in pink, her smile. Dex too so full of promise, his hands thrust to the cuffs into his tux pockets.

The execution on TV was suddenly nothing but sound and fury. Matthew, his penis emblooded and his lobemeat throbbing beneath his ear, stabbed Mute and paused the flogger.

Hugging eight forty-five. He should have turned the damned clock to the wall!

Fifteen minutes to Tweed's phone call if she had been spared. She would make her way back from her assigned spot, passing pay phones, banks of them throughout the building.

He had given her plenty of quarters. More than she needed. He was surprised Tweed hadn't jingled as she left the house.

Matthew rose from the bed. He paced, still erect below, his stiffness a bother. He circled the projection. With the sound off, it seemed unreal.

How could people act the way these two had?

So many children so remorselessly used.

A sheen of floor dirt coated the wrinkles of the woman's soles where her feet hung, knee-bent, above the man's shoulders. He was gripping the arms of the chair, his penis limp upon her cheek.

They had died an hour ago of course. Maybe more. East Coasters were already sated on this couple's prolonged miseries. West Coasters were still awaiting the arrival of dates.

Even the executioner, in her holographic bubble writhing under eager tongues, was in reality on her way home. Maybe she was even concerned with her kid brother's welfare that night at school.

Eight fifty.

This was unbearable.

Year after year, he had taught the prom kill in his sophomore history class as though it were nothing, accepted practice, forgetting the agony he himself had gone through at eighteen.

But it had torqued him, way back then.

It had turned him moody and morose as he turned fifteen. More adult, his folks had said. Until in college, junior year, he had lightened up, discovered song buried in the depths of his wounded heart, and let joy burst from his mouth.

Now, heaven help him, he had delivered his daughter into that same maw.

Even now, she might be . . .

He cut off the thought, a wash of fever at his brow.

Ten more minutes. Give it ten.

She would call. It would be okay. He could breathe easier then.

He thumbed the Flogger, nearly losing his balance as a laser lash seared across his back.

Settling once more into his nest on the bed, Matthew punched up the sound and dug his eyes deep into the couple with the images crawling across their skin.

His flesh and hers hissed beneath a languid electrocution. But that was damned fucking okay with Matthew, they were such slimy shits and good only at the end of their lives (the woman's urine now caught the man full in the face, blinking to avert it) for keeping legions of distraught moms and dads from going insane.

Matthew's fingers scooped up fresh dollops of coconut oil and slathered them on. His penile and lobate tissue responded anew.

Upon the woman's inverted back, a helmeted slitted dome of flesh eased past the thin lips of a blush-lobed lady. Across the man's hairy thigh, twitching beneath a surge, somebody's hand worked a digitally enhanced earlobe deep inside a gaping vagina.

Matthew regained the rhythm.

It lived in the pounding of the music, in the agony of voices, in the faint aroma of roast pork that seeped out of his system (a prelude to the char to come), and in the interwoven throbs of incessantly moving flesh.

He caught that rhythm. He rode it, honed by years of viewing, years of coaxing himself, and being coaxed so by caring lovers, toward the twin consummation of lobe and lingam.

On his way.

9
By the Book

Tweed's chops were just about blown.

The dance band's frantic swing through non-stop charts—heavy on the 'bones and light on the rests—had been more grueling this year than last.

Even the slow numbers felt manic.

Bongo by her side, grabbing at catch-breaths, had been his typical goofball self.

But Dex, Dol, Estlin, and a half-dozen other seniors had acted like square pegs in round holes, hurtling along familiar routes of sound toward two unlucky classmates' moment of truth.

Tweed had been relieved to see Mr. Versailles filling in as chaperone. It meant he wasn't this year's slasher.

But the bristling boxes of riding crops that appeared beside the stage made Tweed shudder, not because she hadn't delivered and received their bare-backed pleasures a time or two in her young life. No, but because when they were dispersed, it would mean that Principal Buttweiler's opening remarks were done and that the moment had arrived to go where the envelope directed, waiting there and cowering.

"The prunes are hot for blood," Bongo cupped into her right ear as she counted.

Glancing into chaperone corner, Tweed saw Mr. and Mrs. Borgstrom edged now on their chairs, in their seventies and shriveled, the adoptive mom and pop of a junior boy whose hair was black and whose ways were sullen and sulky. Their jaws had notches, discolored

jags that marked each year they had been married, a practice fallen away in the fifties.

Then the count clicked over in her brain and her horn rose to join in the final verse of "Lobe Town Blues," a dirge filled with quirky delights and a chance for each section to show off.

Festus Targer, his cymbal shimmering beneath them, held them back. Festus had it in him, assuming he survived next year's prom, to make it big as a drummer.

Jiminy Jones nodded an okay at the principal, who was chatting, hands in his coat pockets, with Nurse Gaskin among the chaperones. Mr. Jones' pudgy fingers brought the band to a skillful close, his satisfied smile's peculiar clash with her fears reminding Tweed how remote his age made him from the coming sacrifice.

The applause seemed heartfelt. Jiminy bowed, waved a section at a time to its feet, then the full ensemble.

Tweed put the trombone, sectioned, back into its case. She wondered who would next reassemble it. Herself? Or its inheritor?

Dex's hand held the envelope. His features were strained.

Damn the rules, she thought. It was insane—her dad more right than she had given him credit for—that people as whole and good as Dexter Poindexter fell each year under the red blade of the slasher. He had promised her father protection he couldn't possibly deliver, but she vowed that she would fight to save Dex too, if it came to that.

Passivity and paralysis were not her style.

Nor his.

Tweed took Dex's hand.

They shared a nervous embrace.

"Ready?" he asked.

"There's gonna be one dead teacher," said Tweed, "if he even *tries* to hurt you."

Dex smiled. "We'll waste him."

Principal Buttweiler stood off to the left on a floor scattered with shags of sawdust.

His hands were crossed straight-arm below his belt, a slim packet of index cards down-angled in one hand. His nods and smiles were more perfunctory than usual, rotating lights turning his strained face blue, then orange, then a sickly shade of yellow.

The poor man had been dealt a savage blow. But Tweed's

sympathy did nothing to dampen the chill she felt as his eyes fell upon her and Dex, deep and unmistakable (or was she just on edge?), the message they shouted: "You two are the ones. Tonight we're going to see you bleed, mourn you, futter you, use the stoppage of your young hearts to remember this night by."

Dex drew her along into the light-shade-light of their horded classmates, come down now, all of them, from the bleachers. They huddled close to the mike where Jiminy Jones had announced each number and where the principal stood, adjusting the mikestand upward.

Nurse Gaskin felt Bix Donner's needy eyes bore into the back of her head. It was hard, wanting to engage this absurd man's spouses in conversation, but knowing that any attempt she made would be interpreted by Bix as encouragement.

When Futzy approached her, Delia had squinted so as to pretend harsh lights were her reason for rotating the axis of their conversation. But in fact it had been to put Mister Pinhead Asshole out of eyeshot.

Now Futzy was knuckling the mike head.

The principal wore his humiliation with dignity. Futzy's lobes reminded her of those of his slain daughter Kitty, Delia's lost heartthrob two decades before.

"Is this on?" he said. "Can everyone hear me?"

The man had class. He didn't even look at them as he asked the question, striking a pose for the ages. They were pieces of shit—he knew it and so did she—and a deserved flush was about to take place. He would flush 'em *all*, as would she, if that were possible.

"It's a momentous night, isn't it, boys and girls?" he began. "In the petting-zoo portion of your time here, we pampered you. While you cut open frogs and pig embryos, we did the same to your brains. We felt along runnels of thought and redirected rivers. And now, poised to leave this slaughterhouse, you, or rather a token couple from those here gathered, shall be sacrificed."

Delia surveyed the faces, mapped memories of a broken arm, prankish debaggings, sneers, jeers, the flow of a dispensatory river of pills and liquids, the probings of countless needles beneath baby-smooth and zit-infested skin—all of it recalling to mind what this graduating class meant to her.

115

She had been their nurse, seen their health impaired, and healed them.

"You and you. And you." He pointed to three seniors close to Delia. "Distribute these riding crops. This is not a new tool, surely, to many of you. It symbolizes the pain I and my staff have taught you to inflict and endure. With care, these crops will last many years. You have found a first love at this school—or, in some cases, the school has had to find one for you, pairing you for an evening—"

An amused ripple moved through the seniors.

"—and soon, the two of you will engage in a search for a third.

"It is customary for your principal to extend his heartfelt wishes at this point, his hopes that you and your love find the threesome you deserve."

Clever man, Kitty's father was. Futzy's tone teetered between making and denying them the wish he had spoken of.

The man's hurt ran deep.

It touched a cold place in Delia.

"Take your time, rummage long and leisurely through the mate-heap roiling before you in the ensuing years. Choose wisely, both in what you do, and in whom you do it with. Most people settle, mindwise, for pretty meager fare. Don't you be one of them."

Yes, she thought, and some never get chosen.

Annoyance and botheration sounded in Delia's ear: "I love this moment."

"What?"

"This *moment*," Bix repeated as she turned. "The fear absolutely sizzles. And the longer their faces are now, the more gleeful they'll be the rest of the evening."

"Hold this for a second?" She handed him her drink, an expectation in her tone, but not in her intent, that she would be right back.

"Sure." He bobbled it but took it.

The fog had begun to thin. The dry ice was nearly evaporated.

"But enough advice from your shortly to be former principal," said Futzy as Delia sauntered coolly away. "Open your envelopes now. No need to use the eraser end of a number two pencil. A finger will do nicely. Go at once to where the pink sheet tells you to be—on pain of death if the detection scanners find you elsewhere—and do not stir from that spot until the ringing of the second bell."

The rapture on the faces of the Borgstroms, as Delia passed them, was an extraordinary sight to behold. Their jaw-notches positively glowed with anticipation.

Peach popped her gum. "Let's go," croaked Cobra, grabbing her wrist.

She jerked about into his tug, reluctant to leave the gym with its orange and blue and green lights, its glints of sequins and spangles. Even the buffed brown of the gym floor struck Peach as beautiful. But delay might mean death, and Cobra's word—*he* thought so, anyway—was law.

In the glow of night light, the hallway was dim and spooky. The click-click of heels and the rustle of pastel dresses beside tuxedo'd boys made everything feel somehow like a movie set, one last masquerade before real life began.

"Where we headed?" she asked.

"Shut it," Cobra snapped.

She did.

He hadn't even shown her the envelope, the one the shop teacher had given them.

Cobra's eyes were a flat gray. That, Peach was convinced, was how he saw the world—if his taste in clothes was any indication.

She had had sex with that weird old guy from Topeka just because she knew Cobra really wanted a coat he kept mentioning, and the fifty-dollar bills the guy peeled off into her hand would buy it.

But when Cobra came back from the store with the coat, it turned out to be the same old lousy leather as always, an uninspired black with three silver studs along the right sleeve. Hardly worth being flogged for. Hardly worth the taste of some grown-up's dick.

A bunch of kids—most of them dorks, though Babs Nealy and Kinny Conner waved at her—hustled up the stairs by the glass doors to the butchery wing.

Cobra hurried her past the stairs, shoving a scrawny hawk-nosed nebbish out of the way. "Move it!" said Cobra, both to the hawk-nosed guy and to her. Peach gave the kid an apologetic look before Cobra yanked her onward.

That was another thing about Cobra: The violence he visited

upon her always arose from smolders of hate. Rarely did he give her the kind of whap, poke, or pinch that signaled true love.

Cobra called that pop-song bullshit. She didn't think so.

Peach watched Tweed Megrim and Dexter Poindexter go into the chem lab. Neat kids. A little unformed for her tastes, but sometimes maybe bland was better.

Twin inverted J's of silver gleamed inside, tall thin spigots over sinks. Then Cobra strong-armed her past the labs.

"Did they stick us on the first floor?" she asked. She was afraid Cobra would try to bulldoze through the shoving mass of students on the stairs to their left.

Instead he dragged her, without reply, toward a darkened classroom set in the corner of the next turn. He yanked open the door and pushed her through.

Desks were shoved together in the center of the room in a logjam of fake-wood planes. Along the walls hung posterboard squares with a number scrawled in black felt-tip pen.

A couple of girls, Dixie Rathbone and Bliss somebody, slumped like stuffed scarecrows on the floor beneath the blackboard.

"Here," Cobra said.

Peach saw their number and beneath it a dark arrow directed downward. Pillows had been placed on the floor, thin as a threadbare blanket but gentler on the butt than hard tile.

She settled in. Cobra humphed down by her side. From where they sat, Peach could see Dixie and Bliss. She wondered if *they* were the ones, if they'd be slaughtered without warning, if she and Cobra and the others arrayed around the classroom would witness the sacrifice. She wiggled fingers at them, but they didn't move, almost as if they were dead already.

Commotion outside the door, raucous boy-talk. From the unclaimed numbers on the walls (she had overheard Bowser mention theirs), Peach guessed Bowser McPhee and his date Fido Jenner. A moment later, they walked in.

Peach had always thought Bowser was cute and little-boy brash and funny, a ferocious mismatch for Fido in her opinion. He had picked up a book she dropped once, then blushed and stammered like an idiot when she kissed his right lobe in thanks.

Now he and Fido started along the far wall, looking for their number.

"Over here," Peach yelled to them.

Cobra smacked her for speaking.

"Thanks," Bowser said. He and Fido collapsed ten feet to her left, beneath their sign.

"Hey weenie," Cobra said, "shut the fuck up."

"Come on, Cobra," Bowser replied, clapping a hand on Fido's knee. "Everybody's up against it tonight. Lighten up, okay? It's a free country."

Cobra tensed beside her.

"Listen, doggie boy. Your fuckin' free country's got two things in it: your face and my fist. You say another word, they're gonna fuckin' connect. It's gonna be one bloody mess of zits, skin, and flesh, you dig, scumwipe?"

She could see Bowser retreat inside his skin, though he glared iron pellets at Cobra. That took more guts than most kids had.

Too bad.

Peach knew, but never told anyone, that when it came right down to it, and without of his gang members around, Cobra would fold.

She had seen, alone late at night, the little boy in him. She knew Cobra was one scared coward hiding beneath layers of protective armor.

She also knew that she was just about ready to dump him.

The bell suddenly clanged. It sent a shock through her system.

Same damn bell signaled the end of one class and the beginning of the next. But in this context, it sounded three times as loud.

All talk ceased. A pall fell over the half dozen in-turned duos seated around the room.

Twenty minutes until the next bell, the one that meant find-the-dead-folks.

Those twenty minutes might be choke-thick with silence.

Or the shiv of a scream might slide into their heads from a nearby classroom, a scream both chilling and relieving.

Or the wall they leaned against might give way and a rough hand draw quick steel across their throats.

On the opposite wall, above two dorky girls in scared embrace, a large clock ticked.

Cobra's hand slipped into hers where no one could see and gave it a private squeeze.

His terror met hers.

10
Defying Gravity

Dark delight.

The school understood perfectly.

Through the glass doors that led into its butchery wing waltzed Flann Beckwith and Brandy Crowe, high-toned worshipers of style, the best slap'n'smack dancers Corundum High had ever seen. Flann and Brandy were odds-on favorites for prom king and queen, despite the run Rocky and Sandy had given them.

Whoever assigned stations—many doubted its much touted randomness—had surely wanted to bring Flann and Brandy down a few pegs.

They'd be pegged *down* all right.

All the way down.

Though the hallway grate below the peephole muffled sound, Flann's voice came through loud and clear. "Christ, what a stench! I thought for sure we'd smelled our last carcass at Monday's final."

Brandy flumphed, "Someone's got it in for us."

"It'll seep into your dress. And my tux."

"I hope they've given us blankets in there," Brandy said. "Even a minute'll get pretty cold."

The taps on Flann's spit-polished shoes came to an abrupt halt outside the refrigeration room. "Nothing we can do about it now. But before the night's over, I'm complaining to somebody. After you, hon."

Sickening.

Even here they moved with grace. Brandy twirled out of view, and Flann's taps followed.

In this part of the school, the backways were tight and ill-lit. They stank of old oak, wet and rotting.

Motor hum from the refrigeration room masked sound from back here. But it also turned the couple, the dapper Flann and his redheaded Brandy with the cinnamon heart, into soundless mouths.

Fortunately, the hanging racks of butchered flesh and the ice sculptures provided ample concealment. Moreover, the large panel farthest from the couple's designated spot had taken two drops of lubricant a half hour before.

Minimal slide, open, shut.

A chilled world stole away all warmth.

Man-sized Ice Ghouls waited here. Legions of them, opaque glassy shapes, sleek and muscled save for a fat howling ghoul who terrified by sheer bulk. Each one raised an icicle dagger, but the howling ghoul's was thickest and most menacing.

Out through their massed numbers, cautious in movement, an ice pick rode tight aslant the killer's torso.

Brandy sneezed.

These two had everything. Good looks. An unending stream of sycophants. A smoothness of manner and tone that erased all grief. Unlimited future prospects. Flann's voice rode upon their assured arrogance. "You okay?"

It would be a pleasure to finish them.

"It's nothing." A sniff, a soft blow, one nostril, then the other. "At least we're out of danger."

"Somebody," Flann insisted, "is gonna lose his job."

"It's okay. It's only ten more minutes. No one ever touches a finalist. That's the law."

"They can't *do* this to Flann Beckwith."

"We're fine," said Brandy. "We're all alone. Just us and nobody else. And you look real sexy. Sexy as money."

"Really? You think so?"

Racks of crayola'd pork flesh serried by as the killer threaded through them.

Sides of meat hung near the doomed pair, a protective veil of butchered beef providing one last barrier if only they'd keep jabbering.

"I'll tell you what I think." Her prom dress rustled. The sounds of thick smooching and shared *mmmm*'s betrayed what they were up to. Then they abruptly stopped. "Did you hear something?" asked Brandy.

Caught breath, three haunches away.

"Hey, relax," said Flann. "All I hear is my heart. And yours."

"Mmmm, you're warm."

"You too." There was a slight rustle, as of tinsel brushing against a glass ornament.

"Do you think we should?" Yield filled her voice.

"Who's to know?" More rustling and Brandy's vulnerable moan. "I'm going to suck my sweetie's lovelobe."

The killer stepped free of concealment.

Flann was stylishly hunched over, almost a choreographed flamenco pose. Brandy's eyelids were closed, her chin nestled upon his left shoulder as he mouthed her lovelobe. From his right hand hung her silken lobebag, limp as a finger puppet.

A gleam of debutante eyes opening. Flann's embroidered suit-back, a stretched target. The brutal drive of cloaked resentment.

Then came a pin-cushion *zit* of pierced felt, the ice pick's keen tip driving through expensive cloth.

The body accepted puncture and impalement as though they were crude afterthoughts, the sudden flair of the ice pick handle stopping its forward hurtle in a pit of depressed serge.

Flann's head pitched forward as three bodies sandwiched unbalanced against the wall. A shove at his suit helped unflesh the weapon.

Brandy's eyes widened. Her mouth readied a scream.

Her boyfriend flailed about, arms whipping wide and ineffectual. The lovelobe his teeth had abruptly severed hung like a blood-engorged tick from his lips. Staggering like a drunk upended in a slippery room, he fell away, his skull making a loud smack against the white wall.

Screams now, muffled in the insulated room.

Screams wrapped in puffs of breath.

Brandy's left hand rose to her maimed ear, blood gush vining down her frail wrist.

The ice pick lifted once. It pinned the girl's right hand rising to resist, pinned it like a stuck butterfly against her left breast, and filled her heart with steel.

122

Her eyes held, even as they clouded with death. Healing lay in Brandy's empty gaze. And in Flann's. Those eyes begged to be icicled, as had Sheriff Blackburn's.

Behind them through racks of meat waited the fat ghoul, an icicle dagger upraised at the end of his massive arm.

That would do fine.

But time pressed.

Do Queen Brandy first. Then her lover. Come out of the cold, regain warm passageways, again dare the fear of heights.

The next bit of payback would be a challenge and a thrill, courage and sheer strength tested to the limit. But close by awaited love and healing and an end to years of torment.

Through the motor hum and the meat racks, the leaden-footed dancers' shoetops scuffed across the floor.

Gerber Waddell sat in his supply closet, the door closed, a dim lightbulb over his head.

Like a great ape after eating, Gerber settled cross-legged on the floor, scratching his belly through janitorial denim.

Thoughts struggled to pierce his rage.

Something not right was seeping through the school tonight. This weren't your ordinary prom, no way, no how.

He was used to grisly thoughts on prom night.

Young bad flesh in rich clothing.

The anticipated *smack*.

That's how Gerber always heard it in his head when they brought the victims in. *Smack!* An echo from the slash that few if any saw, 'cept for its aftermath, which he had to clean up lest it settle into the walls.

Couldn't have it settling into the walls.

Had to make them pristine again.

Well tonight, he was hearing lots more *smack* in his head, some *shuk* and *oof* too, feeling bad things transpire, almost as if he were right there and they were happening in front of him.

He had a feeling there'd be lots more cleanup than usual. Lots more walls to make pristine.

They didn't pay him overtime neither.

He remembered the hospital geeks.

In particular he remembered good ol' Gary the nose-picking nurse, who must've thought Gerber was some piece of meat that cared not a whit about the niceties of living. Nope, good ol' Gary could just, privileged as you please, snuk a finger up into his nostril right in front of the sliced-up brain guy lying on the bed.

Gerber's head had hurt after the operation. But otherwise, he hadn't felt any different. He wanted to shove an ice pick up Gary's nose, get a bloody booger on its tip, maybe take some of *his* brain out along with it.

His hand went to the utility belt: Axe head. Plastic pouch o' screwdrivers. Empty place.

Gerber looked down.

No ice pick.

He sighed.

Always losing stuff. The Bleaks was always getting on him about that, about stuff being lost around the house.

Missus Bleak always pig-yammered at him out of her lipsticked oinker of a yap, till he'd had enough and cried in front of her like a big baby. But in his head she was taken apart, all that flab torn open so the blubber came spilling out on the rug and he weren't about to clean *that* up. But he might, just *might* mind you, dance on it. Nor would he care a tinker's damn about his boots, nope, he'd just make sure he didn't slip on the grease and bang the back of his head where the surgeons had left the deep dimple.

Did they need him at the prom?

Probably so, but goddamn if he would go where they wanted him to go. Not with all the early unscheduled *shuk* and *oof* in his head, not with all the unruly visions of struggle warring up there.

He didn't want to see nobody.

I better get up, he thought. Head off to the next place. Where was that? His feet would know, as they always sooner or later did.

It was quiet in the supply closet. Quiet and close and difficult to breathe. They oughta make these denim suits with air holes, not make a head janitor sweat.

Maybe they wrung 'em out, he thought. Maybe they grabbed 'em out of Missus Bleak's bathroom clothes hamper. Maybe they fueled Corundum High with his sweat.

Gerber smiled.

Them teachers ain't got *nothin'* on me, he thought. Them shitty

124

students, they pass through this place like a digested meal. Gerber, he repairs the walls and linings, frees up blockages, keeps the little shits moving through until they blat out the low-slung buttock end o' things.

But there be rumblings in these walls more than usual. They angered him, and frightened him.

Never you mind that.

Nope, I won't.

He got up, swirling with his palms on the concrete floor and shoving off, then letting his feet figure out where to take him next.

Kyla Gorg looked askance at her lover. "Hey come on, Patrice. The drawing's *random*. Even if it wasn't, and really some muckety-muck picks who's to be killed and where, they wouldn't be stupid enough to use the same location two years running."

"Yeah maybe," said Patrice, worrying a thin layer of chiffon between her pudgy fingers. "But there's always a first time."

"We're safe as a snug bug in a rug here. So chill out, okay?" Kyla thought her date was such a chickenshit.

Generations had survived prom night.

They could too.

"It's so *creepy*." Patrice was scandalized. "I can't believe they'd seat us here. Ugh, you can almost smell the blood."

"Oh, stop it!"

Kyla surveyed the dim cold kitchen, a rare look at a place ordinarily out of bounds.

Two other couples were tucked like ungainly dolls amidst sink units and stoves and preparation tables, murmuring in a darkness lit only by one feeble fixture above the cash register.

The white sign that bore their number had seemed to float on the wall when she and Patrice came to it. In this precise spot, the year before, Melody Jinx and her date had waited and bled and died.

Surely the area had been scrubbed down. But the wall paint was ugly green anyway and what Kyla had touched felt, well, greasy.

Tell herself a million times it was only her imagination, she could still see blotches of gore all around them. Melody's ghost, seeping through the walls and floor where Melody had eaten a cleaver, seemed to wrap them in cold mist.

Again Patrice's worry-wart voice: "I wonder where he is."

"Fido?"

"Of course Fido. Who else?"

"Fido's never going to be ours," Kyla said, with what seemed to her like grown-up resignation. "We have to face it, now that we're graduating."

"Don't *say* that!"

"Come on, Patrice. Folks expect us to triple up with an overweight man, just like on *Fat and Fed Up.*"

"Ugh, I hate that show. And I hate overweight men."

"You like *me*, don't you?" Kyla asked.

"Sure I do." A ghostly jellyfished hand came down on Kyla's knee and orange-juiced there its assurance. "But thin old, wiry old Fido is who I want. He's nice and cuddlable and cute and sweet and kind and scrumptious."

"And out of reach."

"We don't know that. Not for sure. And the night is far from over."

Kyla said nothing.

What was the use?

Give Patrice a last try at her dream, the one she'd first dared to voice in tenth grade.

It had been fun to moon over Fido in private, a secret passion they used to fuel their lovemaking. Kyla had often pictured him with them as her lover's whip cut across his quivering flesh. Once—amazing experience—they had closed their eyes, stroking and sucking at one another, imagining it was him: Fido Jenner, split, blimped, making it with himself.

"I'll bet Ms. Foddereau's the slasher," said Patrice.

Kyla pictured the teacher's flat seamless face. Echoes of her dry humor. The old crone stood before a butcher block, working her bloody hands into an open pork belly.

"I'll bet it *is*," said Kyla.

That sly smile, that seemingly offhand remark about fat, the ripple of a chuckle it had set off in class the year before.

Kyla warmed to the idea. "Boy, if it is, I'd love to see her try to surprise us. I'd love to overpower the superior little bitch and wrench her chin up while you sever her trachea, slicing deep to the spine with that bone saw up there." Among knives on the opposite wall, the bone saw gleamed.

"Yeah, bring her on!"

"We'll filet the smile right off her friggin' face," Kyla said.

"Butcher, cleave thyself."

The grimness silenced her, cutting short her glee. A teacher, probably right this moment, was ending two of her classmates' lives.

Not many friends amongst them, but they were okay kids. The prospect of beholding a slain couple sobered Kyla, even as it touched some atavistic nub of delight inside her.

"Patrice?"

"Yeah?"

"It's freezing in here. Hold my hand?"

"It feels real weird, mister, escaping this way. Almost like you're betraying your friends or something."

Zinc, the smallish second trumpeter, spoke to Bray in the dim obscurity of the girls' gym, half-hearted hallspill providing the only light.

Winnie stood far off, waving her hands and flapping her lips to convince a cluster of young girls about God-knows-what.

"It's nothing you could have prevented," said Bray in an attempt to comfort the kid.

Zinc shook his head, eighteen looking fifteen, his height a paltry five feet. "Doesn't matter. That Russian guy, the scientist with the bushy eyebrows, you know who I mean . . . he says people can control their fate, that there's a psychic link between your deepest desires and what actually happens to you."

"I don't believe that for a second."

"That's what *he* says."

"People say all sorts of wrongheaded things."

The other trumpeter, the defiant-looking one, was resting his elbows on the trampoline pads in the center of the gym. His knuckles thudded an off-rhythm against the thick springs.

He had been clipped and curt when, on their way here, Winnie had offered a compliment on his playing. Now his restless drumming stopped and he strode over to them.

"Hey, Zinc," he said, "let's try it out."

"You don't mean jumping on the tramp?" The kid was incredulous.

Sarcastic: "No, I mean lobesucking. Come on, it'll be a blast." The taller boy, a lick of hair sickled over his forehead, pointedly ignored Bray. *Grown-up, over-the-hill has-been*, Bray could almost hear him thinking.

"Don't, Butch. You'll break your neck."

"Well, jeez, at least spot me. Come on, man. Sailing on up into the darkness? It'll get your juices flowing."

Balancing on one foot, he wrenched a shoe off and tossed it down *thock fwap-fwap-fwap*.

Its mate quickly followed.

"Is he always like this?" asked Bray.

"Only when something's eating him. The prom, you know. Going away to school next year."

The charcoal blur hoisted himself up onto the edge of the trampoline, then hop-rolled onto its yield of canvas.

"Let's spot him."

They skated across the smooth gym floor, a sensation like a layer of ice beneath the soles of their shoes. Other kids were coming in from all directions, and Winnie, turning her head, joined him.

"Couple o' converts?" Bray asked about the girls she had been talking to.

"Discontent is everywhere," said Winnie, "a micron or two beneath the skin. What's with your musician friend?"

The trumpeter had found the discolored center of the canvas. He staggered at first, then eased into a gentle bounce.

"Who knows? Maybe he wants to die."

"Hey, you guys," Butch shouted on the uplift. "It's all a crock. (*Sproing!*) This prom crap. (*Sproing!*) You and me, we can (*Sproing!*) stop it, and we ought to."

Worked up already to nearly ten-fifteen feet, change falling out of his pockets and spinning on the canvas below, Butch stiffed up suddenly, knees bearing the brunt, arms shot out to the sides for balance. He bent and swept the coins off, metal clatters as they waterfalled through the springs, pinging and rolling across the floor.

"Zinc, come on, man," he said.

Then Zinc monkeyed up.

Bray steadied Zinc on the pads, and Butch helped him over the crisscross of springs. His shoes whip-rolled toward Bray, then fell floorward in twin thuds. "I can't believe I'm doing this." Standing, he linked hands with his lover and began a slow seesaw. "Woe, woe, woe!" he said, one at each bounce.

Bray glanced at Winnie. She looked sharp-eyed and stunning, a heartmelt.

"Kids," she commented in awe and disgust.

The seesaw diminished to nothing. The boys bounced now in synch and rising, white cuffs and clasped hands, their moonish faces alight with thrill, their arms angling out on the downfall, then snapping down flat like collapsed umbrella struts as they shot skyward once more.

A drifting horde of seniors, some of them tender, others not, rectangled all about, shouting encouragement and holding their hands up to offer instant rebuff against a bad fall.

Butch and Zinc were ill-lit as they pizza-doughed the canvas and it rebounded them upward. But on the rise, they slipped into even greater obscurity, a sleeve of blackness enveloping them, then releasing them on the downfall.

There was no ceiling visible. Just the one Bray sensed up there, climbing ropes strung up way high like dreams of vines, no limits to how daring the trumpeters might get.

Vanish.

Re-emerge swiftly downward, a plunge through squid ink into the dim ocean below.

Then arrow upward again, squeals of delight rocketing from their mouths.

Bray fancied he heard a noise up above, a metal strut adjusting to chill or weight.

Down again they shot, but Bray kept his eyes above, a dark shift in blackness he assumed he had to be imagining.

Up they rose.

But suddenly there oofed, above, an expulsion of breath, a blow to the belly, and one boy came down empty-handed, a look of terror smeared across his face.

It was the monkey-looking kid, too distraught to keep himself from an upward bounce as lofty as the previous one. Then he too, with a high choking sound, stuck up there.

Swift whickers of pain fell from above. More mechanical

sounds, black on black, loud creaks, a spider dandling its web about trapped flies.

Someone asked stupidly, "Where are they?"

"Get the lights," Winnie called weakly, and it seemed to Bray that she thought she had shouted it.

Yes, I'll do that, he thought. I'll get the lights.

But all Bray could do was stare up into the blackness and listen to the bold shifting sounds, the creaking obscenity of movement and stretched rope, the shifts of some murderous shape about its work.

"They can't *do* that," a girl said. "He's a *tender*."

Others took up her word, the unfairness of it all and the shock in their voices.

In front of him, the trampoline canvas popped like a bedsheet snapped in a breeze.

Then again.

A wash of pops rained down, a sudden shower, foul-smelling.

Bray caught on his chest a slap of liquid, a spray against his face. And a second inundation fell from above as kids backed away.

Bray felt Winnie melt against him. "Jesus, Bray," an echo of her lost strength, "what's our guy doing?"

Above, there sounded a clattering as though a handful of drumsticks were being badly negotiated.

Then something fell, shattering: an icicle, its fragments skating across the darkened canvas, smashing hard, and skidding across the floor.

11

A Ritual Taken to Excess

Sandy leaned against Rocky's back where he fidgeted on a long bench in the boys' locker room, massaging his neck and shoulders. She tried not to breathe smelly gymsuit odor but it couldn't be avoided.

"Is it time yet?" asked Rocky.

"No again, handsome."

Her man sat hunched over, hands clasped, as though he'd been benched for a foul.

He glanced at her and smiled. "We got those two dancers over a barrel, I can feel it."

"No contest, hon. Flann and Brandy, they're a couple of clothesracks. You and me, though, we *do* stuff. Kids cheer your tackles and your field goals. I give them a rise with my pompons and the occasional flash of my butt."

Rocky had worn a clean white jockstrap to bed once. Now she pictured him, his killer teammates too, arrayed down the dim empty bench, big swells of dick held in before them like whips of spackle, their buttock muscles tight, the playful *thwap* of towels against bare bottoms.

"We'll do that throne shit, huh?"

"That's right," she said. "They'll spotlight us. They'll give us a big brassy fanfare, robes, crowns, the whole shootin' match."

"And then the newspaper!"

"Uh huh." She nodded vigorously, relieved that the lesson had finally begun to sink into Rocky's thick skull. "Tonight, big grins to the peons, flashbulb pops, royal waves and armloads of roses. Monday morning, our picture will grace the front page of the *Gazette*—"

"Dead corporate grunts'll've stepped aside at their Sunday afternoon picnics."

"—yes, and there you'll be, ready to take your pick of the jobs opened up by their deaths."

Rocky chuckled.

He rubbed his palms together, like she did when she smoothed hand cream on, but more briskly. "And then," he said, "we'll find a third to round us out."

"Yes. A nice man. Maybe some old guy with a good job and yummy lobes."

Sandy would stay home with the pup. *Which* pup she wasn't sure. But it had frizzy caramel-and-cream fur and a cute wet black nose. She could see the little yapper now. She would hire a landscaper to put in a perfect flower garden, then sit back and spend the money her husbands brought in.

"Nobody from school though," said Rocky, parroting her.

"No one."

Her sights had been raised considerably since their nomination as prom royalty. It had put them safely beyond slaughter. That release from terror had given Sandy a far wider vision of the future, up from the confined sandbox of high school to the unending stretch of beach frontage that lay before them.

"They're all such children here," she said.

"They sure are."

Bending to him, Sandy pressed her breasts against his back and kissed his thick coconut-aroma'd hair.

Gaunt gray lockers aisled off parallel into the gloom, ending at yet another wall of them. Murmurs of other couples arrayed elsewhere back near the showers floated in dim stifles of air. Ghost-voices. Soon to be memories only.

"Is it time yet?"

"Not yet. Soon."

"I swear, I'm gonna cut you a big bleeding hunk of corpse."

"I'd like that, Rocky."

Bobbing knee. "You sure it's not time yet?"

The shrill bell had startled Pill. Gigi, her stuffed goat, huddled close then.

The bell was much louder than when she walked down the halls in the daytime to visit her biology teacher mommy, holding Daddy's hand.

Outside in the hallway, Pill heard heels and giggles. She had just enough time to rush into the coat closet, a nice non-squeaky door that let her leave half an inch and didn't swing open when she took her hand away. It smelled woody, but it was warm enough that cool air blew on her from the thin bright crack.

Two girls came in, noisy and excited. They were very happy to be here.

Pesky, the high-pitched chatterbox of the pair, kept squealing and jumping up and down, to judge from her leathery taps on the tile floor.

And Pill heard laughter in the calmer, lower voice of Flense. It sounded like her daddy when he was agreeing to something Mommy had said but was really patting himself on the back about how much brighter than her he was.

The squealer, the one named Pesky, skipped and danced around the room, hand-kissing stuff on the long counter and peeking into the mini-fridge. Pill caught glimpses of her: a shiny pink ribbon in shiny black hair, her creamy neck and lobe-flesh going by, the gleam of a pleased eye.

Pill was afraid one of them would fling open her closet door and she would get yelled at.

Flense called Pesky a teacher's pet. "*I'm* just along for the ride. Pesky's date," she said. "But they stuck *you* here cuz you kiss their big fat behinds all the time."

"Yep. No blood's gonna be spilled here. What the hey, they're not gonna you-know-what where they eat," said the other girl. "Well I guess, for form's sake and so they don't kill us 'n' shit for disobeying the rules, we ought to sit on the couch, under our number."

They quieted down and hugged a bunch. Among the rustle of dresses and the slaps and slurps and moans they gave out with, the deep-voiced one sometimes shushed the other and asked if she heard any screaming yet.

Pill hugged Gigi and pretend-whispered that these two were silly and a bother, and she hoped they would go back to the dance soon so she could curl up again in the stuffed chair and count the dots in the ceiling tiles.

Then a loud crack startled her. It sounded like a huge toaster popping bread.

The high-pitched one said, though not in reply to anything, "'Mjust askin'!" followed by "But you can't—!" which was cut off by a thud.

Pill hunched up tight and held her breath.

A weak no from Flense gave way to sounds of running and the rattle of a locked door. Then a louder series of no's pierced the air as she was struggled back across the room.

The hunching made Pill's shoulders hurt. She felt light and funny in her head.

She had to keep breathing. Had to trap her whimpers inside.

Through the thrashing, Pill moved her right hand to the closet knob, grasped it, afraid it would creak. Then she froze her arm there. She had been ready to shut the door. But the noise gurgled away, and Gigi warned her not to.

Putting an eye to the crack, Pill saw a glove gripping a tiny pellet. The pellet was all swirly with mist. The gloved hand thrust it between the Flense girl's lips, fingers jammed in, abruptly, in an ungentle way like her old daddy shoving a pill into their cat Puff's pried-open jaws and forcing him to swallow.

Then the glove smacked Flense's face and was gone, and Flense fell out of sight, oddly quiet as the struggle stopped. "Wait!" she said. "What did you—? Leave Pesky alone! Oh jeez, oh shit. Make it stop. Please make it stop." She sounded like she had bad tummy-ache pain, like she wanted to throw up but couldn't.

Someone fell like a sack of potatoes.

Dragging sounds outside.

Grunts of effort.

Pill was suddenly sure that the knocked-out Pesky was going to be shoved into the closet, and that the hurty man with the dark blue arms and the bloody workgloves was going to see her then and do really bad things to her.

Should she scream?

Could she get away if she darted out right now, clonked him with a chair or something, and broke down the door?

Then the shuffling sounds stopped.

The girl who'd been forced to swallow the misty pellet cried and moaned like wind in a lonely cave.

Pill could see the other one through the crack. Her skull knocked hard on the counter top. Then a *shoof* sounded, like some weird heavy car door closing in the distance, and the girl's face bunched up and opened wide into a scream like Pill had never heard before.

Pill started to shiver. She no longer trusted her hand on the knob, but she didn't dare move it.

"My fingers!" came the high scream.

Pill remembered her mother working at that same counter, squaring paper on a green grid and clumphing a curved blade sharply down.

Pesky's face smeared out of the crack as she tried to tear away, but again she was grabbed, to judge from the violent waver in her voice, and the noise grew really loud and close. Pill's fingers flared with pain as the crack shut and the closet door slammed and darkness struck her like a heavy fist.

Pill heard whimpering. When she realized it was her own, she made it go away. Outside, dulled to cotton by the closed door, the fierce fighting went on.

She backed up against warm wood, touching it with one hand and hugging Gigi to her chest with the other.

An angled corner, pillows, her little nest. She inched downward, the walls sliding up around her, soft comfort beneath her as beyond the black muffle the killing continued.

Go away, she prayed.

Go away, go away.

At the Shite House, one side of the split-screen showed the scrubbed teens sitting beneath the number 57, the other the Home Ec teacher poised to spring open the metal panel above them.

She's closing in for the kill," murmured the announcer.

Secretary Wanker suppressed a laugh.

Prom night always fired up the President and his cabinet. The slaughter of the young fueled a year of decisions and proved far more effective a teambuilding effort than any touchy-feely retreat with teams of fake-empathetic facilitators.

To be sure, the cabinet secretaries' juices flowed free, and the naughtiness of their exposed lobes gave everyone that extra jolt.

But the real thrill lay in eavesdropping on two frightened kids thinking someone else had been chosen. And on a teacher who, for one evening of planned mayhem, dropped all pretense of caring for her snot-nosed charges.

It revived memories of their *own* proms even as it firmed up governmental resolve.

But tonight, thought Wanker, something new would be added to the mix.

As if that thought were a signal, the trap was sprung onscreen.

"There she goes!" screamed the announcer.

The blade flashed.

Out popped the Home Ec teacher. The wide-eyed boy sustained a lethal slash to the throat. His date, offering a feeble whine and a feint at struggle, joined him in death.

The beautiful brutality of it brought most of the cabinet over the top, though they were careful that their moans did not top in intensity those of President Windfucker.

Holding back his own release, Willy Wanker spoke softly into his lapel mike: "Now."

The doors burst open.

Everybody turned in mid-spurt at the heavy tromping of boots, taking in a sudden rush of soldiers in camouflage, men and women not much more than high school age themselves, brandishing knives and grimacing with resolve.

The stern-faced suits who tried to protect the President lost fingers to the downslash and were shoved out of the way by the sheer force of numbers.

Cholly Bork took a stab to the neck. The crossbarred airplane control that animated Gilly Windfucker flew out of his hands, and the puppet leader collapsed. Beneath the pummeling, Bork went down, his arms flopping ineffectually this way as he tried to ward off the attack.

A crack crew lofted the inert president into the air. Snips at his strings. Snips where his limbs articulated. His arms and legs were passed on to two solders assigned to snap them over their knees. Others stomped on his head and torso, then tossed the bashed and

12

Zippered Lips and the True Meaning of Fear

Condor had been flying on whatever beautiful shit he had swallowed in the car.

He'd been letting the dance music unfold new eternities inside him. Earing the fear, eying the terror that flaked skin from familiar faces, as old mush-jowled Futzy dispersed 'em all, skelter and yon.

He felt heaven come stairstepping closer as they *shuk-shuk-shuk*ed upward and the handrail, with its hacked worn inked germ-infested splendor, gave them guidance toward a way-the-fuck-up-there staggeringly simplistically functional classroom where once, two years before, Mr. Fink had tossed chalk bits like an outfielder zinging third base to get some kid's attention.

Blayne, darkly brooding all night, had grown darker still, muttering bunches of creepy shit as they sat there alone under the chalkboard behind Mr. Fink's desk.

They had named each possible teacher, looking for a slasher. Their yammering faces oozed out of floor tiles or from the shadows beneath the desk, or they fell from the chalk tray overhead.

Zane Fronemeyer, conjured by an unrelievedly morbid commentary from Blayne, had misted up from a fallen eraser, an oblong devilcake dusted with snow, to menace them with a paintbox of horrors.

Condor had convinced him.

It was Fronemeyer.

Their wacko art teacher!

Then the bell clamored like a floodlight all ablaze. No light shone, yet *all* was light.

Brilliantly limned with light ineffable was this place of salvation. An industrial strength vacuum cleaner of light. A beam of elation. A cockjacking, lobesucking epiphany of hot white jangling lumens.

"We made it!" exclaimed Condor, the drugs surging high in him.

"Yep and it was tough to make," said Blayne. Beneath his continuing brood, an imp peered out from those wide amazing eyes.

"We're *continually* making it, aren't we?"

"The windows, the wastebasket. It's a dull make." Blayne's face turned nasty and smug. "But there's a more interesting make waiting for us out there."

The girls.

"Yeah!" said Condor.

Blayne had lipped Altoona.

Or so he had said in the car.

All night, Condor's radiant head had waggled between death-dread and the black-laced duo they had avoided talking to, relying instead on odd across-gym anticipatory stares and bizarre but weirdly neat circlings, so close they could touch but pretending to ignore one another instead—all of it a buildup to survival and the costume shop.

"I am one primed monkey!" said Condor.

"One prime *mate*!" Blayne corrected.

"Ugh. Squirrelly, real squirrelly." Balls of ticked fur opened up and skittered across the room.

"Squarely so."

"Double ugh, " said Condor. "Let's go get 'em."

He got to his feet and gave one last look at the last place of instruction he'd ever have to be in. The classroom was a fist relaxed into an open palm, reluctant to release him but not all that unfriendly, despite the years of mind-wounds it had inflicted.

In the corridor, puffs and creases of student body flurried by, relieved, hunting, hunting.

Fuck the hunt. *They* were off to snag some *live* game.

A flutter of wings brushed against his face, as two chiffoned quail went birding by: Contusa and Calibrianna, caught up in an unending web of in-turned chatterboxing.

Down the stairs, down the stairs, down the stairs.

A mewling slight spewed like a spitwad from Capper McGee's twist of a mouth as he bounded past them up the stairs. They gave one another fuck-the-silly-bastard looks and wiped McGee's hurl off like so much fartwind.

Condor loved the building's dark dead funk at this time of night.

The place was dying. It was yielding them up. And in the bowels of this bowel of a fuckin' school, behind the scenes, some blood-splashed teacher was right now crimsoning a sink.

As they hit the first floor and headed left toward the auditorium, Condor stopped.

"Hey, watch it!" Blayne bumped him. "What? A glass wall? What?"

"I just had a terrible thought." Condor saw the girls splayed wide, huge fingers punched deep into their bodies, prying then open like so many crabshells. "What if he got *them*?"

"Leapin' Christ, Condor," said Blayne. "Then they'd be dead, we'd be ess-oh-ell, and I'd be so pissed, I'd toilet-paper the turdsucking slasher's front yard for a whole freaking year. Now keep moving, will ya? They're waiting for us."

Condor moved.

Humiliation clamped about his head.

Damn it, Blayne was deep, Blayne was smart.

Whereas *he* was dumb and pokey. He'd never amount to much. Even Pim and Altoona—a couple o' trash-talkin' gals doomed to lives of dirt, snot-nosed brats, squinty-eyed crooked-lipped drags on ciggies that wrinkled their faces toward cronedom years before their time, and endless ineptly-done housework, as far as he could see—would probably reject him, make him watch, get it on in front of him with his best bud, steal him away, and leave poor Condor forever bereft.

"Oh shit, come on." Blayne hugged him as they moved, a cheer-up look on his flushed crazed swirly face. "Look, I'm zipping up my slagging mouth." He did so with a yank, then unyanked the zipper and brushed a finger along the crenelated niobium lining his lover's lower lip.

"I'm sorry," Condor said, feeling better.

"Pas de pro-blay-mo." Blayne tugged open the door to the backstage area and they went in.

Condor heard yells from the auditorium off right. No bodies found yet, though it sounded as if all the seats were being rocked furiously down-up-down-up in the futile search.

They passed a door marked PROPS on the left. Then BOYS' DRESSING ROOM, GIRLS' DRESSING ROOM, and finally, partly ajar, COSTUME SHOP. Blayne, hand to handle, zagged in, Condor behind.

The ceilings were high, but the place felt cramped and confined for all the crap jammed into it. Box after box serried and rose to their right and left. Scrawled labels vied with brittle typed ones for the truth about the boxes' contents.

Shoes lay heaped like war dead below. But before Condor could spook himself too much with the ghostly limbs akimbo'd bodiless out of them, they turned the corner into another larger room, where rack upon rack of fluff and color greeted them, a crazy salad of cloth, sequins, and odd-buttoned garments.

Blayne picked his way through, a jungle hacker amid old-outfit smells. "Yo!" he said. "Anybody home?"

"This way," trilled an amused voice.

Then Condor followed his date around one last switchback of gray-wheeled racks and faded finery gimcracked together.

There the girls waited.

Altoona and Pimlico, two incredible blips of life grinning and shifting and sexing over by the sewing machines, their legs crossed at the ankles, leaning back everywhere.

Futzy's mind churned like a washing machine agitator. Pumps and clunky polished boy-shoes in vast mooing herds of babble were moving along the hallway outside the gym. As the scum scurried by, Futzy nodded at them.

It had been all he could do, speaking over their heads from the band risers, to control his anguish at the papier-mache creature before him and to keep from blasting the little shits with both barrels of his anger.

Now a few of their number were dead, waiting to be discovered and brought to the gym.

Futzy had thought that once this part of the evening arrived, once the Poindexter kid and his date had been dispatched, he'd be in for smooth sailing.

But his bloodlust was nowhere near sated, and he guessed he had known that all along.

"Hello, Mr. Buttweiler." High fluted voice, Charmina Fuchs bubbling by alone. She would make a couple of young studs an obliging breeder some day.

"Charmina," he muttered, stripping her with his eyes, imagining an impossibly long whiplash sweeping swifter than jag-lightning down the young girl's cream-curved torso, her skin blushing beneath the whip sting's fury.

Adora Phipps, wearing her granny clothes and antiquated lobebag, had been strangely attentive tonight. Weird duck, her hair up and wrapped in a tight bun, one strand astray. After the speech, over chaperone refreshments, she'd made feints toward kindness.

Futzy had kept his replies superficial and moved on.

As he watched flocks of boybuddies quickwalk off toward the labs, swivelbutted and gawk-armed, he wondered what the strange lady English teacher, this Adora, would think of his homelife, his cold wives, the spattered blood on his bedroom walls.

Would it shock her?

Would it turn her off?

Or on?

Kitty, holding back her hair with one hand, bent to a drinking fountain.

A rush to Futzy's brain.

Not his daughter of course, but maddening-without-meaning-to-be Wyn Wynans. She stood up, oblivious to him, licking her lips, and went into the gym with her unworthy date.

A sob escaped Futzy's lips. Luckily no one was by to hear. They had to pay—they'd pay in *spades*—for the Ice Ghoul's return.

He would see to it.

By God, he swore he would.

First, Tweed tried the phone bank near the science rooms by the north exit.

"The phones are hosed," said Tad Verle, headed back to the gym in a pink bowtie that accentuated his outstuck ears.

She tried both phones. Tad was right. No dial tone. Dead air.

"That's weird," she said.

"Your dad'll be okay," replied Dex. "Come on."

"He'll be worried." She could feel fret marks on her brow and a tightening in her belly over delaying Dex's stupid hunt for the slain. "Let's try the ones by the front door."

Dex, saying nothing, trailed after her.

Tweed wished he would grow up.

Principal Buttweiler, pacing the hall like a circus bear restive and unbicycled, looked stunned to see them.

He broke eye contact and edged away.

Tweed chalked it up to his unhinged state of mind—the Ice Ghoul, his rumored sado-mates, all of that.

Four phones were located near the entrance, silver corded and stained. Wood partitions scored with graffiti provided token separation between them.

A gaggle of girls were crowded about the left phone. "Shit on a stick," said a knobby-elbowed girl named Relda Weep, whom Tweed had known since first grade and not spoken to once in all that time.

The girls moved off and Tweed found the same damned dead lines here too.

"This is spooky," she said.

"Wonder what the deal is."

"Dad'll be worried, Dex. He'll climb the walls."

Dex looked concerned. "You're really torqued, aren't you?"

She nodded and bit her lip.

Dex hugged her.

Her fears conjured her father at home, his voice shifting into a soft dithering dirge as he eyed the phone and bullets beaded his brow.

"I'm sorry," said Dex. "I wish I could do something. Hey. What if we found Mr. Waddell?"

"The janitor?"

"Sure. *He* could fix it."

Dex was right. Soft doughy congenial Gerber Waddell, head janitor of the quiet ways and kind smile, would rummage around in his hollowed-out skull and come up with the fix, a found treasure glittering in his brain. She hadn't seen much of him since he had switched on the colored lights. "Where do you think he might—?"

A cheer went up beyond the table where Mr. Dunsmore and Daub Murch had sat, signing seniors in. A back-walking, front-walking band of kids appeared, surrounding and egging on a pair of football jocks who were carrying the corpses of two girls.

Oh lovely, came Tweed's first thought. Female dates, just like twenty years before. Wouldn't *that* non-linearize poor old Mr. Buttweiler!

Then she fixed on the victims, their heads rollicking jerkily in the crooks of elbows.

The one with the O'd mouth and not a drop of blood anywhere was Flense, a math whiz and a quick wit. It chilled Tweed to see the wan, slack-jawed face of a long-time friend approach so.

And lumbering by beside her in a crewcutted jock's arms, her fingers missing from the hand in front and a bib of blood splashed like a riotous poinsettia where her belly should have been, was Pescadera Carbone. Pesky. Flighty, funny, and now lifeless.

"Oh, God," said Dex. "It's so . . . ."

"Yeah, no kidding."

Tweed stared at them.

The slow parade rhythmed by, some of the students sobbing, strange grins lighting other faces, all of them awkwardly taking up the pace no one in particular had established.

Dex and Tweed, latching onto the tail, made their way toward the gym. A great pain lanced through Tweed's gut, a pain inscribed with two names: Pesky and Flense.

But also there, and all about, were bright pings of joy, bubble bursts, sniffs of champagne, and each one said, *Not Lon. Not Jerzy. Not Camilla.* Not this friend or that.

The ping which burst most often, again and again, proclaimed, with sweet relief, *Not Dex!*

"Let's go inside," he said softly.

Tweed hugged him, long and teary, and they did.

"Hi, Blayne," Altoona said. Friendly sarcasm and at-lastness colored her words. "See anything you'd like to try on?"

"Yep," he said. "Two things."

147

Condor stood next to him, a hair taller and hyped, his lip-zipper aglisten with fresh licked spittle.

Altoona's left hand lightly gripped the rounded edge of a sewing table. Pim's laced fingers stroked her date's knuckles in high elation.

"Hi, Blayne," Pim said. "Hi, Condor."

"Hello," Condor tried. Something in his tone provoked a round of giggling.

The windowless costume shop had its lights up full. Though the place went on for miles, the myriad racks, choked with costumes and huddled about them, made it feel somehow cozy.

Altoona became aware of her heartbeat, a delicious anticipatory lub-dub, lub-dub.

"You guys sure look sharp," her lover said.

She knew the soft-voiced anticipation that seized Pim in the prelims. That's what Altoona heard now.

It gave moisture and swell to her gens.

"And you girls look rounded in all the right places," said Condor.

It sounded stupid, fake-suave.

When Condor cast a look of embarrassment in Blayne's direction, it led to a second volley of laughter, during which Blayne ushered his friend forward.

"You take the stuff?" she asked. It hadn't done much for her, but Pim was pretty loopy.

"Oh yeah," Blayne said. "A killer coaster."

"Setting mostly," she commented. "But now that we're past the slaughter, ain't nothin' but smooth sailing and clear vistas ahead."

Blayne nodded as he came closer, but it was clear he wasn't one bit interested in listening.

He cobra'd Altoona's eyes. His hand found her free hand, their fingers entwining at their sides as he eased in to kiss her.

There was that warmth again, a zillion times warmer. His rough-nubbed lips pebbled across her pillowy ones. It turned Altoona on.

She tongued metal.

Rise, fall, rise, fall of zipper-teeth.

Cabrille's handiwork indeed. Much like the licking she'd given Pim the night before, but oh so different as well.

Condor and Pim were engaged in an awkward embrace, rocking and swaying, their lips blending.

Blayne's mouth slanted across her cheek to her right earlobe, his zipper moving like a moist blunt blade pretending to cut her face.

Friendship lobe indeed!

It was more like another lefty, her sexlobe's twin, when the metal ring of his lips encased her flesh. She gasped upon his cheek when he fingered her left lobe through its lobebag.

First fondle.

She boldly did likewise to him, diddling him through his thin, flexible leather.

The daring of it! If anybody caught them, they'd be expelled. Denied graduation.

Forced to repeat senior year.

Forced to attend next year's prom.

It made what they were doing explosively exciting.

Pim was moaning beside her.

Glancing over, Altoona saw an inept hand fumble at Pim's lobebag, tug on its bowstrings, yank it swiftly off. The sight of the exposed sexlobe jazzed and juiced her.

Pim's head swung right, her heavy-lidded eyes aglow with drugs and desire, as the usually shy Condor slurped eagerly at her engorged lobe.

Blayne wore a tight elastic designer bag, as did Altoona. He was shimmying hers down and she his, his lobe so nice and thick and warm and sexy beneath her fingers.

Blayne eased her head around.

Racks of courtly costumes hung like dead kings and queens crammed together.

The touch of his tongue, the cool slide of zipper teeth, took her breath away. Her quim was dripping, the swollen labia tight about zip-jags of niobium.

As much as she longed to be sucked into lobate ecstasy, she wanted even more to lick Blayne there too at the same time.

Impossible.

She stopped him and whispered the word into his left ear, her chin at his sexlobe as she spoke: "Foursome." She drew back to see his eyes flare with naughtiness and delight.

Then Altoona was both leading and being led, Blayne hovering at her left shoulder, laughing but mostly keeping his lips at her lobe.

She laughed too.

Into the other couple they toppled, a slow sensual collide, her lips finding Condor's sexlobe while he tongued Pim's.

Blayne's muted moan at her lobe, the tiny pain of zipper teeth biting into her arousal, signaled what she sensed: that Pim's hot mouth had moue'd around his engorged lovelobe, their illegal lovesquare at last complete.

Now all was sucking and being sucked.

Hands roved in every direction. Belts were yanked off, skirts raised.

But head play held sway. It was so majorly mindblowingly incredible, moving higher at each tongued urging, passing them on, grokking that Condor was turning Pim on with the same curled spiral of energy.

And she Blayne.

And on back to Altoona.

Pim climaxed first, that sweet tight sexy childlike *unngh* that Altoona so loved, with the upward flip which led so sweetly from one catch breath to another.

Then they all came, an absurd lovely quartet of uninhibited noise.

In the midst of her orgasm, she felt Blayne ease past her panties, stretching the lacy thigh-hole.

He found what he sought.

Zip-teeth.

Her inner labia behind them.

He used her hot quim to wet her nub, gently circling there, his knuckles knocking lightly at embedded metal.

Then she was off again, thrusting, gripping Blayne about the shoulders, wanting him inside her so badly, wanting his lobe on her nipples, on her clit, wanting it all.

Pim would be there to help, or to be set upon in turn.

And Condor too, damn their warped society so insistent on three! He would make four, and four would be just fine. Then she couldn't think anymore, surges of orgasm rotating the tinseled costume room about her like a carousel.

"Hey, I know!" Blayne said. She only half heard him, hugging him, gasping downward, the sturdy table behind her a blessing to her balance.

"What?" said Condor, too loud but that was okay. The poor dear was excited and riding high on some pretty good shit.

Pim toyed with his zipper pull, there where his smile came to an acute angle that pointed to his friendship lobe.

"Take Pim's clothes off, I'll show you." He had already unzipped Altoona. Now he eased the leather skirt down over her ample hips. She did thigh sways to help out, kicking her pumps off on the thread-wisped floor.

Her leather vest hung open.

His hot hands smoothed over her tummy, her spine, went through her private hair and down her butt slit, caught at lace briefs and eased them off and away.

"We gonna dress 'em up?" Condor asked. He was slower in stripping Altoona's girlfriend, but Pim's succulent body finally came full naked into the costume shop's gaudy light.

"No, stupid."

"Aw, come on, guys," said Pim. "Dress us up."

Blayne leaned over and kissed Altoona's lips. He caressed her sexlobe with one hand and pinched a nipple with the other.

She seized up in that hot frenzied way as if someone had dropped an ice cube down the back of her dress. She didn't mind a bit.

Blayne broke the kiss and said, "I have a better idea than playing dress-up. You're gonna like it."

He knelt before Altoona, using her leather skirt to cushion his knees. Angling his neck to the right, he lined up his lips with her labia.

Condor caught on and did likewise with Pim.

It was a gas, watching Condor and Pim fumble their zippers together, even as she and Blayne did the same. It was like being tickled in lots of yummy places while trying to zip two sleeping bags together with greased fingers.

Blayne slid his zipper pull, the one along his lower lip, into the starter at the base of her right labia. Altoona made a try at hers, joining it with his upper lip starter, but he began to tongue her and that threw her off.

"Wait," she said. "If you keep doing that, I'll never get this in."

He held off.

Then she had it.

It didn't catch on any skin along the way, but glided up as his glided down on the right, making an intimate seal between them.

Everything felt fine and warm and good.

Then his tongue resumed, a wet rouse where their lips conjoined, perfect union, his head giving her its ardency as he rhythmed there.

She glanced at Pim, who was getting off in that special way of hers. Pim looked like a soft pink dream without clothing. And her squirms—as Condor, intimately lip-zipped, lapped her—seemed to say, Robe me in all the world's wonders, wash me in sunlight, let perfect ecstasy swallow me up.

Altoona stretched her right hand toward her girlfriend and Pim seized it in that sweet grip.

Life radiated upon her oval face.

This moment felt like a pinnacle of bliss, which surely it was. Yet it was the beginning of something even greater.

Oh, Jesus.

Her kneeling boy-lover, with his lashable back, killer tush, and steely smile, swept her up into a yummy rhythm. Her joy began to rise again. "That," she said to Blayne. "Yes, that."

Pim's right hand was stroking Condor's hair. "Honey, he's so good," she said to Altoona, almost as if her new boyfriend wasn't there, almost as if he were a trained monkey that couldn't understand. "His mouth is so fucking incredi . . . mmmm . . . oh, yeah!"

Altoona winced. She nodded, unable to speak one word as the tremors seized her. Her hips swayed as Blayne's head moved in perfect harmony. Their blent love surged upward.

Then a hand appeared on Pim's head, grasping her hair and yanking back so hard that her neck made a snapping sound. A blade came across the arched skin, opened up a red blurt-and-spill down the curve of her body and a cascade of blood onto Condor's side-turned head.

A face emerged.

It came toward her.

Blayne struggled below, panic in his eye.

The hand came in rough and scrabbly at her head, her hair, hanks yanked back, a crude tug that wrenched a neck muscle.

Just as the face registered with her, the name rushing in, a tautness bloomed in her throat, too fast for her hands to avert it, then a hot outgush along her breasts and belly, cooling as it came, and no-breath, nothing, nothingness closed upon her.

13
Unearned Sighs
of Relief

Kyla followed Patrice into the gym.

For maybe ten token minutes, they had half-heartedly searched for their classmates' corpses. To hell with school spirit. Then they headed back to the gym to wait for the bodies to be found and brought in.

A bridge had been crossed.

Kyla saw it in the teachers' faces and in the way the chaperones looked at everybody.

Though the grown-ups remained aloof, a new bond, a bond of adulthood, had begun to form between them and the returning survivors.

Mostly, Kyla didn't feel grown up.

But an essential part of her did.

On the bandstand, riding above soft cymbal brushings and steady bass drum thumps, Jiminy Jones noodled ineptly on his downturned muted trumpet. He had one of those bulb-mutes in, the kind that laced his playing with silvery silken regret and caresses that zinged straight to the heart.

"Oh, Kyla," whined Patrice.

Kyla followed her lover's eyes.

She wasn't looking at Pesky and Flense, their bodies lying there like broken dolls beneath the Ice Ghoul's triumphant leer. Nor was she wasting time on the principal, who stood by Miss Phipps holding his speech notes, pale and really upset about something.

No.

Patrice's eyes were trained on Fido Jenner. One hand was stuck in his pants pocket. In the other, he held a paper cup.

Bowser stood beside him.

They were grinning.

Why? Because that slim tramp Peach, Cobra's girl—or from the look of it, Cobra's *ex*-girl—was talking them up, fondling their friendship lobes, hipping and breasting and just generally slinking outrageously before them.

"He's breaking my heart," Patrice went on.

"You can't push the river, sweetie," Kyla said, trying to be as gentle as she could. "If it wants to flow toward us, it will. Besides, he'd have to break up with Bowser, if we were to have a prayer."

Or she and Patrice would have to break up, but Kyla didn't mention that.

Petulant: "Bowser McPhee isn't worthy of Fido. He never has been. And he never will be. It looks to me like Peach is doing one heck of a job pushing *her* river."

Kyla stopped feeding her whining girlfriend. She was feeling jubilant as all get-out. There they were, numbered among the survivors!

Too bad about Pesky.

Too bad about Flense.

But the important thing was that she and Patrice had made it. They were alive and free, a rush of exhilaration coursing through her.

Odd, how you could be shackled and never know it till someone took a sledgehammer to your bonds and set you free.

"I could use some food."

"Get some for me too, okay?" Patrice said, dole-eyed above sultry trumpet sorrow. "I don't want to go *near* him."

"Sure."

Kyla headed off.

Patrice was a tad bit irritating. Kyla had heard that all sorts of splits and new pairings, and sometimes the beginning of threesomes, were often precipitated by surviving the kill.

That was what Fido seemed to be engaged in.

And Peach's scuzzy boyfriend, Cobra, was hip-deep in conversation with—of all people—Sandy Gunderloy and Rocky Stark. He was staring at the cheerleader's breasts, pretending he wasn't upset at Peach's having deserted him.

The creep was miffed though, powerful miffed. Kyla could tell.

Clusters of kids stood around jabbering about the dead girls. Kyla skirted their conversations, the perfect eavesdropper, not being asked to join in, of course. That *never* happened.

The long table of food drew nearer. This was a special night. A binge was definitely in order. The cold cuts called to her in all their splendor.

Kyla glanced back.

Poor Mr. Buttweiler hadn't moved a muscle. He stood by the bandstand, Miss Phipps talking at him. Something was definitely bothering their principal. Something besides his dead daughter.

He just stood there staring at the Ice Ghoul and at the bloody couple splayed before it.

Kyla wondered what special hell he was in that could bring such a low, mean, sorrowful look to his face.

Each kill affirmed the rightness.

And the righteousness.

There'd been a concern that conscience might get in the way. Antiquated, wrongheaded conceit.

Come right down to it, these were acts of *love*, acts that helped heal wounds.

Killing the compromised punkfucks in the costume shop had been a joy. The bloodrush down torsos, the crimson that painted breasts, bore a certain savage grace.

Consumed by the heat of perverse lust, the writhing wantons had, in an instant, flopped dead and cold.

This Pimlico and her Altoona may have jerked about like severed frogslegs as they died. It was impossible to tell, what with their blood-splashed guyfucks struggling to unzip their mouths from the girls' vulvas as the knifeblade opened the throat of one, then the other.

Then, peace reigned everywhere.

Bright, red, wet, and full of love in the costume shop's pure light—such was the calm, a calm more like a cathedral than a high school.

The corpses could have been left the way they were. But it offended one's aesthetics.

Far better to unzip them, despite the sticky blood-bother. Things went smoother, now that the struggles had ceased.

Death simplified matters.

Stick the boys together first. Lined up, rolled out, facing each other, the damned zippers didn't match up, both pulls located on the right lower lip.

Slide one boy around.

Slick leather made the pivot easy, Condor's chin to Blayne's nose and vice versa, the two of them stretched out thin as rolled dough oozed over with burbles of cherry liqueur.

Clots between the zipper teeth made the going tough. But at last, twice over, an upper lip was successfully joined to a lower.

Touching. An insufferably cute kissing pair of bloody punkfuck lowlife losers.

Then a rack of Beefeater costumes was wheeled free of the crammed congestion. Bulky red and black uniforms harrumphed to the floor, moth-musty padded stuff that three years before had strutted and sung, beneath the baton of Jiminy Jones, in a failed attempt at light opera.

The dead zip-mouths were heavy little fucks. But eventually they made it over the thick metal bar, Blayne's nape creased and deeply lined from the weight of his corpse, the abrupt angle of his back-bent head, the wide open smile opened in his neck, the lipstrain of his best bud's zipped body pulling down on the other side.

They looked uncomfortable indeed.

Their skin might give, before anyone found them.

Then again, it might not.

Time for the naked girls, flops of meat and bone that had once tantalized. There was no attraction here now. But the light falling harsh on lifeless, blood-splashed skin carried a certain charm. It touched memories. It soothed them. It gave assurance that this act was not only just but that love's revenge demanded it.

The girls proved more difficult to get right.

Dragging Pim on top of Altoona was easy, one dead face skull-smacking the other.

But managing the zippers was hard.

All that leg flesh. Thighs. The gleam of matched niobium between the anuses was the only part visible, that and the zipper pulls.

No room to maneuver there. None.

These two had been lovers, of which the world was owed proof. Not to zip them together simply wouldn't do. They required the same treatment as the boys, to be racked up there, hanging over the big iron bar by their parts.

Visions of cooked chicken arose, one leg snapped aside to reach meat. Dig a knee into the small of the back, grasp the right thigh with both arms, and lever it sharply up, using every ounce of strength—that was the way to proceed.

Something snapped, a dull pop, a thigh bone dislocated. Discoloration bruised the stretched flesh, a major vein broken by exertion.

But it allowed sufficient access.

The girl's zipper pull slipped over its first tooth and drew up nicely.

An obedient little mechanism.

Her left leg bent back more easily than her right.

There was only one slight vulval snag, halfway up. But backtracking a few zip-teeth set things right again.

Jesus, the lifting! It deepened one's respect for the poor joes who load haunches of beef onto meat trucks.

At last the females were up, slid onto the bar next to the dead boys but not touching them. Propriety had to be maintained.

Heads down. Blood would have dripped from them if there'd been any left.

The stocky one—it felt wrong to call this dead thing Altoona—threatened the balance. But the other girl's oddly angled, disjointed thighs tipped sufficiently in the opposing direction to steady them on the clothesrack.

As the rack rumbled toward the passageway, the foursome swayed like commuters on a subway car.

It would be good to position them where the others would discover them.

Raise a few hackles.

Make the little shits shit their britches, get the blood pumping, their adrenalin flowing, divide and conquer them.

Perhaps at some point, the hunger would be satisfied.

But there were plenty of worthy victims out there, the evening was still young, and after all, wasn't prom night made for love?

Peach felt sexy and free.

And her own damned woman at last.

As she and Cobra, him with his back turned, had risen from their waiting spot, Bowser smiled, blew her a kiss, and left with Fido.

That had been enough to jazz her.

Almost before the echo of the find-the-dead-folks alarm was finished, Peach blurted out that they were through. In spite of Cobra's stunned disbelief, she held her ground, taking his abuse and riding out his little-boy tempest, knowing in her heart that what she was doing was right.

Now, having sauntered brazenly up to Bowser and his increasingly okay date Fido, Peach Popkin was suddenly on top of a world she hadn't known could exist.

Blue, red, and orange lights maundered high in the gym, catching balloons and streamers up by the rafters. Wherever her gaze fell, young gods and goddesses looked back, disbelief and elation in their eyes.

Peach had worried that Cobra would make a scene. But he didn't. Sandy and Rocky, of all people, had caught his attention. He even ignored his gang members, almost as if they had split up too.

"Yeah, well you're cute too," said Peach. "You're both cute. Isn't it neat?"

Fido's clownish look made her laugh.

Bowser said, "You mean surviving? Yep. Too bad about Pesky and Flense, but I guess someone had to bite it."

"No, silly," she said, "I meant isn't it neat that we feel so good together? I love your lobes. Do you love my lobes?"

They averred that they did, very much.

"Do you think you two could, I don't know, futter me a nipple or something? I'd love you forever."

"I'll bet Bowser could," Fido said. There was a hint of fear in his voice.

But he was wiry. Peach recalled his supple way of threading the hallways between classes, a skim past the lowing herds without touching them, almost balletic in his grace.

Fido was a mercurial sort. Come futtering time, he would slip past a flurry of cuts and rends as the senior class tore into the sacrificed girls. Beneath it all, his butcher knife would zip in, copping a prize Peach would cherish for years to come.

"I'll bet *you* could too. You and Bowser *both*," she said, moving in to plant a lush kiss on Fido's friendship lobe. In doing so, her breasts splayed shamelessly against the poor boy's suit front. Peach heard him gasp.

"Would you crop us if we did?" he said.

"Hmmm, neat idea," cracked Bowser. He mock-leered at her, but he was one excited boy, as his tented crotch made clear.

"Sure I would," said Peach.

Cobra'd always been the one to crop, to whip, to slap and smack. It did neat things to her head to imagine doling it out instead.

"I'd crop you both with such love, your flesh would throb for days and days."

Cobra's violence had been so ugly and mean. While that had had its appeal, what Peach felt now seemed so much more limitless and pure.

"And you know what?"

"What?" asked Fido.

"Sometimes,"—she brought their heads near her mouth, Fido's friendship lobe on her right, Bowser's bagged sexlobe on her left— "sometimes, I'll want the two of you to crop *me!*"

Her hands cupped their napes where a barber's razor had edged off stubble. Dry fear-sweat mixed there with some sort of yummy fruity cologne.

Their hips came close enough to hers that she could feel hints of hard cock on either side.

At any moment, Futzy Buttweiler would have his say. They would dance and dance and finally futter the dead couple. Then it was off to some place private, a place where she could show these cute boys lots of good things to share.

On the far edge of the gym, still near the hallway, stood Dex and Tweed holding hands.

There would be time enough to get closer to the Ice Ghoul, check out the sprawl of Pesky and Flense, how their bodies were arrayed and how best to approach them when midnight came.

At the moment, Dex felt oddly detached from it all.

The phones had unsettled him.

The dead girls as well, dripping blood down the hallway.

And now the principal.

Mr. Buttweiler and Miss Phipps were huddled by the bandstand. They had been huddled there for some time.

What was the delay? Why didn't he start?

The doors to the gym were clear, everyone but a few stragglers inside again.

But something kept Mr. Buttweiler from the mike, and now Mr. Versailles and Miss Brindisi came in to confer as well.

Dex thought he must be imagining it, but their eyes seemed often to peek up and glare at him and Tweed.

Had they done something wrong? Had the paperwork been screwed up? Had they been sitting under the wrong number? What was the penalty for that? And would they get a chance to show what had been written in their packet before the law came down, by mistake, on them?

Dex patted his coat. Something springy responded from the inside pocket. Relief. The paper with their location and number.

"What?" asked Tweed.

"Nothing."

"Come on."

"Just making sure the paper's there."

"What paper? Oh you mean the one about where to sit. Why?"

"Nervous habit. I don't know. What if we sat in the wrong place?"

Tweed squeezed his hand. "Silly, we did just what the paper told us to do. Besides, what difference does it make? We've got our designated victims. Jeepers, I can hardly see them through the crowd."

"Yeah, you're right," said Dex. "I wonder what the hangup is."

"Mr. Jones can't play for beans, can he?"

Dex laughed. "Sure can't."

Yet another reason for the principal to start speaking. Shut up the noodling muted trumpet and Festus Targer's random bass thumps and steel-brush cymbal circlings.

Futzy Buttweiler would release some hot air about the girls, about sacrifice, prom spirit, motherhood, and apple pie.

Then Jiminy Jones would call the band members back to the stand. Tweed would pick up her 'bone and Dex would strap his sax to his neck and stick a reed in his mouth to moisten it and secure it on the mouthpiece and they'd be off and away into the music again, flying high.

But the minutes slid by and Futzy Buttweiler kept conferring with the faculty.

Dex's elation at surviving had begun to turn into something else, something unsettled, an uh-oh not yet fully understood.

"My God," said Tweed in a dreamy voice, "this is a special night. There's ozone in the air."

Dex sniffed. "If you say so."

"Silly. I *do* say so. And it *is* so. So let's have a smile. There, that's better. Is my yummynums impatient for Mr. Buttweiler's immortal words? Me too. Just soak in the atmosphere, Dex. Okay? We're not gonna pass this way again."

"Right-o," said Dex, giving Tweed's hand a squeeze.

But in his heart, the dread just got thicker and thicker. Come on, Futzy, he thought. Say it. Get this show on the road.

And for the love of Christ, stop *staring* at us!

14

Prom Askewity

Tweed's dad shut off the TV and his Personal Flogger. Wincing from the welts, he shrugged out of the device and wiped his eyes with a tissue.

The same damned dirge rose from his lips, his voice quavering as Tweed's memory persisted.

Smiling.

Standing at the door.

"Good night."

A vision. The sudden flash of her life. She had popped from Cam's womb, growing much too fast toward womanhood.

And now?

The answering machine on his nightstand caught his attention.

A one. Not a zero.

A deep red number one, staring back at him.

Why hadn't he noticed it there on the phone?

How had he missed the ringing?

Before his bath. Toothbrushing as sinkwater furied from the faucet. Humming a foamy *fossil-fossil-fossil* mazurka.

Matthew bet—no, he *knew*—that that was when the call had come.

He hit Play.

An unfamiliar woman's voice scoured inside his head, using his daughter's name. She berated him and confirmed his worst fears.

Matthew had to play it twice to get it all, its harsh message of death and possible salvation so unsettled his mind.

There was a tight fear in him and a sobbing.

But there was also anger. At himself, at Corundum High, at the entire warped ritual so ingrained in the culture.

If this unknown caller spoke the truth—and her words carried conviction—Tweed and Dex were either dead or saved. Either way, it was too late to do anything about it.

But his anger grew. It refused all reason, shaping its own reasons, acts that impelled.

Kill the killer.

Leap to the gym lectern and grab the mike.

Shame the entire student body, the faculty, with an impassioned speech that would haunt them the rest of their days, that would force them into battling against the custom's continuation, that would at the very least halt the futtering of his daughter and her boyfriend.

He would bring them home in one piece. He and the Poindexters would join hands, mourn for the dead, speak from the heart in support of the anti-slasher movement.

Matthew dressed, muttering, singing a song quick and curt and choppy. The sobs that welled up threatened to crush him. But he gritted back his tears and pressed on.

Insane, this pointless flurrying, he thought. Tweed is dead. Stolen from him.

But his fingers vigorously zipped and buttoned, thrusting wallet, keys, coins, and handkerchief into his pants pockets.

He bounded down the stairs.

Stopped on the last one and stared.

By the front door beyond her fluxidermed moms, Tweed at her loveliest looked back.

"Good night."

Matthew's palm arced on the newel post. He headed away from the vestibule, into the back of the house and along a hallway.

"I'll get them." The phrase matched his stride, drums and percussion sounding in the background. "I'll *get* them, I'll *get* them."

Into the laundry room, past washer and dryer, he tore open the door to the garage and hit the button, shoulder-high on his left. The garage door rumbled up.

His eye caught the hatchet on the wall, nails angled to hold it, a worn leather cover sleeved on it like the hood over a hawk's eyes.

He grabbed it. Solid heft. It bounced once on the passenger seat.

Then he fired up the car, intent on getting to Tweed, on saving her or making them pay for her life.

Something. Anything.

It was against the law for anyone but the designated slasher to use the school's backways.

But the law wasn't going to stand in his way. Not tonight. He wouldn't allow it.

Matthew backed out too fast, rotating the wheel. Drumming filled his head. Percussion. A surge of fierce melody. The garage door jiggle-rumbled down in counterpoint. The roadway at the end of his driveway curved and reversed beneath him.

He gave a bitter laugh.

"I'll *get* them," he sang. "I'll *get* them."

Crazed father to the rescue.

The trumpet wept and wailed like an old man slumped over, smoking a cigarette, eyelids heavy, against a moonlit wall in an alleyway.

Sandy's boyfriend looked dazed, as he often did. Rocky rarely gave himself credit for having any brains. "But I thought," he said, "our third would be some guy *outside* of school."

"I did say that," said Sandy. "But Cobra is different."

Cobra was staring at her breasts, but she could tell his attention was divided. His glance flicked toward Peach Popkin, who was cozying up to two losers. "Hey Rocky, come on," he said. "I've *never* been part of this fuckin' school, and you know it."

Sandy felt exceedingly jazzed, as if her entire being were drenched in lubricant and every move she made, down to the least breath, turned her on even more.

She was used to erectile eyes painting sex patterns on her body. Mostly, that had been a subliminal annoyance. Not until this moment had she herself felt a fraction of the fantasized sensuality at play in those eyes.

The concluding bell had done it.

It sparked something in her. It planted a seed. When she and Rocky burst out of that smelly locker room with the other kids, it felt as though she rode on a wave of freedom.

She was free to be whatever she wanted. No limits. The balloting was done, Rocky would be king, she'd be queen, and no one could coerce her into fulfilling some fantasy of theirs.

Not any more.

They would test-drive, at least, this Cobra. He was different. He was dangerous. It would be fun to jump his bones. Fun too to watch the hood and the jock turn one another on.

She couldn't wait.

"Well, Sandy knows best," said Rocky.

"Damn fuckin' straight, she does." Cobra's hands did spastic fidgets, a nicotine jag. His eyes slipped up her dress and licked between her thighs.

"But none o' that drug stuff." Rocky sat high on his horse, the one whose saddlehorn Coach Frink had stuck up Rocky's butt.

Cobra looked sharply at him. "Drugs? What are they? I never heard of any dee-are-ugs, not in my whole fuckin' life. You clear on that, muscle man?"

Sandy imagined the whip in his hand. It made her heart race.

"Hey, but I thought you . . . I heard that you—"

"It's all lies, man. Bad rap's done stuck me with a bad *rep* all the goddamn time in this fuckin' shithole. They never get off your back once they climb on. They're like a Flogger stuck on High with the straps sewn shut. But nobody never proved a thing on me, not one."

"Sorry, Cobra," Rocky said, looking cowed. "I didn't mean nothin' by it."

Rocky could have torn Cobra in half without raising a sweat. But Sandy guessed years of bull-headed coaches had made him malleable. She and this dark-eyed mini-thug had years of fun ahead, making Rocky perform for them.

"That's it, guys," she said. "Be friends. We have a whole dance to feel this thing out—"

"—I'm gonna feel *you* out—"

"—and I for one am planning to enjoy it." She could already sense a dark texture to the air, a miasma of thin-lipped disapproval from students and teachers alike, judging the three of them.

It did nothing but turn her on.

The trumpet music stopped. The drummer began a roll, soft, then faster and louder until finally he spangled off a cymbal shining gold and shimmery in the spotlight.

"Fuckin' Futzy's up," muttered Cobra, "ready to spout more prom bullshit."

The principal held folded papers in one hand and tapped the mike with the other. He was gazing out, white in the face, beyond the gathered masses toward the Ice Ghoul.

Mr. Buttweiler, a really nice man who winked at Sandy a lot, looked seriously psycho tonight. Too bad the prom committee, many of them friends of hers, had trampled on his feelings.

But he would get over it. Maybe it would help him overcome his twenty-year-old funk.

And if it didn't?

Well fuck him, she thought, amazed at the crudity of her musings. Fuck him to hell and back. He was nothing, now that school was out, over, and done with forever. He was pasteboard where power had stood. Wink at some *other* piece of tail, you jackass, she thought.

It made her laugh.

"What's so funny?" Rocky asked.

"Yeah, babe. What gives?"

"None o' your beeswax," she said.

Soft sadness through the speakers. "Can you all hear me?" A squeal. He backed off. The feedback died.

"Maybe not now," Cobra said with a leer, "but me 'n' old Rocky here'll crop it out of you later. See if we don't."

"Yeah, Sandy." Rocky adopted Cobra's macho stance. "Double welts for you tonight!"

"Promises, promises," she said.

She caught Mimsy and Bubbler pointing at her, fellow cheerleaders who were a longstanding item. The prissy pair of boob-and-panty-flashers acted stunned.

Well, fuck them too, she thought.

Futzy Buttweiler tapped on the mike, leaned around looking, tapped it again, looked closer and flicked a switch on its neck, then tapped it once more. This time, thunks sounded.

He cleared his throat.

Gerber felt like a shirker.

He'd done the flag thing, the colored light thing, the setting up of the mike, the series of bells by which the senior class got herded here and there for the slaughter and the okay-you-can-get-up-now stuff.

All that stuff.

From where he stood, looking down on the prom, he had done all the right things. But he hadn't hovered as he usually did. He hadn't been seen by all the right people.

Gerber was spooked.

Maybe it was the big red monster in the center of the gym. Its face was plenty creepy. The ferocity of its stance made electricity shoot up his spine and into his partial brain. He could shut his eyes, or go as far away as his shoes would carry him. But still, them lightning sparks did their upshoot thing and the cold eyes stuck in that wicked red face penetrated deep inside him and urged him to do bad things.

He gazed down.

Ants. The spotlit bandstand. The big red monster and the dead girls. Spiffed-up seniors milled or stood in clumps on the sawdust.

Something kept Gerber company that night, but he didn't really want company.

Shadows moved.

Even up here.

Was it him? His feet suggested where to go next. He could already see himself there.

Life weren't fair.

You grew up, got overzealous, maybe one or two people died what ain't hadn't oughta.

So what?

But that weren't how society saw it. Nope, they cut the bad urges out of your brainpan and chucked the cut part in the trash. Made you safe again. They thought. Made you productive and put you in a janitor suit so's you could serve a good function for your fellow man. They thought.

Huh.

Their knives weren't so smart.

But he wasn't about to tell them so. Maybe he knew shit little, like they said. But he knew that if he told them, they would open up his skull all over again, take out the whole damn thing this time, and toss it in the trash.

Ol' Gerber was too wily for that!

But he was spooked tonight, for sure. He would catch hell for doing or not doing some shit, though he'd done everything he was sposta oughta. Maybe that was the meaning of the shadows and the sounds.

Guilt goblins.

Conscience. That thing without which he'd been operating before they sliced his head open. Maybe it was filling in the empty spaces.

Great. Useless stuff. Hope I don't catch any o' that, he thought.

Then he saw the shadow again, even way up here. And he lowered his head and put his big hands on top of it, cringing and feeling tears come into his eyes.

Go away, he thought. Go away.

His feet wanted to move again.

Jonquil stood less than ten feet from the slain girls, sniffing the as-yet subtle smell of death.

No, that wasn't quite right.

Pesky's ribboned belly had begun to steam with a stenchy redolence that pleased her, that stoked her lust and made her think of later.

For the past many years, Jonquil had taken to marauding after the prom. She would find some neighborhood in an obscure section of Corundum, draw a bead on some lonely guy or gal or couple through their window, and fuck the juice out of them. Totally anonymous, dressed like a slut on the troll, she acted with complete abandon.

She loved it.

"Ladies and gentlemen . . ."

Futzy's voice faltered. He struggled to regain his composure.

Jonquil wondered where Gerber Waddell was. He hadn't been around all night. Usually he hung about on the periphery of the prom. In some ways Gerber *was* the prom, hints of violence behind his soothing exterior.

She found other reasons to wonder.

There was something strange about Flense's body. The solid white of her gown was now wet with blood. It hadn't been so when they carried her in. An inner wound only now soaking through? Jonquil didn't think so.

"You have passed a very important stage in your life, a stage that . . . ." Futzy paused.

A blotch suddenly bloomed on Flense's right breast, a bright red blotch completely separate from the ribside Jonquil had been looking at.

The blood wasn't coming from inside Flense at all.

From Pesky? Not a chance. Her corpse faced another way.

Jonquil looked up, noting moisture on the Ice Ghoul's cheek, a drop at the tip of its beakish nose. Leaks in the roof, Claude had guessed. She watched the drop elongate and detach. A spangle of rain. She fancied she could see the spatter hit Flense and widen the red blotch.

A neuron fired in Jonquil's brain.

Not water. Not water at all.

"My friends," said Futzy, departing from his text, "I have to admit to some confusion. Sheriff Blackburn should have been here by now."

That was true, thought Jonquil. Futzy had made no big deal about it, which was perhaps why she hadn't noticed it before. Ordinarily, the sheriff would remove the padlock from the gym's outer door and slip in. By now, he should have been standing by the bandstand, ready to spout his drivel about the community, their new role in it, all that grown-up crap.

"What gives?" Claude came up beside her.

"I don't know."

"But there's something far worse," said Futzy, "than the sheriff's absence."

"Oh my," Claude murmured, "our beloved leader's about to lose it."

"With good reason, I'm afraid," she said. Through a sea of bobbing heads, near chaperone corner, she noticed the strange couple, Brayton and his date. They had this look, a look that bespoke knowledge.

Interesting.

Something more than bloodlust wriggled its sensuous way through Jonquil. She felt, in that tip-tilted gym, as if they were all standing on the deck of a vast ship. Below them, a boiler stoked with rage—more rage than Jonquil had felt in years—was poised to explode.

Futzy's halting words, the blood dripping from above, the odd couple whose presence somehow tied it all together—these things caressed her so violently, she teetered on the brink of jumping her snooty colleague's bones right there on the dance floor.

On Flense's chest, fingers of blood stretched to grope the dead girl's breast, a clotted palm moist upon her nipple.

"The slain pair you have brought in . . . ," said Futzy.

Oh my God, Jonquil thought. Sometimes you knew, by the way someone began, how they'd end.

And he did. "The slain pair you have brought in," he repeated, "are not those who were slated to die."

There was a beat before the sound began.

Then it was suddenly there, like waves of ants scurrying underfoot at the destruction of their anthill.

Jonquil herself gave a sharp *ah*, her hand to her mouth. She saw Brayton squint and grab his date's arm. Raven had gone white, but the starch hadn't left her face, that stubborn grit Jonquil had found so alluring when they met.

"Pescadera Carbone and her escort are not the designated victims. I . . ."

"Great," said Claude over the tumult. "Just when the school needs a true leader, our beloved Futzy crumbles."

Then the tenders whose birth timing and the luck of the draw had spared came deadmarching into the gym with their dates. A couple of wrestlers carried the corpses of Butch and Zinc.

"Oh my God." This over the mike. "Sheriff Blackburn should be . . . does anyone know where the sheriff is?"

A second dead couple, one of them a tender.

Jonquil felt her knees buckle at the sight. She clung to Claude's arm, moved in, wanting so badly to kiss him.

But he reared back. "Wait now," came his objection.

Then she heard the sound above, like a diver leaving a springboard. She looked up and saw the falling body.

Impressions through colored light. Something unraveling. A sandbag. Stocky like their missing sheriff. It *was* Sheriff Blackburn, his eyes bugged out in disbelief, thin glistening erections of zoom. It made not an ounce of sense.

Then he hit the end of the rope, a groan and hold above, and the glistening erections shot from his eyes.

What were they?

One smashed on the floor and skittered like a scattering of hockey broken parts into a waiting trash can for the bonfire Wanker had scheduled at midnight on the Shite House lawn.

All of this a trio of filmers filmed, cameras perched like parrots on their shoulders, eyepieces to their eyes, close enough but not too close to be caught up in the melee.

So as not to detract from the slaughters being carried out across the nation, the footage would be aired on late-night news. This would be a capper, not a distraction.

So the Committee to Assassinate the President had planned it, and so it would be.

Wanker was pleased with himself.

He was able then, at last, to relax into the ride of his orgasm, his huddled privacy set aside for a brief instant as he moved into the flow and gave all he had for his country.

"I think we've made it," said Tweed, barely whispering. The darkened chem lab, with its odd stifle of odors and its solid workbenches, would suffer nothing louder.

Dex confided, "I think you're right."

"Did you hear screaming?"

"I might have." He gestured in the same direction she had fancied muffled sounds coming from moments ago. "Off that way."

"Yes, just ringings in my ear," she said. "I thought I was only spooking myself."

It might be, thought Tweed, nothing but a shared deception. Right this moment, the square grate above Dex might be kicked spangling across the classroom and the killing begin.

Or now. Or now.

But she felt a lifting in the lab, as if it and its ghostly pairs of seniors arrayed against the wall were being raised heavenward. Intuition, sure. But that was something she and her sister Jenna excelled in.

"I wonder who bit it," Dex said.

"I love you, Dex."

He looked into her eyes and smiled through a sadness, a good wish toward somebody now defunct. "Love ya, Tweed."

"No, I mean more than ever."

Relief flooded her body. Dex looked so good, so indescribably good, that she thought she might burst.

"I mean," a laugh escaped, his eyes steady on hers, "I mean," she said, putting her hands to the sides of his head, his earlobes warm between thumb and forefinger, "I mean I really sincerely truly *love* you, Dexter Poindexter."

Then her lips pressed against his.

His hand touched her back.

A lip tingle, like spot-on trombone playing but a kajillion times more gratifying, softened her. She grew moist as if Dex were fondling her, her earlobes beating hot with passion.

Her fingertips found something smooth at his lapel. With a laugh, she broke the kiss.

"What?" he asked.

"You still have your sax strap on," she replied.

"Makes me feel saxy."

"Old joke." Bubbles of joy effervesced in Tweed's head.

"Besides," said Dex, "I knew, one way or the other, that we were going to survive this. I just knew it."

A bell shattered the silence, so loud and so sustained that gasps and shouts and a flurry of startled obscenities erupted in the classroom.

Tweed hugged Dex anew, taking his friendship lobe between thumb and forefinger as though it were a fat velvet button.

"Let's go," said Dex, helping her up. "Time to hunt for the victims."

Whichever couple found the dead folks first won some silly prize. But Tweed didn't care about that. She only cared that she and Dex were out of the woods—a murkier and more wicked place than she had imagined—and she told him so.

"Yeah, yeah, I know," he said. "But let's get into the spirit of the thing anyway. We did it. We're survivors!"

"I've got to call Dad first."

Dex took her hand.

Futterware and cleavers swaying in tandem, they headed for the hall, which was already choked with kids on the move. This was the beginning of an unencumbered life together for her-and-Dex-and-whomever.

And it felt wonderful!

PART THREE
THE GAME CHANGES

"The future smells of blood and leather, of godlessness and incessant whipping. Our grandchildren would be well advised to come into the world with extremely thick skin on their backs."
　　—Heinrich Heine

"When you skin your customers, it's a good idea to leave a little skin behind to regenerate, so you can skin them again."
　　—Nikita Khrushchev

the gym. It's the safest place to be. The killer could be anywhere out there. There's safety in numbers."

Use fear to halt the mass exodus before it begins.

"I want you to spread calm. Not panic. There's no need for panic. Hold one another. Assure one another. We're in control here."

Jesus, what a lie.

"Teachers and chaperones, please make your way to the bandstand. That's it. Steady as she goes. We're in control here. We'll figure out the best course of action and restore order, calm, peace, serenity. That's it. We're doing fine. Everything's under control."

Adora Phipps was standing close by.

Elwood Dunsmore sidled his way through the crowd on the right.

Jonquil Brindisi, clutching Claude Versailles' arm, wore a strange shiny-eyed smile as they approached.

"You folks are handling this just fine."

He raised one finger in a be-right-back gesture. Then he crouched at the edge of the riser.

The Borgstroms, the white-haired notched elders, had risen and were coming forward.

Nurse Gaskin hesitated, unsure whether faculty and chaperones meant her. Futzy motioned her over, blue dress, short dark hair, Kitty's age had she lived.

"Delia," he said to the nurse, "try to find Gerber so we can get the lights turned on full. Elwood, I want you and . . ." Brest Donner's husband Bix arrived on the left. "I want you and Bix to hack down the sheriff's body, if you will. Then toss a blanket or something over Jiminy Jones. Please."

"No problem, Futzy," said Elwood, his army brainwashing kicking in. Bix looked less certain. But he nodded and started to leave with the shop teacher.

"Oh, wait, Elwood." Almost let him get away. Chaos contrived sometimes to muddle the brain.

"Something else?"

"You don't have a key to the front padlock?"

"No, sir. Only the sheriff has that."

"Search him. I doubt you'll find it. How soon could you saw through the padlock? It's pretty thick."

Dunsmore grimaced. "Hell'd freeze over first. Maybe an acetylene torch. Get one from the shop, wheel it over, heat up the steel, lever a blast of oxygen at it, we ought to be through in two minutes. I'll need to have a look at the lock though. They've come up with a new tempered steel that resists just about everything."

"Try it anyway." Futzy dismissed him. "Jonquil, take over the mike. Talk about the vices in that winning way of yours. Harden them. Calm them. Make them ready for whatever might be coming down the pike."

"What about you?" Jonquil asked, a defiant little bitch as usual, forever implying inadequacies in him.

"I'll be back soon. I'm going to my office—"

"I'll go with you," Miss Phipps chimed in.

"—try the phone there, call for help if the line's up, get my gun in any case. Claude, check the pay phones. Rumor has it they're dead, but I want to be sure. Be super cautious out there and return straight to the gym when you're done, give Jonquil some backup at the mike."

"How about us?" Mr. Borgstrom radiated a soft savage bloodlust that was lovely to behold. "What can we do?"

Futzy nodded. "You and your wife stay close by. Provide moral support. With your help, we'll survive this."

The eager old couple grinned, their lobes long sucked dry of juice and withered with age. Oldsters were usually a royal pain, their rutted thought patterns blocking the crosscut blasts of creativity. Not these two. An engaging insanity lit their limpid eyes.

Futzy rose again to the mike.

He had cobbled together a plan. Was it any good? He had no idea. Sometimes it sufficed, at least for a time, just to have one.

He summarized it for the senior class.

Then he turned the mike over to Jonquil Brindisi and headed, Adora Phipps at his heels, toward his office.

Tweed suddenly wanted very badly to be home under her comforter. She didn't feel at all like a grown-up. She felt like a sniveling little kid in need of serious daddying.

Through mercurochrome swirls of light were carried the bloody corpses of Butch and Zinc, the two trumpeters who would trumpet no more. Broken necks, torn eye sockets, deep ripped slashes across their chests. Zinc had been a tender, exempt from all violence, a fortunate white-ball plucker who had struggled to suppress a smile as he walked off the auditorium stage a week ago Thursday. That made his death unspeakably worse.

The wrestlers carrying them laid them before the Ice Ghoul. There was room beside the pair of slain girls. Sheriff Blackburn's body swayed from its rope at one edge of the sacrificial platter.

The principal tried to calm everyone. But it was hard to process his words.

Tweed's father had reason to fret. The phones had been dead. Maybe he would call the cops. Maybe they'd break in any moment now to rescue them. Her knees felt weak. *Now*, she thought. Break in *now*. But the nightmare continued.

Wherever her eyes alighted, looks of panic punched through a restless mill of classmates.

Her boyfriend shivered audibly.

"Oh, Dex, I'm scared."

"You're telling me," he said, admitting his own terror.

The killer's malevolence lay everywhere, eye and hand full of power. Dex's sax strap. Tweed had a sudden fear that it might be yanked up at any moment. His neck would snap. She gripped it, wrenched it over his head, and flung it into the churning crowd.

"Hey, what're you—?"

Tweed hugged Dex fiercely. His balance went haywire. But he steadied himself and hugged her too, his warm sweet head tucked alongside hers. "I love you, Dex."

"It's okay. We'll get through this." His words were an echo of Mr. Buttweiler's. "We'll stay here like Futzy says and we'll be safe. He and the teachers'll figure something out."

"Whoever's doing this is gonna kill us all."

"No he won't."

"He will. I know it." It wasn't over yet. Not by a longshot.

"Don't work yourself up," said Dex. "You're spooking *me* now. It'll be okay. You'll see." His hands comforted Tweed at her waist.

Everyone had so bunched toward the front that the gym felt suddenly packed, dense with fear and restlessness. Towering above, the Ice Ghoul, its face set in chill triumph, seemed to see many more bodies strewn before it. It lusted after broken bones, torn limbs, futtered flesh—far more sacrifices than had been laid before it.

Knife raised high.

Crude cock viciously erect.

Knees and bent legs. Feet like a runner's poised at the starting block. Buttocks splayed over one heel.

Its hunger was limitless, its cruel red maw only now beginning to be filled. Tweed hugged Dex closer. She wanted to turn away from those dark eyes, but they held her in their sway, made her look, made her shudder.

Trilby feared she would pass out when rumor came, then was confirmed, that the slain girls had been found in the faculty lounge. Brest held her. A wash of sound rushed through her brain, white noise before a swoon.

"But *Pill* is in there," she said. "We've got to—"

"Come on," said Brest. "Bix, you stay here."

"I'd better go with you."

"No, Futzy's gonna need your help," insisted Brest. "Me and Trilby'll be careful."

Trilby had resisted fainting, the gymnasium taking on its painful reality around her. She followed Brest past the refreshment table to the entrance.

The corridor shone with a feeble light full of shadows and menace. That didn't matter. Nothing mattered but finding her way to Pill. Trilby prayed her daughter hadn't been killed.

Or maimed.

Or kidnapped.

At a run, they passed by the array of phones, a wall of glassed-in trophies, the entrance doors secured with the lock Elwood Dunsmore had snapped shut. The faculty lounge at the far corner of the building seemed miles away.

"Pill? Honey?"

Trilby shouted the words. Fear gave them a sharp edge. She worried it would terrorize Pill further.

The cherry-stained door of the lounge hung ajar, but no reply came.

Brest shoved the door wide open.

Trilby rushed past.

Spatters of blood by the paper cutter. On the floor. On the—Oh, my God!—on *and running down* the splintered wood of the coat closet.

"Pill?" A sob choked her. "Pill? It's Mommy."

Brest grabbed the knob, silver smeared with streaks of blood.

Trilby would have eased the door open, but Brest, always more violent and impetuous, flung it back and held her splayed fingers out to catch the rebound as it banged off the wall.

Pill sat cowering in the corner.

No blood.

In her arms, held so tight as to deform its plush body, Gigi the goat tried to comfort her.

Her face held shock. Her eyes took their time focusing. She looked smaller, every limb tight, as if the muscles tensed around her bones drew all her flesh inward.

"Come on out, Pill," Brest said.

But Trilby tore past her, went into the coat closet, crouched to her child and peeled her from the flimsy wood walls and into her arms. Her skin felt ice cold.

"Mommy?" A voice barely audible. "Mommy?"

"Yes, Pill. It's Mommy. Mommy's here. You're safe now." Nothing mattered but holding and soothing her little girl.

Brest's attempts to break them free of Bix and trio them up with Delia Gaskin, Bix's openly expressed wish for extramarital affairs, Trilby's own subservience to Bix and Brest, not just under the riding crop but in everyday life—none of that mattered now.

The one thing of importance in the world was hugging Pill. Bringing her back. Healing her in the days ahead, once this nightmare was over.

"He killed them, Mommy."

"I know he did, Pill. But he's gone now and Mommy is here and you're safe. Safe as can be."

"The man in the janitor suit. I saw his hand. It had a knife in it. The girl was just asking. That's what she said. I'm just asking. But he killed her." Her voice, weak as tea, lanced Trilby's ear with hurt.

She rocked her little girl there on the floor of the coat closet.

Brest's shadow fell on them.

The child suddenly let go of her goat and groped at her mother, her head nestling deep into Trilby's neck, her hands as clingy as claws high up where the shoulderblades nearly met over her mother's spine.

"He killed them both, Mommy."

"I know he did, Pill," she soothed. "I know."

16

In the Midst of Mayhem, Love

Bray and Winnie had entered the gym with the bodies of the dead trumpeters, stunned at the savagery of the kill.

Bray nodded as his date—that's how he had begun thinking about Winnie—angrily abandoned her optimism. They followed the seniors, attached to the crowd but not integral to it, off far enough that no one could hear their conversation.

She understood now, she said, that their killer friend wasn't the champion she had believed him to be.

Disillusionment lay bitter upon her face.

Then they had seen the slain girls and "Oh, Jesus," Winnie had said, nearly in synch with his unspoken thoughts.

The sheriff had fallen.

The bandleader.

And Bray understood that he and Winnie, there under false colors and archly eyed by the amazing Miss Brindisi, were quite possibly in the deepest of shit one could be in.

Through the principal's speech, through the huddle of faculty and the uneasy buzz of students, Bray held Winnie. She seemed airless, without focus. A forlorn sylph. Even in her distraught state, he thought, she was gorgeous.

He would protect her.

He felt brave. He didn't know why such a feeling had come to him, but it had.

While Winnie, gung-ho for glory at the start, had deflated, Bray had somehow gained in strength. Poor lamb. They would survive this night somehow. Then they'd go off and start a life together.

Her head suddenly twisted up, her eyes newly flaring. "Where's that packet from Fronemeyer's house?"

"In the car. Why?"

She slumped back down. "Great."

"Except for this." He reached into his tuxedo jacket and pulled out the thick sheaf of twice-folded paper. "In case we wanted to go exploring, I thought—"

"The map!"

He unfolded it like a flower coming into bloom. Four pages, stapled, the top one with a three-digit combination Bray guessed allowed the designated slasher, and him only, access to the school's secret passageways.

"We could—"

It occurred to him too. "Of course." Their means of escape. Why hadn't he thought of it?

"—find him," she said, "and reason with him."

"It's our way out." Then Winnie's words registered. "Hey, wait a minute. I'm not gonna let you get *near* our madman. He's wigged out. He'll kill us both."

"No, listen." Winnie paused.

Bray could tell she had been ready to go at him again. To attack his cowardice. But now her mind slipped into gear, more furious in its cogitations than he'd ever seen it.

Jonquil Brindisi stood at the mike. Two men were near the Ice Ghoul, hacking at the rope that held the dead sheriff aloft.

Winnie's hands danced in colored light as she pieced things together. "We find him," she said. "We sneak up on him, overcome him, maybe knock him out. Then we reason with him, we talk to him, for as long as it takes. We get in touch with his problem, soothe him, convince him he's already done enough to solve it. Then we get him to confess, give himself up, make a speech to the press, go national."

"Oh sure, Winnie. And he's just gonna go along—"

"Yes. He will."

Bray stopped speaking. Her certainty never ceased to amaze him.

179

"He *will*. No two ways about it. I can do it. I can convince anybody of anything."

"I've got a better plan," he said.

They blended into the crowd in a reasonable fashion. But Bray felt that a spotlight had been trained on them. At any moment, Jonquil Brindisi would point an accusatory finger at them and have them torn apart, futter bait for the frenzy that lay just beneath the surface for the poor panic-stricken kids around them.

"Here's what we do," he went on. "We escape into the hidden backways. We find the designated slasher's private parking area. Using his car, we blow this town, this state, this whole wretched nation. And we start a new life together, plain and simple, somewhere else."

"They hunt us down." She said it as if she could see it. "They scapegoat us for tonight's outrages. They toy with us on the tube. They tear us apart, they torture us. They put us on *Notorious* next year, an extra special three-hour version, a slow hellacious juicing."

She made him see it.

The pauses between sentences, the stare full of import and meaning, made him see it.

Winnie's arms came about him, her lips near his friendship lobe. "Bray, my strange lovely man, one way or another, they'll fry us. Finding the killer is our only choice."

Bray could hear Jonquil's words at the mike. Tough talk, thrusting iron rods up into youthful backbones. Without looking at her, he knew she was brooding on them. Her accusation might come at any moment.

Winnie felt warm and solid in his arms.

"Do you understand?" she murmured.

He kissed her neck, her cheek, her lips. Her nape felt so perfect against his palm.

"Let's go," he said, determined. "Let's find him."

Winnie took his hand. They sauntered toward the door the two women had rushed out of.

Bray thought they'd be halted at any moment. "Wait a minute," her stern sexy voice would rise, "where do you think *you're* sneaking off to?"

But through his envelope of fear, past the refreshments and out the door to the hallway, Bray and Winnie walked hand in hand, toward a meeting Bray wasn't looking forward to at all.

On the way to his office, Futzy wracked his brain for a suspect, sharing those that came to mind with meek mousy Miss Phipps.

Maybe Zane Fronemeyer had gone insane. But anyone acquainted with Zane would scoff at the very idea.

Might it be the mean-eyed, blubber-chinned cashier in the cafeteria, Skaya something, whose face looked as though she'd been pickled in bile from the moment she was born?

Or one of the newer faculty members, the untried, untested, unknown, indeed unknowable ones fresh out of college?

"Gerber Waddell," Miss Phipps suggested.

Futzy stopped on the stairs.

The building smelled musty, layered with dust.

"Gerber," he repeated, mulling it.

They continued upstairs. Futzy was deep in thought. He hadn't seen the janitor since the lights dimmed and rainbowed. Had Gerber, in his years of subservience, finally somehow triumphed over the intent of his lobotomy?

Each year, Gerber changed the designated slasher's combination to the backways. He wrote it on the map contained in the slasher's packet. Did anyone else know it? No one at all. Gerber always surreptitiously slipped it in, last thing before delivery. Futzy himself made a special point to avert his eyes when he gaped the mouth of the envelope to receive it.

Futzy opened his office door for Miss Phipps. As she walked past him, he caught a hint of her perfume. Lilac? Some old lady scent. Her dress was dark velvet, swaying at the ankles. Old lady dress. A crime. Behind her gold-rimmed glasses, her young face made a thin oval.

"Find the snubnose," he said. "Top drawer, I think. I'll check the phone. Be careful with the gun. It's loaded."

"All right."

He moved to the desk and lifted the receiver.

No dial tone.

The lines had likely been cut somewhere deep in the building. But it felt as if his lair had been violated.

Gerber, the shy feeb.

It had to be him. Somehow, Futzy would find him, put a bullet

181

in what was left of his brain, spare him the torment of being sentient when the graduating class sailed into him.

Miss Phipps rummaged in the desk drawer and lifted something out. She raised it. Against her delicate fingers, Futzy saw the velvet backing. "Is this her?" she asked. "Your daughter?"

"How . . ." *dare you*, he was about to say.

She picked up on it, flustered: "I'm sorry, I—"

"No, wait. It's all right." Futzy approached Miss Phipps, her look of fright softening at his reassurance. "That's her. Yes. That's my little girl. My Kitty."

"She's beautiful."

"She is," he said. "She was."

Miss Phipps sensed the rawness in his voice. She set the picture facedown in its drawer, which she closed. Her eyes glowed with compassion. Her body moved closer.

"Now wait a minute," he said.

Something was blossoming in her eyes, behind those prim frames.

"I don't *want* to wait any more," she said.

Futzy took in her ache, her mouse-beauty, the look he had always assumed meant nothing more than bland respect. Now, as she came near, that look softened into something else, something warm and inviting.

"You're . . . I'm—"

She surged toward him, a velvet dream, her lobebag angling as her head tilted in. A tight lipline puffed and swelled and touched his mouth, tasty, warm, moistening beneath the flicker of her tonguetip.

Some women came at you, when the moment finally arrived for such a bold move, tentatively, their hips seemingly dead, their torsos not much better. Adora Phipps wasn't like that.

Her whole body, behind its deceptive folds of old-lady velvet, exuded urgency, pushing against him in a solid wave of *give me, give me*.

Futzy's hands glided past her waist to her rump. The fabric slid over naked curves of flesh.

No undergarments.

Adora broke the kiss and hugged him fiercely, grinding herself into him.

"I don't think we should—"

"Shut up, you!" she said, forcing his lips open with hers, tonguing him as her hands snaked below his belt and found his zipper. The mousy little English teacher, bold as any whore, had backed him up against his desk.

His hands rose and clutched as they bunched up vast accumulations of velvet, shoving them up her body like rolls of hippo fat, gathering more and more of the stuff to make them heavier still.

His organ popped out into Adora's hand, just that little bit longer and fatter for the Tuffskin he had beefed himself up with.

She eased him back. Futzy felt hem, naked thighs, and perfectly cuppable buttocks, her cleft moist and jesus christ warm and wondrous where his fingers brushed it.

Something, a pen set, jabbed against his coat. Then it gave way, propelled off the front of the desk to smash against the floor.

Adora pillowed Futzy's head on an unabridged dictionary and climbed aboard him, an animal, this prudish covert brainy genius thrusting her taut love-sleeve down about him, deep to the balls, riding him, her hips in sexy sway, her face hypnotic, her eyelids shut, a sheen of lovesweat even now beginning to glow upon her brow.

Futzy swam in revelation.

Opaque encounters now came clear, the many odd looks she had given him: her love for him, and, far stranger, his love for her.

He wanted her, he needed her, he adored her.

In a matchless conjoining of flesh, Adora rode him, her balance precarious but for Futzy's hold upon her waist. He worried about her knees, a hard polished glass surface to either side of the blotter. But Adora, consumed in ecstasy, paid them no mind. She muffle-moaned into his mouth, getting off, her hip thrusts and her fierce climax bringing him off as well.

Into her sweet waiting lovewomb, Futzy arced his seed, the pair's urgency fueled by years of denial and by what was transpiring in the gym.

Adora collapsed upon him, exhausted, laughing aloud. He fancied the glass top, stretched almost to shattering, might give way beneath them.

"Whew."

"No kidding," he said. "I think you found the gun."

"I most assuredly did." Her eyes glistened above their shared laughter.

He looked at her. "You're my wife!"

"I don't think so."

"No, I mean *really* you are. We're in a tight spot—"

"Well *you* certainly are." She gave his cock a vulval squeeze.

"—we, unnngh, I mean there's no time for bullshit at a time like this. We could die at any moment. You and me are crazy to be doing this and I love it. I love *you*. In the morning, if we're still alive, I'm reclaiming my life, I'm putting my foot down, I'm ordering the sorry bitches I married to pack up and get out."

"They've hurt you," she said. "I've heard stories."

"I let them do it. I needed it. I don't need it any more." It was true. Adora had broken a logjam in him, one that had robbed him of years of happiness.

Right now, however, he had a school full of terrified students to save. *They may be shits*, thought Futzy, *but they're all mine.* Eventually the little savages would throw off their inanities and insensitivities, straighten the warps in their warped little noggins, and grow into the imperfect adults we've somehow managed, the rest of us, to become.

"I love you, Futzy."

"I love you too, my sweet Adora Phipps." He gave her a quick kiss. "We've got to go." She nodded. "But this isn't over. This has only begun, you understand?"

"I do."

A humming kicked on. The service elevator on the far side of the wall was in operation. During school hours, a host of sounds masked it. But here, at night, with the throb of music no longer pounding in the gym, the elevator's hum could not be mistaken.

They heard its door open.

Something rumbled out, into the hallway, just outside the principal's office.

Futzy helped Adora off, the flesh that joined them reluctant to let go. The snubnose lay in the middle drawer. He drew it out, moving swiftly and soundlessly to the door.

Adora swayed behind him.

Get back, he motioned. Then he yanked the door open.

The stench of death assaulted them.

A clothesrack. A confused tangle of limbs, oddly bent, more flesh than went with two bodies.

Then Adora gasped and Futzy resolved what he was seeing.

Not two but four bodies.

The zipper-mouthed boys zipped together, clothed and bloody.

And the girls who went crazy over them, naked, broken-limbed, somehow joined at the crotch. Bloody gleams of zipper. The rumors about them were true.

Adora gripped him from behind. She bit his shoulder through a thickness of suitcoat, saying nothing. Then her sobs took on volume, and the depth of her fright set his own mood plunging.

Matthew Megrim had never been the designated slasher. But he knew, as did most teachers, the location of the unassuming, vine-hidden, slightly rundown garage a block east of school.

It was tucked into a quiet residential alley. A punch code that ought to have changed each year, but never did, secured the garage. The teachers knew it and kept it secret to avoid the inevitable student pranks.

Rolling down his window, Matthew punched in FUTZYB. The garage door opened. His mind dwelt on the unknown slasher, on his daughter, and on his drowned wives, fluxidermed in the vestibule of his home.

Cam and Arly's death had been terrible and swift, an act of God.

Tweed's death, if indeed it had happened, would be a perversion, the assumption of godlike power by mere mortals.

Inside, a bend of lights lit a ramp that corkscrewed down out of sight. To hell with the law, thought Matthew, and drove ahead. In the rearview mirror, as his descent began, the garage door rumbled shut.

The dirge once more filled his mouth, wordless, full of ire and regret, an opera hero, treacherously murdered, gone down to death. The song, as did his mind, danced with fire. Someone must pay, it said. Wrongful death must not go unpunished.

But hope burned strong as well.

On the phone, the woman's voice had spoken of possible salvation, as if she, whoever she might be, would do her best to stop it.

Matthew had passed the school, its skull-flag flapping in the night breeze.

185

Now, parallel fluorescent lights led the way down the ramp, affixed where the damp gray cement walls met cement ceiling. A slow steady half-block of driving drew his car beneath Corundum High.

The ramp widened onto the slasher's parking area. There sat a bulky powder-blue car waiting for its owner.

Whose was it?

On school days, Matthew tended to arrive early and leave late. So his knowledge of other teachers' vehicles was spotty.

No time to rummage. It would be clear once he met the slasher, and there'd be only one such roaming the backways.

Matthew parked beside the powder-blue car, yanked up on his handbrake, and killed the engine.

"I'll *get* them," he hummed fiercely beneath his breath, "I'll *get* them."

On the driver's side of the slasher's car, in harsh light, stood an elevator.

What a joyless grimy hellhole this was. It ought to have been more inviting, a dark version of the faculty lounge perhaps.

What was he thinking?

More societal indoctrination. Years of it drummed into him, into them all.

They ought rather to shut *down* this vile place, bulldoze earth into it, strike flat the garage, close off the backways at school, close off all backways everywhere at every last high school in the Demented States of America.

It was nothing short of barbaric, this ritual slaughter of the young.

Matthew stared at the hatchet on the passenger seat. Fool thing wouldn't be needed. The anger had drained from him, leaving urgency, yes, and regret. What was done was done, though he much feared what that might be.

Leaving his car, he approached the elevator, its metal surface scarred and dinged red with age. He punched a battered silver button.

Nothing.

He tried it again, held it down.

Something connected. Motor sounds, rumblings from above. Would they betray his coming?

What did it matter?

He would find the slasher, verify the phone lady's story, milk his colleague—assuming said colleague hadn't died at Dex's hand—for details about Tweed's murder, details he would then use to shame the promgoers.

There would be no animosity, hard feelings, nor thirst for revenge against the one chosen to carry out the slash. That was an impersonal task. An honor. One did the deed, then let it fade into collective memory. To some, it was a revered act of heroism.

To others, it was a scandal.

Krantor Berryman, the earth science teacher, had been routinely shunned for years.

He had been chosen once.

Rather than take part in what he called the country's shame, he had paid his fine and served a year in prison.

Now, Matthew, as the elevator door opened and a blast of rank air billowed forth, vowed to join forces with poor Berryman.

He had gone along with the others, shunning the outspoken anti, like the rest. But all that, he vowed, would change.

Do it, thought Matthew, the sound of those words trumpeting in his ears like a clarion call.

New waves of anxiety about Tweed flooded him as he ducked into the elevator and punched for ascent.

17
Darkness Descends

As she left on her assigned search for the janitor, Delia Gaskin met Brest and Trilby Donner heading for the gym.

Her longed-for lovers.

Pill clung to Trilby. the little girl's tear-stained face, blanched to the lobes, was scooped hollow. She seemed to have staggered off a rollercoaster, vowing never to ride one again.

"What is it?" asked Delia, laying a concerned hand on Brest's arm.

"She'll be okay," said Brest. "Trilby and I thought Pill would be safe in the faculty lounge. She heard Pesky and Flense being slaughtered. She even saw part of it through a crack in the closet door."

Concern washed through Delia. "Does she need to lie down? There's a nice comfy bed in the dispensary."

"Do you want to, honey?" Trilby asked.

Pill shook her head decisively. She gripped her mommy's waist tighter than ever.

There would be no chance, thought Delia, to do her nurse number on the frightened child.

Not yet anyway.

"The poor girl's really upset," Delia said. "Did she get a good look at the slasher?"

"Not from what we can tell," replied Brest. "Just a lot of noise and voices, a knife flashing by, an arm in a dark blue sleeve."

"Sounds like Gerber Waddell."

"That's what we're starting to think. We're wondering if maybe the surgeons missed one small chunk of brain and his dormant urges are just now catching up with him. He's reverting to what he was."

"Futzy sent me to find him and get him to turn the gym lights up full. Sounds like you two haven't seen him."

"Not a sign," said Trilby, Pill staring up at Delia from her mommy's waist. "I haven't seen him all night."

"Well, I guess I'll check the band room."

"Be careful," said Brest, glints of lust peering through her concern.

"Don't worry. I'm stronger than I look." Delia smiled grimly and left them.

Glancing back, she saw Bix come up to them, his gaze drawn to the child, then shooting along the hallway toward her.

Fucking nuisance. The one damned thing that stood between her and his wives.

She reached the band room door and tossed another glance backward. There was Bix, still staring at her as his hand caressed the back of his child's head.

He would come after her. Delia could sense it. He would make his move.

And she would make hers.

She pushed open the door. The shadows were darker in here, a lone dim lightbulb casting much of the room into obscurity. It was a decidedly creepy place, what with the tall gray semicircle of doors, each concealing instruments and music stands. And possibly more.

It was quiet here too. The stillness of a volcano readying to erupt.

No janitor of course. Delia had known she wouldn't find Gerber here. But she supposed she ought to try a few doors, if only to go through the motions.

A noise behind her.

Big surprise: Bix Donner walked in.

She hoped he had been circumspect.

"Hi, there." Almost a whisper in church. "Mind some company?"

"You never give up, do you?"

Bix chuckled softly. "Nope, not where a beautiful babe like you is concerned. Cupid's arrows pierce deep." He approached her, each

189

level of wood flooring groaning as he ascended.

"Did you tell your wives where you were going?"

"I told them I'd take a spin past the science labs, see if our killer shows himself. He's gotta be one sick gent, a real nutcase. But if I could come at him *mano a mano*, I'll bet I could take him."

"Heroics, huh?"

Bix shrugged. "Why not? Maybe that's the way to my Delia's heart. Unless of course . . . you'd like to give in to your little Bixie-poo right now."

He took a step closer.

Delia held her ground.

"Unless," he said, "you'd like him to kiss you right where you stand."

She sensed heat and a faint whiff of musk lifting off his body. His hungry eyes peered out of the obscurity, searchlights slashing nightfog to ribbons.

"I'll tell you what I'd like," said Delia, swaying with him, almost touching him, toying, tantalizing, turning him on. "I'd like you to find our killer—"

"Ummm hmmm?"

"Walk right up to him—"

"Ummm?" Smug smile.

"And do this."

Delia's right fist was pulled close by her side, tense as a steel spring. She had kept her tone calm and casual. Now the fist shot out, a dark thunderbolt to Bix's solar plexus, knuckled, swift, deeply damaging.

He went to his knees.

Big man brought low.

His hands fumbled at her dress.

She backed away, then turned to the standing lamp.

He would take a good few minutes to recover, but Delia saw no need to wait that long.

The lamp pole was thick and securely screwed into a heavy base, an ample supply of cord coiled beside it that snaked off to a wall socket.

Delia lifted the lamp and upended it.

The on-off pull jinked against its lightbulb like a distant tricycle bell.

This is for Trilby, she thought, swinging the lamp base against the side of Bix's head with all her might.

And this is for Brest.

The first blow had collapsed him. The second came down squarely on his face, staving it in beneath the eyes. A big iron smile punched across his nose and cheeks, a pleased dent that spewed bloody ecstasy.

Damned pole wasn't long enough to keep his blood from spattering her dress.

Stability returned to the rocking room. The one pale light, moving with her attack, had made shadows dance. Now they calmed.

The Bixmeister was stone-cold dead. Could she be sure? Delia righted the lamp, slipped out of a shoe, and pressed her foot against his chest.

No heartbeat.

She toyed with smashing the lightbulb. She would grind hot shards of glass into his eyes in the darkness she had brought on, just to be sure.

But other matters needed attending to.

And the air wasn't moving above his nostrils.

Delia slipped her foot back into the shoe and wiped down the lampstand.

Should she check on the janitor? No need. His bonds were surely as secure as the last time she had checked and the time before that.

Her heart thrilled with love.

Maybe Kitty Buttweiler had been lost to her twenty years before, Kitty and her cute date slain in sacrifice to the Ice Ghoul.

But there lay now before Delia, if she played the game right, the sweet prospect of loving Brest and Trilby Donner in secret.

She had to resist the temptation to keep on killing, as strong as that temptation was. More precisely, she needed to fit each remaining death into a grand scheme that would divert suspicion to Gerber Waddell.

She turned away from the tall doors and the false walls behind them, the myriad entrances to the backways.

No.

She would leave by the band room door.

She would run in panic down the corridors to the gym.

Had blood splashed her gown? If so, that was all to the

good. It would corroborate her story, make it more chilling, more convincing.

Behind her, as she left, all was still and silent.

"You're squeezing my hand," said Tweed.

Dex became aware how tense he was, from his shoulders to his fingers. He let go. "Sorry."

"It's okay."

He stroked the small of her back and gave a nervous laugh. "I'm just . . ." He set his punch glass on the refreshment table. "It's just that it's *hard* standing here doing nothing when some . . . some son of a bitch is—"

"I know, Dex."

"And Jiminy Jones. He was so *serious*, with his bristle mustache and his catch phrases about music and notes—you know, that stuff about the white is the paper and the black, *all* of it, is the music—and his angry baton slashes when the trumpets rushed."

"I liked Mr. Jones too."

Dex hung his head.

All his life, he had been steeling himself for this night, ready to fend off attack despite his fear, eager for the moment when the bell that meant freedom sounded at last.

Now that bell had rung and he had felt the elation of survival. Then he had discovered, as had they all, that their survival was by no means assured. Attack could come at random, from any quarter. It was no longer a controlled quantity within a measurable slice of time.

Dex turned to Tweed. "I want to be brave. But it's so hard. He could be anyone. He could be within reach of us right now."

"I know."

"I'm scared, Tweed. It's one thing to . . . how can I defend us from this? I'm just some stupid kid who . . . no, wait, I'm a *man*, I can do this thing, I can do it."

Then the tears came, and Tweed crushed her crinkly dress against his body. She hugged him fiercely, braver by far than he.

It wasn't fair.

He would lose her for being a coward. She would pretend nurture now, but when they were out of the woods, she would drop him for some other guy.

He had felt brave earlier. He had *prepped* for braveness. He had even secretly lusted to go into teaching one day, instilling in the young a love of the greater vices perhaps.

Like Jonquil Brindisi.

What moved people to do what they did? The question had always fascinated him. Besides, it would give him a shot at being the designated slasher some day, taking out bullies like Stymie Glumm or Angelo Manglebaum.

He would never tell Tweed's father that. Nor would he argue against the anti-slasher cause with him.

No. The law said Mr. Megrim was entitled to his opinion, as long as he limited himself to talk alone. In time, he would come to accept his son-in-law's differing stance on the issue.

Dex's tears began anew.

All of that was past.

"I've got to . . . to get it together."

"Dex," soothed Tweed in his ear, "let it fall apart for a while, okay? You're in my arms. You're safe here. Just let it fall apart. It'll come together soon enough."

Dex buried his sobs in her hair, the aroma of hair spray cloying but comforting.

As distraught as they all were, he didn't want his classmates to see him crying.

They would remember afterwards, when this nightmare was over. It might ruin his rep. It might condemn him and Tweed and their chosen mate to a life of poverty and scorn on the outskirts of society. Prom bravery counted for much. Tonight *might* be judged differently, but he didn't want to bank on that.

"I guess," he said, calming, "I guess I just prefer . . . you know, everything in its place."

"You do." Tweed stroked his hair. "You're that way. But tonight we've got to roll with the punches. It's tougher than we thought it would be, that's all."

"It is."

"Dex, just know that I love you and I'm with you, no matter what happens. Whoever's doing this will be caught, and killed, and torn apart. Futzy and his staff will see to that. They've *got* to, they really do. Have faith in them."

"I will," he said, wiping the tears on his tuxedo sleeve.

But inside, Dex had no faith at all in Principal Buttweiler and his staff, who, from the look on their faces, had not the slightest clue about how to bring the rogue killer to justice.

Peach had never seen anyone look as stunned as Bowser McPhee.

To tell the truth, Peach couldn't believe what was going on either.

The multiplying bodies were bad enough.

Some teacher had gone off his nut.

Eventually, she had no doubt, he would be found and futtered. A few more classmates would eat it and the school would gain some notoriety, but Peach was sure she would survive.

Death—her own, that is—was not within the realm of possibility.

Bowser was a bit more upset by the killings than she. But what really seemed to torque him out, and how could Peach blame him, was Fido's reaction.

Fido had paled and woozed—and simply walked away from her and Bowser.

Right straight to the fat chicks over yonder, a pair of mustachioed slugs pup-tented in plug-ugly, wallpaper-inspired dresses whose green and magenta blooms splashed garishly everywhere.

In-fucking-credible!

"I can't believe he *did* that," Bowser repeated. "The simpering little bastard took a hike."

"He wants to marry a couple of blimps!" The nerve of anyone rejecting her for two lard-lugging losers like Kyla Gorg and Patrice Menuci.

"He was my *guy*," said Bowser. "We were gonna be together *forever*." The poor boy was really broken up. "How's he gonna get home? What'll I tell my folks?"

Ms. Brindisi and Mr. Versailles were speaking at the mike like Academy Award presenters.

The sheriff's body had been carried to the band risers, a tarp thrown over him and the music teacher.

Peach wished they had joined the other dead folks in front of the Ice Ghoul. Putting them on the risers seemed to expand the ghoul's dominion, as though the huddle of frightened seniors between the creature and the wall behind the bandstand now fell beneath its sway.

"Whynchu take Fido aside and talk it over?"

"I don't know," said Bowser, stunned all over again. "I guess I oughta do that. But I feel like saying, Fuck it to hell and back. He's not worth it, walking away like we meant nothing to one another. We were everything, Peach, I shit you not, *everything* to one another."

"So take him aside and tell him that."

And do it, oh please God yes, she thought, do it before he touches those blubbering tent-sprawls of noxious girlflab.

"I won't," said Bowser. He gritted his teeth and flexed his fists. "I can't, but I will." But before he took his first step, the teachers at the mike were saying, "Make way for her."

Make way? Who was there to make way for?

Peach, hearing fresh rumblings ripple through the crowd, craned her neck to see.

Nurse Gaskin's bobbing head moved off to the left, her hands raised to slice through a dappled sea of bodies. Someone near Peach passed along rumors of blood on her dress.

"They're saying her dress is bloody," said Bowser.

"I hear them," said Peach.

Beneath a glisten of blue and pink and orange lights, the nurse passed through a jostle of students to the risers and the mike.

She looked shaken as she shouldered the two teachers aside and clung to the mikestand, a grasp at salvation.

"It's . . . ."

She covered the mike and spoke briefly to Mr. Versailles, then back, as distraught as Peach had ever seen anyone.

"It's the janitor. We were in the band room, me and Bix Donner."

On Peach's right, a high hoot sounded from a woman holding a little girl. The woman raised a hand to her mouth. Brest Donner, Peach's biology teacher, gripped her fiercely in her arms.

Oh yeah, Ms. Donner's wife.

"I . . . ." The nurse brushed off Jonquil Brindisi's hand.

The stains on her dress sickened Peach.

She pictured Ms. Donner's husband—this Bix guy the nurse was yammering on and on about, who had helped Mr. Dunsmore cut down the sheriff's body—being stabbed by the feeb janitor, blood from the wounds spraying upward to splash Nurse Gaskin's dress.

"I yelled at Gerber," she said. "I tried to stop him. He just kept coming at Bix. Then he swung the lampstand up and slammed it down—"

The nurse covered her mouth, her eyes hot with tears.

In an instant, Ms. Brindisi was beside her again, speaking words Peach couldn't hear.

Nurse Gaskin nodded.

A final thought occurred to her.

She dipped again to the mike: "Trilby? Brest? I'm sorry."

She almost seemed to regret her own survival.

"I've always treated the poor man well. We all have. Gerber couldn't help what he was, and what he's become again. He vanished through the band room doors into the backways. I . . ."

Her hand fumbled for a tissue in her right pocket.

That's when the lights went out.

There was a loud noise, like a big switch being thrown *ker-chunk*.

The image of Ms. Brindisi and the nurse hung in a ghostly afterglow, then wiped away to black.

Peach, fear ballooning in her like a sudden burst of fever, found Bowser's waist and clung to him.

"Jesus Christ," he said.

Peach saw the janitor coming at her from all directions, that benign wisp of a grin cracking open to reveal madness, bloodlust, a rapacious urge to kill.

A voice began, booming from the PA system.

At first, she thought it was the janitor's. But the fear that quavered in the words and their deeper pitch identified the dead sheriff, speaking no doubt under duress.

"Boys and girls," said Sheriff Blackburn's voice, "the front entrance to the school is open. You must not stay in the gym. If you stay here, you will die. I repeat—"

But the voice repeated nothing.

Peach could almost see him looking up from a scripted text, looking up to see a sudden blade come sweeping in. A rushed shoved grunt of impalement had been caught on the tape, chilling in how nearby it sounded.

Faintly, over a renewed sweep of crowd noise, Peach heard Ms. Brindisi.

"Stay where you are!"

But that was futile advice.

Peach wanted out of there that instant, and every one of her classmates wanted the same.

The babble surged.

The bodies moved her, shoved her, precisely where they all wanted to go. Screams lanced through the panic. A few seniors went down in the crush. Or maybe Gerber Waddell had swept in to slaughter them. Who could say? Peach only knew she had to escape, and fast.

The opening to the dim hallway loomed before her. She shoved the kid in front of her, *Sorry* on her lips. But she wasn't sorry at all. Nor were those in back who propelled her forward.

Above the melee, loud and distorted, a sad gentle singer from the fifties sighed, "I'm Mister Blue, wah-o-wah-ooh." Interspersed, Gerber Waddell's familiar chirp stole in, sharp and piercing: "Hi there, hi there."

"Oh my god, he's got me," shouted some frightened boy. The janitor strode among them, cutting, slashing, killing whatever got in his way.

Peach squeezed through the dim rectangular archway. A crush of bodies threatened to snap her ribs, so great was the pressure on all sides. But she made it to the corridor, holding miraculously to the back of Bowser's suitcoat.

The air cooled.

The flow of students carried her as swiftly as before, but with less threat of violence.

They would escape.

She knew they would.

She and Bowser, they'd be all right, no matter who else fell to the killer loose in the school.

The corridor still lit with its dim lights, the crowd rushed and shuffled toward freedom.

But screams arose from those who reached the front entrance first. Word rippled back, even as they pressed on, of fresh corpses awaiting them there.

Peach and Bowser rounded the corner.

Miss Phipps and the principal, ashen-faced, stood beside a grotesque clothesrack they had just wheeled in. It bore four broken bodies.

Elwood Dunsmore, the shop teacher, his face blasted and blackened by a smashed blowtorch, lay propped against the padlocked doors.

And impaled on the upraised knife-arm of a sculpted Ice Ghoul, dripping blood and water down the cold crystal of its body, were the corpses of Brandy Crowe and Flann Beckwith. A fresh icicle jutted from each eye, crazy antennae in a mad game of Cootie.

Frenzy surged in Peach.

And in the crowd.

Bowser's face looked ready to explode. "We've gotta get out of here," he yelled. Peach could hardly hear him through the din.

She grabbed his hand and together they raced off through fractures in the crowd.

Everybody had been set off, ping-pong balls and mousetraps.

Rude slams and brushes buffeted her, like the best of slap'n'smack dancing, only far more hectic and nowhere near as fun.

They would break free, she and Bowser.

There *had* to be a way out.

And they'd find it, her classmates be damned.

A mad scurry filled every glance she threw.

They were *all* out for survival, thought Peach. And not one of them would survive.

PART FOUR
Catching the Ice Ghoul

"Most people have ears, but few have judgment; tickle those ears, and depend upon it, you will catch their judgments, such as they are."
  —Lord Chesterfield

"Trust not one night's ice."
  —George Herbert

18
Fear and Weapons

In the spiffy outfits the State had given them for their delivery into Zane Fronemeyer's hands, Bray felt—as they explored Corundum High's backways—like a prince with his princess passing through the scullery, the cramped living quarters of the poor.

Winnie's gown snagged on a nail and ripped.

The backways were ill-lit and dank, choked with spiderwebs and the threat of rats. The air was close and confining, hot enough to make Bray wish his tux were made of lighter stuff.

"Where are we?" asked Winnie.

"Let's see," Bray said, moving toward the next dim lightbulb, waist-high on his right.

Randomly placed along the walls, the bulbs were of minimal wattage. They glowed rather than shone. That and faint copying made the map barely readable, even when it was held inches from the light.

The designated slasher clearly needed a tiny flashlight. Bray supposed that whoever had killed Fronemeyer had taken one from the packet.

Why hadn't he taken the map? Perhaps he was already acquainted with the backways, a slasher from years past.

"I think we're beyond the auditorium. We've dipped under the corridor on the east. That way," Bray gestured right, "is the band room. See how it curves off?"

"I'll take your word for it. What's over there?"

"Cafeteria, I think. Can't tell though if it's the dining area or the kitchen."

Truth was, they could be completely turned around. Disorientation crowded all about and may already have claimed them. An adventure that had begun with confidence, as they slipped through a panel by the auditorium, now felt full of uncertainty and trepidation.

"Let's peek out and see."

"What if there's someone there? A couple of seniors?" he asked.

"What *if?*" Winnie was exasperated.

"They see us, they think we're behind the killings, a crazed student body somehow gets us, it's all over."

"Christ, Bray," she said, "do you expect to spend the rest of your life in here?"

"It's just safer, that's all. It's the prudent thing to do. He's in here somewhere, I know it."

"You're a fucking wimp."

"We'll find him. Or he'll find us." We'll fight him and kill him, he thought. "You can talk to him, you're good at that."

"That's why you jumped your prom. That's why you ran."

"You can reason with him, bring the poor guy out into the public spotlight like you want to."

"You've got no guts," she said. "I say we have a look." Even in insulting him, she was beautiful.

No way was their friendly slasher going to hold still for a dollop of argument. It was kill or be killed. That's what it would come down to.

And he'd have to save Winnie. He'd have to rip the bastard's guts out, to keep Winnie from harm and to prove to her he was no coward.

"You're wrong about me," he said.

"If only."

"Okay, let's have a look."

The panels were clearly marked, bold and readable. A large white number, in this case a 975, was painted above the release.

Bray pressed the release and the panel slid open. Cooler air and indirect light rushed in, sudden unexpected friends.

No one there.

He breathed easier.

"Bunch of tables," said Winnie behind him.

"Yes."

Six chairs were upturned on each tabletop, their metal legs like TV antennas aligned, roof after roof. Bray peered out, his thumb keeping the panel retracted.

Somewhere in the distance arose a muffled hubbub. But other than pillows against the walls and posterboard with student numbers inscribed, the cafeteria was empty.

Winnie shouldered him aside, angling for a clearer view. Her body was warm and wonderful beside him. "I guess this shows you can read a map, at least," she said.

Bray had a sudden image of someone creeping up on them in the narrow passageway, behind their backs, a knife raised, ready to fall.

"What is it?" Winnie asked.

He realized he had tensed.

"Nothing," he said.

But he drew back and Winnie came with him. He let the panel shut with a faint whoosh.

It was damned dark in here. The dank heat, woody as a fresh pine box, crept in around them again.

Bray wished his eyes would adapt more quickly to the darkness. But even when the faint outlines of the backways resolved themselves, he had the persistent feeling that someone or something held them in its gaze, waiting, waiting to rush them or to strike as they passed by.

"This is hopeless," said Winnie. "It's an endless maze. He could be anywhere. Maybe even gone home by now."

Winnie was full of surprises, thought Bray. Fired up one moment, now suddenly discouraged.

"Nope, our killer's still here," he said. "I can feel it."

"Maybe."

"No maybes. He's not finished. Sooner or later, we'll meet him. And somehow we'll stop him."

"We'll talk him down. Coax the fight out of him," she said, more assured.

"You got it," said Bray, imagining a quick tussle with an unknown assailant, tackling him from the darkness, a flashing blade, Bray's hand seizing a descending wrist to keep death at bay.

It could come at any time, from any place.

Or the knife blade might slip into them now, now, with no chance to fight back.

No.

He couldn't afford to think that way.

They'd be prepared, they'd have their chance.

He and Winnie would subdue him, slay him or deliver him up to Corundum High's freaked-out kids and faculty. Winnie would have her media moments of glory and persuasion. And one way or another, society would welcome them back into its embrace, where they could begin a life together, unharassed and free.

"All right," said Winnie with renewed resolve. "What are we waiting for? Let's press on."

"Why not," he said.

And on they pressed.

Kyla had never seen Patrice so worked up, so turned on by Fido's sudden interest in them and off by the dangers that surrounded them.

Thank God that *she* at least had kept her wits about her.

To be sure, she tickled her fancy with the riotous times that awaited their threesome, should they be lucky enough to survive prom night. But survival came first in Kyla's book, and it fell to her to figure out how to assure it.

"Keep up, you two," she said.

Behind her, a sequoia to a sapling, Patrice hugged Fido to her and hurried along, her eyes impossibly large with fright.

They had left most of the kids by the front entrance, where a futile attempt was underway to ram open the heavily reinforced doors.

Ranks of peach-colored lockers marched by on either side, any one of them ready to explode into violence. Kyla kept them moving down the center of this gauntlet, their ultimate destination Lily Foddereau's butchery wing in the back part of the school.

The least they could do was to arm themselves with *real* cleavers, not the futtering ones, sharp but small, that hung from everyone's belt.

"Kyla, I'm scared," whined Patrice. It had become an annoying mantra, as if admitting her fear could ward off the thing that frightened her.

Kyla's cowardly lover didn't even expect an answer. But Fido, who had settled into a litany of reassurance, piped up: "We'll be fine, honey lamb. He won't get us."

Kyla understood they were both stressed to the max. But so was she.

And she didn't like how it felt when the three of them were under pressure. If indeed they survived the night, she thought there was a good chance their relationship wouldn't.

Kyla held open the glass door to the butchery wing, nose-wrinkling whiffs of gore lifting off the tile and wood as they passed. She followed after Patrice and Fido.

The stench of slaughter raised her hackles.

Curiously, it comforted her as well.

Very few students were roaming these blood-encrusted halls. Kyla guessed it was because butchery, the favorite subject of few, was far too near the night's events.

Patrice, on the other hand, loved it.

As did she.

The two of them had in fact first met, first touched eyes, over the bloody spews of a lopped chicken head. Their love, such as it was, had grown out of the slaughter of pigs and lambs and wide-eyed cattle, neck slice, abrupt collapse of unsteady legs. They had a history here, she and Patrice Menuci.

"I don't like this," said Fido.

Maybe, thought Kyla, Fido were best to have remained a fantasy. The reality was beginning to wear thin.

"It's okay, baby," Patrice simpered back. "We'll get us some steel and hole up somewhere until they rescue us."

"In here," Kyla said.

Over many years, mists of gore, especially during finals week, had turned the grout between the tiles from tan to rust. Ditto the hinges of the doors. This door's pattern of bloodspray was nearly invisible, so much a part of the woodgrain had it become.

They slipped through.

A wall of cutlery winked at them from behind Miss Smiling-Bitch Foddereau's chopping block. On the pegboard, chalked outlines surrounded each tool.

There were missing knives. But then a few knives had *always* been missing, gone astray over years of instruction and never replaced.

"Take two each," said Kyla.

She reached her heavy arms upward for her favorite hackers and hewers, huffing from the exertion. Kyla loved the heft of them, their shaped grips and perfect balance.

Fido and Patrice obeyed, laying hands on the pegboard as if it were a prayer wall and they were penitents. They came away clutching the handles of honed steel.

"What now?" Patrice asked.

She held two long carving knives, severed leg ends of a gleaming insect.

Fido had found a pair of meat cleavers.

Kyla looked at Fido and Patrice. Bedroom longings rose in her at the sextuple threat of violence that filled their fists.

In the meaty air, soft wafts of lust blew past her nostrils.

If this be life, thought Kyla, let it last forever.

Outside the band room door, Trilby hugged her little girl. Delia Gaskin had taken Brest inside to view Bix's body. Soon she would come out for Trilby.

Pill had stopped talking altogether.

Trilby thought she had seen Pill at her most frightened. But her father's death, announced so vividly at the bandstand by Delia, had driven her deeper into herself. She had shut down, drawn in tighter, her skin almost bloodless, near as white as meringue.

"It's okay, Pill," she said.

But it wasn't.

The door opened.

Delia and Brest emerged arm in arm. Brest's eyes were moist. She gave Trilby a dour look.

It seemed out of place, since Brest had, many years before, confided having fallen out of love with their husband. But even withered feelings of affection tend to sink their hooks deep into one's heart, early and enduring.

"Pill?" The girl clung to her, trying to bury herself in her mother's body. "Stay with Brest now. I need to leave you for just a little while."

Pill's fingernails deepened uncomfortably, crab claws at Trilby's back. The child moaned.

It was unbearable.

Trilby wanted to embrace her always. But she needed to see Bix in death's grip, needed the grim closure it would provide.

Brest knelt and tried to pry their daughter free. Pill's moan became a whine, then a keening.

"There, there," Trilby soothed.

Pill was a sight. A shattered child who couldn't bear, for one second, the denial of her mother's embrace.

But at last, the three of them overcame her resistance, and like a magnet giving up one steel surface for another, she lunged for Brest, almost knocking her over with the zeal of her need.

Brest awkwardly patted Pill's back, starting several times to speak but saying nothing.

Delia prompted Trilby to rise. How kind and full of caring she is, Trilby thought.

Inside the band room, the air was rank with warring odors of death.

Bix's bowels had emptied. The night before, Brest had made spaghetti. From years of marriage, Trilby knew how spaghetti altered Bix's bathroom smells. That smell now infused the band room, stenchy, homey, strangely comforting yet out of place.

Her eyes fixed on his corpse.

Bix lay there like a tosser-and-turner in a mattress ad. He had grown a little chubby around the waist as Pill advanced beyond toddlerdom.

His frilled shirt was wrenched out of his cummerbund. Trilby could see his navel and the wiry black hairs that surrounded it. The skin at his paunch did not move.

One never noticed a motion so perpetual until it ceased.

No inhale at all. No exhale.

It was maddening.

It terrified her.

Her breath caught, refusing to release. She raised a hand to her mouth.

Delia Gaskin hugged her from the side. "You okay?" she asked.

Trilby nodded. She suffered Delia's embrace, leaning on her for support.

Bix's face was an outrage.

His skull was broken and bashed. The skin at his exposed ear had shifted, a fallen fracture of shale. Blood spilled from that fracture.

His nose, crushed—the bone snapped upward at an obscene angle—sat atop a deep spewed gash, the punch of a steel fist having left moist wrinkles in the crater-edges of his flesh.

His skin had been rent asunder, as if the killer had wanted to see the man beneath the face, the secret Bix that Trilby had always suspected was there. But all that showed was inert muscle and bone.

Trilby felt faint.

But she could not tear her eyes away.

The next thing she knew, she was sitting on the edge of one of the band room's rising levels, something sharp and bitter broken under her nose. She reared back and felt Delia's arms supporting her.

"Steady, now," the nurse said.

"I'm okay," she tried to say.

She took a deep breath and closed her eyes. Her face seized up in a cry. On the inhale, she smelled her husband's corpse behind her. Then the tears subsided.

Delia offered her a tissue.

Trilby blew her nose and daubed the edges of her eyes. "You're so kind," she said. Poor lonely woman. Poor Delia.

Brest had been after her to start an affair with Delia. She had heart. Depth of character. She really cared, not just in a nursely way. It was more genuine than that.

Society called same-sex threesomes perverse.

What did society know of such things?

It wouldn't be perverse, not in the least. It would feel good and natural.

Now was hardly the time for it, but Trilby felt the nub inside her, the pull she hadn't quite felt before, the feeling Brest had, with far too much zeal, urged upon her.

Its eventuality lay before her.

"Help me out the door?" she said, her words faint.

"Of course," came Delia's concerned voice.

And the nurse's firm grip, surprisingly strong in one so trim and feminine, came about Trilby.

She rose to her feet.

19

At the Mercy of the Ice Ghoul

Life was such a bitch, Sandy thought as she followed Cobra and Rocky along the second floor corridor.

Things had been thrown topsy-turvy.

There were rules. If you obeyed them, everything went fine for you. Yet, somehow—

(Just one crazy. Keep reminding yourself. It's one wacked-out maniac.)

—the rules had been thrown out the window. No rule book at all.

Waiting in the boys' locker room, Sandy and Rocky had thought themselves immune. Designated slashers never laid a *finger* on potential prom royalty. But now? Sandy shuddered. They hadn't been safe at all. Flann and Brandy had bitten it in the refrigeration room. Rival nominees. Then an exempt tender had been killed, for the love of Christ. No one was safe from the rogue janitor.

It put her entire world in doubt.

Striding alongside Rocky, Cobra reached back an index finger, hooked it into her cleavage, and pulled Sandy forward as though she were wearing a harness.

"Come on, bitch, keep up," he said, nearly pulling her off her pumps. "The Ice Ghoul'll getcha if you don't."

Cobra chuckled, digging the weirdness around them. The turn of events had confusedly torqued Rocky. Her too. But their new boyfriend seemed to be getting way the heck into it.

Crazy strength.

When Peach jilted him, they had waifed the poor dejected creep in. Then the killings began to multiply, the world tilt into Cobra's sullen territory. Now Mister Bigshot Heel-Clicking Hood was steering the threesome wherever he liked.

Did that concern her?

She had no idea.

Nothing made sense but survival and Sandy's mind could only hold to that one overriding idea. There'd be time later to sort out their lives.

Twice they had counterclockwised the vast square that was the second floor hallway. Twice they had passed the same damned lockers and clocks, the same damned classrooms where she had been forced to endure Home Ec and Art and Algebra and Spanish and the ill-named "teachers" who had inflicted all of that boring crap on her.

Visions of hell.

Sandy guessed that Cobra's strategy, if he had one, was to keep going, to stay within the maundering crowd and steer clear of doorways.

He released her and lit up a cigarette, never stopping, moving forward in a confident stride.

"Hey," said Rocky, "you can't smoke in here."

"What're they gonna do?" Cobra asked with a sneer. "Kill me?"

"No, but they might expel you."

Cobra, bemused, flashed Sandy a look of exasperation. "I'll take my chances, jocko."

Rocky pointed. "There's Mr. Buttweiler's office."

"I'm acquainted with it," said Cobra.

Some kids shuffled through the principal's door, their chosen place of refuge. Had he left it unlocked? Or had the janitor's key opened it as a lure?

"Our next set of corpses."

"Come on, Cobra," said Sandy. "Don't joke about it."

"Who's joking? Those dweebs are dead."

Bloodslicks stained the tile floor outside Futzy's office. Drippings from the zippermouths. Sandy had been royally grossed out by what the killer had done—not to mention what the zipheads *themselves* had done—to their bodies.

"Can we settle someplace?" she complained.

"Good idea," said Rocky.

"No way." Cobra nixed it. His heels clacked as they walked. "Shut your traps a sec and let me think." Fumes drifted past his ears. "I got it!"

Abruptly he veered off.

They followed.

There would be time, when this was over, to right the balance. For now it was okay with her to let Cobra set the agenda.

Humming a soft song of grim determination, Matthew Megrim pressed on through the backways.

Ten minutes before, he had stepped off the elevator; it felt as if an eternity had passed.

He'd had a similar feeling years before, descending a tower of spiral stone steps in an ancient cathedral. The sameness of what passed before his eyes, then and now, drew him into a sort of circular time, his footsteps seeming not to advance him at all.

In the obscurity ahead, Matthew thought he saw a flash of white, the distant rustle of bunched cloth. An organdy dress?

He hurried onward, suppressing the urge to call out. No need to alert the slasher or put him or her on the defensive.

By the time he had gained the bend where the vision had appeared, it was gone.

Still, he pressed on more hurriedly, losing his way but trusting to luck to bring him at last into the presence of Tweed's killer.

Earlier, he had attained the walkways above the gym, a dizzying drop downward past balloons and crepe hangings and a flat-browed Ice Ghoul.

Why, he wondered, was the gym without lights? And it was so quiet, as though everyone had fled elsewhere. The only illumination came from bulbs around him, light-hoarders as always, and from the doors to the backways below.

Matthew's fancy strained downward, a platter of corpses trying to resolve itself before the Ice Ghoul.

Were there any bodies lying there at all? He couldn't tell. One moment, there were none. The next? Two, or three, or four. Inert lumps of black on black that might just as well be tricks of the air.

He thought to call out but felt it would be useless. There was no one down there to answer. And if there were, they'd know he was breaking the law and have him arrested.

Instead, he had made his way along the narrow path, crawling, feeling the smooth edges with his outstretched fingers, then taking laddered steps down into the backways again. Their familiar cloy and hug had seemed comforting for a moment. But quickly, they became once more a bewildering and hopeless maze.

The tune that circled in Matthew's head was low and ominous. Limited in scope. The noble revenge of "I'll *get* them, I'll *get* them" had been replaced with a cavelike chant in Latinate grumbles.

It didn't echo.

Even if he had let it out full instead of hoarding it inside his mouth, it wouldn't have echoed.

The close, airless wood and stone of the backways absorbed all sound, closing over it like rent skin healing after a flurry of welt-wounds. Matthew felt as if he were in a diving bell, cut off and confined, steeped in his surroundings but observing apart from them.

Into this cauldron of physical and temporal disorientation fell his hopes and fears about Tweed. One moment, his daughter was already dead and he was embarked on a fool's errand. The next, she had survived and the two of them, aided by an anti-slasher groundswell, would turn this nation around.

They were only two people.

But sometimes you got lucky. Sometimes, forces came together like waves, and you rode them and fed them until things changed.

Yes, and sometimes idiots deluded themselves and fell off the deep end into quixotic crusades. Naked emperors on parade they were, thinking they were arrayed in the finest cloth, hearing not the hoots of the mob but high hosannahs.

Something caught Matthew's eye. A shadow of darkness straight ahead roiled with movement.

Once one saw a *real* being in this impossible obscurity, one's imaginings dropped away as obvious frauds.

This vision was distant, the slow roll of a back perhaps, dark restlessness upon darkness, a form reaching for existence as it passed weak bulbs, then lapsing again into nothingness.

But always a restless motion forward.

Matthew stalked it, thinking he was gaining on it, thinking it had disappeared into the gloom, then catching sight of it once more.

An excitement grew in him, the soft melody acquiring an upbeat rhythm in its steady movement onward.

Tweed didn't like leaving Dex in the hallway. But she had to pee and this *was* the girls' room.

Inside, she found the lights on full. That was a relief. No one here, she thought.

But as she rounded a baffle, an ankle came into view, a dress hem, telltale red slut-heels. And there was Peach the floozy, leaning against Bowser McPhee.

"Hey, come on, you guys," Tweed said. "Boys don't belong in here."

The back of Bowser's dark combed head, an odd warped plane of skin and hair, reflected in the mirror. His coatback creased like twists of milk against the shiny jut of a sink. Dreamy-eyed, he wallowed in bliss.

"Buzz off, Tweediebird," said Peach. "Me and him are sticking together for protection."

Bowser said, "Maybe I should—"

"Hey, baby," said Peach, rubbing herself against him, "we're just getting started. Don't you move a muscle. Not *this* one anyway." Her hand slid down along his zipper, gripping the cream-white bulge below.

"Sure, cool, why not?" said Tweed, not trying to disguise her disgust. She flounced to the nearest stall, went in, and locked the door.

Let them suck lobe. Let them strip and do it right there on the scuzzy tile floor, within reach of sink pipes, scurries of hair, and decades of impacted scum no janitor's mop would ever touch.

Tweed didn't care.

Peach was a slut and Bowser was bratty and obnoxious. Fuck 'em, she thought, fuck 'em both to hell and back.

She set her purse on the silver shelf and rustled her gown and panties this way and that, planting her naked bottom on the commode's cool seat. She leaned forward intently. Her rustlings fell away. In their place, low moans and groans assaulted her ears.

Her bladder refused to cooperate.

Jesus, at a time like this!

Dex was waiting outside in the hallway, skittish as a colt, while her dad fretted at home.

By all report, the backs of restroom stalls were solid. But what if this one wasn't?

An insane janitor could do whatever he liked. He could prepare for years, breaking every rule in the book just like he'd broken a bunch tonight.

Then there was Bowser and Peach.

Sure, they were into each other. That much their ugly gruntings made clear.

But Tweed bet they each had half an ear on her, picturing her bare-bummed, waiting for that first quick splash of liquid on liquid, then a full stream.

The seconds crept by.

Nothing.

Nothing.

Soon they would notice.

They would stop what they were doing and giggle. Peach would chime in with a crude remark and Tweed's bladder muscle would seize up tighter than ever.

The pressure mounted, but the dam refused to burst. Come on, she thought, come on.

Think of something else. Let the body take over. The past hour's killings came welling up: blood, icicles, Sheriff Blackburn dropping like a sack of flour.

Strangely enough, for all his prim stiffness while he lived, it was the death of Jiminy Jones that prompted much of Tweed's shock. Short in stature, an imitative trumpet player, Mr. Jones nonetheless displayed always an infectious love of music, a love that had inspired her and Dex, that made them reach beyond the norm in their playing and in what they listened to.

She couldn't believe Mr. Jones was dead, his corpse tarped upon the risers he would no longer break down or set up. His short fat arms would no longer wave a baton at them. His tinny dictator's voice would no longer bark, "Don't *rush*, don't *rush*," in time to the strict beat he heard in his head.

Tweed's bladder let go.

Thoughts of Peach and Bowser came rushing in. But the process had been set in motion, a steady stream that would go to completion.

Did she detect any increase in their moans, anything to signal an untoward interest in her bodily functions?

None.

Surely, it had all been in her head. As usual, she had been too damned self-conscious. Her father had made a Broadway show tune out of it, even softshoeing to it and brandishing an imaginary cane and straw boater. "Get out of your head," he had sung, "and into my heart, bah-pitty bah-bah bah-pitty bah-bah-*bah*."

Tweed wiped, stood, adjusted her prom dress, and flushed.

When she emerged from the stall, she spied Bowser's white sleeve, the gold cufflink, where his right hand had disappeared in a flurry of red frills hiked high up on Peach's stockinged outer thigh.

Tweed couldn't see what Peach's hand was up to. But from her arm movements and Bowser's muffled *ung ung* where their lips met, it was easy to guess. He was so turned on that even his friendship lobe appeared to blush and swell.

Tweed pretended nonchalance.

Standing at the sink next to them, she took out a tube of lipstick, leaning forward to apply it. Smart pert babe in the mirror.

She appeared untouched by the horrors around her. But she wasn't. You couldn't tell anything from a person's outer show.

Fingers fell on Tweed's waist.

She froze.

It was Peach's free hand, caressing clumsily, working its way down the curve of her butt.

"What do you think you're doing?" asked Tweed, moving abruptly left so that the hand withdrew as from an oven burn.

Peach turned upon Bowser's lips, speaking through his mindless unfocused barrage of guppy kisses. "You *want* us, Miss Prissy Perfect. It's the end of the world. Join in, indulge your whims, share the fun."

Tweed said, "Why don't you go find Cobra? Or Fido?" She put a spin on it. I've got Dex, she was saying. You two creeps have dumped your boyfriends like noseblown kleenex.

"You're here," Peach said. "They're not. Bowser's hard, I'm

wet, and you look pretty tasty. Doesn't she, Bowser, sweetie?"

"Arf, arf," he said, giving Tweed a dark, zitful leer.

Tweed glared. "Not interested."

She looked back at herself in the mirror.

One last touchup.

Somewhere nearby, she had the sudden sense of . . . something awful.

She couldn't pinpoint it.

It felt all-surrounding, as if the mirror's reflexiveness threw off her instincts, her fight-or-flight response.

"Fine," said Peach. "Be that way, bitch."

Tweed blushed, warm from the insult but also reacting to something else. There was something very wrong here, a thing more terrible for being undefined and out of reach.

An image of Dex waiting in the corridor came to her. She had to get back to him. She had to be sure he was all right.

Tweed stuffed her lipstick in her purse, then glanced over. Bowser McPhee, staring at her, was fingering the slut's lobebag, tugging it down, down, down, not intending to stop, not *being* stopped by his new lover. It slipped lower, then fell to the floor, sweet aroused girlflesh hanging there naked and exposed.

The sight thrilled Tweed.

She was dumbstruck, frozen where she stood, wanting to be with Dex right now, wanting just as much to stay and watch, maybe even partake in the events unfolding before her.

This is crazy, thought Tweed. This is way past crazy and I oughta move, go, get out.

Right now!

Dex stood there in the hallway spooked.

Why hadn't they headed for a more heavily trafficked area, instead of these out-of-the-way restrooms?

He could stand to go himself, but the frosted glass door with BOYS etched on it was dark and foreboding. He would have to snake a hand inside it to turn on the lights.

Why were the lights off anyway?

It was a trap. Gerber Waddell waited inside, knife dripping. If Dex held really still, he could probably hear drops of blood hitting the tile floor.

Besides, what if Tweed emerged, missed him, went off by herself to look for him? She would be attacked for sure, and Dex would live his life knowing that his negligence had led to her death.

No. He would wait here. His bladder could wait too. No matter that it was spooky here and there were far too many shadows oozing up out of the age-old grime where wall met floor. No matter that things gleamed in those shadows.

He had his moves down.

He just needed to be vigilant.

Ah but what if the mad janitor was in the girls' room right now, holding his hand over Tweed's mouth and readying his blade for her throat?

Dex felt like bursting in.

But no. No sound other than a flush came from inside. No scuffles. His ears were attuned to the slightest noise, even imagined ones.

I can't trust my senses, he thought.

But there's stuff you *know* your mind is making up, and there's no mistaking the real thing when it happens.

Yeah, but by then it'll be too late.

It's the girls' room, he kept telling himself. The girls' room.

No boys allowed.

Only pervies would be interested in sneaking in. And he was no pervy. Dexter Poindexter was a straight arrow, and always would be.

It was good to be a straight arrow in a world that was falling apart. His parents said so. They told him they were proud of him for it.

Just be on the alert, he thought. Be ready to fend off attack, darting out from any doorway or any secret snap-back-able portion of any wall. Steer clear of walls.

And try not to piss your goddamn pants.

Explain *that* to the tuxedo rental place.

He laughed. Here his life was in danger, and he was worried about being embarrassed in the face of some dumb-ass clerk.

Dex checked his watch.

What was taking her so long?

Something snapped in the distance. His ears went up. Was it close by? Had it come from the restroom?

20

A White Knight Felled

Delia Gaskin slipped into her third janitor suit. There were two clean ones left, lying before her on a folding chair in the backways.

The thought of trying to tug a soiled pair of coveralls back on over her legs and up her torso appalled her. The stench of gore-soaked denim, the clammy feel of it as it slid over skin, nearly turned her stomach. At night's end, she would fling them all into the basement furnace. That would happen soon after Gerber Waddell had been thrust into the frenzied masses to be scapegoated and futtered.

Ahead of her hung two floating rectangles of light, innerlit jellyfish exhibits in a darkened aquarium. She recognized them as belonging to the ground floor restrooms in the school's northeast sector. Fluorescent light bled out of one-way mirrors above the restroom sinks, casting short swatches of light into back corridors, the wood here gone to mold, dust, and disrepair.

Each restroom was viewable from an alcove, a four-foot recess from the backways to the surface of the mirror. On Delia's first pass through this area, she had chanced upon a folding chair leaning against the alcove wall, CORUNDUM HIGH SCHOOL stenciled in white on the back.

Damned janitor had been a guilty little bugger after all, breaking legions of laws by being in the backways for other than upkeep (and precious little of *that* there had been), wanking off no doubt to flashes of girlflesh. Delia hadn't yet checked the showers in the girls' gym, but she was willing to bet that Gerber the perv had a peephole and a folding chair there as well.

She turned into the first alcove, hoping for victims. Bingo! Three of them. A girl and a guy going at it hot and heavy, right up against the sinks. And Tweed Megrim, pooching out her lips as she painted them.

Delia gripped the handle of her carving knife. This kill would be easy. A quick swing of the mirror panel and a lunge.

She told herself she ought to wrap things up soon. Have the janitor snuffed, comfort Brest and Trilby, free the rest.

But she liked setting the superior little snots a-scurrying.

She loved to terrify them, reducing smug instructors to fear and quivering, slashing the life out of yet another wretch and watching the river of panicked ants roil and boil and jump its banks, a seethe of insectual panic that empowered her after years of powerlessness and scorn.

She reached for the mirror's catch.

Behind her a voice spoke up.

Or rather it sang.

Delia nearly leaped back in fright. She bit down upon a scream. Blood pounded in her brain. As she turned, she had the wherewithal to conceal the carving knife at her side.

"Wait now," he sang, "just wait now."

There stood Matthew Megrim, history teacher and daddy to the bitch who'd been slated to die tonight. By chance, Delia had spared this man's daughter, though now she was preparing to strike the unlucky girl down in the restroom.

"Hello, Mr. Megrim," she said.

All the teachers used first names with each other and with the staff. But the staff, herself included, were expected to use titles when they addressed the faculty. It made her feel small. Tonight, she felt bigger.

Her greeting sounded a tad sardonic.

"A question," he sang. "I have a question."

Seniors loved this man, whose history lessons were always spontaneous and sung. To Delia, it seemed an affectation.

This sad sack's past had dealt him an unknown blow, one that drove him into this vocal refuge. His singing voice was smooth and beautiful. It would be a shame to silence it, but she clearly had no choice.

He was wary. Would he think she was the designated slasher? For an instant. Then he would realize that a mere nurse had no business in the backways.

In an instant he would run. Or more likely, he would stand and defend his little girl. Either way, she had to regain the advantage.

"Matthew," she said in sultry tones.

"What're you doing back here?" he sang, his notes and rich delivery starting to falter as he registered her words and her manner of speaking.

Her free left hand flew to her sexlobe and snatched off the bag. Her head tilted at a bold come-hither angle.

With thoughts of love did Delia light her eyes. But deep inside, an impulse traveled from head to hand. Her right arm rose, the steel blade as rigid as her guile was soft.

He saw it. Saw what she hid.

Observant bastard.

The teacher's resolve was swift. He tried to leap at her, to seize her attacking wrist.

But he bobbled. The forbidden sight of the nurse's sexlobe threw him.

It was enough. The honed blade sheared through his moving fingers, no stop, no averting as it swept up to cut where his shoulder met his neck.

They danced a brutal ballet.

His death leap threatened to hurl them both against the mirror. The kids, frightened off by the report, would slip out of her grasp.

She spun their axis about, even as she swept the knife across his throat. He pitched forward and she slithered behind him, gripping his hair, letting go the knife, and yanking him backward with all her might.

Matthew's neckslit grinned open.

But Delia had succeeded in slowing him to a dull soundless thud against the glass. A gush of blood sheened down his daughter's face as she put the finishing touches on her lips and headed past the necking couple.

A death wheeze burbled from Matthew Megrim's throat: melodic, rhythmic, optimistic even in the grip of excruciating pain. The poor fuck had once more saved his child, who walked oblivious out of the girls' room, flouncing away from death for the second time this evening.

Delia let his corpse collapse and retrieved the knife from where it had fallen. Not sharp enough for the neckers.

She recovered her blue chiffon lobebag and slipped it back on. From the gym bag lying beside the folding chair she drew a thick rubber mallet. Hefted it. She would stun 'em and drag 'em off to the machine shop for fun and games.

No time to waste.

Kitty Buttweiler's memory demanded far more honoring. Love by death stolen away could never be regained. But by God, that love could be revered, and she was determined to revere it.

There was nothing like human skin split wide—down to muscle, organ, bone, and marrow—to rouse the blood and focus the attention.

Delia unlatched the mirror and swung it open.

The lust bunnies, Bowser and Peach, an odd pair, separated their kissy lips and arched back to check out the noise, the cool draft, the sudden disorientation.

Delia reached over the sink, a perfect swing to her arm, and smacked the bare-lobed slut first. The fallen Peach pinned her mate, which made it a breeze to lay open his forehead. He fell silent, inert, as she had done before him.

The girl first, then the boy, Delia drew up into the alcove beside the dead teacher. With wraps of twine, she secured their wrists behind their backs.

The going was rough, the way tight.

But foot by foot, Delia dragged them along the backways, fired by thoughts of the machine shop and its possibilities for mayhem.

The restroom door swung shut behind Tweed, a rush, then a catch, slowing a foot from closure.

Dex wasn't there.

Then he emerged from the shadows. She ran to him, let him gather her into a bear hug.

"I was afraid for you," he said.

"Me too, for you," she said. "It was awful."

From the restroom came a boy's voice, lonely, hurt, and anxious. His yelps of pleasure sounded like pain.

Dex tensed.

"It's only Bowser McPhee," said Tweed. "Him and Peach. They're going at it."

The high-pitched voice fell silent, falling off its odd orgasm. Tweed imagined white ribbons of sperm jetting across the red frills of Peach's dress. The image fascinated and revolted her.

She was glad to have resisted, glad to be in Dex's arms.

A group of promgoers swept past them.

In their midst moved the old chaperones with the notched jawflesh. Arm in arm they went, their eyes aglow with perverse delight. If you shut your eyes, you could smell wilted violets.

"Where to now?" Tweed asked.

He shrugged. "Back to the dance?"

She pictured the Ice Ghoul rising out of the darkness the gym had been plunged into. "No way. I bet he's there waiting for the first stragglers to wander in."

Dex snapped his fingers. "The band room."

Not more than an hour before, her biology teacher's spouse had been killed there. His blood would be lying in fresh pools on the planking, near where the French horns sat. Moreover, the room held fond memories of Mr. Jones.

Tweed didn't want to go there.

But how likely was it that the slasher would return to the site of a recent kill?

"Let's do it," she said, taking Dex's arm.

Against the counterclockwise flow they walked, pressed uncomfortably near the lockers. But the band room lay less than half a corridor away.

When they entered, fresh death-smell still befouled the air. The corpse, thank God, had been removed. No one else was there. The lampstand, bloodstained from the bludgeoning, gave off its feeble glow. Tall gray doors curved around the room, menacing and quiet.

"I don't think we should . . ."

"This is home," Dex said. "I say we take our chances here. Don't worry. I'll die before I let him hurt you or get near you."

Though Tweed had misgivings, she relented. "I feel safe with you." That was both true and untrue.

"Good, let's get comfortable."

In the obscure gloom, Dex removed his white tuxedo jacket, folded it, lining out, and draped it on the floor against the tall door which on a normal day held sax cases. He was gambling, and Tweed went along, that it didn't hold something else tonight.

Dexter Poindexter, risk taker.

She loved that about him.

She loved lots of things about him. Pulling herself over, she planted a kiss on his friendship lobe.

"What's that about?" he asked.

"It's about how I love you."

He smiled and gripped her hand where it rested on his arm. "I love you too," he said.

And he did.

Cries of pain interrupted Bray and Winnie's embrace there in the backways. It was unclear to either of them how far or from what direction the cries came.

A young male voice.

Two sharp grunts.

It raised Bray's hackles. Winnie's too, to judge from her reaction.

Bray had halted her onward hurtle, drawn her into his arms, felt her body melt against his, her mouth open to his lips.

Now the pitch of another victim's pain shot lightning bolts through her and split them apart.

"Come on," she said, pulling him along.

"Wait. Where?"

"I'm pretty sure it came from over there." She pressed forward again.

Winnie must have the night vision of a cat, thought Bray. Or my kisses have energized her.

She gripped his hand as the close warm air breezed past them. The walls swept by like batter made of rotting wood, curving out of the pitch black on either side, dim disconcerting rollers crashing without sound about them. An occasional nail snagged his suit.

The bulbs were burnt out in this section of the backways, but that didn't stop Winnie. It felt to Bray like an endless roil of dreamtime. He had to remind himself that a knife-wielding maniac might leap out at them from anywhere at any time.

"Are you sure you're—"

"Quiet," she shot back.

In their first moments behind the scenes, Winnie had spoken of trusting to instinct. Now she had clearly slipped into that mode.

Shifts in temperature and air currents and an impression of black-on-black crossings signaled intersections. Winnie barreled through them, taking her and Bray left or right without a moment's hesitation.

Abruptly she slowed, stopped. "That's the place. I'm sure of it." She raised her arm and pointed.

Two boxes of light floated ahead, canted at a peculiar angle. Bray felt imbalanced in their presence. They hovered there like pointillist paintings stippled in gradations of gray, a sense of menace emanating from them.

"Careful now," said Bray, tensing to grapple with their killer friend.

To the right of each box was a recess, the place from which the light was coming. Bray imagined a figure crouched to spring. Winnie wouldn't have a chance.

"Let me by," he said.

He gripped her, turned her, maneuvering past her. Do it, he thought, don't let fear creep in. He raised his hands defensively as he walked into the light and turned toward the recess.

Nothing.

No . . . but . . .tricked!

The slasher was there below, ready to spring. Bray's skin flushed with quick sweeps of heat. His eyes were still adjusting. The slasher charging at him had the advantage.

A knife lunged from the darkness.

Nothing.

No movement at all. No slasher. No knife.

Winnie came up to him. She peered down, then averted her eyes. "Christ," she said.

Crouching closer, he saw what Winnie had seen. Another victim, some old guy, a teacher type, someone he'd never seen. The angle the man's head lay at made no sense.

Then Bray saw that his neck had been brutally sliced open. There was blood everywhere. A crude parabola of gore coated one segment of the glass, a window onto an empty restroom.

I'm not seeing this, he told himself.

"Bray?" Winnie's throat was flayed raw.

He rose, the shock flooding him.

He wanted someone, anyone, to comfort him. Winnie. She would do. Her arms came about him, and he realized *she* was seeking comfort from *him*.

Frantically, they embraced, grappling for elusive assurance, finding it and craving more.

Dumb, he thought.

He and Winnie had laid themselves wide open for attack.

They would die here. At any moment the mad slasher would leap out and cut them to ribbons. But even as he let his mind career about in panic, Bray held Winnie in a numb, shocked embrace, his body as calm as a grave.

Deadened. Dead. One way or another, they were as good as dead already. They would become victims. Or they would be accused and convicted of tonight's killings.

The cards were stacked against them.

Winnie tensed. A soft cry issued from her. Her head lifted as she seemed to sniff something new and terrible, a sharp miasma of misery on the cloying air.

"What?" Bray thought he said.

But Winnie's head was angled back, frozen in attentiveness like the snapshot of a mustang, its mane tossed about, its nostrils flaring wide from the scent of a predator on the wind.

21

Aerated and Tumbled Dry

Two things awakened Peach.

A warm slap of fluid across her cheeks.

And Bowser's screams.

Aches sang all over her body. Her knees and elbows, her thighs and back, her now-unshod feet, and every part of her head. All of it felt as if she had been drubbed unmercifully. Her hands lay like two comatose crabs, trapped and numb beneath the weight of her torso.

Peach opened her eyes, one puffy eyelid like a nagging fear in her peripheral vision. Shiny snips of tin, like crimped moons, lay scattered about a blunt iron base. Washes of blood coated the dull gray metal.

A low ominous hum came from above.

The machine shop. Elwood Dunsmore's preserve, where humiliation of the inept held sway. Peach hated it.

Fluid spattered her face like gobs of hawked spit. Some of it landed on her lips and splashed into her mouth, salty and rude.

Bowser's screams redoubled.

Peach looked up.

Like a piston frozen in an upthrust position, a silver square plattered Bowser above the blunt iron base. His head hung down, bent back at the neck, hair askew. His shoulders angled awkwardly as he lay upon his bound hands, the white coat of his tux scored and scuffed with dirt.

Off the other side of the square, his legs hung dumbly asplay, the bottoms of his trousers puffed up like wads of bloody gauze, dripping, drinking, o'erspilling.

Peach saw janitor overalls rising from odd shoes, powder blue and dressy. A woman's hand grasped a red knob in a cross of knobs and eased it down.

Nurse Gaskin!

How could it be Nurse Gaskin?

Her eyes were taut, intense, narrowed to an insane point.

Again the hidden drill bit into Peach's new boyfriend, a spew of screamed denial issuing from his lips. Blood shot out from above, swatted her brow, forced her eyelids shut.

She opened them, the sting of blood prompting tears. Wimpy old nurse lady, mateless, over the hill. When they had spoken of her at all, it had been with sneers or innuendo. Now she'd gone over the edge.

A skilled hand reversed the cross of knobs, dropped to tug Bowser a few inches farther on, then found again a red knob. She was punching buttonholes deep into Bowser's body, working her way toward his head as if she were making a human cribbage board.

And Peach was next.

She wanted to cry out, to scream for help.

But all sound had drained from her. Her body, an empty gourd, shook and shivered. Like a sudden blush below, her bladder released. The warmth became clammy and chill. The odor of undiluted urine invaded her nostrils.

Above, a new gush of blood fountained. A spurt of Bowser's heartpump rained again across Peach's face.

Bray felt like a mule tugged along by some crazed prospector, as twists and turns of backway were carved out of nothingness by the womanshape that impelled him on.

Winnie's instincts were up.

Since they'd left the restroom victim, Bray had lost his sense of direction. For all he knew, they had reached China.

Winnie's step did not falter.

"Are we getting closer?" he called out.

Her hand raised to wave him silent. Then he abruptly ran into her halted body. He clutched her as if he had meant to.

"Oaf," she said. "Listen."

Bray couldn't hear anything but his own heart and the settling of ancient dust. Then he made it out: The faint whine of a buzzsaw, a gnat at his left ear.

Winnie said, "This way," and again they were off, like Alice and the Red Queen trying furiously to stay in place.

He concentrated on staying near the receding rustle of Winnie's dress. His eyes struggled to keep it in view.

Oddly, there in the oppressive confines of the backways they swept through, Bray's thoughts turned less to the danger they were in and the corpses they had seen, than to Jonquil Brindisi.

It was almost as if the obscure grayness in front of them were a moving projection screen.

Upon it he saw the thick-lipped looker, the flaming redheaded instructress of the greater vices, sizing him up, sizing them *both* up, from their first meeting.

There she stood at the mike, keeping the kids from panicking. Her strength thrilled him, turned him on, setting off flares of worry at the thought of her accusatory finger suddenly pointed in their direction.

Generous breasts, earlobes to die for, a hot steely look in her eyes: He craved it all, the promise, speaking perhaps only in his mind, that this woman would be the perfect complement to his and Winnie's love.

They stopped again.

The whine was louder.

Winnie's mouth touched his ear. "We've got him!" The triumph, the high flush of arousal in her voice thrilled him. Then she took off again, hurtling faster, a great bird of prey swooping down the obscure passageway, drawing him along in her wake.

He loved Winnie. He loved her determination, her naivete, her shape and smell, the totality of her. If they survived this night, their life together would be glorious.

Another halt. This time, he nearly knocked her off her feet.

The high whine came louder still, edged this time with a scream, a piercing girl-sound. Then that was choked off and the whine ceased.

Dead silence descended upon the backways.

Winnie swore.

"We've lost him," said Bray.

"Not yet," she shot back, nearly sniffing the air to find their killer. "We're almost on him."

"He's gone."

She thrust her face into his. "Look, there's no time for your bullshit, okay?"

No recrimination in her words. Just love and a forgiving, a statement of fact, a simple urging to follow her as she turned and flew off once more on sheer hunch.

Seconds later, an eternity later, Bray saw a flash over Winnie's right shoulder.

It fluttered. A distant figure came through a panel. A moving smudge. He was headed straight for them! Then clearly no.

The closing panel sheered away the light and Bray saw the figure recede, something swinging from its right hand.

"Wait! Hey you! Stop!" Winnie shouted.

After the briefest of pauses—would he kill them?—the flat sound of running echoed along the backways. Their savior had no interest in chatting. Nor it seemed in confrontation. Not now, at any rate, while he and Winnie had the upper hand.

Bray saw a sickly white 654 above the panel as they passed it. "Shouldn't we—" he began, but Winnie flew on, then jerked to a halt.

A muffled thud. No running sounds.

Another panel had shut.

They were alone in the backways.

He felt Winnie deflate. "He's escaped."

"No, he hasn't," protested Bray. "We can still catch him." His body was suddenly in overdrive, straining to go on. "How many panels can there be up ahead?"

"I *had* the bastard." She made a gesture, an expression of despair, her certainty gone. "Now he's vanished."

"Yeah but couldn't we—"

"It'd be a waste of time. I'll bet he wants us to do that. Then, while we're mucking about looking for him, he'll kill again. A few more victims."

"Speaking of victims . . . ."

"Yes," said Winnie. "Let's. He may have left a clue to his identity."

They doubled back and found 654 again.

Bray found the catch and released it.

And the abattoir that had been a machine shop opened its vile red stench to them, an outrageous glimpse into hell.

In the school's basement where they had gone to ground, Kyla looked upon the antics of Patrice and Fido with sheer disgust.

She could understand giddy. Hysterical was even in her purview. But throwing caution to the wind, acting like puppystruck schoolkids, shouting juvenile defiance at the walls? It drained the love right out of her, new as well as old.

For years, Patrice had felt like part of her, a hairy wen one accepted and even grew perversely fond of. It stunned Kyla how fleeting eternal love could be, how in one instant over something that seemed trivial, it could crumble, leaving you alone again in the ashes of solitude.

She was sitting crosslegged against a cheaply paneled wall. But the wall felt solid. You could sense—*she* could anyway—whether or not a wall was hollow. This one had no boobytrap, nothing to give the slasher an advantage.

Out on the concrete floor, Fido brandished his cleavers, Patrice her knives. They circled one another at a safe distance: Jack Spratt sparring with his wife.

"Quiet, you two," said Kyla.

Again they ignored her.

Giggles.

High-pitched come-out-come-out-wherever-you-are's.

Safe feints at mutual mayhem.

By God, Kyla wanted to slaughter them both. Impulse twitched in her hands, there where she clutched her own cutting tools.

All part of this evening's madness, she thought. It would be easy to best them, to put her past behind her, to blame two more deaths on the janitor—who was futtermeat, surely, as soon as he showed his face.

"Me 'n' Patrice are ready for you!" crowed Fido.

His skin, whose touch for the longest time she and Patrice had craved, seemed loathsome to her now. She despised as well the visual blat of his friendship lobe, an odd bit of flesh that last night she had dreamt of kissing.

Patrice's knives danced like daggers of rain in the harsh light, a safe distance from Fido's.

Few kids knew the school *had* a basement, let alone how to reach it. Fido had hit upon the idea of hiding here. He had convinced them it would be a swell idea, the slasher concentrating on the upper floors for his victims. Now Kyla had her doubts.

Their new beau was too damned cocksure.

Patrice had soaked up his confidence, going giddy in the head, her chubby figure twirling like a hippo in heat.

The gargantuan furnace hummed low and ominous, a row of double bass players bowing hushed subliminal tones from their instruments. Angled pipes rose and fell like thick strands of dark spaghetti, their shadows and smudges hiding just about anything, any*one*, Kyla's imagination could conjure.

Beyond the mad dance of her companions, a laundry chute curved down. Its indistinct length faced her squarely.

There was something dark and nasty, something threatening, about it. It hung there like a big gaping elephant's trunk, the light of a lone bulb throwing shadows into it that glinted, suggesting moisture where dryness surely prevailed.

It reminded Kyla of her fluxidermed granny, her vulval opening as big and blaring as a tuba mouthpiece. Daddy had kept his dead mother in his bedroom closet. He hadn't bothered to have his fathers fluxed, which made him an oddity among grown-ups, Kyla had later realized. One parent only had been fluxidermed.

Nor did he display it in the vestibule, as normal grown-ups did. When Kyla came home before her father, she would go into his dark bedroom and peer into the closet, past forests of hanging suits and shirts, at the bare buttocks of her grandmother. From that dusty dark ruddy pucker had her daddy dropped, a dark ominous ancestral privacy. That's what this gaping laundry chute reminded her of, as the huge furnace rumbled in Kyla's gut and Fido and Patrice flurried knives at one another.

An ancient laundry basket on wheels, its canvas sides bulging with huge mounds of soiled towels and sheets, awaited the laundry chute's next disgorging.

"Will you two shut the fuck *up*?"

She said it loud if laconically, knowing they would blow her off. But some things just got said cuz they needed saying. Maybe a failed warning would be sufficient to ward off the killer.

Maybe not.

Probably not.

Then something clanged overhead.

It put a halt to her companions' silly little dance of death. It raised the hairs on the back of Kyla's neck, blasting prickly heat straight up into her backbrain.

"What was that?" Patrice wondered aloud.

A rumble began like distant muffled timpani, as the clang reversed itself. Some sliding door wrenched up, then juddered decisively shut, almost the confident slice of a guillotine blade falling home into its groove.

The rumble bumbled about above, growing louder, the beat of it coming faster and more violent.

Kyla couldn't fix on it. Then her ears peeled the sound from its echo. She focused on the dark downdrop that gaped before her.

Fido and Patrice gazed about wildly. A brandish of knifes angled out to ward off any attacker.

Before Kyla could warn them, even as words took shape in her confused brain, she saw the thing tumble into view, a dark furball in the darkness, coming quick, separating itself from the chute and leaping free.

Was it a huge black spider rolled into a ball, ready to spear out its legs and scuttle murderously toward them, stinger out, its dark dangle of limbs silently going *dandle-dandle-dandle*?

The thing bounced once on the heaped laundry, leaving a blotch of gore across the white expanse. Then it smacked the concrete by Fido's feet. The crack of a bat upon a skull. Splintered bone. It rolled furiously, *flop-flop* it rolled *flop-flop*, hair-face-hair-face.

Bowser McPhee, Fido's ex-boyfriend.

His skin was gray verging on blue, bruised, upsplashed with blood to the jowls.

The neck had been sheered through in one clean sharp slice.

Kyla wondered why Fido's screams sounded so high. Then she realized all three of them had merged their screams, a braid of terror tightly stranded together.

She froze. The head before her, with its baleful blinkless stare, held her in thrall.

If the killer happened to appear now, Kyla realized, she would be as helpless and doomed as a deer startled into dumbness on a dark highway, creamed by the rig that pinned it to the night with its high beams.

22
A Proliferation of Deaths

Dex and Tweed huddled together on the band room floor against a ten-foot-tall gray-painted door. A fan of such doors swept off in either direction. Theirs housed sax cases, the others timpani, trombones, tubas, every band member's weapon of choice.

They couldn't be sure, of course, that the storage space behind one of those doors hadn't been emptied out before anyone arrived, an easy point of access for the killer.

One level down, the lone dim bulb atop its stand feebled light into the room. At its base was a dried pool of blood, hastily mopped, from the death of Bix Donner, the husband of Tweed's tenth grade bio teacher.

Dex had thought the rogue slasher would not return to the scene of his crime.

He wasn't so sure any more.

The crazy bastard's preternatural vision, Dex was starting to fear, had them in his sights. The slow cold hand of paranoia slid its fingers along his spine and dug its nails into his brain.

Yet perhaps the cause of his rising panic was not paranoia at all, but survival instinct.

"Poor Mr. Donner," Tweed whispered, breaking the silence like a shout.

Dex raised a finger to his lips. At her ear: "Keep an eye out. He could rush us from anywhere. If you even *think* a shadow moved, let me know. Don't assume you're imagining it, okay?"

Tweed nodded.

She mouthed something soundless. Dex thought it was "I love you," though the weak light made it impossible to be sure.

The bulb flickered as if a moth flitted back and forth over it. Then it went out. Blackness rushed in to surround them.

One squat upper window glowed with enfeebled moonlight that shot down head-high to carve a far sliver out of one wall.

We're sitting ducks, thought Dex, we've got to get away from these doors.

He took Tweed's hand and helped her up, the rustle of her dress concealing perhaps the groan of a tall gray door's hinges.

Dex felt a breeze. The passing of someone's body before them? At any moment, Tweed would cry out from a lethal wound. Or a knife blade would violate him, pricking out the heart of his life.

"Hold me," said Tweed.

Dex gave her a quick fierce hug, then said, "Come on."

Holding Tweed's hand, Dex slid his right shoe along the platform. He was no longer certain of the four-inch drop to the next level, where the trumpets and French horns sat.

It wouldn't do to trip and tumble. They'd be dead in an instant.

Tweed said, "Not so fast!" Panic at being dragged along in the darkness. She bumped him, then regained her balance.

"Another level now, watch your step," he said. "Clarinet section. Okay, we're off the risers. Past the piano. I can make out the band room door, coming up on the blackboard now."

He felt along it. Soon the door.

The killer's eyes burrowed into their backs. He would never let them escape.

But what if he were right *outside* the door, waiting for them in the hallway?

Tweed tugged him to a halt. "Dex, I heard something. Out there."

And the band room door opened, gray on black. A figure slipped through. The door hissed closed behind it. Dex rushed whoever it was, grappling with the shape, his fists darting out, trying to stun their attacker, to get the upper hand.

No resistance. A woman's voice shouted out, "Hey, wait . . . what—?"

"Miss Phipps!" said Tweed.

Adora Phipps, Dex thought. She's safe. But he felt down her wrists just in case.

Empty hands.

"I'm sorry," he said. "It's us. Me and Tweed. We thought you were—"

"I'm not. But I'll be damned if I know who is. Listen we're trying to round everyone up, get them back to the gym. It's the safest place, and Mr. Buttweiler's got a plan. Come with?"

Dex nodded.

"You bet," said Tweed relieved.

"Ditto," said Dex, realizing his nod had failed to register.

"Good, let's go."

After groping about for it, the door made a vertical gray line. Then that line gaped into a rectangle wide enough for them to pass through one at a time.

Jonquil Brindisi walked as if she had been thoroughly oiled, her lubricious limbs animated by sheer desire. She loved the mayhem, the chaos, loved them to distraction.

Once Gerber Waddell was found, she would join in the futtering. But if *she* found him first, she planned to fuck the simple dweeb, feeling his lovely violence invade her as she tied him down and rode him.

Just imagining it made her gasp.

She had already dragged Claude into a supply closet after Elwood Dunsmore had been found torch-faced by the entranceway and Futzy'd rolled in the mutilated zippermouths. Claude kept up his but-I'm-married routine until she yanked his fly open and filled her throat close to choking.

Then his pretzel of words, the syntactically convoluted bullshit he had made a part of himself, turned into barnyard grunts and oh-yeahs and suck-me-darlin's. She had left him panting, his organ still thick despite its hot spew. He tasted like pea soup pureed with pearl onions.

Thus, Jonquil had mused, do the greater vices ever overwhelm the lesser.

Now she was on Gerber's trail.

More precisely, she was up for whatever the fates delivered. She *craved* the killer. And she felt that the strength of her craving ought to be enough to draw him out.

Until now, Gerber had been a sexless dolt of muscles and nods, thinning hair and stupid grins. Who would ever have guessed at the dynamo of hatred which had clearly simmered inside him for years, exploding at last into this amazing orgy of bloodletting?

Swimming upstream of the fleeing students, Jonquil had heard talk of terrible screams and the whining of buzzsaws. Up ahead, she saw the closed classroom door.

No noise came from the machine shop. But a bright light inside cut through wires of opaque glass in the lower half of the door, throwing sprays of dark diamonds across the corridor.

Something had gone on here. She sensed it. Perhaps her demented janitor awaited her, crouched to kill but ready for seduction if she played him right.

Jonquil grasped the doorknob and moved boldly inside, into the full light of the shop. Bulks of machinery stood gleaming and silent everywhere.

Tensed to repel attack, she took in Brayton and Raven standing by the far wall. Their soiled prom clothes had been torn. Their faces were forlorn and bereft, their eyes unable to stray from what they beheld.

Then she strode toward them. A large lathe moved out of her way, and there before her—wafts of deathstench turning the air moist and oozy and charged with sexual energy—were a pair of mauled, mutilated kids.

An unidentifiable male, headless, lay akimbo upon the tile floor. His off-white tuxedo was as pinkish red as bleeding gums. His chest looked as if it had, from neck to navel, once sprouted teeth, all of them yanked out now. Gaping holes pooled there, crimson fleshcups that made Jonquil swoon.

But it was the female that truly got Jonquil off, what with its slutty red-frilled frock and the sizzling-as-hot-blacktop body, no mistaking it, of Peach Popkin, whose face alone would have made identification problematic.

The Popkin girl had been caught in a swan dive, her arms extended, her bare back arched up into a U upon the platform that housed the table saw. Her breasts met the table's smooth surface at nipplepoint, their tips pushed flat beneath her blanched aureoles.

Beyond the blade, the girl's strawberry blond hair, streaked a deep red, wisped forward. Her coiffure had been mussed from the killer's having pressed her forehead forward into the gray blur of a spinning blade.

At rest now, the blade stuck deep, through skin and skullbone, parting the halves of her brain. Though sprays of gore had spattered her flesh, most of it had shot across the room like spoutings from a dying whale's blowhole.

The scene was breathtaking.

"We can explain," came Brayton's voice, a warmth to it that moistened Jonquil further.

"Oh no you can't," she said, not accusing but filled with the wonder she felt.

"We were in the backways," said Raven. "We saw the killer come out of here. He had the boy's head by the hair. He got away."

"Marvelous," said Jonquil. The woman before her was one succulent saucy wench. Then it struck her. "How did you break into the backways? Only the slasher's supposed to know the combination, him and the janitor."

"Should we tell her?" Brayton asked.

Raven made a face. "What choice?"

He shrugged. "Zane Fronemeyer was chosen to be your school's slasher. He's dead. The janitor axed him in his basement. Fronemeyer's wives are dead too."

Jonquil shuddered. "Zane was a scumsucking zit from the word go. He wanted to suck *my* scum. He kept nagging, long after I made it clear he was less than zero in my book. Camille and Hedda deserved better. But the question remains: How do you two know all this?"

Brayton tried to speak, then gave up.

"Let's show her," his date said. She raised her hand to her left ear.

Brayton did likewise.

Christ! In the presence of death, these two sexy people, thought Jonquil, are about to expose their sexlobes to me. They're as turned on by all this as *I* am.

Ripples of come-need treadled through her loins. The right word, the right look, would set her off without a touch.

Their lobebags fell away.

And there, in all their glory . . . .

But Raven's exposed lobe was dyed a godawful green, some ridiculous protest among the homeless-by-choice. And Brayton yanked and peeled and his sexlobe, his friendship lobe too, came away in his hands like some spent Cyrano's nose putty.

The crude puckers of flesh which punctuated the question marks of his ears meant but one thing.

"You and Raven . . . you're—"

He nodded.

"My name's Winnie," the woman said.

"They took us off the streets, drugged us, delivered us to Fronemeyer. But Gerber Waddell killed him before he could kill us."

This changed everything.

A couple of freaks.

From the look of his severed lobes, Brayton was a promjumper. No way would Jonquil deign to suck on the vestigial stump of anyone's sexlobe, least of all some joker who had dodged his prom. Why, blowing a fucking eunuch would be about as frustrating and far more humiliating.

Jonquil sublimated her lust and grew cool.

"You've got no business being here," she said. "I ought to have you, I *will* have you arrested."

Brayton raised his hands. "Hey now—"

"We're your best chance of catching the killer. You need access to the backways, and we've got it."

The feisty little slut was right.

Jonquil still had the hots for Gerber Waddell. If she expected to fuck him before he was futtered, that could only happen by playing along with these two.

She deflated and stood down. "I give," she said. "The backways it is. Let's find him."

"This way," said Brayton, putting his lobebag back on. He punched a tiny keypad over the panel they stood before.

Winnie entered first, a soiled doll returned to the dingy package it had arrived in.

Jonquil went next, loving all over again the musk Brayton wore as she passed him and regretting what she'd learned about him. He'd have made an irresistible bedmate.

Brayton trailed after her.

The panel slid shut as the musty backways swallowed them up. Fired up at the prospect of finding the janitor, Jonquil moved between the homeless pair as though she were a convict and they her jailers.

Sandy glanced about nervously.

The larger stairwells, wide and step-scuffed at the four corners of the school, always teemed with students between classes.

But halfway along the east, north, and west sides of the school were less-frequented stairs, shut off at top and bottom by steel safety doors. The lights burned harsh here, throwing hard-edged shadows across pink-tiled walls.

The stairwell, which stank of Lysol, was a place of loneliness and crushed cigarette butts.

Rocky was squatting against one wall.

Beside him stood Cobra, his knee bent and one cleated heel stuck to the wall like a magnet. His back bent, he puffed on a coffin nail.

Sandy feared the lulls, those times when the three of them were here alone. Rushes of kids would come by from above and below, the bars of the steel doors clanging and releasing, latches raucously catching as they swung shut. Then for a time, no one. Ominous stillness. All a-fidget, she would long for the next wave of promgoers, her friends, Rocky's friends.

Or total geeks, it didn't matter.

Anyone to suggest safety in numbers.

They had hit another lull.

"Let's go some place else," she said.

Rocky, on automatic, began to rise.

Cobra's free hand restrained him. "Stay put. Don't get me wrong. I like Sandy's sweet ass and I'm planning on having plenty of stiff-poled fun licking her lobes and knockers. But *I'm* calling the shots now. I say we hang here."

The door opened below. Then it swung shut. Faster than usual, Sandy thought.

From the landing, only part of the upper door was visible.

A snapping, like the quick sharp shake of a chain, sounded below. The door rattled as if the person who had come through it were trying to open it again.

Then a woman dressed in blue appeared, her short hair in mid-shake as she—Sandy recognized Nurse Gaskin—bounded up the stairs, clutching a large brown folder, the kind with accordion pockets like a briefcase. Bloodstains dappled her dress, reminders of her having witnessed the death of Mrs. Donner's husband in the band room.

The nurse glanced at them as she sped past, her face full of frowns like grown-ups often got, her fists clenched into tight balls.

She wanted to say something as she went by, but she held back until she was almost at the top. Then: "The bastard locked the door behind me."

Sandy didn't need to ask who she meant.

None of them did.

They glanced at one another, then moved as one in sheer terror. Sandy's head surged with hot flushes of panic.

Gripping the gray railing, she followed Cobra and Rocky, gearing that the janitor would somehow magically rise about them, bursting out of one of the panels fitted into the tile walls. Her flats pounded up the steps. A gray wad of gum lay like squashed putty on the edge of one step.

As Nurse Gaskin shot her hand to the door, Sandy heard another sharp snap, twin to the one below.

Did the sound come before, at, or after the nurse touched the door? It was too confusing to tell. It must have been just before.

Ms. Gaskin's hand pulled back from the door as if from a jolt of electricity. She jammed the folder under one arm and hit the bar, full force, with both hands, leaning into it.

The door refused to budge.

Sandy and her men had nearly reached the top platform.

Her mind raced.

They would die here. At any moment, darkness would come crashing down upon them. Hands would shoot out in a quick grasp at her ankles, yanking her off her feet.

No! They would shove the door open, the four of them exerting maximum effort to gain freedom.

But what lay in wait for them when the door flew open?

The nurse turned to them. She glanced with sudden alarm over Rocky's shoulder. He had one foot on the top step and began to look backward.

Sandy was spooked to the max.

She felt the janitor behind her, ready to grab them, skewer them. He was ready to unleash another outbreak of bloodletting.

Then the nurse's face bloomed with hatred.

She slammed full-force into Rocky, upsetting his balance, sending him flailing off the step.

Then she grabbed Cobra by the hair, yanking him across eight feet of ineffective arm-waving, head-first into the tile wall.

"Whoa," he had said, "wait a—"

But the headslam cut off his rising protest, and the nurse repeated that headslam as if she had been possessed by a mad plan to butt their way to freedom. A bullseye reddened on the tile wall.

Down below, Rocky landed badly, crying out in pain and disbelief as his body struck stairs and railings, meat and bone out of control.

Sandy froze, unable to move or think.

This wasn't happening.

The nurse was kind and meek and dorky. It was *Gerber Waddell* they had to look out for.

But kindly Nurse Gaskin released Cobra with an upward flurry of hands and bent for the brown folder.

Rocky was crawling painfully up the steps toward them, his legs weirdly skewed, his right temple smeared with blood.

Cobra fell, no sound from his mouth, just a resounding smack as his skull struck the floor.

"Don't," Sandy whimpered or thought she did.

The brown folder tumbled end over end like a flipped playing card, and in the nurse's hand was a ball peen hammer. As she passed, she threw Sandy a look of contempt that pinned her to the wall like a moth to cardboard.

Sandy trembled. She was unable to summon the will to cry out or stop the attack on Rocky.

The nurse's arm swung up.

It swung down.

And Sandy watched the hammer crack open a crater in her boyfriend's skull, staving it in like the thin hollow shell of a chocolate bunny. His body shook with the viciousness of each blow. Sandy couldn't look away, no matter how much she wanted to.

Rocky's cries stopped.

He became a big bloody ragdoll.

Only the nurse's savage grunts remained, a counterpart to her swung thunks into red flesh. Above those sounds sailed the wisps of Sandy's whimpering.

At last, the nurse turned away from Rocky and fixed Sandy in her stare. She rose up the steps toward her. Sandy's legs gave out and she slid down the wall.

Tears blurred her vision.

She was falling and the monster was rising.

"Three's a charm," said Nurse Gaskin, low, heavy, and harsh.

She crouched before the girl.

Cold wet metal touched her brow. A tickle slanted across it, a cool drop of blood.

The hammerhead lifted.

Another diagonal, crosswise to the first, traveled Sandy's forehead.

"Don't," she whimpered.

"Hold still now." Ms. Gaskin gripped Sandy's ponytail and wrenched it tight. "This will only hurt for a second."

The blur pulled back and then the punch came swiftly in, leaping beyond all bound, violating Sandy, opening her up.

The stairwell vanished and a rush of stars rode in on a black wave of night.

23
True to Their School

Despite the chaos that had befallen Corundum High, and faced with mounting reports of fresh victims, Futzy Buttweiler had never felt so much in command.

Some enterprising jock had brought several dozen small flashlights from one of the science labs. Their beams now angled crazily across the gym. They had ended up primarily in the hands of natural-born leader types, but other kids held them too, infiltrating the privileged few around the bandstand.

Beyond the people Futzy addressed, the Ice Ghoul loomed out of the darkness. But the papier-mache monster didn't cow him any longer. Neither did it bring forth memories of Kitty's death and futtering.

Tonight, Futzy would strike back.

He would triumph over the Ice Ghoul.

Before the night was out, he would see that Gerber Waddell was tracked down and torn apart.

Adora Phipps hugged him.

There would be no more bullshit in his life. He loved this woman. Why should he hide it? He wanted every godforsaken soul in the *world* to know that Futzy Buttweiler loved Adora Phipps.

He returned her hug. Then he spoke to the crowd massed before him.

There stood the Borgstroms, their eagerness to savage some deserving bastard, *any* deserving bastard, shining out even in darkness.

Beside the Borgstroms were Dexter Poindexter and Tweed Megrim, the night's intended victims who had by some strange chance escaped their fate and were now willing, brave souls, to tempt it again.

And, for all Futzy knew to the contrary, beyond their narrow perimeter of flitting torches, sick dimwitted Gerber Waddell himself lent an ear, knife in hand, ready to rush them at any moment.

Futzy kept his voice low, both to draw close their conspiratorial circle and to shut out the janitor, if indeed he were listening in.

"We're in the midst of a grave crisis, my friends," he began.

"Hey, Futzy," one of the newer teachers piped up. "Cut the crap, will you? There's no time for it."

That stung.

Futzy felt tempted to sting back.

Then he admitted to the merits of the remark, simplified, clarified, and began anew.

"I suggest," he said, "that we stay in pairs, divvy up the school, and move out, one flashlight to a pair. Everyone is to be armed. Adora and I have gathered some cutlery." He gestured to a pile of knives at his feet. "Take a couple. If you find the janitor, strike first and save your questions for later. Don't be jittery and don't go off half-cocked. Be *fully* cocked and ready for anything."

"What about the students?" asked Claude.

It struck Futzy for the first time: Jonquil Brindisi, who usually cleaved to Claude at these affairs, was nowhere to be seen. He prayed she hadn't come to a bad end. He would miss her spice and spirit.

Nurse Gaskin was absent as well, she who had witnessed the death of Bix Donner and been unable to stop it. Futzy hoped the poor woman wouldn't be permanently scarred by that experience.

"The students," said Futzy. "An excellent point, Claude. As you comb your portion of the school, gather them up, keep them close about you. And shout out to Gerber to give himself up. Offer him clemency, leniency, anything to lure him out of the backways. Our kids are smart. They'll go along to save their necks. But Gerber, despite the cunning he seems to have displayed tonight, is still at heart a simple-minded feeb. He'll buy into the big lie. Then we'll savage him."

It was tempting to speak up, but Futzy kept his remarks close to the chest. The Ice Ghoul seemed to strain forward to hear, struggling to split itself off from the darkness, rise to its full height, crane its bull neck, lumber forward, and kill them all.

A crazy notion came over the principal: He fancied that the janitor had squeezed up into the Ice Ghoul's hollowed-out head, directional mikes in its ears, and heard his entire plan.

Futzy dismissed that as paranoia.

Directly before him, hand in hand, stood Dex and Tweed. Adora, finding them hunkered down in the band room, had persuaded them to come along to the gym.

She gave Futzy's arm a squeeze.

It was time.

"Mr. and Mrs. Borgstrom, you two explore the butchery wing. Claude, I want you and . . . and Brest—Trilby, you stay here with Pill—to scour the science labs. Dexter and Tweed, you've got the stairwells."

Futzy's inner map of Corundum High flashed by as he doled out sector after sector. He didn't want any place overlooked. To himself and Adora, he assigned the band room.

"Take time to do it right," he said. "Don't skimp, don't shortchange. When you're finished, bring yourselves and any kids you've rounded up to the auditorium. If you find Gerber Waddell, send runners there.

"And good luck to you all."

Crowding forward, their flashlights crazily stabbing downward, they delved into the cutlery, as somber a group as Futzy had ever seen. He was reminded of the solemn clatter of communion trays passed hand to hand, tiny glasses of grape juice lifted out with a clink.

Adora squeezed his hand and brought it to her lips. "Good plan, darling."

"We'll get him," he assured her.

"I love you, Futzy," said Adora, her eyes beaming with pride.

"And I love you, dear lady."

Futzy felt no cause for confidence.

Yet oddly enough he was confident.

He looked forward to tossing Trusk and Torment out of his life for good—they would be amazed at the new vigor in him as he threw their sorry asses off the front porch—and installing Adora Phipps there instead.

She would glow.

So would he.

And Kitty, at last, would be laid to rest.

But first—Futzy stooped and grabbed a shish kabob skewer to complement his snubnose—they had a rogue janitor to subdue.

Trilby sat in a folding chair behind the refreshments. Pill lay slumped on her lap, a thumb stuck deep in her mouth.

Stroking her daughter's hair, Trilby made soothing sounds and gently rocked her.

Above them, among the rafters, floated the dim shape of a basketball hoop and backboard that had been cranked up and away. From the ill-lit expanse before them rose the Ice Ghoul, the lines of its frame harsh and cutting, its face obscured by shadow.

But Trilby was unafraid.

A madman had murdered her husband, spooked her little girl, and thrown her household into chaos. Yet she feared neither for her life nor for Pill's.

They would survive and grow strong.

Before Brest left with Claude Versailles to check out the science labs, she had hugged Trilby and Pill. "Sit tight," she had said. "We'll be back soon." But as she said it, she had worn her stone face, tight and drawn, her eyes clamped down upon her feelings. There was no telling how tonight's mayhem had affected her, nor how it had affected their future.

Don't think about it.

Pay attention to Pill.

Pill had witnessed a murder, under threat of discovery and slaughter herself. She had heard her father's death announced before a frightened crowd of promgoers.

"There, there," she said. "That's my Pill." Her hand stroked the angel-smooth hair above her daughter's neck. Tonight's terrors might cause Pill to develop too early her lust for blood.

Or she might never do so.

Trilby didn't know which would be worse.

No, that wasn't so.

If Pill were inadequately socialized, she would be treated as an odd duck, open to taunts and jeers and the most hurtful kind of bullying.

Worse, she might join the anti's.

Pill had a fiercely independent streak. If she were permanently damaged over this—and the magnitude of tonight's trauma threatened to make that a certainty—she might join the crazies who, as they claimed, used violence to *end* violence. Eventually, she would be taken out by government forces.

Stop, she thought. You're hurtling into a terrible future. This *will not* come to pass!

"We'll come through this okay, honey," she said, her voice catching. "We just have . . . to be strong." She wiped her eyes with the back of her hand.

Pill lay against her like an inert sack of pudding and bone, her eyes open but unfocused, slow blinks lidded upon them like an infant dull with sleep. Her thumb-sucking came and went but the thumb stayed firmed ensconced in her mouth.

Random shouts issued from distant hallways, coming from bunches of aroused, terrorized kids joining in a hunt for the slasher. At some point, that sick soul would be found and futtered. Then they would all be free.

She stifled a laugh.

Free.

Free to build a new life around the obsessive kernel of this night, a nightmare forever revived, recreated, relived.

No, she thought. We will get beyond this. We will process it and go on.

"We will, honey," she said. "We will."

It was almost time to thrust the drugged fucker into the mob. Almost time for him to be royally futtered.

Delia had developed a taste for blood.

But for the sake of Kitty, and to assure triumph in her pursuit of Brest and Trilby, she would wrap things up now. Call it quits. Slake the frenzied bloodthirst of the crowd with good ol' Gerber Waddell.

And emerge a survivor.

There'd be time enough, after bedding her grieving girlfriends, to maraud and slaughter once more, carefully, selectively, at random intervals.

The janitor lay propped against the wall of a corridor, a lone lightbulb throwing a harsh glare across him. Alarm lit his eyes.

She wondered if she had trussed him up too tight. Had she cut off his circulation? Would his walk be convincing? Or would they see evidence, assuming there was anything left to autopsy, that he had been bound and gagged for over an hour?

Slumped that way, Gerber looked so small.

Her toy, her plaything.

It was an odd responsibility she had taken on, this being in charge of lives and deaths, this manipulation. It made her feel creepy, and virtuous, and *powerful* all at once.

Stooping she put a hand on his shoulder and felt his muscles strain in resistance.

"You okay, big fella?"

Sweat stood on Gerber's blunt brow.

"Yeah, I thought you were."

Beyond the wall, not six feet from her roped hostage, lay the gym's north side, the bandstand where the principal spoke in low murmurs.

A squat stool on her left held a small kit of medical supplies. The syringe was out and ready, resting upon a leather pouch.

She worked Gerber's right sleeve up under the ropes, baring his arm just above the elbow. Tied him off. Smacked two fingertips against his skin. Squinted in the dim light. Found what felt like a vein and jabbed the needle in.

"This will only hurt a lot, and for a long time," she said.

She had drawn the entire ampule of liquid into the hypodermic. Now she shot it home, hard supreme power in the steady closure of her thumb, encircled by metal and slowly pressing down to dope him up good.

The janitor's eyes glazed over.

Needle out. No need for cotton. Let him bleed. Soon there'd be plenty more blood.

Delia returned the syringe to the stool and worked at his bonds. They were tight, but they were not impossible. Soon she had them off.

Gerber's eyelids had grown heavy. She undid his gag and vigorously rubbed his legs.

"No more pins and needles," she said. "It's meat-cleaver, serving-fork, and carving-knife time for you."

She had to get him up. Walk him about. He had to be convincing when she shoved him out.

At first he stumbled.

Heavy, drugged guy.

It felt as if they were on an unsteady deck, rolling and heaving with the waves.

Then he grew used to it, moving more like an obedient automaton.

His arm lay heavy across her shoulders. His big, denim-clad body stank of confinement.

"Only a little farther," she said, hoping she was right.

Years before, there'd been a math teacher, a designated slasher, who had, contrary to all law, ushered Delia into the backways the day after the prom. He had shown her about, doing his best then—and his best was piss poor—to prick her, up against the outer curves of the band room.

Her memory had sponged up the details, where they were, how they had arrived there.

Even so, the backways tended to disorient. She concentrated on direction, staggering under Gerber's unsteady weight. The things she needed to complete his condemnation waited in the walls behind the auditorium stage.

He mumbled something, his breath close and reeky.

"That's right, Gerber," she said. "It's time to die. Would you like that?"

Gerber's head lolled, his lips open and drooly. He looked vacuous and thirsty.

His janitorial boots galumphed obediently along as they walked. Though they threatened to stomp her blue bloodcaked pumps, they never quite did so.

They turned a bend.

Ah!

The series of panels on stage left appeared. A cramped three feet separated that wall from the black legs, the array of curtains that hid actors about to enter the stage proper.

A tiny table held a rag.

On the rag was an ice pick. And next to it, soaking the rag, lay an icicle, one of many Delia had found in an obscure corner of Lily Foddereau's refrigeration room, where a leak in the overhead pipes had created an inverted forest of them.

A noise sounded behind her.

Delia froze.

All night, a pair of somebodies had been cramping her style. They had almost caught sight of her leaving the machine shop with the McPhee boy's head swinging from her hand.

Again it sounded, an exchange of words.

Still distant, but that wouldn't count for shit if they saw her.

"Stand up," commanded Delia in a whisper. A large 525 hovered ghostly white above them.

The dumb fuck cooperated.

She grabbed the ice pick. Then the icicle, cold, wet, stubbornly sticking to the rag.

"Take these," she said.

Gerber's hands opened at the touch of them and closed again feebly. She gripped them tighter about the handle and the icicle.

Huge hands, loam hands.

Fumbling for the catch on the panel, she jabbed it, missed, jabbed again, and felt the mechanism obey. The panel slid open, a soft *shuck* sound. At her feet, a shaft of light fell.

The intruders were almost upon them.

"Go!" she told Gerber. "Through those curtains."

By some miracle, she got him over the lip of the panel. He moved away from her, marching like an obedient clockwork toy, just where she wanted him to go.

"Yes, that way lies good things, Gerber."

Not a moment to lose.

Should she step through after him, or hide in the backways?

Her mind dithered.

Delia chose to step through, swift in the instant of decision, feeling eyes about to light on her.

Gerber was moving, brushing black velvet but passing between the hanging legs.

Any second now he would be visible. The clamor would begin.

Fleeing to a prop closet upstage of the legs, Delia hid herself behind it.

The space was maddeningly shallow.

All it would take was one glance her way and the game would be up.

But the strange, soiled couple that emerged from the backways, and Jonquil Brindisi behind them, had eyes only for the denim-clad man making his slow entrance onto the stage.

From the first, as she and Dex explored the stairwells, Tweed had been bold in calling out to Gerber Waddell.

Reckless even.

She had known it, but her giddy state led her to take risks. And because they were brandishing some pretty mean cutlery, she felt safe.

Tweed could tell the wandering students were impressed by her and Dex's role as deputies. They had picked up strays in the hall and in the first two stairwells they examined.

In the close confines of tile and steel and gum-encrusted steps, their shouts to the janitor doubled back upon them in weird echoes.

When they reached the east stairwell, they found an odd lot of sober kids outside the door. Another lot stood inside the stairwell, their eyes fastened upon a trio of corpses.

The old feeling of helplessness flooded into Tweed again. Suddenly she had no will to hold up her knives.

Her heart held not much fondness for Cobra, Rocky, or Sandy. But violent death levels all victims.

Somehow Dex rallied.

Somehow he said just what everybody needed to hear to start them on their way toward the auditorium. Something about the principal having a plan, though Tweed couldn't recall Futzy saying anything planworthy in the gym.

Now they were sitting with their contingent of strays in the left front block of seats, as other unsuccessful troops straggled in emptyhanded.

Their flashlight beams did a feeble dance along the sloping aisles as they walked.

Someone slow-scanned, high across the auditorium's stage-right wall, the motto painted in large gold letters: "The strength of a nation lies in the regimentation of its youth."

No one said much.

Faces were drawn.

Young shoulders slumped forlornly.

Mr. Buttweiler and Miss Phipps sat side by side on the edge of the stage. They had no plan. Dex had been speaking from some wishful place in his head. But no one, certainly not Tweed, seemed in any mood to ding him for it.

The principal's spindly legs rhythmed at random, shoe heels nearly knocking against the stage front. Hands clasped earnestly in his lap, he leaned to say something to Miss Phipps.

She nodded.

Grimacing, he began to rise.

But when he was halfway up, Tweed's attention shot to the right.

Onstage, someone was emerging from between hanging dark curtains.

Hands, arms, chest.

Objects gleamed from his fists—

It was Gerber Waddell!

—shiny objects, a thin one, a thick one.

The janitor's face was shrouded in washes of death, the deaths he had brought about.

Futzy stood in shock, a hand at one pocket. His head hung dumbly, as if he'd just been told his best friend had died.

Tweed's brain teemed.

It's the slasher, said one part of her mind. Run!

But voices, high and fast and full of anger, were rising all about her. Another part of her mind latched onto them, found resonance with that feeling, and rose with them.

Dex shouted beside her, his face as red as a newborn robin cheeping for worms.

Sounds were issuing too from her.

The air was full of movement. Flutterings. Hard young bodies rushing forward.

Across the black floor of the stage staggered the head janitor, a dumb slow feeb of a slasher. Tweed wondered how he had surprised or bested *anyone.*

Futzy stood transfixed. Then his hand was fumbling in his pocket and he pulled out a gun, the great unequalizer, death-power packed in a fistful of metal. With a deafening blow, Futzy punched the air before him.

The feeb's left shoulder yanked back. A man and woman entered from the wings behind him.

Far from stopping Tweed and the others, the gunshot drove them into a greater frenzy. Down the aisles they teemed, surging up the stairs in a rush of bodies.

Tweed watched the couple—odd correspondence student types—seize the janitor and wrest the ice pick from him. The man drove it into his neck and left it there.

Jonquil Brindisi came onstage.

Then Tweed swept into a surge of prom fabric that rushed past the principal, rudely thrusting Futzy Buttweiler aside like flotsam in a stream. The steel gleam of futtering cleavers winked in every hand, her own hand, Dex's too, their long knives absurdly left at their seats.

But that was okay.

One cut, one slice among the hundreds now sweeping in, would be enough.

The stage thundered as a choke of bodies came in all about. Despite the collisions, one purpose thrived. One thirst that kept the bodies honed in on the falling janitor, the hacked man whose denim suit shredded off in tufts of cloth and flesh.

In they dove, young birdbodies, a sharp hack and away, circling to swoop down for more.

Deep-hued as barbecue sauce, Gerber's blood splashed suits and dresses. *Tweed's* dress. She grew high and giddy, gaiety and rage intermingled in the sounds she made.

A man lay stripped before her, more exposed as each moment passed, bits of cloth, flesh, and organs filling the air like blood-tinged chokes of cottonwood.

She breathed meat.

She breathed madness.

Their victim's mind, sick and vicious even under attack, unspooled itself in death, flinging out darts of vileness.

But she—and all of them, this happy band of hackers and hewers—resisted those darts. In the shaping of communal grave-clouts were they caught up, weaving it, shuttled, hack by flurried hack, upon a loom of common cause.

Righteous was their wrath and beautiful.

She would tell all of this joy to her dad.

Her sister Jenna too, whose prom would be a cakewalk after this.

Through a turmoil of bodies, slapping and smacking in earnest—by God, the dance only *hinted* at it—Tweed saw her means of ingress. She seized it, rode it in, war whoops in her throat, her hand coming down, no choice really in what prize she would slice off, all of it a matter of fate and luck.

Like a coelacanth's mouth still moist from feeding, a meaty flesh-hole wuttered up at her. Its wet, red, ragged regret ovaled out to yield a slice of organ.

Slash! She held it against the blade as she pulled out, a nub of gore trapped between thumb and steel. Ms. Foddereau's butchery class paid off in spades.

"I got a nipple!" Dex screamed. "I got a nipple!"

Tweed became Dex's magnet, retiring with him upstage. Behind them, the pounding and battering of bodies kept up. In another moment, the killer would be reduced to bone, and soon that would be divvied up as well.

Tweed tugged at Dex's sleeve. "Look," she said. "Our teachers are up to their elbows in it too."

The air was misty with blood. But the spray was fine enough, atomized even, that they clearly saw Nurse Gaskin sail in; Claude Versailles, whose outsized body belied the deftness of his killer cuts; Ms. Brindisi, Miss Phipps, Mr. Buttweiler, and the others.

Tweed billowed with pride in Corundum High.

Out of a night of trauma, they were pulling together. Students and faculty alike.

For all the hell they had endured, a special bond would unite them forever, a bond as tight and conjoining as the mad janitor's futtered body was loose and undergoing disjointure.

Tweed gripped her bloody prize and smiled at Dex, who beamed back at her and held up the ruddy whorl of his catch.

Something jinged like a spun quarter at her feet. She looked down. "A key," she said.

It was gold and thick and angled. The word YALE gleamed upon it.

"The key to the padlock on the front door is my guess," said Dex. He bent to pick it up. "The one he took from the sheriff."

Tweed touched it in Dex's hand. Hard planes. The key was wet from the janitor's futtering, warm from his pocket.

She slid a finger along its length. She kept sliding, clasped Dex's hand, palm to palm, the key to their salvation trapped between. Then she lost herself in her boyfriend's eyes.

24
The Mouths of Babes

Friday, October twenty-sixth.

Jonquil Brindisi, her long legs crossed, sat in Claude's generous futon chair, sipping a banana daiquiri as she listened to Futzy Buttweiler and Delia Gaskin hold forth from the couch.

Futzy had called them all together, the major players who had survived the prom. They needed some sort of closure, he said, and he was right.

A lot of changes had come down.

Claude had divorced his wives and swiftly remarried. His new mates? The couple Jonquil herself had lusted after until the state of their earlobes had cooled her passions.

The three of them sat now in clunky dining room chairs, listening and nodding.

Lovey-dovey motherfuckers.

Futzy had replaced his pair of hellions with Adora Phipps. While they insisted a third would *surely* come along any day now, Jonquil doubted they were looking in any serious way.

And no secret to anyone and not a scandal to the unbigoted, Delia Gaskin, while maintaining the fiction of a separate residence, was deep in lust with Bix Donner's widows, Trilby and Brest, their threesome a virtual marriage.

Trilby's little whistleblower knelt alone on the living room carpet. Pill busied herself with a deck of cards, some weird sorting exercise whose rules only an eight-year-old could divine.

Near Pill sat Tweed and her kid sister Jenna, crosslegged on

256

pillows. They bookended a chipper Dexter Poindexter, who had replaced a slaughtered bank clerk at First National soon after the prom.

"Now that the media brouhaha has died down," continued Futzy, Adora's loving eyes on him, "I thought a nice quiet evening of putting the pieces together would benefit us all."

Claude nodded and spoke. "A final look at things, one last breath and benediction before we move on with our lives. Is that what you mean?"

Jonquil, bemused, said nothing.

What a load of crap this was. Were they a bunch of fucking wimps? She could take on such a night again easily. Truth be told, she missed it already. The terror, the hunt, the futtering of the crazy janitor whose bones she had wanted to leap but had ended up breaking instead.

Might it somehow happen again?

She thrilled at the thought.

"Yes," said Nurse Gaskin. "Victims of major traumas tend to obsess about them. We should look on this retelling as a ritual signpost, a mark of punctuation on the way to healing."

"Back to normal after tonight, eh?" said Jonquil. The looks Bray and Winnie gave her reinforced her doubt.

"By no means." Nurse Gaskin's eyes flared with hatred.

Then she smoothed it over.

Delia Gaskin, in Jonquil's opinion, needed to be taken down a few notches. The upstart bitch in whites had far too lofty an opinion of herself.

"The horror of that night," the nurse said, "will haunt us for the rest of our lives. But going over the ground again may make it in some sense manageable."

With that, she and Futzy launched into a retelling of the events of prom night.

Like obedient little androids, the others, everyone but Jonquil, chimed in with one part of the story or another.

Jonquil clinked and sipped, remarking what odd ducks she had fallen in with. Between bouts of savage fucking in the supply closet, she liked to regale Benji Rubblerum, the new head janitor, with stories about her colleagues and how very odd they were.

Then the weird thing happened.

Futzy and the school nurse, caught up in their tale, came to the killing of Pesky and Flense in the faculty lounge.

Jonquil saw seeds of worry sprout in Trilby Donner's eyes.

Her little girl looked up from her playing cards, listening and staring.

Jonquil might have jumped in to deflect the telling. But she loved to witness the fruits of violence, especially violence inflicted in all innocence.

"Then," said the nurse, who wore a stylish denim dress, long-sleeved, with embroidery that suggested cowboy motifs, "it's my guess that old Gerber took a pellet of dry ice in his gloved fist and forced the poor girl to swallow it."

Her hands illustrated as she spoke.

"Miss Gaskin!" said Trilby, ever the mom.

Then Pill's eyes bugged out. Her eyelids fluttered and she keeled over. No one was near enough to break her fall.

But the girl, on her knees already, did not fall far. In a glancing blow, her scalp knocked against the futon frame. The cards she cupped in her hands fanned out over the carpet, a sprawl of red and black and white.

Jonquil observed it all coolly.

She clinked her ice.

It looked as if the poor girl was choking on her tongue.

She would die if no one helped.

But the nurse barreled in to clear the girl's passageway, hovering like a benevolent angel. She rubbed Pill's hands vigorously, feeling for pulse and heartbeat, moving deft fingers everywhere on her body. "She'll be all right, I think. Claude, do you have maybe a day bed Pill can lie down on?"

"There's the guest room upstairs, with the coats. Just shove them aside."

"Trilby, why don't you stay with her, out of earshot of the rest of this?" Delia said.

Upstart bitch.

Granted, Little Miss Nursiepoo was caught up in a minicrisis. But that gave her no excuse for addressing Claude as Claude, for calling Trilby Trilby. It ought to have been Mr. Versailles and Ms. Donner, even outside working hours.

In the privacy of her threesome, the bitch could use first names all she liked. But in mixed company, it was unseemly, an affront to all decent Americans.

The two women took Pill upstairs.

Delia Gaskin returned and the tale continued. But no one was into it much any more.

Jonquil, when she wasn't mulling how best to puncture the nurse's inflated ego, saw that Pill's fainting spell had brought back the terror of that night in everyone here.

Jenna Megrim, a sweet senior whose prom would occur six months from now, who had lost her father and almost her sister as well, seemed most upset.

But the pall lay upon them all.

Delicious.

When they stood up to disperse, Brest checked with Trilby and Pill upstairs.

Then she left with Delia Gaskin.

It saved time, *lots* of time, Jonquil later realized, that the rest of them were still mixing and milling when Pill, holding her mother's hand, appeared on the stairs and began to tell them why she had fainted.

When Pill awoke, she didn't know at first where she was. Mommy was holding her hand and feeling her forehead, and Mommy's new secret sort-of-wife Delia was standing over her, saying, "I think she's coming out of it."

A huge turned-away snoozing bear lay beside Pill on the bed.

Coats.

A lamp with a frilly green shade cast a soft glow from the nightstand. The overhead light had been switched off.

Then Pill remembered.

But she managed not to show it, not even when Delia stared right into her eyes.

"You okay, Pill?" Mommy asked.

"Uh huh."

Delia said, "You gave us a scare."

"I'm sorry, Delia," she said.

Mommy bent and laughed and kissed Pill on the cheek and told her not to worry, that she was just delighted to have her back among the living.

Delia examined her, holding her wrist tight with a concentrated frown, and then moving Pill's head in strange ways by the neck and jaw.

Pill didn't much like Delia. She hadn't much liked her since Daddy died, or even before. But her two mommies seemed to like her a whole bunch, especially Brest.

So Pill only shared the way she really felt with Gigi the goat. In whispers, late at night, under the covers.

But now, she *especially* didn't like Delia.

Luckily Delia left and Mommy stayed behind.

"Mommy?" Pill said.

"Yes, dear?"

"I need to tell you something."

The telling was hard. At one point, Mommy began to cry and Pill almost wished she hadn't told her anything at all.

But in spite of her crying, Mommy was a tough lady. Pill knew that already, from the rough love her mommy sometimes shared with Daddy and Brest. She knew it from her limps and winces and from the way moonlight lit her bruises when she came in late at night to kiss Pill on the cheek, and Pill pretended to be sleeping.

Mommy cried and sighed and blew her nose.

But when Brest came up and said she and Delia would be off and asked was Pill okay, Mommy said, "She's fine."

Then her face got all dark. She added, "Make some excuse. Drop Delia off at her place and come back without her."

"I don't understand," Pill's second mommy said. "Is there—"

"I'll explain when you come back."

Pill was proud of her mother.

"Don't let on that anything's out of the ordinary, okay?"

Brest said she wouldn't. She found her coat in the pile on the bed, Delia's too, and left the room.

Mommy held Pill. She told her she was her sweet pumpkin. "We'll give them five minutes," she said. "Then we'll go downstairs."

But Mommy kept looking at her watch and Pill knew that nowhere near five minutes had passed when Mommy told her it was time, hustle her buns, chop-chop.

It felt strange, like being in a fishbowl, to leave the bedroom holding Mommy's hand and see all the grown-ups standing in clumps downstairs.

They stopped when Mommy said something. They all looked up.

Then Pill told them.

Just like she told Mommy.

It was really hard this time. It felt as if she were back in that closet again, but this time Mommy was with her.

It was okay to see the hand moving again, *Delia's* hand in that same gesture, the dry ice pellet in her glove.

And it was okay to hear *Mjust askin'!* again, realizing now that the big girl saying it was really saying *Miss Gaskin!*.

Pill worried at first that she wouldn't be able to tell it the way it happened, so the grown-ups would get a clear picture. But she saw from their faces that they did.

They got it clear all right, Mr. Buttweiler, the principal, most of all. Pill could see that in the blush of his blotchy skin.

And in what came next.

Futzy looked at little Pill on the landing, listening as she drew the correct conclusion from that terrible night. She was an angel, and this was her annunciation.

If he tried, he could hear her voice deepen into his slain daughter's voice. He could see her sprout a foot taller, her breasts plump out, her first lobebag being slipped over her lovelobe when she came of age. She was Kitty all over again.

Kitty had come back, his beloved girl, to set things right.

Adora had enriched his homelife.

Now his daughter had returned to fix the rest of it.

When Pill finished, she gazed up at her mom.

"Oh wow," said Jenna Megrim.

Heads turned.

"What is it, Jenna?" Futzy asked.

"I was parking cars that night. I remember, after it was all over, wondering why the janitor's car was parked in the faculty and staff lot. But then I figured he knew the combination into the backways and didn't need to drive into the so-called, not-really-secret garage everybody knows about and use the underground elevator.

"What I didn't see, until Pill was talking just now, was that—and I've gone over this a hundred times in my head—the nurse's blue clunker was *never* in the parking lot, at least not up to the moment the school was padlocked shut."

"She was inside long before then," Jonquil said coolly.

Futzy recalled how quickly Delia had left that night, not through the front door like floods of relieved seniors did. Ten minutes later, when Jonquil, Adora, Winnie, and Bray joined him in exploring the backways, Matthew Megrim had been discovered. Soon after, they found the hapless history teacher's car by the elevator. Hints of gas fumes suggested that the motor had recently been on, though that made no sense.

It hadn't been his fumes at all.

It had been Delia's.

So Futzy told the gathering of survivors.

"Something else," Winnie said from the couch, holding Claude's hand and Bray's. "The coroner's report repeatedly mentioned right-handed stabs to the bodies. Now I remember the janitor at the light bank lifting a hand to adjust the lights just before the music started. Did anyone else see that?"

Tweed spoke up. "We were on the bandstand. Me and Dex." She looked up to recapture it. "The janitor was raising his left hand, kinda drifting it hazily over the switches, struggling to recall which ones he was supposed to throw."

Futzy brought back other scenes. Gerber Waddell screwing in lightbulbs, triangulating an American flag, weeding flower beds in front of the school. He saw Gerber's left hand moving, ever moving, his right hand idle or thumb-tucked into his belt.

Futzy looked at Trilby Donner's little girl. "Pill," he said, "which hand did you see holding that dry ice pellet? Can you remember?"

"I think so," the little girl said.

Gripping the oak railing, she brought the scene back with a squinch and a twist to her face. The narrow crack through which she had seen the killer's arm.

Her hands let go, shaping a slow fog before her. First the left rose, then stopped, falling back into place. Then with increasing certainty, the other, the right, lifted, finding its fixed place in the air, holding the invisible pellet, the arm, the hand, a gesture of strength mixed with delicacy.

The movement of Pill's hand matched precisely Delia's gesture on the couch, right before the little girl had fainted.

Trilby Donner, once more in shock and torn umpteen ways, listened as the questions confirmed what all this had been leading to.

Delia Gaskin, Brest's hush-hush lover and her own, had, by dint of damning evidence, just been convicted of multiple deaths: Zane Fronemeyer and his wives, Sheriff Blackburn, Jiminy Jones, a slew of seniors in the midst of a night of terror, and then, to redirect the finger of accusation, poor innocent Gerber Waddell, a feeb falsely futtered, his reputation forever besmirched.

Trilby felt shame.

And violation.

How could a person seem so decent, mouth all the words of love one could ever hope to hear, yet beneath that facade be monstrous?

She and Brest were still deep in grief over Bix's death.

Now, their relationship had once again been ripped raw. A betrayer had wrapped herself about their ailing hearts, a snake whose hooded guile had penetrated deep to the soul.

Trilby's hand went to her mouth.

Her eyes teared up.

Keep it together, keep it together.

Focus on Pill.

Focus on her beautiful innocent girl, nodding to this or that question from the gathered adults, her words pure and carefully chosen.

Pill was not the easiest child to raise. She tested for boundaries. She gave guff. She pushed back.

But always, Trilby sensed her child's secret delight in being reined in, in knowing where the limits were.

Trilby had feared, coming off the prom, a shattering. She had seen Pill move this way and that in new psychic space, struggling to keep her balance in a world rearranged, a world from which her father had been violently ripped.

But now, here in Claude Versailles' living room (how she wished Brest could witness it), Pill was taking confident steps onto solid ground. In this precious eight-year-old girl, her childlike honesty in full display, Trilby had her first glimpse of the proud woman her daughter would become.

This vision anchored her.

These were her friends and colleagues, their eyes afire with appalled awe at the deception and temerity of Delia Gaskin. But primarily their eyes brimmed with wonder at the emergence of Pill, *her* Pill, her lovely daughter, getting near to being gangly of limb, a slim barely-there little girl in bib overalls and close-skulled brown hair.

Her friends could not save Trilby from the madness of the moment, but Pill could. For all her quiet frailty, Pill would pull her mother through; Trilby sensed it deep in her heart.

So too would it be with Brest.

Somehow they would survive this time, keeping a dread secret from the monster in their lives, as would Pill (her innocence wily enough not to tell Delia a thing), until this close-knit community took its proper revenge upon her.

That revenge would not be long in coming.

Already, as the final questions to Pill were asked and answered, Trilby saw wheels turning.

In Futzy Buttweiler.

In Jonquil Brindisi.

In Claude Versailles.

Retribution would be swift and sure.

She and Brest, newly wounded and raw, would be seen after.

More important, Pill would see her father's murderer dealt with. She would forgive her mommies for their bad choice, rectified at once and explained when she was much older. And she would find firm footing in this marvelous society in the greatest country on the face of the planet.

From the midst of torment, a new seed of hope and solidarity would sprout.

Trilby had never loved her daughter more than she did at this moment. That's what her tears, freely flowing now, announced to all who cared to observe them.

Hope was justified, she thought, even when life seemed most hopeless.

25

Piecing Together What Was Torn Asunder

Bray looked up at the sound of Claude's front door opening. In walked Brest Donner from having dropped Delia Gaskin home.

Brest was a hard woman, he thought. Beauty edged with greed, an inturned nature. Before too many years had passed, her great-eagle sweep and flare would droop into something vulturish.

Bray considered the abomination this woman had instigated: a female threesome.

He couldn't help but be judgmental about such a perverted combination of partners. Despite his years as an outcast and the prejudicial treatment he had suffered, there were certain personal choices that struck him as simply wrong. Three women in a sexual entanglement was one of them. Didn't the Bible have a few prohibitions against that sort of thing? He believed it did.

"Okay, what's up?" said Brest. "A surprise party?"

Everyone spoke at once. While the confusion was sorting itself out, Bray whispered to Winnie, "They'll slap us in jail."

She goggled at him. "Jeepers, Bray, *now* what's your problem?"

"We were heroes, weren't we? You and me, the two social pariahs, especially. We did the media circuit and the world changed, a tiny bit anyway."

"So?"

"So now the story will turn way the fuck around: We made a

265

mistake, we got fooled, we fucked up. They'll take everything back, they'll try us for Gerber's murder, they'll demonize us, it'll be *Notorious* for sure."

Claude leaned to Winnie. "Is our handsome yummy-nums lapsing into Bray-mode again?"

"He sure is," Winnie said.

"Be not dismayed, hubby ours," Claude said. "Everyone in this room, without exception, was Delia's dupe."

That was true. Claude had a way of cutting to the heart. He was also a mean flogger when the mood struck him.

"*All* of us made a mistake," continued Claude, "which we simply must, with all deliberate speed, rectify. If we visit right retribution upon our wayward school nurse, they'll make us heroes all over again. The public loves seeing justice meted out. Calm down, Bray, sweetie. Let come what may."

Claude sat back, not waiting to see if Bray followed his advice. Claude *knew* he would. His confidence, Bray thought, was irritating, but it wasn't misplaced. Claude knew him.

Claude knew them both.

Had sexy Jonquil Brindisi not been so deeply bigoted, it would have been sweet and savory for them to have tripled up with her. But Claude, the more he and Winnie got to know him, was a pretty decent companion. He treated them well, he was fun to listen to, and he cooked a mean omelette.

"I just don't like it," Bray muttered, but only for form's sake.

Winnie's look said, I love you, you doofus, despite your fretting and moaning.

Meanwhile, Brest had clearly been struggling to make sense of the babble. As everyone spoke up, fitting in this or that piece of the puzzle for her, Trilby held her hand.

Pill leaned against her mother and listened, looking tired but otherwise like any other eight-year-old up past her bedtime.

Bray twiddled his fingers at her, a spastic butterfly caught chest high. Pill gave a wisp of a smile and twiddled back.

The plan for dealing with Delia Gaskin came in part from Futzy Buttweiler and in part—indeed the *killer* part—from Jenna Megrim.

Bray listened in fascination as their plan gathered shape and momentum. Carrying it out, he sensed, would provide the healing for which they had come together. As one part of the plan meshed with another, their conspiratorial circle took on centripetal force. Heads angled in like sharpened stakes in a concealed pit.

Only Jonquil held back, sipping her drink.

Bray gave her a brief look of wistful lust, to which Jonquil dutifully shot back an intolerant glare full of fire and fuck-you.

Still, her compact, killer, curvaceous legs, crossed just so, boggled Bray's brain. He longed to uncross them, to shred those dark stockings, to dip down into the warm moist fire of her loins and tongue up the juices that sizzled there.

Right, he thought. Not in this lifetime.

Winnie elbowed him. Listen up, Bray, her look commanded him.

Bray listened.

Dex sat on the floor against an overstuffed armchair, intent on the grown-ups' conversation.

Tweed sat huggably close on his right, her sister Jenna's head on his left thigh.

Despite Dex's graduation the previous spring and his coming-up-on six months at First National, clerking away as if he'd done it forever, he still felt very much a kid.

The terrors of the prom had indeed aged him. And this evening's revelations went even further toward drawing his youth to a close. But maturity wasn't something you snapped on like a toolbelt.

It was strange being a boy.

Boys were expected to show strength. Not to cry, or only on special occasions.

But really the girls were in charge.

With *decent* boys anyway.

He had heard of the rougher sort of guys, who threw their rage around and made things nasty for the women in their lives. They were just wacked-out dudes, far as he was concerned.

But among normal people, the women held sway and everybody knew it.

There were even jokes about it.

Now he had learned that it wasn't sick-guy Gerber Waddell, but sick-girl Delia Gaskin, who had been the prom killer.

Poor Gerber, a kind retard with a nasty past and a brain pruned back to cut out his nastiness, they had futtered by mistake.

And Miss Gaskin walked about, bold as brass, wearing a mask of innocence, even trysting on the sly with the widows of the same Bix Donner whose life she herself had ended.

She had to be insane.

To think that he had visited the nurse's office, what, at least half a dozen times during his four-year stint at Corundum High. She could have sliced him up, fed him poison pills, or God knows *what*-all.

She could have done that to *anyone*.

Maybe she had.

No doubt there would be an investigation. Odd incidents at the school. Rumors of excess pain, of prolonged illnesses, the examination of pill bottles in medicine chests.

Dex didn't think anyone had died, but maybe he was wrong. Probably though, what with all the ribbing the nurse took, she had simply snapped.

On his left, Jenna stirred.

Tweed cuddled against him, almost hiding her head beneath his arm. Perhaps she was reliving those awful moments at the prom, and the death of her father. Dex would have to soothe her tonight, to assure her that she was safe in his arms and adored to the max.

But Tweed's kid sister squirmed in a most delightful fashion at his thigh. As he watched her take in each speaker in the room, Dex could feel the tension in her body.

Jenna was a pert thing, a little more compact than Tweed but otherwise a knock-off of her.

And a knock-out.

Dex mused.

Sister-wives were not unheard of.

Jenna was currently nursing a crush on the sprightly Pish Balthasar and on Bo Meacham, a hot-shot quarterback with nothing but brawn and looks to recommend him.

Maybe after her prom, she would wise up and gaze upon her brother-in-law in a new way.

Dex hoped so.

But he thought it best to let that unfold on its own. It was inconceivable to bring it up with her. Maybe he could plant a seed in Tweed's ear, letting sisterly magic weave its gossamer web.

Shame on him!

With all the upset and outrage sweeping through Mr. Versailles' living room, here *he* was firmly focused on lust.

Maybe Tweed would chastise him tonight.

He loved their Private Flogger.

And he was glad it made such a racket, the buzz-build, the *thwap*!

Jenna, down the hall from their bedroom, was most likely listening, lying there stroking her lovelobe. Most likely, she had Pish and Bo on her mind as she stroked, but maybe not, maybe not.

He could dream, couldn't he?

Tweed clung to Dex.

She missed her father's melodious voice.

At first, her house had seemed empty without him. But Dex's love for her had so filled it, and so filled her heart, that the ache of her father's death had lost its edge in recent months.

Jenna's presence helped too.

Their sisterly rivalry, always minor, had vanished completely in the sudden maturity prom night had brought on.

Jenna had recently taken up with Bo Meacham, whose outsized nose and dorkish grins were more than offset by his dropdead looks and a stellar career this year as lead quarterback. She had dropped hints to Tweed, snickering over popcorn while Dex was off hitting the bars with his work buddies, that noselength, at least in Bo's case, did indeed nicely correspond to genlength.

But more important to Tweed was her sister's near-certain crowning as prom queen. Next spring, the designated slasher's victim would come as usual from the pool of the non-exempt, a pool which would *not* include Jenna.

Proper protocol would be observed at Corundum High. Mr. Buttweiler would see to it. No doubt, the entire Demented States of America would tune in that night to witness the restoration of order in Corundum, Kansas.

Pillowed on Dex's thigh on the floor, Jenna was following intensely the how-shall-we-kill-her debate which filled the living room.

Tweed watched a lightbulb struggle to go on in her sister's head.

Later, she swore she heard the tinny tinsel clink of the pullchain as Jenna's eyes lit up.

"Wait! I've got it!" she said, interrupting a savage suggestion from Jonquil Brindisi. Jenna had always been bold with adults. "We mustn't rip her apart. Not quickly. Not slowly. Not with drops of acid steaming pain into her wounds. Not with starved, rabid rats dangling within a jaw's bite of her flesh. Nope! We've got to keep her skin intact!"

A razor stropped in Miss Brindisi's voice. "The woman deserves slow dismemberment." End of argument.

Had Jenna already taken her course in the greater vices? Yes. Tweed remembered the B+ on her sister's report card the winter before. No reprisals were possible from that quarter.

"Jonquil," said Mr. Buttweiler, "let's hear what Jenna has to say, shall we?"

"She's a real pistol," whispered Tweed to Dex, who nodded and squeezed her hand.

Jenna's prodigious zest, her zeal when she latched onto the meat of an idea, was a favorite topic of conversation between them. That, even more than Jenna's beauty, explained her popularity.

"*Here's* how we'll kill her!"

Tweed observed the others as Jenna talked.

Trilby and Brest, torn by warring emotions, nodded with enthusiasm as her plan unfolded. Miss Phipps' eyes saucered behind her gold wire rims. Futzy Buttweiler's eyebrows looked like a couple of fat caterpillars working overtime at pushups. Claude Versailles and his formerly homeless lovers were utterly enthralled by Jenna's words.

Even Jonquil Brindisi's defiance softened to neutrality there in that armchair. Her sips grew more deliberate, her body shifting in what Tweed suspected was growing arousal.

"Once she's dead," said Jenna, "we'll have her fluxidermed. Her body will be on display just inside Corundum High's front door. Kids'll get to paint her. Or scrawl graffiti on her. Or maybe do some other stuff the prom committee thinks up or approves. But nobody's allowed to steal her. And no one can, like, remove her arms or legs or anything, because everyone will understand what her role at the prom will be and just be *dying* of anticipation all year."

Jonquil Brindisi's long legs dandled against one another as

she leaned forward.

"Her role at the prom?" she asked.

Ms. Brindisi's friendship lobe blushed with bloodlust, her lovelobe's gray-paisley bag seeming to throb with a stung-thumb swelling.

Tweed's pride in Jenna flowered as her plan spilled out with renewed energy. The living room, once solemn, was now abuzz with fresh dreams of collective revenge. Jenna's stunning imagination pictured the gym, months in the future.

She showed them, all of them, how it would be on that terror-filled night.

Where precisely the slaughtered couple would pillow their heads.

And how the climax of the evening would at last put the community's anguish—and the anguish of an entire nation—to rest.

"I was a blackened corpse
among the living, and in this hour
I am the fire of life
and my flame burns up
the darkness in the world.
My face must be whiter
than the glowing white face of the moon.
. . . .
Do you see my face?
Do you see the light that shines out of me?
Ah! Love kills!
But no one dies
without having known love!"
    —Richard Strauss's *Elektra*,
       trans. Holland and Chalmers

". . . the secret ministry of frost
Shall hang them up in silent icicles,
Quietly shining to the quiet moon."
    —Samuel Taylor Coleridge,
      Frost at Midnight

EPILOGUE
Atonement and Payback

Futzy Buttweiler and Adora Phipps, bundled up in overcoats, observed from the sidewalk in front of the Bleak residence, where Gerber Waddell had once been housed and fed.

"It's marvelous," said Futzy, "how everything came together in little more than a day."

"It is, darling," came Adora's reply. "I'm glad Tweed and Dexter suggested it."

Adora had softened him.

Students he had thought of as rapscallionly turdsuckers on prom night, he now saw anew.

On this chilly Halloween eve, an hour after sunset, candles wuttering in one hand, Futterware containers clutched in the other, grim-faced grads made their way in slow procession along the street and up onto the lawn.

Singles, couples, and triples, Futzy forgave them all, loved them all.

The Bleaks, touched by the attention, stood on their front porch. Shyler Bleak, looking old and stooped, waved and nodded at no one in particular. His hefty wife dabbed at her eyes with the corner of a hanky. From all accounts, they had treated Gerber well.

Along Halloween sidewalks, costumed rug-rats, some holding a parent's hand, roved from house to house, ringing doorbells, shouting a high-pitched threat, and suffering the toss and smack against face or torso of twisted bags of candy, coins, or God knows what, before the doors slammed in their masked faces.

Sensing perhaps that an event of great import was transpiring outside the Bleak residence, not one of them crossed the long parade of processing students to demand treats there.

Dex and Tweed did them all proud.

They stood at one corner of an old brown comforter unfolded on the lawn, softly greeting each penitent, or simply nodding, as he or she laid down a futtered cut of janitor within the stenciled outline of the slain man.

Bits of bone.

Nubs of sun-dried flesh.

Snailings of some internal organ.

Only by an extraordinary feat of imagination could this symbolic feint at defuttering be said to reconstitute the poor man these promgoers had hacked to pieces.

Yet it felt to Futzy that Gerber Waddell did indeed, in some significant way, manifest in these feeble tailings.

Amidst the moonlit scumble of his flesh, good old Gerber returned to forgive and forget, to fire them up for the revenge that lay ahead.

A lone child in a skeleton suit and mask, its pre-teen lobes absurdly scored with painted bone-shapes, stopped to tug on the principal's sleeve and ask, "Aren't you Futzy Buttweiler?"

The girl (or boy) held a grocery bag weighted with goodies, half of which, if statistics compiled the previous year held, were tainted with rat poison, razors, or finely ground glass. From the tone of the question, Futzy's TV notoriety had sunk a deep set of roots into at least one little mind in Corundum.

"Yes, I am," he admitted.

"You could use this," said the kid, reaching into his bag and drawing out a wrapped lollipop, which thrust up from a skeletal hand: a scepter, a sucker, a challenge.

Futzy took it. "Thank you," he said.

"You need to put it in your *mouf*, Futzy."

That was what TV fame did for you. It gave everybody the right to call you by your first name. Even some upstart brat.

Adora's hand tensed on his arm.

"I'll have it later," said Futzy.

"No, now," said the child, its moon-white chin bobbing beneath a stiff mask edge. "I want to watch you suck on it. I need to see the stick pokin' outa your lips."

"Don't," cautioned Adora.

But he had to.

There was no urgency, no brattiness, in the kid. If Futzy held firm, he would probably shrug and pass on.

It was simply a matter of mood.

The ritual that was unfolding before him made the space where they stood feel charmed, blessed, and strangely . . . safe.

Futzy patted his wife's hand. He undid the brown twist of paper, eyed the amber glisten of a moonlit sphere of candy, and popped it into his mouth.

Hard ball roofing his palate.

Root beer.

Was there another flavor? Some toxin being released? Beginning its lethal work?

Futzy didn't think so.

He slurped it out and said, "Mmmm." Then, "Thank you, my good man."

"I'm a *girl!*" objected the trick-or-treater with puffed-up annoyance and went her way, her bag brushing noisily against her bone-suit.

"So you are," said Futzy, craning about to watch her painted hipbones fluoresce on down the sidewalk.

"Are you okay?" asked Adora, alarmed.

"Yes," he said. "Want a lick?"

She thought a second, then shook her head as if ashamed of her decision.

Futzy popped it back in.

Root beer.

He observed the older boys and girls, his former charges. There on the lawn of the Bleak residence, they were learning a critical lesson in solemnity and sobriety, one that no school could teach. When they were done, they huddled around Gerber's remains for a good long while, letting their candles burn down.

Before long, Claude and Jonquil would arrive with the implements they needed for Delia Gaskin's comeuppance. Then all of them would proceed, in a different mood entirely, to the town cemetery.

Futzy felt the eagerness building.

In himself and in everyone present.

Delia Gaskin checked her face in the hall mirror at Brest and Trilby's house, where she had pretty much taken up residence.

Funny how you could kill people, going right straight counter to the law, and still appear as normal as everyone else. Even Wigwag hadn't seen a change in her, loving her without reserve right up to the day she'd brought him to the vet and had him put down; but then dogs were just that way.

One thing was clear: There weren't no God. And there weren't no voice of conscience neither. All of that was part and parcel of the contrived guilt society heaped on your head and jabbed into your mind, hoping to corral your nastier impulses.

I'm a pretty little number when I get gussied up, thought Delia, indulging in a moment's preen. All spiffed up for the delight of Brest and Trilby. She would turn them way the fuck on.

And they her.

Glancing one last time at her suit—no lint, no dandruff, lookin' fine—Delia ventured out into the night.

The evening before, when her lovers returned from Claude's house without Pill, they'd told her the little girl was doing fine. Tweed and Dexter Poindexter, the young fools who had escaped the blade on prom night, had begged to have Pill sleep over so they could take her out tonight for trick-or-treating.

Though Delia's bedmates begged off sex, they made her hot with plans to meet them this evening near the crypt Bix Donner was immured in for some steamy lobeplay.

The graveyard lay less than a mile from their house. Delia saw no need to drive. Besides, it was a beautiful night to watch the starlight spill across square after square of sidewalk, her heels hard and sharp as she walked.

Monsters and goblins parted to let her pass.

Delia gave cheery hi-there's to clusters of them. She exchanged good-natured grins with moms and dads holding some apparition's little hand.

One foolish vampire, out all by himself, she swatted with sufficient force that he rose nearly a foot into the air. The solitary tyke's glow-in-the-dark fangs flew out of his mouth and skittered across the pavement, as did his candy, his apples, and his coins. He ran off bawling into the night.

That'd teach the little dummy a lesson in safety, thought Delia. She ought to have dragged the little shit behind a bush and broken his neck. Up out of the flesh-twist of his throat would his final breath have struggled, his blanched makeup a deathmask ready-made.

But Delia had sex on her mind.

When that was so, little else mattered.

She reached the end of Pine Street, went one block north to Maple, and turned west.

A hundred yards ahead lay the entrance to the cemetery. The long swung locked metal gate kept cars out, but night visitors on foot could easily and legally sidestep it.

Her old flame, Kitty Buttweiler, was buried in the far corner of the cemetery. Kitty was no doubt resting easier since the night Delia had avenged her death.

It had been the right thing to do.

Of that she was certain.

But it was good that Bix's crypt lay farther south, in a different part of the grounds.

As Delia approached it, she marveled anew at the upkeep Corundum put into its cemetery: Tall dark oaks lofting like dancers into the night sky. Immaculately kept lawns. Fat gravestones huddled close together. All of it attested to the town's wealth and neighborliness.

She didn't notice the wisps of . . . could it be fog? . . . until they began to curl about her ankles.

Odd.

The night air felt on the edge of nippy.

But fog, even the slightest lick of it, seemed not quite right.

For the first time in ages, Delia tasted fear, a cold thumb on the back of her neck that sent shivers up into her brain and down along her spine.

But then Brest appeared, Trilby too, around a corner of the crypt.

Brest blew her a kiss.

Delia waved and swept forward. The low white fog now definitely lingered longer, claiming more ground. It coiled in cable-thick wisps that appeared, absurdly, to seep from the crypt itself.

Dry ice, came the recognition.

And the next: *I've got to get out of here.*

Then the fog darkened up from behind the markers. Only it wasn't fog.

It was heads and torsos.

As if by prearranged signal they emerged, and Delia backed into arms, arms that enfolded her and rushed her forward.

Her feet left the ground.

She fell back and up, secured from falling, abruptly horizontal, the stars going by overhead, imperfections underfoot making the way unsteady.

Her limbs were caught in vises.

As she craned about, Delia recognized the faces of those that carried her.

Students. Faculty. Fellow staffers. They refused to meet her eyes. Their faces grim-set, they ignored her protests.

Delia twisted and strained.

To no avail.

It was like her frustration when her older brother locked her in whatever wrestling grip he liked back when she was eight.

"No!" she cried. Deaf ears. "Please!"

The principal and mousy Miss Phipps joined Brest and Trilby. Futzy made a gesture and the mass of people swung around the crypt.

A burly figure lofted into moonlight.

The Ice Ghoul.

Or what had been left of it and retrievable from the theater prop room.

His head and half of his chest topped a tall pair of stepladders, his height half what it had been last May, but his angle of menace caught to perfection.

Between the shoulders of two of the heedless automatons that carried her, Delia saw Jonquil Brindisi and Claude Versailles standing beside the homeless pair who had, in the wake of prom night, become media darlings.

"Mr. Versailles, Ms. Brindisi!" she cried. "Help me!"

The planes of Jonquil Brindisi's face were as cold and smooth as sheared ice. It was clear she took umbrage at Delia's direct address.

Her chiseled slip of a nose flared. Her eyes glowered.

"Strip her," she commanded, rasping the order in offended tones. "Tie her up."

Hands mauled her, lowered her.

They ripped her garments, the blouse collar choking her until it tore free.

Cool air kissed her naked breasts, working its way through young rough hands and arms.

Her hips, her thighs, her legs twisted as though machine-caught in the mob's rip of skirt fabric, pantyhose, and frilly crotchless silken panties.

They exposed her, somehow never letting go their grip on her limbs, giving her no chance to escape.

A cool thick clamp snapped about one ankle, about the other. The press of bodies concealed them from view. But the same sensation gripped her wrists, and then she saw the rope. It was thick. Shiny new. Thin sharp bristles randomly porcupined from the twisted wheaten cable.

Rope-ties were tugged and tightened.

Were they trying to quarter her?

Delia guessed not. But the muscles of her thighs strained like whipped sails and the ball sockets at her shoulders threatened to dislocate.

At last, the hands that had held her lifted away. Night air touched her everywhere.

If she failed to tense her neck muscles, her head flopped back onto nothing.

She was stretched taut. Relentless pulls on her arms and legs came from four thick, angled, toddler-high posts sunk in the ground and notched to secure the rope. The moon illumined the flesh-shelf her body made.

By name she appealed to them. The students, Dex, Tweed, Jenna. Pye Pringle, a wispy junior who hung around Jenna and whom Delia, two days prior, had patched up in the nurse's office.

Pye looked away.

Then the principal stepped in. "All right," he said, his face harsh and rough, "peel it off."

They *wouldn't*.

That was her first thought.

Then it was too late for any thought at all.

They surged in. The urgency of their mass move puffed a night chill across her naked body.

"Wait, no!" she said.

But the air filled with shouting.

Crudely wielded scalpels carpeted up layers of skin, as fingernails dug into the soft yield of her flesh and tore it away, patch by patch.

Agony sheeted her limbs.

Ankles, calves, thighs, then her arms, caught fire and turned to flameless torches.

Up hip, down torso, at her navel, the flames spread and met. The shock to Delia's system suspended her between screaming and blacking out.

Then they slid the blades beneath the skin on her face, peeling upward from the neck, over chin and cheek, pulling at her eyelids so severely that the inflamed lids were almost torn off before they plipped back down on her eyes.

Clots of hair, as had happened below, came up in impatient hands. Her body became a living suit of ravagement.

Black dots danced amid red. Delia's tears stung like acid as they runneled down her temples.

Her tormentors backed off. The night breeze rippled razors, thin and multitudinous, along the neural skintorch Delia had become. She willed herself, despite the steady eruption of pain, to escape into oblivion.

But oblivion refused her.

Then she heard a familiar sound, multiplied a hundred times, again, again.

Rustles of burst-open plastic wrap.

The restless sound of many fingers finding their careful way around metal.

Out of the hubbub of mob noise, one word seeped through over and over on hushed, hissed esses.

Syringe.

When Delia's tears cleared, she took in the surround of bodies.

The poised hands.

Chest-high about the moonlit circle, there shimmered, like ice, thin silver down-stabs of frozen rain.

"Slowly," the principal said. "Carefully. Stay away from the vital organs. We want this to last."

Then they began to needle her.

Dex stood arm in arm with Tweed, detached from the melee of torture.

If a press of bodies obscured his view, he let it. So did Tweed.

They were ageless, he thought. An aggrieved couple watching justice meted out but not fired up with bloodlust.

He felt excited and jazzed, of course.

What self-respecting American wouldn't?

But more than that, Dex felt pity.

This was one twisted woman. A betrayer, a violator, the executioner of young folks who did not deserve to die.

Oddly enough, she was also his savior.

And Tweed's.

Futzy Buttweiler, in a moment of rare candor, had confided to them that Zane Fronemeyer's packet held his name and Tweed's that night.

A chill had coursed through him.

For all his bluster, Dex would have been no match for Mr. Fronemeyer. He would have suffered the fatal wound. Then he'd have seen Tweed fall beneath the knife blade, feeling the life ebb from him as she, in agony, struggled and died.

They felt relief.

And guilt.

Their slaughter would have fallen into the normal course of events, a sacrifice sad but accepted.

But the slaughter of Tweed's dad, of the sheriff, Jiminy Jones, the Fronemeyers, and all those kids? Those killings were perverse. They cut across the grain of all that was right and proper in American society.

Nurse Gaskin's deserved death would punctuate these atrocities. The media would, as ever, find renewed closure and new reasons to fret about whatever turned their fret-brains on and made their subscription rates rise.

But her death would not *undo* her atrocities, not even when the dead woman did her stint, the following spring, as a pinata.

Tweed had said as much, and Dex agreed.

Maybe that was what growing up was all about.

You got to see how ragged-edged life was, and how tidy the *stories* about life were.

It was a comfort, to confuse one for the other. But it was also a comfort, and a sanity, to know the difference and quietly accept it.

Dex gave his wife a squeeze.

"I love you," he said.

"What did you say?" she shouted over the melee.

"I said I love you!"

Tweed's eyes twinkled. She gave him a kiss, then turned her gaze again toward the staked and sought-after murderess before them.

Jenna had been one of the first students to sink a needle into Nurse Gaskin.

She had chosen a spot on the right arm, where the nurse's strained biceps ramped along above her elbow.

Jenna thrust it in deep enough that when she released it and stepped back, it only angled down a little and stayed stuck there. But she left an inch or so out, so that those who came later, the kids without a syringe of their own, could shove hers in deeper.

That was the considerate thing to do.

Share the vengeance.

Some kids slid under her and put theirs in from below. Those didn't stay stuck, of course. Gravity wouldn't allow it.

So some of them shoved it in again along her sides as they regained their feet.

Others circled around for another stab into buttock or back, the blood from earlier puncture wounds anointing them as dry-ice mist curled about them.

"Cripes," some kid said. "Nursie's a fuckin' pin cushion, ain't she?"

Jenna and Pish exchanged get-a-clue looks.

Guys were so transparent when they wanted to hit on you, a window onto Geek City.

They ignored him.

He got the hint and drifted away. Some boys were so dense though. Surely everyone knew about her and Bo Meacham, about her and Pish Balthasar.

Jenna was off limits and happy to be so.

Pish of the smoky eyes said, "She's beautiful when she writhes." She was staring at the nurse's parted legs.

The hypos were so numerous, they seemed to weave weird metallic leggings, or some sort of oriental armor that halted at the parts most in need of protection.

Beautiful?

Yes, thought Jenna.

An image came to her of a cautiously smiling beekeeper covered in bees.

In her fight against pain, against death, the nurse seemed larger than life. Like a living suit, the forest of hypos magnified the nurse's body, the jerk of her movements.

Hers was a dance of denial.

It was also, strangely enough, a dance of affirmation, a struggle to embrace death.

"She *is* beautiful," said Jenna, touching Pish's friendship lobe so that the pretty dark-haired genius shut her eyelids in a gesture of surrender. "She'll look super, hanging up."

"Mmmmm," murmured Pish, looking like a Manx with a dead goldfish in its mouth.

For an instant, but how glorious an instant, Jenna imagined the fluxidermed nurse swaying above the warmth of the prom.

Her body was stuffed with blood sweets, hard circles of cinnamon and cherry, wrapped in twists of plastic and shaped like platelets.

She hung from ropes, those same ropes Sheriff Blackburn had dangled from, as an amazing sweep of lights played over her.

In Jenna's vision, the dance band was playing dreamy, caramel-taffy music.

Below the unclothed nurse lay two slain seniors.

She and Pish would survive.

They *had* to, to see this beautiful scene, and to be a part of it.

Midnight would arrive.

Then they would futter the couple. Futter them so fiercely, the blood would spew up, paint the nurse's bloated belly, and drip back down.

And when at last the orgy of futtering was done and the corpses not much more than memory, everyone would be given sticks tipped in needles only a little shorter than tonight's.

They would poke and jab, watching the dead nurse's body jiggle and swing at rope's end.

Her skin would rip open.

And out would spill a gorefall of candy, pelting them, battering their laughing blood-smeared faces and raining into their upthrust hands.

Taffy music would cream upon them.

Pish and Bo, in their bloody prom clothing, would smother Jenna in delirious hugs.

And life would begin in earnest.

At the last minute, Tweed handed her syringe to a former classmate. He had given a rebel yell and surged in, his body as thick and bulky as a rhino.

Dex had watched her give it to him.

Tweed shrugged, and Dex understood. Their minds were that attuned.

She felt no hard feelings toward the nurse. The wild scene unfolding before them seemed, even as it happened, a vivid memory. She nudged Dex, whose eyes were glued to the controlled carnage, the invaded body, the stream of needlers flowing in, out, and around Nurse Gaskin.

He turned to look at Tweed.

"Over here," she said, taking his arm.

Her father's plot lay close by. The screams, the mob sounds, were scarcely muted.

Above the top of the crypt, an illumined ridge of red papier-mache resolved itself into a slice of scalp, the twist of a ghoulish ear.

Tweed's gaze caressed the letters cut into her father's headstone. BORN SINGING, they said. And below that, SINGING STILL.

"He would have sung some interesting things tonight," said Dex, his voice full and fond.

"Life is short," said Tweed. "Dad knew that."

"Should we go? Or do you want to watch her die and hear what Mr. Buttweiler has to say?"

She shook her head. "There's no need."

"Okay."

"But I would like something else."

When Dex asked what that might be, Tweed knelt to her

backpack, which she had set against her father's gravestone.

I love you, Dad, she thought. She wished he could be there for this.

Unzipping the pack, she reached deep into its cloth wound.

"Ms. Gaskin sure can scream," Dex said.

It thrilled Tweed, that sound.

The screams felt as if they were coming from Nurse Gaskin's deepest secret self, as hidden as the murderous part of her, close to the angels, a dark rich soil given voice.

It made sense of the universe.

And it offered a perfect backdrop for Tweed's revelation.

She withdrew a thermos and a tall tumbler.

When Dex turned back from the scream, he saw what she was doing and broke into tears.

"Oh, Tweed. Really?"

"Yes," she said.

She rose, uncapped it, poured until the glass swirled brimful of moonlight.

Then she set the thermos on stone, took a long cool swallow, and held the tumbler out to the father-to-be.

Nurse Gaskin's howls of pain corona'd Dex's head. He was crying.

How lovely her man was.

They would make a beautiful baby.

Tweed touched his friendship lobe, warmed it in her fingers, and kissed it with sweet ardency.

Then she took Dex's right hand and fisted it about the tumbler.

"Drink," she said. "For our love."

And he did.

His tears subsided. Through what remained of them, he smiled.

Then he raised the glass.

Over wounded-gazelle screams, a benediction from a supportive cosmos, Tweed watched the water glug down his throat, its silver backwash sloshing at his upper lip.

When he had emptied it, he smashed it against her father's headstone. Lifting her in his arms, Dex gave Tweed the deepest, wettest, sloppiest, most soul-stirring kiss she had ever known.

Life was good indeed.

And it was about to get a whole lot better.

ABOUT THE AUTHOR

Robert Devereaux made his professional debut in *Pulphouse Magazine* in the late 1980's, attended the 1990 Clarion West Writers Workshop, and soon placed stories in such major venues as *Crank!, Weird Tales*, and Dennis Etchison's anthology *MetaHorror*. Two of his stories made the final ballot for the Bram Stoker and World Fantasy Awards.

Robert has a well-deserved reputation as an author who pushes every envelope, though he would claim, with a stage actor's assurance, that as long as one's writing illuminates characters in all their kinks, quirks, kindnesses, and extremes, the imagination must be free to explore nasty places as well as nice, or what's the point?

Robert lives in sunny northern Colorado with the delightful Victoria, making up stuff that tickles his fancy and, he hopes, those of his readers.

Visit him online at: www.robertdevereaux.com

Bizarro books

CATALOG   SPRING 2010

Bizarro Books publishes under the following imprints:

www.rawdogscreamingpress.com

www.eraserheadpress.com

www.afterbirthbooks.com

www.swallowdownpress.com

For all your Bizarro needs visit:

WWW.BIZARROCENTRAL.COM

Introduce yourselves to the bizarro genre and all of its authors with the Bizarro Starter Kit series. Each volume features short novels and short stories by ten of the leading bizarro authors, designed to give you a perfect sampling of the genre for only $5 plus shipping.

BB-0X1
"The Bizarro Starter Kit"
(Orange)

Featuring D. Harlan Wilson, Carlton Mellick III, Jeremy Robert Johnson, Kevin L Donihe, Gina Ranalli, Andre Duza, Vincent W. Sakowski, Steve Beard, John Edward Lawson, and Bruce Taylor.

236 pages $5

BB-0X2
"The Bizarro Starter Kit"
(Blue)

Featuring Ray Fracalossy, Jeremy C. Shipp, Jordan Krall, Mykle Hansen, Andersen Prunty, Eckhard Gerdes, Bradley Sands, Steve Aylett, Christian TeBordo, and Tony Rauch.

244 pages $5

BB-001 **"The Kafka Effekt" D. Harlan Wilson** - A collection of forty-four irreal short stories loosely written in the vein of Franz Kafka, with more than a pinch of William S. Burroughs sprinkled on top. **211 pages $14**

BB-002 **"Satan Burger" Carlton Mellick III** - The cult novel that put Carlton Mellick III on the map ... Six punks get jobs at a fast food restaurant owned by the devil in a city violently overpopulated by surreal alien cultures. **236 pages $14**

BB-003 **"Some Things Are Better Left Unplugged" Vincent Sakwoski** - Join The Man and his Nemesis, the obese tabby, for a nightmare roller coaster ride into this postmodern fantasy. **152 pages $10**

BB-004 **"Shall We Gather At the Garden?" Kevin L Donihe** - Donihe's Debut novel. Midgets take over the world, The Church of Lionel Richie vs. The Church of the Byrds, plant porn and more! **244 pages $14**

BB-005 **"Razor Wire Pubic Hair" Carlton Mellick III** - A genderless humandildo is purchased by a razor dominatrix and brought into her nightmarish world of bizarre sex and mutilation. **176 pages $11**

BB-006 **"Stranger on the Loose" D. Harlan Wilson** - The fiction of Wilson's 2nd collection is planted in the soil of normalcy, but what grows out of that soil is a dark, witty, otherworldly jungle... **228 pages $14**

BB-007 **"The Baby Jesus Butt Plug" Carlton Mellick III** - Using clones of the Baby Jesus for anal sex will be the hip sex fetish of the future. **92 pages $10**

BB-008 **"Fishyfleshed" Carlton Mellick III** - The world of the past is an illogical flatland lacking in dimension and color, a sick-scape of crispy squid people wandering the desert for no apparent reason. **260 pages $14**

BB-009 **"Dead Bitch Army" Andre Duza** - Step into a world filled with racist teenagers, cannibals, 100 warped Uncle Sams, automobiles with razor-sharp teeth, living graffiti, and a pissed-off zombie bitch out for revenge. **344 pages $16**

BB-010 **"The Menstruating Mall" Carlton Mellick III** - "The Breakfast Club meets Chopping Mall as directed by David Lynch." - Brian Keene **212 pages $12**

BB-011 **"Angel Dust Apocalypse" Jeremy Robert Johnson** - Meth-heads, man-made monsters, and murderous Neo-Nazis. "Seriously amazing short stories..." - Chuck Palahniuk, author of Fight Club **184 pages $11**

BB-012 **"Ocean of Lard" Kevin L Donihe / Carlton Mellick III** - A parody of those old Choose Your Own Adventure kid's books about some very odd pirates sailing on a sea made of animal fat. **176 pages $12**

BB-013 **"Last Burn in Hell" John Edward Lawson** - From his lurid angst-affair with a lesbian music diva to his ascendance as unlikely pop icon the one constant for Kenrick Brimley, official state prison gigolo, is he's got no clue what he's doing. **172 pages $14**

BB-014 **"Tangerinephant" Kevin Dole 2** - TV-obsessed aliens have abducted Michael Tangerinephant in this bizarro combination of science fiction, satire, and surrealism. **164 pages $11**

BB-015 **"Foop!" Chris Genoa** - Strange happenings are going on at Dactyl, Inc, the world's first and only time travel tourism company.
"A surreal pie in the face!" - Christopher Moore **300 pages $14**

BB-016 **"Spider Pie" Alyssa Sturgill** - A one-way trip down a rabbit hole inhabited by sexual deviants and friendly monsters, fairytale beginnings and hideous endings. **104 pages $11**

BB-017 "The Unauthorized Woman" Efrem Emerson - Enter the world of the inner freak, a landscape populated by the pre-dead and morticioners, by cockroaches and 300-lb robots. **104 pages $11**

BB-018 "Fugue XXIX" Forrest Aguirre - Tales from the fringe of speculative literary fiction where innovative minds dream up the future's uncharted territories while mining forgotten treasures of the past. **220 pages $16**

BB-019 "Pocket Full of Loose Razorblades" John Edward Lawson - A collection of dark bizarro stories. From a giant rectum to a foot-fungus factory to a girl with a biforked tongue. **190 pages $13**

BB-020 "Punk Land" Carlton Mellick III - In the punk version of Heaven, the anarchist utopia is threatened by corporate fascism and only Goblin, Mortician's sperm, and a blue-mohawked female assassin named Shark Girl can stop them. **284 pages $15**

 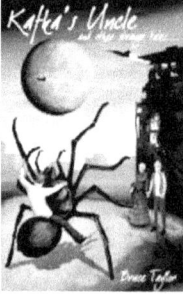  

BB-021 "Pseudo-City" D. Harlan Wilson - Pseudo-City exposes what waits in the bathroom stall, under the manhole cover and in the corporate boardroom, all in a way that can only be described as mind-bogglingly irreal. **220 pages $16**

BB-022 "Kafka's Uncle and Other Strange Tales" Bruce Taylor - Anslenot and his giant tarantula (tormentor? fri-end?) wander a desecrated world in this novel and collection of stories from Mr. Magic Realism Himself. **348 pages $17**

BB-023 "Sex and Death In Television Town" Carlton Mellick III - In the old west, a gang of hermaphrodite gunslingers take refuge from a demon plague in Telos: a town where its citizens have televisions instead of heads. **184 pages $12**

BB-024 "It Came From Below The Belt" Bradley Sands - What can Grover Goldstein do when his severed, sentient penis forces him to return to high school and help it win the presidential election? **204 pages $13**

BB-025 "Sick: An Anthology of Illness" John Lawson, editor - These Sick stories are horrendous and hilarious dissections of creative minds on the scalpel's edge. **296 pages $16**

BB-026 "Tempting Disaster" John Lawson, editor - A shocking and alluring anthology from the fringe that examines our culture's obsession with taboos. **260 pages $16**

BB-027 "Siren Promised" Jeremy Robert Johnson & Alan M Clark - Nominated for the Bram Stoker Award. A potent mix of bad drugs, bad dreams, brutal bad guys, and surreal/incredible art by Alan M. Clark. **190 pages $13**

BB-028 "Chemical Gardens" Gina Ranalli - Ro and punk band Green is the Enemy find Kreepkins, a surfer-dude warlock, a vengeful demon, and a Metal Priestess in their way as they try to escape an underground nightmare. **188 pages $13**

  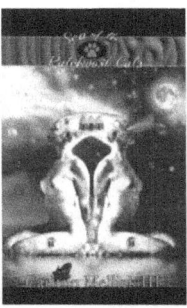 

BB-029 "Jesus Freaks" Andre Duza - For God so loved the world that he gave his only two begotten sons… and a few million zombies. **400 pages $16**

BB-030 "Grape City" Kevin L. Donihe - More Donihe-style comedic bizarro about a demon named Charles who is forced to work a minimum wage job on Earth after Hell goes out of business. **108 pages $10**

BB-031"Sea of the Patchwork Cats" Carlton Mellick III - A quiet dreamlike tale set in the ashes of the human race. For Mellick enthusiasts who also adore The Twilight Zone. **112 pages $10**

BB-032 "Extinction Journals" Jeremy Robert Johnson - An uncanny voyage across a newly nuclear America where one man must confront the problems associated with loneliness, insane dieties, radiation, love, and an ever-evolving cockroach suit with a mind of its own. **104 pages $10**

BB-033 **"Meat Puppet Cabaret" Steve Beard** - At last! The secret connection between Jack the Ripper and Princess Diana's death revealed! **240 pages $16 / $30**

BB-034 **"The Greatest Fucking Moment in Sports" Kevin L. Donihe**
- In the tradition of the surreal anti-sitcom Get A Life comes a tale of triumph and agape love from the master of comedic bizarro. **108 pages $10**

BB-035 **"The Troublesome Amputee" John Edward Lawson** - Disturbing verse from a man who truly believes nothing is sacred and intends to prove it. **104 pages $9**

BB-036 **"Deity" Vic Mudd** - God (who doesn't like to be called "God") comes down to a typical, suburban, Ohio family for a little vacation—but it doesn't turn out to be as relaxing as He had hoped it would be... **168 pages $12**

BB-037 **"The Haunted Vagina" Carlton Mellick III** - It's difficult to love a woman whose vagina is a gateway to the world of the dead. **132 pages $10**

BB-038 **"Tales from the Vinegar Wasteland" Ray Fracalossy** - Witness: a man is slowly losing his face, a neighbor who periodically screams out for no apparent reason, and a house with a room that doesn't actually exist. **240 pages $14**

BB-039 **"Suicide Girls in the Afterlife" Gina Ranalli** - After Pogue commits suicide, she unexpectedly finds herself an unwilling "guest" at a hotel in the Afterlife, where she meets a group of bizarre characters, including a goth Satan, a hippie Jesus, and an alien-human hybrid. **100 pages $9**

BB-040 **"And Your Point Is?" Steve Aylett** - In this follow-up to LINT multiple authors provide critical commentary and essays about Jeff Lint's mind-bending literature. **104 pages $11**

BB-041 **"Not Quite One of the Boys"** Vincent Sakowski - While drug-dealer Maxi drinks with Dante in purgatory, God and Satan play a little tri-level chess and do a little bargaining over his business partner, Vinnie, who is still left on earth. **220 pages $14**

BB-042 **"Teeth and Tongue Landscape" Carlton Mellick III** - On a planet made out of meat, a socially-obsessive monophobic man tries to find his place amongst the strange creatures and communities that he comes across. **110 pages $10**

BB-043 **"War Slut" Carlton Mellick III** - Part "1984," part "Waiting for Godot," and part action horror video game adaptation of John Carpenter's "The Thing." **116 pages $10**

BB-044 **"All Encompassing Trip" Nicole Del Sesto** - In a world where coffee is no longer available, the only television shows are reality TV re-runs, and the animals are talking back, Nikki, Amber and a singing Coyote in a do-rag are out to restore the light **308 pages $15**

BB-045 **"Dr. Identity" D. Harlan Wilson** - Follow the Dystopian Duo on a killing spree of epic proportions through the irreal postcapitalist city of Bliptown where time ticks sideways, artificial Bug-Eyed Monsters punish citizens for consumer-capitalist lethargy, and ultraviolence is as essential as a daily multivitamin. **208 pages $15**

BB-046 **"The Million-Year Centipede" Eckhard Gerdes** - Wakelin, frontman for 'The Hinge,' wrote a poem so prophetic that to ignore it dooms a person to drown in blood. **130 pages $12**

BB-047 **"Sausagey Santa" Carlton Mellick III** - A bizarro Christmas tale featuring Santa as a piratey mutant with a body made of sausages. 124 pages $10

BB-048 **"Misadventures in a Thumbnail Universe" Vincent Sakowski** - Dive deep into the surreal and satirical realms of neo-classical Blender Fiction, filled with television shoes and flesh-filled skies. **120 pages $10**

BB-049 **"Vacation" Jeremy C. Shipp** - Blueblood Bernard Johnson leaved his boring life behind to go on The Vacation, a year-long corporate sponsored odyssey. But instead of seeing the world, Bernard is captured by terrorists, becomes a key figure in secret drug wars, and, worse, doesn't once miss his secure American Dream. **160 pages $14**

BB-051 **"13 Thorns" Gina Ranalli** - Thirteen tales of twisted, bizarro horror. **240 pages $13**

BB-050 **"Discouraging at Best" John Edward Lawson** - A collection where the absurdity of the mundane expands exponentially creating a tidal wave that sweeps reason away. For those who enjoy satire, bizarro, or a good old-fashioned slap to the senses.   **208 pages $15**

BB-052 **"Better Ways of Being Dead" Christian TeBordo** - In this class, the students have to keep one palm down on the table at all times, and listen to lectures about a panda who speaks Chinese. **216 pages $14**

BB-053 **"Ballad of a Slow Poisoner" Andrew Goldfarb** Millford Mutterwurst sat down on a Tuesday to take his afternoon tea, and made the unpleasant discovery that his elbows were becoming flatter. **128 pages $10**

BB-054 **"Wall of Kiss" Gina Ranalli** - A woman... A wall... Sometimes love blooms in the strangest of places. **108 pages $9**

BB-055 **"HELP! A Bear is Eating Me" Mykle Hansen** - The bizarro, heartwarming, magical tale of poor planning, hubris and severe blood loss... **150 pages $11**

BB-056 **"Piecemeal June" Jordan Krall** - A man falls in love with a living sex doll, but with love comes danger when her creator comes after her with crab-squid assassins. **90 pages $9**

BB-057 **"Laredo" Tony Rauch** - Dreamlike, surreal stories by Tony Rauch. **180 pages $12**

BB-058 **"The Overwhelming Urge" Andersen Prunty** - A collection of bizarro tales by Andersen Prunty. **150 pages $11**

BB-059 **"Adolf in Wonderland" Carlton Mellick III** - A dreamlike adventure that takes a young descendant of Adolf Hitler's design and sends him down the rabbit hole into a world of imperfection and disorder. **180 pages $11**

BB-060 **"Super Cell Anemia" Duncan B. Barlow** - "Unrelentingly bizarre and mysterious, unsettling in all the right ways..." - Brian Evenson. **180 pages $12**

BB-061 **"Ultra Fuckers" Carlton Mellick III** - Absurdist suburban horror about a couple who enter an upper middle class gated community but can't find their way out. **108 pages $9**

BB-062 **"House of Houses" Kevin L. Donihe** - An odd man wants to marry his house. Unfortunately, all of the houses in the world collapse at the same time in the Great House Holocaust. Now he must travel to House Heaven to find his departed fiancee. **172 pages $11**

BB-063 **"Necro Sex Machine" Andre Duza** - The Dead Bitch returns in this follow-up to the bizarro zombie epic Dead Bitch Army. **400 pages $16**

BB-064 **"Squid Pulp Blues" Jordan Krall** - In these three bizarro-noir novellas, the reader is thrown into a world of murderers, drugs made from squid parts, deformed gun-toting veterans, and a mischievous apocalyptic donkey. **204 pages $12**

BB-065 **"Jack and Mr. Grin" Andersen Prunty** - "When Mr. Grin calls you can hear a smile in his voice. Not a warm and friendly smile, but the kind that seizes your spine in fear. You don't need to pay your phone bill to hear it. That smile is in every line of Prunty's prose." - Tom Bradley. **208 pages $12**

BB-066 **"Cybernetrix" Carlton Mellick III** - What would you do if your normal everyday world was slowly mutating into the video game world from Tron? **212 pages $12**

BB-067 **"Lemur" Tom Bradley** - Spencer Sproul is a would-be serial-killing bus boy who can't manage to murder, injure, or even scare anybody. However, there are other ways to do damage to far more people and do it legally... **120 pages $12**

BB-068 **"Cocoon of Terror" Jason Earls** - Decapitated corpses...a sculpture of terror...Zelian's masterpiece, his Cocoon of Terror, will trigger a supernatural disaster for everyone on Earth. **196 pages $14**

BB-069 **"Mother Puncher" Gina Ranalli** - The world has become tragically over-populated and now the government strongly opposes procreation. Ed is employed by the government as a mother-puncher. He doesn't relish his job, but he knows it has to be done and he knows he's the best one to do it. **120 pages $9**

BB-070 **"My Landlady the Lobotomist" Eckhard Gerdes** - The brains of past tenants line the shelves of my boarding house, soaking in a mysterious elixir. One more slip-up and the landlady might just add my frontal lobe to her collection. **116 pages $12**

BB-071 **"CPR for Dummies" Mickey Z.** - This hilarious freakshow at the world's end is the fragmented, sobering debut novel by acclaimed nonfiction author Mickey Z. **216 pages $14**

BB-072 **"Zerostrata" Andersen Prunty** - Hansel Nothing lives in a tree house, suffers from memory loss, has a very eccentric family, and falls in love with a woman who runs naked through the woods every night. **144 pages $11**

BB-073 **"The Egg Man" Carlton Mellick III** - It is a world where humans reproduce like insects. Children are the property of corporations, and having an enormous ten-foot brain implanted into your skull is a grotesque sexual fetish. Mellick's industrial urban dystopia is one of his darkest and grittiest to date. **184 pages $11**

BB-074 **"Shark Hunting in Paradise Garden" Cameron Pierce** - A group of strange humanoid religious fanatics travel back in time to the Garden of Eden to discover it is invested with hundreds of giant flying maneating sharks. **150 pages $10**

BB-075 **"Apeshit" Carlton Mellick III** - Friday the 13th meets Visitor Q. Six hipster teens go to a cabin in the woods inhabited by a deformed killer. An incredibly fucked-up parody of B-horror movies with a bizarro slant. **192 pages $12**

BB-076 **"Rampaging Fuckers of Everything on the Crazy Shitting Planet of the Vomit At smosphere" Mykle Hansen** - 3 bizarro satires. Monster Cocks, Journey to the Center of Agnes Cuddlebottom, and Crazy Shitting Planet. **228 pages $12**

BB-077 **"The Kissing Bug" Daniel Scott Buck** - In the tradition of Roald Dahl, Tim Burton, and Edward Gorey, comes this bizarro anti-war children's story about a bohemian conenose kissing bug who falls in love with a human woman. **116 pages $10**

BB-078 **"MachoPoni" Lotus Rose** - It's My Little Pony... *Bizarro* style! A long time ago Poniworld was split in two. On one side of the Jagged Line is the Pastel Kingdom, a magical land of music, parties, and positivity. On the other side of the Jagged Line is Dark Kingdom inhabited by an army of undead ponies. **148 pages $11**

BB-079 **"The Faggiest Vampire" Carlton Mellick III** - A Roald Dahl-esque children's story about two faggy vampires who partake in a mustache competition to find out which one is truly the faggiest. **104 pages $10**

BB-080 **"Sky Tongues" Gina Ranalli** - The autobiography of Sky Tongues, the biracial hermaphrodite actress with tongues for fingers. Follow her strange life story as she rises from freak to fame. **204 pages $12**

BB-081 **"Washer Mouth" Kevin L. Donihe -** A washing machine becomes human and pursues his dream of meeting his favorite soap opera star. **244 pages $11**

BB-082 **"Shatnerquake" Jeff Burk -** All of the characters ever played by William Shatner are suddenly sucked into our world. Their mission: hunt down and destroy the real William Shatner. **100 pages $10**

BB-083 **"The Cannibals of Candyland" Carlton Mellick III** - There exists a race of cannibals that are made of candy. They live in an underground world made out of candy. One man has dedicated his life to killing them all. **170 pages $11**

BB-084 **"Slub Glub in the Weird World of the Weeping Willows"** **Andrew Goldfarb** - The charming tale of a blue glob named Slub Glub who helps the weeping willows whose tears are flooding the earth. There are also hyenas, ghosts, and a voodoo priest **100 pages $10**

BB-085 **"Super Fetus" Adam Pepper -** Try to abort this fetus and he'll kick your ass! **104 pages $10**

BB-086 **"Fistful of Feet" Jordan Krall -** A bizarro tribute to spaghetti westerns, featuring Cthulhu-worshipping Indians, a woman with four feet, a crazed gunman who is obsessed with sucking on candy, Syphilis-ridden mutants, sexually transmitted tattoos, and a house devoted to the freakiest fetishes. **228 pages $12**

BB-087 **"Ass Goblins of Auschwitz" Cameron Pierce** - It's Monty Python meets Nazi exploitation in a surreal nightmare as can only be imagined by Bizarro author Cameron Pierce. **104 pages $10**

BB-088 **"Silent Weapons for Quiet Wars" Cody Goodfellow** - "This is high-end psychological surrealist horror meets bottom-feeding low-life crime in a techno-thrilling science fiction world full of Lovecraft and magic..." -John Skipp **212 pages $12**

BB-089 "Warrior Wolf Women of the Wasteland" Carlton Mellick III
Road Warrior Werewolves versus McDonaldland Mutants...post-apocalyptic fiction has never been quite like this. **316 pages $13**

BB-090 "Cursed" Jeremy C Shipp - The story of a group of characters who believe they are cursed and attempt to figure out who cursed them and why. A tale of stylish absurdism and suspenseful horror. **218 pages $15**

BB-091 "Super Giant Monster Time" Jeff Burk - A tribute to choose your own adventures and Godzilla movies. Will you escape the giant monsters that are rampaging the fuck out of your city and shit? Or will you join the mob of alien-controlled punk rockers causing chaos in the streets? What happens next depends on you. **188 pages $12**

BB-092 "Perfect Union" Cody Goodfellow - "Cronenberg's THE FLY on a grand scale: human/insect gene-spliced body horror, where the human hive politics are as shocking as the gore." -John Skipp. **272 pages $13**

BB-093 "Sunset with a Beard" Carlton Mellick III - 14 stories of surreal science fiction. **200 pages $12**

BB-094 "My Fake War" Andersen Prunty - The absurd tale of an unlikely soldier forced to fight a war that, quite possibly, does not exist. It's Rambo meets Waiting for Godot in this subversive satire of American values and the scope of the human imagination. **128 pages $11**

BB-095"Lost in Cat Brain Land" Cameron Pierce - Sad stories from a surreal world. A fascist mustache, the ghost of Franz Kafka, a desert inside a dead cat. Primordial entities mourn the death of their child. The desperate serve tea to mysterious creatures. A hopeless romantic falls in love with a pterodactyl. And much more. **152 pages $11**

BB-096 "The Kobold Wizard's Dildo of Enlightenment +2" Carlton Mellick III - A Dungeons and Dragons parody about a group of people who learn they are only made up characters in an AD&D campaign and must find a way to resist their nerdy teenaged players and retarded dungeon master in order to survive. 232 **pages $12**

ORDER FORM

TITLES	QTY	PRICE	TOTAL

Please make checks and moneyorders payable to ROSE O'KEEFE / BIZARRO BOOKS in U.S. funds only. Please don't send bad checks! Allow 2-6 weeks for delivery. International orders may take longer. If you'd like to pay online via PAYPAL.COM, send payments to publisher@eraserheadpress.com.

SHIPPING: US ORDERS - $2 for the first book, $1 for each additional book. For priority shipping, add an additional $4. INT'L ORDERS - $5 for the first book, $3 for each additional book. Add an additional $5 per book for global priority shipping.

Send payment to:

BIZARRO BOOKS
 C/O Rose O'Keefe
 205 NE Bryant
 Portland, OR 97211

Address

City   State   Zip

Email   Phone